TWO'S A
CHARM

Heather Spellman is an Australian author based in southern California. She has slept in a cemetery, has a friend who was bullied by a prince and has lived in a haunted house in a haunted town. *Two's a Charm* is her third published book for adults.

TWO'S A CHARM

HEATHER SPELLMAN

PAN BOOKS

First published 2025 by Pan Books
an imprint of Pan Macmillan
The Smithson, 6 Briset Street, London EC1M 5NR
EU representative: Macmillan Publishers Ireland Ltd, 1st Floor,
The Liffey Trust Centre, 117–126 Sheriff Street Upper,
Dublin 1 D01 YC43
Associated companies throughout the world

ISBN 978-1-0350-8306-0

1 3 5 7 9 8 6 4 2

A CIP catalogue record for this book is available from the British Library.

Typeset in Stempel Garamond LT Pro by
Palimpsest Book Production Ltd, Falkirk, Stirlingshire
Printed and bound in the UK using 100% Renewable Electricity by
CPI Group (UK) Ltd

MIX
Paper | Supporting
responsible forestry
FSC www.fsc.org
FSC® C116313

Visit **www.panmacmillan.com** to read more about all our books
and to buy them.

To Anna and Darcie, my magical sisters

Chapter 1

JUST SAY THE MAGIC WORD

Effie

Bong.

The ornate clock tower on Yellowbrick Grove's town hall tolled six, jerking Effie Chalmers out of a quaint imaginary world in which alarming electric bills and dead mothers did not exist.

Alas, back in reality, such things were omnipresent. Even Effie's book-lined bedroom, with its cosy striped reading chair and magnificent pothos plant, was haunted with memories of her mother's quick smile, her careful way with a watering can, and the bedtime stories that had kept a young Effie and her younger sister Bonnie bespelled for weeks at a time. So too was the household to-do list, written on a starry notepad that read *From the Escritoire (and Heart) of Lyra Chalmers.* Effie knew it was silly, but using her mother's stationery made her feel like Mom was still there: that when Effie jotted out a note or a particularly captivating passage from a book, it was actually her mother doing the transcribing. And after the year she'd had navigating wills and funeral arrangements and pitying, prying conversations from the townsfolk, Effie needed that presence. Even if it was one that shimmered, just out of sight, at the corner of her bespectacled eye.

A leaf-blower, courtesy of three-time Yellowbrick Grove Garden of Perfection winner Freddie Noonan five doors down, revved in time with the clock tower. Effie's book, a marble-edged edition she'd snuck from the rare books room of the library where she worked, slipped from her hand. Its pages flapped in consternation – and in warning of a book restoration bill that was about to join the electric one.

No. Unexpected expenses (exhibit A: the aforementioned electric bill) were Bonnie's remit, not Effie's. Effie did not abide the unplanned, the spontaneous, the ill-considered. Certainly not since the weight of the entire household had come to rest upon her shoulders like a leaden cloak of responsibility. She knew she could never replace their mother. But she did have to walk in her shoes if the sisters were to keep their childhood home safe from opportunistic property developers – and if Bonnie were to make it to thirty without a divorce, a bankruptcy or a flirtation with cult membership (it was not looking good).

A snap of her fingers, and an emerald stream of magic righted the book, setting it back on the side table and tucking in Effie's favourite bookmark, a faded photo collage of her mother that a younger, more carefree Effie had carefully printed and laminated.

Mom's smile – oh, how Effie missed that kind, generous smile – poked out from the top of the book, watching with love as Effie gathered her outfit for her evening library shift, one of the many extras she'd taken on to avoid being at home alone with Bonnie. Not that her wardrobe required much gathering. Effie's habitual attire consisted of a rotating series of cardigans, high-waisted pants, and T-shirts with literary quotes on them that drew approving nods from the library patrons and exasperated sighs from her sister, a perfectly put-together blonde who had tried numerous times to turn the drably brunette Effie into someone more photogenic and outgoing. Effie, who *did* have an appreciation for fashion, albeit one mostly shaped by her favourite books – Anne of Green Gables' puffed sleeves, Miss Marple's knitwear – had pushed back. None of it had felt right. And now, as the polite face of the family's grief, Effie simply wanted to go through life without being perceived. The less you stood out, the fewer questions you got about how you were doing or how long it had been or whether you had anything planned for the upcoming anniversary of your mother's constantly whispered-about demise.

In the bathroom, Effie spun the faucet and stepped beneath the temperamental flow of water – then stepped straight back out again, muttering every expletive that came to mind. (Given that a young Effie had read the dictionary cover to cover for fun, this was quite a few.)

The water was positively arctic, as it so often was after Bonnie yelled those three fateful words: *getting ready, Eff!* Bonnie's magic wasn't as strong as Effie's, but she was certainly able to inflict the curse of a freezing cold shower upon her sister with a regularity that suggested that if she actually put her mind to spellcasting instead of reality TV bingeing, she might be a force to be reckoned with.

But for now, Effie – freezing cold Effie who was aghast thinking about just how much electricity was used to heat a whole boiler of water – was the one to be reckoned with.

Grumbling, Effie pulled Mom's embroidered dressing gown from the hook on the back of the bathroom door and grabbed an armful of clothes. Then she stalked, shivering, down the photo-lined hallway to Bonnie's bedroom, a profusion of pink that the two sisters had mutually dubbed 'the Flamingo Room' back when they were teens and their completely different interests hadn't yet caused the rift between them to widen into a gulf. There'd been a time when Effie had been the aspirational sister simply by virtue of being older – and therefore trusted with things like choosing which chocolates to buy from the corner store or being the de facto adult supervision when their mother had volunteered to cover yet another shift at the Toto Hotel. (She'd never mentioned the bills, although looking back, Effie could see that Mom's shoulders had drooped under the same existential cloak that she now found herself draped in.) But that had promptly faded when, at fourteen, Bonnie had made a rapid transition from freckly, gangly kid into *the pretty one*, and had quickly distanced herself from her sister's introversion and embarrassing glasses-and-braces aesthetic.

Now, ten years later, Bonnie was still the pretty one, and Effie, well, she was *the other one*.

The distance between the sisters had broadened over the past year, with Effie trying so hard to fill the gap that their mother had left, and Bonnie bristling at her every attempt. Effie knew that she could never replace Mom, that she couldn't come close to her warmth and generosity. But someone had to be the adult in the room, the one who kept up with the Jeep's oil changes, who replaced the smoke detector batteries, who did the taxes. Even if sometimes after work Effie drove to the outlook at the top of the tallest hill in town and screamed, *Not me! Can it for once not be me!*

Tonight, Effie suspected, was going to be such a night.

'Hey, babe. You're dripping water on my rug.' Bonnie was perched on a fluffy pink chair, clad in a sequinned minidress that involved about as much fabric as a dish towel. The long blonde hair draped over her shoulders was the only thing that kept her from looking utterly indecent. She was midway through painting her toenails, something she always seemed to be midway through. Especially when Effie needed her help taking out the trash or returning Pickles, the wayward French bulldog who apparently wished he lived on their side of the street.

Effie pulled on her pants, scowling as she caught her reflection in Bonnie's full-length mirror: with her wet hair slicked back around her cat's-eye glasses, she looked like a drowned rat. 'How do you manage to use up an entire boiler of hot water every time?'

'Want me to warm it up again?' Shrugging, Bonnie rubbed

her thumb and finger together as though about to cast one of her disastrous spells. Her hand glowed faintly purple beneath the swirl of floral tattoos she'd splurged on for her eighteenth birthday. Effie was not a tattoo hater by any means, having a few secret bookish tattoos of her own, but she'd never understood that decision. Bonnie's magic was weak, but it still made her special. It made her a Chalmers sister. It was one of the few things that the two of them shared, and seeing it blotted over with meaningless irises and lilies had hurt Effie in a way she hadn't been able to articulate.

'With *your* magic? Only if you plan on shelling out for the insurance deductible,' said Effie drily as she pulled on her favourite Booktrovert T-shirt.

Bonnie dropped her hand, now rubbing at a spot on her toe where she'd overshot with her sparkly nail polish. Effie knew the jab about her sister's magic had landed, and she felt a twinge of guilt. But Bonnie had everything else going for her. The effervescent personality, the ability to worm her way out of speeding tickets, the constant job offers for things she was clearly unqualified for, and the sheer *freedom* of being the younger, carefree sister. Effie, who, at twenty-eight had a white streak in her dark hair and some alarming frown lines appearing between her brows, deserved to have *something*. Even if she had to keep that something under wraps to avoid the attention of the town, which exhibited a deep and annoying interest in the comings and goings of the Chalmers sisters.

Bonnie had social charms. Effie had magical ones. It was only fair.

'I figured you weren't going out, so the hot water was fair game.' Bonnie returned her nail polish to an overflowing drawer, then picked up her hair curler – which Effie demanded she keep on a ceramic plate after the time she'd almost burned down their sprawling Queen Anne home. Times, plural.

'Your reading chair isn't going to judge you if your hair's

a bit oily,' Bonnie added as she admired her own gleaming golden hair. 'Or you've got a case of BO.'

Now fully cardiganed and therefore imbued with her librarian superpowers – which mostly involved doing excellent story-time voices and resetting wi-fi connections – Effie grabbed a fluffy, googly-eyed pillow and flung it at her sister. Half-heartedly, but the kind of half that Bonnie would give herself when slicing up a pizza to share.

Bonnie caught it easily, hence why she'd been basketball captain and Effie had been, well, a familiar face in the Yellowbrick Grove High School library.

'Not Mr Fluffles!' exclaimed Bonnie, giving the pillow a hug. She sighed, then held up a pinkie finger stacked with tiny chevron-shaped rings. 'I promise to warn you next time I need all the hot water. Which will probably be when I get home from my shift. We're hosting a welcome party for that new guy in town tonight.' She waggled a perfectly shaped eyebrow with practised sultriness. 'Maybe I'll need a cold shower instead.'

Effie lifted her glasses to rub at the bridge of her nose. Fabulous. She couldn't wait to help pick up the pieces when the inexorable love affair inevitably went awry. 'Well, I for one have a date with the circulation desk.'

'Sounds dusty.' Bonnie grimaced, then extended an olive branch the only way she knew how: with a pout and a finger waggle that served as an alternative to a hug. Effie, of course, did not do hugs, unless the warm embrace of a book counted. 'Sorry, I didn't realize you were leaving the house.'

'I always work Thursdays.' Effie knew that her tone sounded cold, but rightly so! She *was* cold. Literally cold, all thanks to her sister's lack of consideration, which was an ongoing theme in the book of their lives.

'Oh, right.' This appeared to be breaking news to Bonnie.

'I'm not a hermit. I have a job. And friends.' All right, just the one friend, Tessa, but an excellent friend.

'I know, I know.' Bonnie ran her fingers through the perfect golden waves of her hair. 'This whole bar thing – it's taken up so much more of my energy than I thought. And my money.'

Absolutely not. They were not having this conversation. It was not Effie's fault that Bonnie had spent her entire inheritance on a *bar* instead of investing it carefully in a three-fund account that would return seven per cent in compounding returns over a lifetime. Or that she'd had four years of back taxes to reckon with. Or that she'd financed a vintage Cadillac at an interest rate straight out of *The Sopranos*.

And still, Effie was expected to put down her book and offer guidance and commiseration every single day.

But not this day. Not this freezing-shower, late-to-work, mildly-jealous-that-Bonnie-might-meet-the-hot-neighbour-first day. Especially without a *please* or a *thank you* in the mix.

Muttering a quick excuse about a library emergency, Effie snapped her fingers, lightly increasing the humidity in the room just enough to make her sister's hair frizz.

'Wait, what? No!' moaned Bonnie, reaching for a bottle of hair serum.

Biting back a smile, Effie grabbed her bag and ran downstairs to her second-favourite place after her beloved reading chair: the Yellowbrick Grove Public Library.

Chapter 2

UNDER A STRANGER'S SPELL

Bonnie

The bar was Bonnie's happy place. Although to be fair, for most of her life, Bonnie's happy place had been all of Yellowbrick Grove. She'd lived a charmed existence, and she was well aware of it. Mostly because Effie had made a point of making her aware. But it wasn't *Bonnie's* fault that she had a natural charisma, or that Effie made a concerted effort to exist on the periphery of her own life. Their town might be small, but it was home, and it came with all the wonderful things that home delivered when you made the tiniest bit of an effort. Yes, Bonnie was popular, but that was because she actively worked to be part of the community. She'd played (and coached) basketball for years. She'd been on the dance team, the improv team and the entrepreneurship team. She'd hosted bake sales, car washes, pep rallies, everything. It wasn't as though she'd just been sitting around watching soap operas and eating Girl Scout cookies (she'd also topped the Girl Scout cookie-seller leader board) while Effie had shouldered the weight of the family.

Besides, Effie had *decided* to take on that role. And frankly, Bonnie resented her for it. It suggested that Mom hadn't done enough to support and look after them, when she'd worked herself to the bone to give them a wonderful childhood. Leaf-kicking trips through the autumnal parks, stomach-wrenching turns around the fairground rides, family movie nights in front of the ancient TV, all of it. Effie had become even more insufferable in the wake of their mom's death. Instead of letting Bonnie grieve, instead of respecting the special space that Mom had held in their lives, she'd tried to fill it with all of her fussing and fastidiousness and *admin*. Bonnie, frankly, couldn't give a shit about admin. Especially after this past year, which had demanded she reprioritize her entire life.

Bonnie squared her shoulders and swanned into The Silver Slipper, which she'd bought using her inheritance. It still remained her greatest accomplishment. Unlike Effie, who'd thrown her half of the life insurance pay-out into something called an index, Bonnie wanted to create something that would help remember their mother.

The bar was exactly the sort of place that Lyra would have enjoyed visiting on her days off from the hotel or on the nights when her shifts let out early enough: a former corner-block diner with green-tinged windows and globe-shaped pendant lights that somehow captured everyone's best possible angle. The main action took place on the ground floor, but there was a private area upstairs for parties or special occasions (on Sunday nights the local tango dancers gathered for a milonga, and they'd burn through the bar's entire allotment of Quilmes beer and Torrontés wine). Not to mention the upstairs attic that Bonnie eventually planned to turn into an apartment. Out front, set against a backdrop of ivy and well-fed flower baskets, were half a dozen cosy benches over-hung by Moroccan-style lanterns that cast starry light over the streets as they twisted in the breeze.

Unsurprisingly, the townsfolk had flocked to the bar since its grand opening four months earlier, and Bonnie couldn't be prouder. She could tell from her sister's huffy looks that Effie thought it was all luck, or perhaps the Bonnie glamour she was so jealous of, but the bar's success had been the result of sheer blood, sweat and tears. (All right, only a bit of blood – that time she'd gashed her toe while helping with the tiling – and not *so* many tears. Most of those had been for Mom, really. But the sweat was real. Hence all the showers Effie was so opposed to.)

'Bonnie, babe!' chorused Hannah, Kirsty and Alana, Bonnie's own personal Greek chorus. According to Effie, anyway. Bonnie hadn't paid *that* much attention in literature class at school. She'd been focused on more pragmatic things, like building her social networks and jostling for personal references. Besides, what was a deep understanding of *Medea* going to get you other than some trauma and maybe a gig at a museum?

'Babes!' Bonnie swept in for a cheek-kissing extravaganza. 'How's the party shaping up? Sorry I'm late. Effie issues.'

'The worst,' groaned Kirsty, a svelte brunette who had an impressively negative opinion of just about everyone. Which worked for Bonnie as it gave her a chance to freely unload whenever her sister did something to irritate her, which was most days.

'Tell me our guest of honour isn't here yet?' asked Bonnie, glancing around.

She wasn't quite sure how she wanted them to answer. Obviously, as the bar owner, it was good form for her to be ready and waiting for when recent arrival-from-the-city Theo Carmel, the subject of *much* gossip among the townsfolk, darkened the bar's already dimly lit doors. But the other part of Bonnie desperately wanted to be fashionably late. To be the one that everyone saw making an entrance. To be beheld rather than the one doing the beholding.

'No sightings yet, babe. Although we're prepared.' Prim Hannah, who was indeed always prepared, ran her fingers through her perfectly straight hair as her enormous eyes scanned the bar for fresh blood. This was, of course, one of the downsides of living in a small town: you knew everyone, and the pool of eligible partners was vanishingly small.

Especially when you had to excise people from your list of possibilities based on their prior dalliances with anyone in your immediate friendship group.

Thankfully Yellowbrick Grove was still close to the city, and picturesque enough to be a popular tourist destination for people looking for something between a staycation and an actual getaway. During the on-season weekends (fall, when the trees turned an astonishing combination of fiery colours, and spring, when the blossoms ran riot), the streets were packed with visitors looking to spend their hard-earned cash at the bar, and their precious time off with Bonnie, who needed a warm body every now and then.

'According to my research, he comes from a prominent banking family,' said Kirsty, whose social media stalking skills were unrivalled. In another lifetime, Kirsty would have been a Pulitzer-winning investigative journalist, but in this one she ran a moderately successful blog about life in Yellowbrick Grove, with some social media consulting on the side. She'd stopped just short of becoming an influencer, thankfully, because Bonnie could only afford to give away so much free booze before the bar's bank account started making warning sounds.

'And there was a breakup,' added Alana, a fashionable bohemian whose heavily pierced ears had a preternatural ability to absorb gossip, and a job as a yoga instructor that was extremely conducive to hearing it. 'His childhood sweetheart ripped his heart in two. On their anniversary, would you believe?'

Bonnie filed this away for future use. She'd never personally been in a relationship long enough to be able to mark an anniversary, but she was sure that would hurt. Actually, she'd never been the dumpee, either, something she was quite proud of. It took a lot to reach the grand old age of twenty-five without having had someone throw your heart to the crows. She always made it a point to get in first and do the dumping, usually when the uncomfortable reality of feelings was starting to set in.

'We could do with a top-up on table four, sweets,' said Winston Wakefield, head of the Yellowbrick Grove Old Darts team, and who always wore a hat advertising this fact. Winston was so ancient and so well known that it felt as though the entire town had grown up around him. He was like one of those 200-year-old tortoises that you hear about a family passing down through the generations, its startled, wrinkly face privy to decades of change. (Shelby, the turtle who lived in the town fountain, was the closest Yellowbrick Grove came to this particular phenomenon.) Winston and his similarly wrinkly friends had been keeping the place in business since its diner days, and Bonnie was grateful they were creatures of habit. Even if they did have annoying superstitions like keeping anyone in green away from their board, and forcing anyone who'd played a nine-darter to sit at the next table for the following week (which meant they ended up doing shots with students from the college – never a good idea).

But Yellowbrick Grove was full of odd superstitions and proclivities. You learned to roll with them, or you'd spend your days like Effie: huffing and puffing at every little thing that didn't make sense. Uncle Oswald sure had – he ran a revoltingly overpriced shop down an alleyway off the square catering to every occult-like and spiritual whim you might have. Even if you didn't have such whims, Uncle Oswald, who'd graduated with honours from the School of Pushy Sales Tactics, would definitely help you whip some up. But given that right now Bonnie could spot a moon-phase pendant, an electromagnetic field-blocking phone cover, a bouquet of rosemary poking out of a purse, and a set of tarot cards being pored over on a nearby table, it was fair to say that the whims in this town were plentiful. And why not? In a world where things grew ever more complicated, people could hardly be faulted for seeking solace in magic.

Especially in a town like this, where half the buildings were supposedly haunted (including the apartment upstairs), where the moon hung a tad too low in the sky, and where black cats lurked skittishly in every dark corner. The Chalmers sisters might be the only two individuals in town with *real* magic – something they hid carefully – but everyone else was trying to find their own, and the internet made that easy. Every day, Bonnie would hand over a drink to a girl scrolling through videos of palm readings, or she'd clear the plates of someone who'd clearly been trying to discern their future in the sauce of their home-made chocolate brownie.

Effie might judge them for their efforts (*dilettantes* was the term she used), but Bonnie didn't mind it at all: it made it easier for Bonnie and Effie to hide their true selves.

Besides, she enjoyed reading the horoscopes in the *Yellowbrick Grove Gazette*. Especially since they'd been taken over by the mysterious Madame Destinée, whose identity remained secret, no matter how much begging the locals did. Which reminded her: she hadn't read today's. Fortunately, Winston had a copy of the paper sticking out from one of the huge pockets of his faded jeans.

'Beers coming up, just so long as you read me my horoscope. I'm a Leo.'

'Leo, huh?' Winston rattled through the paper, pausing to share some of the more fascinating headlines. 'Ooh, sale on barbecues this week. And Edna Furling is doing an art show in Emerald. I liked her work with the circles. Very circle-y. And your uncle has some new cat statues in from Egypt! La-di-da! Ah, here we go! Leo. *Business unusual is more interesting than business as usual. Meanwhile, love is closer than it seems. Always has been. Always will be.* Well, that's a bit enigmatic, isn't it?'

'Sounds like I need to watch out for someone peeping in my bedroom window,' said Bonnie, pouring half a dozen pilsners for Winston's friends, and a shandy for Gerald Ho, who was from New Zealand, where they did things just slightly, annoyingly differently from here. And apparently called flip-flops jandals, which Bonnie wasn't sure was a real thing, or whether Gerald was just, as he put it, 'having a lark'.

'Ah, this is a safe town – no one's going to be doing that. I don't know how Officer Brigsley isn't bored out of his brains. Do you want me to read mine? What's the sheep again?'

'Aries. The ram.'

'That's the one! Aries. *Keep your eye on the target, or sharp disappointment awaits.*'

Bonnie chuckled. 'That could've been written for you specifically.'

'Maybe I've got my own peeper, eh?' Winston waggled his thick eyebrows as he cast a look around the room for said peeping Tom, before jamming a fistful of bills in the tip jar on the counter. 'Thanks, sweets. I'll be back in an hour or so.'

Winston hurried off with his tray, which he clutched to his chest as though it were the Sid Waddell darts trophy.

'My god, that man can talk,' droned Hannah in her famous monotone, which was so persistent that during high school the orchestra conductor would bring her in to help tune the brass instruments.

Bonnie grinned. 'Some people try to get their ten thousand steps in daily. Winston aims for ten thousand words.'

'So, how are we liking the decorations?' Hannah gestured with long, manicured fingers. At Bonnie's request, Hannah had spent the afternoon hanging colourful bunting and blowing up balloons. She'd even sourced confetti cannons from her mom's impressive wedding-planner arsenal. Bonnie suspected that this might be overdoing it. But could you really overdo it at a party? Especially when you were dealing with someone from the city, where things were bigger and brighter just by their very nature?

'Very demure, very mindful,' said Bonnie appreciatively.

'*And* I grabbed a welcome agate heart from Behind the Curtain.' Hannah flashed a dramatically gilded cardboard giftbox from Uncle Oswald's shop. 'Oswald said it's really important to start a new journey with the right kind of energy. I'm going to start buying these for my clients as housewarming gifts. Money trees are so passé.'

Bonnie nodded along, because that was safer than opening her mouth. Uncle Oswald was what some might generously call a grifter, and others, less generously, a conman. Mom had called him a charlatan, and a few other choice names. They'd never really got along, in large part because they viewed the responsibilities of magic in entirely divergent ways. Lyra had always considered magic a great privilege that should be used sparingly and for good. Oswald, on the other hand, saw it as an opportunity for personal enrichment – and since the family magic had a tendency to bypass its men, he'd spent most of his life pressing Mom for insight into her spells or begging for a quick enchantment to support his latest trick.

In fairness, Uncle Oswald lived in a gorgeous storybook house overlooking the town's Botanic Gardens and had never complained about the electric bill, so, magic or not, he was doing something right.

Kirsty, who'd been keeping a close eye on the smart doorbell, waved her Lululemon-clad arms frantically. (Kirsty was always dressed in athleisure, citing the need for freedom of movement before the front-facing camera that formed the bulk of her career.) 'Here he is!'

Here he was indeed. Bonnie had only met Theo once before, but her first impression of him had been, well, a bit of a tingly one. Theo was tall and well built – so much so that Bonnie wondered whether she needed to invest in a taller, wider front door. He wore casually expensive pants, a pair of leather loafers Bonnie associated with Wall Street, and had the kind of disarming smile that suggested he knew precisely the kind of impression he made on people when he entered a room.

Bonnie was all too familiar with that expression. It was the smile of someone who knew that the world was on their side, who experienced only pleasant interactions, because when you looked a certain way, doors opened for you. Bonnie knew that expression, because it was her own.

'Theo!' She hurried up with an Old Fashioned in hand, figuring it was hard to go wrong with a classic. 'Welcome to The Silver Slipper, and to our charming little town! Are you feeling all settled in?'

She passed him the drink, ensuring their hands brushed just so.

Theo sipped his Old Fashioned – a bit nervously, it seemed. Was she having the same impact on him he'd had on her? Hopefully she was, and even more so.

'Getting there. I've got a few boxes left to unpack.'

Theo cast his green-eyed gaze around the bustling bar, which Bonnie was pleased to note was packed with cheerful revellers dressed up to the nines. (She had a strict look-your-best dress code that she rarely relaxed. Well, except for the darts players. Their shlubbiness was grandfathered in.)

'Nice place. It's yours, right?'

'All mine,' said Bonnie, her tone betraying her subtext: *just like you'll be*. And, of course, he would eventually be. It was how things went in town.

'Hi,' drawled Hannah, appearing beside Bonnie, the very picture of a wide-eyed ingenue. Hannah wasn't a threat, though – between her realtor's schedule and caring for her dad, who'd been diagnosed with early onset Alzheimer's a year earlier, she'd decided that dating was a hobby she didn't particularly need to invest in. 'Yellowbrick Grove is going to love having you. What we lack in size we make up for in charm. And property values.'

'And don't worry. Whatever happens here stays here,' added

Alana, meaningfully. This was true, since gossipy though she was, she never left town long enough to share said gossip beyond the hills that bordered it.

'Sorry, can I get through? Don't mind me . . .' Bobby, the Chalmers sisters' floppy-haired, soft-eyed next-door neighbour, awkwardly wheeled a keg through the front door, despite the fact that Bonnie had requested multiple times that he go around the back.

'Hey, Bonnie! Where do you want this?' he asked, mopping his brow with the back of his wrist, around which he wore the friendship bracelet his little brother Kevvie had made several months back.

'Ugh,' muttered Kirsty, as she did every time Bobby made an appearance.

Bonnie felt a pang of sympathy. Yes, Bobby was far from the coolest guy in town, and he was way too interested in tabletop gaming and birdwatching. But he was kind, and he always brought over cookies when his dad, who owned The Golden Hour Bakery, was testing out a new recipe. And, most importantly of all, he did Bonnie's bidding without complaint and without expectation of payment, which was a decent asset when you were trying to get a new business off the ground.

'Behind the bar. Can you hook it up?'

'Can do, boss.' He smiled affably, flashing a chipped tooth that had been a teenage Bonnie's fault – she'd dared him to climb the largest tree at the Botanic Gardens on a particularly rainy day. 'Anything else while I'm there?'

'I'll take a top-up,' said Kirsty, waving her glass at him.

'Same,' droned Hannah, squeezing her half-empty glass into the crook of his elbow.

'Cucumber water, with extra ice, but only if it's distilled,' said Alana, who was constantly detoxing from one thing or another. Although, for someone who made a point of not drinking, she was quite helpful behind the bar.

Hannah tapped Bonnie's shoulder with a glimmering nail. 'Babe, you'd better get your claws in before Winston does.'

Theo had strolled over to the darts board and was now affably shaking hands with the darts team, who were merrily recounting the time they'd won a rotisserie chicken package after beating out The Chairmen of the Board, their competitors from the neighbouring town of Emerald.

Oh goddess, they were going to scare him right back to the city.

'Do you need rescuing there?' she whispered in his ear.

'Sorry, what was that?' Theo turned, his brows furrowed over his emerald eyes. Jensen Ackles' eyes, thought Bonnie, who'd watched *Supernatural* an unhealthy number of times. But that was something that would forever remain in the diary she kept under her mattress.

'How about a tour?'

Theo looked suspiciously as though this was the last thing in the world he wanted. 'Um, sure.'

Bonnie shot him an irresistible grin, then invoked her murder weapon. A curl of hair twisted around her perfectly manicured finger.

Theo seemed to falter. Success.

With a well-practised Marilyn Monroe sway to her hips, Bonnie walked Theo through her tour of The Silver Slipper.

'Downstairs is pretty self-explanatory,' she said, also evoking Marilyn's breathy way of speaking for good measure. 'Amazing cocktails, a solid beer and wine list, darts – not my choice, but it was a contingency when I bought the place. Through this door we have the pool table and pinball machines. You should see the lines for those after about 10 p.m. They single-handedly pay the staff.'

'You pay your staff in quarters?'

'Sure, it's how we do things here.'

Theo frowned, as though he wasn't sure if she was serious. This, thought Bonnie, was one of the hardest parts of looking a certain way. Guys never expected you to be funny. In fact, they never expected you to be anything else, really. Personally, Bonnie thought that her sense of humour was one of the best things she had going for her. She'd spent a lot of time cultivating it to survive life with Effie.

'Ready for some stairs?' She gave him an assessing up-and-down look. He passed with buff, flying colours. 'You look like you can handle them.'

Bonnie grabbed the banister, a glorious knot of antique wood studded with a brass sculpture of a griffin, and led Theo upstairs.

'Interesting art,' he mused, taking in the framed paintings that covered the walls in an explosion of abstract colour – mostly greens, golds and purples, the colours of their family magic, their auras.

'My mom painted them,' said Bonnie, trying to suppress the hesitation in her voice that always threatened to arise every time she brought up her mother. She rubbed at her tattooed wrist, where a floral explosion of lilies and tulips hid the purple marks that flared beneath her skin when she drew upon her magic. She'd raced out to Clock Heart Tattoos the day she turned eighteen, desperate to hide the thing that made her different from everyone else. And not even in a good way; not like Effie's magic, which actually did what her sister asked. Bonnie, meanwhile, was lucky if she could charm the wrinkles out of a shirt or bespell that thing on the top shelf within reaching range. More often than not, this would result in scorch marks on said shirt or that thing on the top shelf smashing on the floor. Magic was an imprecise art.

'This one's my favourite,' she said, pausing before a small canvas where swirls of green, gold and purple all melded together in a gorgeous, calming swirl. Lyra, Effie and Bonnie's magic, all together as equals. It made Bonnie think of better times, when the three of them had been inseparable, an arm-in-arm gang of joy and daisy crowns and pizza so deep-dish it might as well be lasagne, and black-and-white movie marathons that they'd talked over, inventing their own terrible dialogue. Of before Effie had abruptly distanced herself when Bonnie had turned fourteen, shutting her out like there was something wrong with her, like she was . . . *unserious*. Of before Mom's death had ripped their lives in two, leaving something too painful to even consider in its wake. Something that Bonnie had done her best to plaster over with endless activities and events and Boss Babe goals.

Theo folded his muscular arms, contemplating. He'd clearly realized that the vibes were suddenly off and was trying to get things back on track. 'Not this weird brownish one over here?'

Bonnie recoiled. 'Definitely not that one.'

Bonnie had never known why Mom had painted this particular one. It was Uncle Oswald, through and through, but not his magic – he had no magic as far as she knew – but rather a representation of how Mom saw his aura. Why paint such an unsettling brown? Why let it live on for ever on a canvas?

And yet it was one of Mom's paintings. Bonnie couldn't just throw it away or hide it. It *had* lived for a while above the downstairs toilet, until the patrons had complained of feeling ill while peeing.

Theo tapped a finger against the painting's frame. 'I guess the value of a piece of art is in the eye of the beholder. Or the gallery owner.'

Bonnie chuckled. She was liking this new addition to their town. He was hot, if a bit acerbic.

'That's enough art criticism for now,' she said, leading him up to the second floor. She pushed open the door to the private events room, which was being prepared for an engagement party being hosted tomorrow.

'Congratulations?' mused Theo. 'It's a bit early for that, isn't it?'

'I would've given you your own space, but Devon and Amanda have had a save the date for months. And I'd rather risk your ire than theirs.'

'You say that, but I'm going to leave a one-star review admonishing you for the lack of personal attention.'

'Should've given me more notice you were moving to town, then.'

'Next time. Wow, vintage.'

Beneath all the balloons and streamers, the room was rich with antique wood from the local mill, and stained-glass windows crafted by the former hippie artist lover of Mom's best friend Sabine. Bonnie loved every inch of it, and never could resist showing it off: the massive hanging light fixture sourced from a factory up in Maine, the higgledy-piggledy hammered-tin ceiling, the grooved floorboards that had been loved, and abused, by generations of high heels and rolling carts.

'Really cool space though. This is all yours?' Theo brushed his fingers over a retro light switch. Bonnie didn't blame him. She fiddled with the brass toggles every time she came in as well. Although they did kind of look like boobs, now that she thought of it. Was Theo a boobs man? Bonnie hoisted hers up in her bra, even though it was already doing a fair bit of hoisting. There was more suspension going on here than in your typical garage door.

'Since about four months ago. But this place has been an institution since before I was a twinkle in my mom's eye.'

'Your dad's, don't you mean?'

Bonnie shook her head. 'Mom raised us. If my dad didn't have the good sense to stick around to raise a human being as excellent as I am, I don't want anything to do with him.'

'Noted. It's good to have boundaries. Trust me.' Theo looked as though he were about to add something, but changed his mind. Bonnie leaned suggestively against the railing, inviting him to make the inevitable move. And yet, much to Bonnie's utter confusion, he did not.

Usually by now, especially after one of Bonnie's extremely strong drinks, a guy would be all over her. Or if not then at least in her personal space. He'd certainly be pressing further about the third level of the building, which wasn't *yet* a proper apartment, but could do in a pinch if you weren't too concerned about splinters or asbestos. It was still better than the Flamingo Room back at the house, from which many a gentleman caller had done the walk of shame at five in the morning before Effie, always an early riser, started knocking on the door and asking whether Bonnie had heard the poltergeist banging away last night.

'Should we . . . head downstairs?' suggested Theo. 'I'm worried that if I get much deeper into this Old Fashioned I'll trip over the diamond ring piñata or stumble into a balloon display that someone's definitely spent a solid day working on.'

Bonnie tried not to frown. Was he immune to her charms? This was not how things worked.

Her wrists were growing warm and she could feel magic sparking inside her. Her wayward, infuriating magic was the only thing in her life other than Effie that refused to bend to her bidding. Maybe this time it would do what she intended it to.

C'mon, Mom, she thought, focusing on the swirling paintings in the hallway, the lilac patterns twirling and flaring like smoke. *Help me out here with some mood lighting.*

Bonnie's wrists glowed lavender beneath her tattoos, and magic crackled from her fingers. Not towards the light fixture as she'd hoped, but rather in the direction of the balloon display, popping each one in rapid turn, like a series of rubbery firecrackers.

Then, in a horrifying cascade of dominoes, the candles lying on the table next to the balloon display spontaneously caught fire, in turn setting alight the paper tablecloth. Acrid smoke filled the air as the smoke alarm started shrieking like a banshee.

Theo sprang into action.

'Shit!' he exclaimed. He grabbed a fire extinguisher and pulled the pin, spraying foam all around the room – including over Bonnie, whose brand-new sequinned dress would never be the same.

Shit indeed, she thought, staring down at her ruined ensemble. She had planned on returning it tomorrow and exchanging it for a fresh dress to wear the next night. But that was hardly going to happen now. And her hair, she thought, catching a glimpse of herself in the mirrored edging of one of the leadlight windows. She'd curled it twice, for this?

'Tissue?' Theo grabbed a saturated napkin from a stack that had been sitting next to an array of paper plates, ready to be used for cake. Not for horrendous, magically precipitated wardrobe malfunctions.

'No, no, I'm good,' said Bonnie with a brave smile. 'Luckily the shaving foam convention is coming to town on Sunday. I'll be right on trend.'

'You can have my jacket.' Theo doffed it and held it out. She hesitated, then accepted it gratefully.

'Do you mind if I roll up the sleeves?' The jacket arms were so long that she felt like one of the sky dancers outside the local car dealership.

'Roll away. And let me pay for the dry cleaning. I feel terrible.' He did indeed sound mortified. Rightly so, especially because mortification suited him. The flush brought out his cheekbones, and the way he was cringing in his tight shirt highlighted the outline of his biceps.

'Don't, don't. These things happen,' she said airily. 'Especially owning a place like this. We like to keep things interesting. If you stop by tomorrow, you might spot me in a chicken costume. Or dancing on the bar.'

'Careful, I hear health and safety frowns on that.'

'Could you turn around for a moment?'

Bonnie made a twirling motion with her finger, indicating that Theo should avert his eyes. Then, keeping his jacket on, she wriggled out of her dress, grateful that there hadn't been much to it in the first place. It hardly took being a magician to worm your way out of some spaghetti straps and a handkerchief's-worth of stretchy fabric.

'All right. You can turn back now.'

'Oh,' said Theo. 'Um.'

'Just call me Houdini!'

Scraping her hair back into a slightly foamy ponytail, Bonnie led Theo back downstairs, where things were starting to get rambunctious.

Hannah, spying Bonnie's dishevelled appearance and change of outfit, wasted no time in jumping to conclusions. 'Look at *you*.'

Alana, who'd been helping Bobby out behind the bar, thoughtfully tapped a sprig of mint to her cheek. 'I see you've made our guest welcome.'

Kirsty's eyes narrowed slightly, and Bonnie inwardly preened. She loved Kirsty, she did. But the girl was *so* competitive. It was refreshing to put her in her place, which Bonnie strove to do at least once every day. It was what made a healthy relationship, of course.

And then there was Bobby. Dear, sweet, innocent Bobby. Bobby, who never turned her in for cheating during every pin-the-tail-on-the-donkey game of their childhood. Who'd happily corroborated the excuses she fabricated for the countless exams she'd missed during high school. Who, over the years, had escorted no fewer than three possums out of their house after Bonnie had left the back door propped open during her late-night exploits.

What would she do without him?

Get in a lot more trouble, probably.

'Everything all right, Bon?' Bobby hurried out from behind the counter, still polishing the glass he'd been cleaning. 'I thought I heard the fire alarm, but these three said it was just figurative smoke.'

'*Rawr*,' purred Hannah, making a clawing motion with her extremely sharp, glittery nails.

'More than fine.' Bonnie grabbed an Old Fashioned off the counter – Alana *was* a solid helper – then passed it to Theo with a wink. 'Isn't that so?'

Chapter 3

YOU PUT A SPELL ON ME

Effie

The upstairs reading room at the library had an excellent view of the downtown area, and Effie, who was preparing to close up for the night, could see that the party was still going strong at The Silver Slipper – of course. Bonnie had an innate capacity for stretching any social gathering to its limit. She was the queen of after-parties, and after-after parties, and all too often those parties came with her to the Chalmers family home, keeping Effie up all night and forcing her to fabricate pointed stories about poltergeist infestations to avoid addressing her sister's shenanigans and how they disrupted her sleep. Not that Effie was shaming her sister. Bonnie was welcome to do what she wanted with whom she wanted, so long as it was consensual (and legal). But did she have to be quite so loud about it? Frankly, if you were able to be heard through double-brick walls, you were being a bit much.

'Any good reading plans tonight, love?' asked Bowow Walker, who was sitting at the large central table, her heavily made-up face – and habitually clashing attire – aglow under one of the green banker's lamps. Bowow was not her real name, obviously, or anything even close to it. Effie wasn't entirely sure where the nickname had come from, but it probably had something to do with the fact that Bowow was a founding member of the Yellowbrick Kennel Society, and also the local dog whisperer. If you had a problem pup,

Bowow was your girl. Although not girl, really, given she was probably as old as the library, which was showing its years in the temperamental plumbing in the downstairs bathroom, and the 'butterfly enclosure', which, far from being a zoological wonder just meant that moths had got into the ancient periodicals. Thankfully, Effie's magic had kept most of the more expensive problems at bay. Why, she'd won an award just this year for her fiscal stewardship and record number of days without a pigeon incursion. Which she could also thank her magic for.

Heading over to the side table by the window, Effie gathered a stack of discarded *National Geographic* volumes. She grimaced as she realized someone had cut out half the images. Great. The college kids were doing summoning circles again. 'Always. I have a fabulous murder mystery series on the go – the protagonist is a cheesemaker. And yourself?'

Bowow's eyes twinkled behind her reading glasses as she patted her usual foot-high stack of cowboy romance novels. 'A night in with my boys. And the Pomeranians.'

'Those yappy things,' muttered Bruce Dickens, an old rocker type who seemed to think he was Bruce Dickinson, the frontman of Iron Maiden. Every now and then a tourist would mistake the two, and the non-famous Bruce would lean heavily into the fallacy, affecting a British accent and talking about his cosy little spot in Paris. Needless to say, Bowow had absolutely no interest in anything Bruce had to say. Especially since he did not actually own a cosy little spot in Paris, France, although he *did* own a dilapidated cabin outside Paris, Tennessee. Which was almost the same thing. 'Don't know what you see in a dog like that. Cats. Now cats are where it's at. Cats have boundaries.'

'Unlike some,' muttered Bowow, gathering her stack of books and setting them down in her wheelie basket (another of Effie's additions to library operations). 'Can I borrow these, love? Ooh, was that lightning?'

No, not lightning. Rather, a flash of purple magic from The Silver Slipper, reflecting off the library window. Effie groaned inwardly. Bonnie was at it again, trying to magic her way out of a situation – or worse, into one. Surely her sister had figured out by now that nothing good ever came of using magic on *people* (mild hair-frizzing spells aside). Magic was safest used sparingly, surreptitiously and as a process efficiency helper.

'Just some bright headlights,' Effie told Bowow. 'All right, everyone. Fifteen minutes until closing. Could you return any books and periodicals to the cart and bring anything you want to borrow down to the front counter?'

She turned to Derek and George, the library's resident chess obsessives, then Tammi, the library's resident snacker. 'Derek and George, I promise no one will touch your board until tomorrow. And Tammi, do you need a napkin for those crumbs?'

'No, boss,' whispered Tammi, swiping the crumbs off the table and into her voluminous purse. Effie closed her eyes, counted to three, then opened them again. At least Tammi had resolved the situation, even if it had been in a particularly unappealing way. And on the plus side, Tammi carried a separate bag for books, so the crumbs weren't going to ruin any library volumes.

Waving goodbye to the stragglers and making sure that old Thomas who slept in the parking lot was warm and had charged his phone, Effie closed up for the night.

Her giant tote bag of books swung as she tried to drag the massive front doors closed, failing the first time, as she always did. The carved stone gargoyles on either side of the door regarded her disdainfully, the same way Bonnie would whenever she went to haul a box of books from the Jeep.

'A little bit of core strength goes a long way,' she'd say, tapping her perfect midsection.

Well, so did a little bit of magic. Glancing around to make

sure she couldn't be seen, Effie clenched her fists. A thin stream of green flared from her wrists, pulling the doors closed and yanking the lock firmly into place.

Then, clomping down the lengthy stone front steps – the library was a charming Carnegie one, and predated accessibility laws – she ensured that the side entrance with the lift, a fundraising effort from the Friends of the Library group she'd chaired for several years, was properly closed.

The chairs were tidied, the lights off and the doors locked. There was no more procrastinating. It was time to go by Bonnie's bar and put in an appearance at the welcome party for the town's newest resident.

The night around the stone-walled library was cool and crisp, and Effie drank in the autumnal feeling of it all as she made her way along the winding path that led back to the quiet road.

All around, the trees wore shaggy coats of amber and red, and cheerful chrysanthemums formed bright potted pompoms along garden paths and outside quiet garages. Pigeons pecked merrily at scraps and seeds, and cats' eyes flashed as the car lights and street lamps reached out to pet them.

Soon enough, the shops of the downtown square came into view: Pawsitively Purrfect Pet Grooming, the Tough as Nails salon, Cooking the Books (a cookbook shop), Plant Food (a vegan bakery), and down the alleyway, Uncle Oswald's shop, Behind the Curtain. Which Bonnie, who admittedly had her witty moments, called the 'Griftertorium'.

Effie approached The Silver Slipper apprehensively, already overwhelmed by the thudding bass and warblings of something that might have been karaoke or just someone loudly lamenting their partner's texting etiquette. The flagstones outside smelt yeasty with spilled beer, and Effie didn't want to know the provenance of that puddle of . . . ugh, carrots and corn.

Turning her head as she always did to avoid eye contact

with Pete the Plumber, who liked to sit in the patio area and show anyone who'd listen the latest and greatest moments from the parts catalogue he'd put together, Effie and her overstuffed book bag collided with a flower basket someone had left sitting on the wall.

Sunflowers, dianthus, lilies and fern fronds landed with a botanical thud, inviting some amused finger-pointing from a few kids Effie recognized as the local supermarket staff poring over dream journals around a mountain of half-empty beer glasses. Were they even old enough to drink, or had Effie just reached the point where anyone under the age of twenty-five looked like a baby?

'Rats,' Effie whispered, stooping to regard the damaged basket. Hiding her wrists behind her book bag, she coaxed forward a thin stream of green magic, enticing it to return the uprooted plants to their rightful places.

'Not a plant lady, huh?' came a voice with the sharp cadence of someone from the city. Effie glanced up to see a tall guy with tousled hair and piercing green eyes – eyes the same colour as her magic – taking her in. He visibly shivered. It must have been much warmer inside because he was wearing only a thin shirt and jeans. Well, and designer shoes, and a watch so clearly expensive it looked as if it had been made from the smelted contents of Fort Knox.

Drink in hand, he stepped out into the same part of the patio that Effie always made a beeline for when Bonnie demanded that she show her face in the name of sisterly solidarity – the bit where the music never quite reached, and the lighting was just right to pull out a paperback on the Balinese love seat if you needed to. Bonnie didn't know this, but Effie had a perpetual charm running on this particular spot, just in case.

'I brought that,' admitted the guy, helping Effie pick it back up and place it on the patio ledge. It teetered, then found its footing. 'A thanks-for-having-me gift.'

'Ah. You must be Theo,' said Effie. He did fit the bill: he looked exactly how she imagined a rich banking heir from the city would look. Right down to the perfect teeth and the starched collar of his shirt – a professional job, not the half-hearted effort with the iron and the quick charm that the Chalmers sisters made do with.

Theo picked up the drink he'd set down on the wall and took a sip. 'Guilty.'

Effie plopped her bag at her feet and gestured around at the quirky, low-rise buildings with their thatched roofs and decorative tiles, some of which were presently being captured in night-time tourist selfies. 'Welcome to Yellowbrick Grove. I hope the town isn't too much of a disappointment after the city.'

'No, no, it's great. I love the skyline. Very restrained.'

'We do have some great stargazing here. I love watching the Pleiades emerge in their cluster and jostle for attention. It hits close to home.'

Theo chuckled – he must have siblings of his own. 'Ah. Personally, I'm a fan of Sirius. I have a soft spot for dogs.'

'You should talk to Bowow Walker, head of our kennel association.'

'Bowow, huh? Is she related to the rapper?'

'Second cousin, twice removed,' said Effie, deadpan. 'Nice flowers, by the way. Did you get those from A Pocket Full of Posies?'

'I did. I'm a bit disappointed they didn't fit in my pocket, though. Misleading advertising,' he replied, with a touch of sarcasm.

'You just need bigger pockets.' Effie showed off the voluminous pockets on her skirt.

'You could smuggle a whole pie in those things.'

'I can, and have. You should see me over the holidays.'

Theo looked impressed. 'I try not to arrive empty-handed, but it's not like you can bring a bottle of wine to a bar. Well, you can, depending on the venue, and the wine. But I was worried that a place called The Silver Slipper might be more about chugging beer from shoes than cellaring fancy vintages.'

Effie chuckled in spite of herself. Was she actually enjoying conversing with this handsome stranger? Bonnie usually had the gift of the gab around men, while Effie hid away, caught up in her anxieties about how she was being perceived and whether she'd be found wanting. It was different at the library, though. That was *her* realm, where her knowledge and her skills (and her secret, magical ability to get books from the top shelves) mattered.

'You would be correct,' she said. 'The only type of vintage my sister has room for is 90s fashion from Etsy.'

'Your sister?' Theo looked confused, as though he were trying to connect Effie to any of the party animals he'd met tonight.

Effie sighed: the *does-not-compute* moment was imminent. Every time a newcomer learned that she and Bonnie were related, you could hear the mental record scratch as they tried to figure it out. Did they have different parents? Was one adopted? Had one been raised in a basement and the other at Disneyland?

'Bonnie,' she said, defeated. 'The one in the sequinned dress with the entourage of harpies.'

Theo blinked. 'But you're nothing like—'

Ah, there it was. The admission that she was the lesser sister, the one that charisma had overlooked, the one whose headstone would eventually read 'Survived by her seventeen cats'.

'Yes. I know,' she said irritably, grabbing her book bag, which was now damp at the bottom. Fabulous. She could only hope the lining had held up, and that spilled beer wasn't seeping up through the stack of mystery novels she was carrying. Not to mention the googly-eyed frog cosy, courtesy of Tessa, that encased her favourite lunchbox.

A blast of music roared as the bar's door swung open and Bonnie emerged, wearing nothing but a man's jacket and a pair of high heels. The jacket was buttoned, at least, making the overall ensemble quite tame by Bonnie's standards.

'Theo, babe, are you hiding out here?' called Bonnie. 'It's no fun without the guest of the hour.'

Theo flinched, but only slightly. Forcing a smile, he turned, waving with his glass. 'Sure. I was just talking to . . . Hey, wait up!'

But Effie and her books were already on their way back home.

Chapter 4

DO I HAVE TO SPELL IT OUT?

Bonnie

Ouch, her head. Bonnie's skull was inhabited by a thousand galloping stallions, who with each pounding hoof sent a clap of thunder pounding right behind her eyes. Even her biggest, darkest sunglasses and her strongest painkillers were not cutting it.

'Big night?' asked Terrance, one of the cute baristas at The Winged Monkey, the town's highly photogenic coffee shop. Wedged beneath a rabbit warren of offices and apartments, it was an airy space crammed with plants and pottery. Whoever had furnished it had been given a clear mission to select items that were either rickety or cosy (not both), and as a result, the seating options were plush, deep couches and hanging egg chairs surrounding cute little tables that habitually spilled cookies and coffee all over the floor.

'The welcome party for the new banker from the city,' said Bonnie. Every consonant sounded like a particularly zealous percussionist bashing a set of timpani between her ears. Bonnie wasn't allowed to drink on the clock – an annoying law that admittedly did make sense – but she'd made up for lost time after they'd shut down the bar and continued the party on the back patio of the Dorothy House, an adorable cottage that Hannah was in the process of selling.

'There could be a buyer among us, right?' she'd asked the group, who'd responded with a drunken roll call of credit scores.

Apparently, just as you shouldn't feed gremlins after midnight, you also shouldn't do shots after 2 a.m.

'Banker, huh. I'm studying business, you know,' said Terrance hopefully as he whipped up Bonnie's usual triple chai cinnamon latte. 'I'm also working on cultivating a photographic memory. I can do half a deck of cards. The full deck is going to be my audition for College Kids Got Talent.'

'Good for you, child.' Unfortunately for Terrance, anyone with a mullet was officially too young for Bonnie, and card memorization was definitely not on her list of sexy hobbies. It was up there with Bobby's D&D fascination, which she'd never understood. Although, the way Bobby's eyes lit up when he was talking about gnomes or whatever *was* a bit endearing.

Terrance pouted, but recovered quickly. He spun around the iPad. 'And with your discount . . .'

Bonnie smiled as she added her tip. She had a discount at most places in town, which she thought only fair given the contribution she made to the local economy, and the generous pours she provided at The Silver Slipper, where you definitely got your money's worth in every glass.

Bonnie staggered off to the twin pink velvet couches that she and her entourage claimed every Saturday morning. Regrets. So many regrets. Not least that for all of her flirting and sassing and all the preparatory Googling she'd done on foreign exchange and hedge funds, her guest of honour had been decidedly uninterested.

'I don't understand.' Bonnie traced the heart that Terrance had drawn on her cup. 'I literally took off my dress *right in front of him*, and he didn't react.'

Her wrists glimmered lightly, and she placed her hands beneath the table.

'Maybe he's asexual,' mused Hannah, polishing off a muffin so large that it must have been stolen from atop a beanstalk.

'Maybe the breakup broke him,' said Kirsty. 'He *was* talking to your sister. On purpose.'

Kirsty had a point. Perhaps he was avoiding putting his heart out there, and what better way to sidestep that risk than by engaging Effie, of all people, in conversation. After all, there was nothing like participating in an episode of Effie's long-running show, *Who Wants to Feel Bad About Their Life Choices?*, to put you off diving back into the dating waters.

Alana downed her wheatgrass shot. The bell sleeves on her kaftan almost knocked over Bonnie's very much needed coffee as she gestured for Terrance to rustle up another. 'You know what always works? Jealousy. Competition. *Emotional unavailability.*'

'I'm listening,' said Bonnie. This sounded like a scheme, which was one of Bonnie's favourite ways to spend her time. Especially if Bonnie got to be at the heart of said scheme.

Alana pulled out her pill case and started popping multi-vitamins like Bonnie might M&Ms. 'We need to make it look like you're off the market – or close to it. He'll think if he doesn't act soon, he's going to miss out altogether.'

'The scarcity principle, huh.' Bonnie had learned about this during her short course on business marketing the college had opened up to the public earlier in the year.

'You could use Bobby,' suggested Hannah, ostensibly touching up her lip gloss. Like any good friend, she was actually using her compact mirror to see who might be listening. 'He follows you around like a puppy anyway. You might as well put him to good use.'

'The bar certainly isn't his calling,' agreed Kirsty. Her long nails flashed as she swirled her espresso in her cup. 'You know he used house vodka in my drink? House. Vodka. He should know that I'm top shelf or nothing!'

Hearing the word 'vodka' made Bonnie's head hurt. She rubbed her temple.

'Bobby means well,' she said. 'And the amount of free labour I get out of him is criminal. Besides . . .'

Hannah regarded her curiously over the remains of her muffin. 'Besides?'

Bonnie *had* been going to say that she'd always thought Bobby was kind of cute, and moreover, actually one of the kindest people she knew, but she wasn't about to give her friends that kind of ammunition. The one thing about being queen bee was that you never, ever showed weakness, especially when that weakness manifested as questionable taste in men. Ugh, this hangover was doing a number on her.

'It's a great idea,' she said, toasting with her mug. 'Two boys, one stone-cold fox.'

Chuckling, her friends toasted back.

'To killing the boys with babehood,' said Hannah.

Kirsty leaned back in her chair, squinting at the outside through the plant-smothered window. 'Wait, is that Theo? Where's he off to this early?'

Trying to get a better look, Bonnie dragged her Ray-Bans down over her nose. Instant regret. She promptly popped the sunglasses back up, blinking as her poor, dehydrated brain tried to find equilibrium.

'Not yoga,' decided Alana, taking in Theo's running clothes: understated but designer, and marred with sweat, even given the chilly morning. 'Although he could do both. Runners do have weak glutes – yoga can help with that.'

Kirsty chugged her espresso and stood. 'I can give him my loyalty card. I'm only two stars off a free session.'

'Good idea, Kirst.' Trying to keep her tone light, Bonnie snatched the punch card out of Kirsty's hand and hurried to the door. 'Can you clear the mugs for me, babe?'

'Sure thing, babe!' said Kirsty, her smile tighter than Bonnie's favourite pair of jeans.

Bonnie blew her a kiss. 'I have the best friends a girl could ask for,' she said cheerily as her eyes narrowed. *Watch yourself, Kirsty*.

'Are you going for a run, or are you being chased?'

Bonnie stepped out from behind the fountain at Linda Park, one of the four small parks that formed an emerald of green around the downtown square, and which Theo had chosen as his jogging track. Startled by her sudden appearance, a trio of green-throated ducks waddled off towards the turtle pond, forcing an approaching skateboarder to leap to one side to avoid a situation that would have sent feathers flying. Shelby, the long-necked centenarian turtle who hung out in the fountain, blinked disparagingly. No doubt Shelby had seen plenty of engineered meet-cutes over the years.

All right, perhaps this wasn't one of the better ones. But *you* try catching a runner. And besides, Bonnie wasn't usually the one doing the chasing. She was a novice when it came to this particular type of courtship.

Acknowledging her with the wave of a sweaty hand, Theo stopped in his tracks, then dropped his head, placing his hands to his knees as he tried to catch his breath. Sweat streamed down his neck and chest, forming a damp trail around a knotted leather necklace. Leather – an interesting choice. Bonnie wasn't sure how she felt about that. Was he a surfer? A time traveller?

No, she was not about to get the ick. Not over something as tiny as a necklace. Not when she had an entire scheme going. Especially not when Kirsty was eyeing an elevated spot in the pecking order. She had a reputation to uphold, not to mention physical needs. Once this hangover passed, anyway.

Catching his eye, Bonnie repeated her 'being chased' line, but Theo looked at her as though she was an alien who had asked him his thoughts on interstellar travel.

'Sorry, podcast,' he said, tapping a white earphone. He stretched out an Achilles. 'What was that?'

You could manage an impeccable delivery once. A decent

delivery a second time. But the third time? Why bother. Bonnie wasn't going to lower herself by repeating it.

'Never mind,' she said easily, even though her inner voice was having quite the monologue. 'I just saw you out and about and wanted to see how you're getting on.'

'Good. Great.' His finger hovered over his earphone. Bonnie had never seen anyone so anxious to get back to his podcast. What was he listening to? Serial-killer true crime? Movie recaps? Hopefully not a bald gym-bro guy. 'This is a really sweet little town,' he added, seeing that Bonnie wasn't going to let him go that easily. 'Everyone's been so welcoming.'

Bonnie took a step back to allow a power-walking mom with a double stroller past. The mom was video-calling in an extreme outdoor voice about the perks of astral travel when you were stuck at home with the kids.

Fair enough.

'Do you need any help finding anything?' pressed Bonnie. 'Groceries, doughnuts, dry cleaners? I know all the best spots. And I can get you hooked up with mates' rates.'

Theo raised an eyebrow. 'Mates' rates, huh?'

Aha, a multi-syllabic response! Not all was lost.

'It's one of Gerald Ho's weird New Zealand sayings,' she explained.

'Ah. But I'm good, thanks. I've got my GPS to show me around.' Theo tapped his watch, which wasn't the fancy one from the night before, but a smartwatch that flashed with his vital signs. Hmm, his heart rate was dropping instead of increasing, which meant that Bonnie was *not* doing her job. But Bonnie was a problem-solver by nature.

With Theo's attention away from her and on his watch, Bonnie covered her wrist with her hand and focused her magic, sending it streaming towards Theo's watch. The watch grew warm – so warm that an alarmed look crossed Theo's face and he stripped off the rubber band, hurling it to the ground.

'Did my eyes deceive me, or did I just see sparks fly?' joked Bonnie, as Theo stared confusedly down at his watch, which was glowing red on the yellow brick paving stones that the town stubbornly stuck with some 200 years after its founding. The bricks were made from local clay, from a quarry that was apparently bottomless, but which had a decent swimming hollow nearby. Poor Officer Brigsley had to escort particularly rowdy members of the town's youth from it on a daily basis.

'Weird. It's like you're some sort of bad luck charm,' said Theo. 'No offence. But after the fire last night, and now this . . .'

Bonnie forced a smile, or maybe bared her teeth. She wasn't close enough to a mirror to tell. But hopefully Theo hadn't noticed the emotion behind the expression. In fact, he probably hadn't, because he was busy prodding his watch with a stick. A bad luck charm! Now *that* was a first – the odd snide remark from Kirsty aside. Bonnie was the opposite of a bad luck charm: she brought wit and cookies and an elevated likelihood of ending up on the local news wherever she went!

'At least I have Apple Care. Is there an—'

Bonnie guffawed. 'There is absolutely not an Apple Store around here. Sure you don't need help with that GPS?' She scrunched her eyes at the corners in the way she'd been told was irresistible.

Until now.

Theo mopped his neck with the collar of his shirt. 'I can definitely find my way around a place too small to have an Apple Store.'

'Well, the town is on a grid system.' Bonnie was doing her best to be charitable. 'I believe in you. If you end up at the base of the mountain near the Toto Hotel, you've gone too far. If you end up back at the bar, you've gone just far enough.'

'Noted.' Theo grinned, flashing his astonishingly white teeth. 'Oh hey, I wanted to ask about your sister.'

'Effie?' Bonnie failed to keep the disbelief from her voice.

'Effie,' repeated Theo, rolling it around in his mouth in a way that left Bonnie feeling as though she'd disappeared into Opposite Land. 'I didn't get her name last night. But if you see her, can you let her know I'm sorry? I think we got off on the wrong foot.'

'Everyone gets off on the wrong foot with Effie.' Bonnie waved an exasperated hand. 'That's just Effie. She's not happy unless she's miserable. But we live together, so I'm sure I'll get a chance to tell her.'

Theo put his dead watch back on. 'You live together, huh? Must be like living in a sitcom.'

'Definitely not as many laughs,' said Bonnie. 'She needs to borrow some books on humour from that library of hers.'

Theo nodded thoughtfully, giving Bonnie the very odd feeling that the social order had somehow shifted, and that this handsome stranger might be interested in . . . Effie? It couldn't be. She must be misreading the signals.

'Not that our library has anything on the ones in the city,' Bonnie hurriedly backtracked, suddenly worried that Theo might take it upon himself to visit the town's library. Was he a reader? Were bankers bookish types? Did the library have a subscription to the *Financial Times*? 'There's absolutely no reason to see it. It's just *old*. With these big, cracked steps, and *gargoyles*. And a creepy guy who lurks out back.'

'Sure.' Theo tapped his earphone, and the tinny sounds of his podcast crackled from his ear. 'I'm gonna get back to it before I have to warm up all over again. These knees aren't what they used to be.'

Ah, the self-deprecating young-person-pretending-to-be-an-old-person jokes. Maybe Bonnie had been right about the ick. Perhaps Theo wasn't love interest material after all. He probably had a 9 p.m. bedtime and dragged himself out of bed early to meditate. Which meant he'd likely frequent

Alana's yoga studio after all, thought Bonnie, eyes narrowed. Or, given the knotted leather strap she'd noticed around his neck, maybe Uncle Oswald's Griftertorium, home to the town's most sought-after, fraudulent crystals and moon-charged, possibly diphtheria-infused water.

'Great! Well, see you at the bar some time!' Bonnie waved uselessly as Theo jogged off through the park in a blissful state of 360-degree podcast audio.

As she stalked back across the park and towards the bar, an odd concern twisted at her stomach: something had changed, and for the first time since she'd turned fourteen, this town might no longer be wholly hers.

Chapter 5

A WOLF IN WIZARD'S CLOTHING

Effie

If you invited Effie to wax lyrical about her perfect day, it would not involve visiting Uncle Oswald's shop. Of all the humans in Yellowbrick Grove, Uncle Oswald was among those she least wanted to spend time around, and that included Bonnie's Greek chorus of harpies. (All right, so she was mixing her mythologies – though remixes were in, judging by the borrowing uptick she'd seen in genre mashups.)

But Uncle Oswald had apparently dug up a photo of Mom that he thought she might like, and she wasn't about to say no to that. Even though she knew that the gift was almost certainly not without strings. Uncle Oswald was absolutely going to request that Effie gently hex some of his crystals or apply a charm to his useless potions. Depending on the quality of the photo, she might give some of his nicer products a light glimmer, but that was where her assistance would end.

Fortunately, Tessa was coming along for moral support, although this was less about helping Effie fend off Uncle Oswald's endless beseeching requests and more about the cat statue one of the townsfolk had told her about: the one that apparently Uncle Oswald had sourced from an Egyptian vendor of all things magical. Tessa and her cousin Claudette, who lived in rural South Carolina, had a running bet where they bought each other cat figurines and paraphernalia, a game that would only ever end if one of them bought the other a piece she already had. They'd been going strong with it for over a decade, and the cats were getting more obscure and increasingly abstract. There were a few that Effie wasn't entirely sure sat under the feline umbrella, but she wasn't about to bring that up and risk having to play cat statue adjudicator.

'Cat statue. Lyra photo. We both win.' Tessa tied back her cloud of curls with a bandanna and rolled up the cuffs of her jeans before unchaining her bike from the novelty rack outside the library, which was made from curved yellow metal shaped to spell out READ. Balancing on one pedal, she rode alongside Effie, who was on foot. 'Although next time you should bring your skates.'

'Shh!' Swiping her white streak of hair behind her ear, Effie glanced around. She'd been learning to roller-skate on her days off, and the last few times she had even managed to travel in a straight line without falling on her butt. But she definitely didn't need Bonnie finding out about her efforts. Or worse, Alana, who would spread the news around town like some highly contagious disease until it somehow ended up on Kirsty's blog.

'All right, all right.' Tessa pushed her oversized glasses up her nose – only Tessa could make a giant's glasses look good. 'Thanks for squeezing it in on your break, though. I know it's hard to leave the siren call of the book stacks. And the very exciting peanut butter and jelly sandwich I know you packed.'

'On extra-seedy brown bread,' agreed Effie, shooting Tessa a grin. All right, so maybe she could stand to be a *tad* more adventurous in life. 'And it was almost as hard as leaving the twins, I bet.'

Tessa chuckled. In the past year she'd given up a lucrative accounting career for the much lower-stress job of walking the neighbourhood dogs. Although this was a financially questionable choice, it was mostly a great one – except when it came to the two extremely barky, extremely vicious chihuahuas that she and Effie had nicknamed the twins. Effie had never met any other creatures so murderously inclined. Anyone who came within six feet of them feared for their ankles. But worrying about your ankles was preferable to having to desperately piece together a company's finances using the receipts they'd shoved into a plastic bag.

'So, how's the new guy in town?' asked Tessa shrewdly, once they were headed towards the town square. 'Did you get to meet him?'

Effie grimaced. 'I did. He was appropriately baffled by how little I resemble the great and charismatic Bonnie.'

Tessa curved her bike around a bright wildflower growing up from a crack in the ground. 'One of those, huh.'

'One of the many. At least they always get it out of the way fast.'

'It's better than wondering, I suppose.' Tessa lapsed into silence, frowning. Effie suspected she was wondering about Alana, whose yoga sessions she'd been assiduously attending since the studio had opened. Tessa had never openly mentioned her crush, but she'd clearly been pining for the least evil of the harpy entourage since their high-school days.

'How's teen crochet night coming along?' asked Effie presently, trying to change the subject from love and feelings, two things that usually only resulted in pain. Just look at the entire gothic romance genre.

'Oh, we're going to have a blast! We're doing turtles in honour of Shelby's hundredth birthday.' In addition to being exceptional at mathematics, Tessa was also exceptional at crafts, and was capable of creating cute things via any craft method you could dream up. She hosted the teens craft club at the library, and always got rave reviews. In the past few months, she'd helped her loyal gang of thirteen-year-olds bead pens, make stained glass, and fashion friendship bracelets for each other. Next up, according to the photo Tessa was flashing on her bedazzled phone as she coasted along, was crochet turtles.

'We should definitely do a turtle display,' mused Effie. 'Although is it really Shelby's centenary?'

Tessa grinned mischievously. 'That's my story, and I'm sticking to it. Besides, it's rude to ask a turtle their age.'

They were downtown now, cruising up to the picturesque square, all brightly painted gabled buildings covered with ivy and hanging flower baskets and cheerful shrubs in enormous pots. Sculptures and murals adorned every side wall and plinth, and curved streetlights glowed with antique globes. Outside the old bank, Carlos the busker strummed away at his guitar. A few families were sitting on the steps listening, their kids dancing and clapping away in time with his upbeat tunes.

There were so many reasons to love the town, and with its charming shops and picnic benches, the town square was definitely somewhere at the top of the list. Well, except for the rent-a-scooters that were constantly strewn all over. When Effie was alone, she'd either haul or magic them back into their racks.

'Obstacle course incoming.' With Effie in tow, Tessa carefully wove her bike around a clump of scooters.

The cheerful tune of Carlos's guitar followed them as they made their way across the bumpy cobblestones of the square and down the alleyway that housed Uncle Oswald's shop. Dreamily painted with a sprawling mural of night-blooming flowers, and strung back and forth with rows of cafe lights, the alleyway was a favourite of the influencer set and tipsy couples. Tessa leaned her bike on the wall outside Uncle Oswald's shop, a wonky brick building painted black and patterned with splotches of gold, set between a gourmet spice shop and a small art gallery sponsored by the college. The shop's window display featured two crystal hands whose fingers were draped with glittering gold charms and their palms stacked with gleaming rock cairns. Around them were candles of all shapes and sizes, each with their prices proudly displayed.

Painted in huge gold letters on the façade were the words *Behind the Curtain*.

'All right. Let's go get a weird cat sculpture!' Tessa made cat claws with her stubby nails.

Family awkwardness, here I come. Effie squared her shoulders, preparing to be assaulted with incense-thick air and the warbling tones of Enya, and followed her friend in.

A gong rumbled through the room as they stepped over the threshold, pushing their way through the clinking beaded curtain that overhung the door. Inside, the shop was a rabbit warren of kitschy, pricey displays: there was nothing that didn't have a handwritten price tag hanging from it. Yin and yang tapestries hung from the ceiling, while Turkish rugs covered every inch of the floor in floral splendour. Salt lamps spilled magma-hued light over towers of Wadjet eye magnets and the alien-head pins spilling out of myriad crystal bowls. Black and purple tea candles formed pyramids on the rickety furniture, while the bowls of tumbled crystals reminded Effie of the vegetable displays at the Sunday farmers' market that set up in the square.

Bells and chimes jangled as Tessa brushed past them in search of her cat sculpture. Effie, hurrying after her, stubbed her toe on a massive geode. She swore, sparking her magic at it to increase its visibility for the next unsuspecting guest.

But things were about to get even worse than a toe-stubbing. Uncle Oswald had emerged, and was schooling a group of students in the healing properties of crystals.

'Welcome to Behind the Curtain! I see you're dealing with . . . anxiety issues, no?'

The students all nodded. Holding up a finger, Uncle Oswald emptied a black velvet bag onto the hammered-brass elephant table in front of him. A series of watermelon-coloured gemstones landed on the elephant.

'Tourmaline,' whispered Uncle Oswald, twirling his awful moustache with a finger – ugh, Effie hated that moustache. He whipped his cape from side to side in a practised move. 'Now, this one becomes electrically charged when heated or squeezed, helping you move those toxins and stressors out of your body and into your crystal.'

The students exchanged unimpressed looks.

'Keep it close, and you'll see it work its magic on your circulation, bones and teeth, and, perhaps most importantly, bloating.'

'I reiki my own crystals,' whispered a student in dayglo Birkenstocks to their friend, who wore a pink beanie perched atop her waist-length hair. 'I saw this great video on it. I'll show you.'

'Truly, if it's stress management and sleep support you're looking for, in addition to a *hundred* other things, tourmaline is the panacea.' Realizing he was losing his audience, Uncle Oswald unfurled a scroll detailing the ways that tourmaline could heal the body, support the heart and save the soul. 'Who wants to pick up a piece and feel it take on their warmth?'

The students shrugged, looking at each other and waiting for someone else to take the lead. Finally, apparently feeling bad for Oswald, the girl in the pink beanie took the watermelon-coloured stone.

'It's kinda warm, I think?' she said after a moment. She passed it to another girl clad in a Little Mermaid T-shirt roughly ten sizes too big. 'Here, you try.'

'It's pretty?' offered the girl. 'Although my CBD pen is pretty good for stress relief. And it's way cheaper.'

'You won't get prices better than these – or purer gems,' Oswald reassured her. 'We're looking at just $300 for a carat of the green, and about double that for the watermelon samples. For the Paraíba blue, the sought-after Brazilian option, we'll talk out back. And remember, every gemstone in Behind the Curtain has been blessed under a full moon, doubling its efficacy and its protective nature.'

The students hesitated.

'I do my own moon-charging,' murmured a girl with green-and-white striped hair that Effie wasn't sure was deliberate or the result of a terrible accident involving household bleach.

'I can do $250 for the green,' offered Uncle Oswald, who was slightly sheened with sweat. Apparently the evil within was coming to the surface for a breather. 'I can feel the elevated stress levels you're giving off. Your auras, they're positively buzzing with it.'

The students now looked anxiously tempted, and Effie wanted nothing more than to step in and tell them to spend their money on some books instead. Or even better, to keep their money and sign up for a library card. She felt her wrists growing warm. Perhaps she could disrupt the 5G signal in here and prevent any payments from going through. But Effie wasn't one to meddle, especially not through magic. Mom had always emphasized how *impractical* magic could be, that in spite of your best efforts and most charitable goals, it had a habit of going wrong, especially when used on other people. Not only that, but it invited questions, and questions invited attention. Too much attention, and you ended up staring out at a yard full of pitchfork-toting townsfolk, like Great-Aunt Grace, who – well, the less said about that, the better.

'Aha! Found it!' exclaimed Tessa. She hefted a Bastet cat sculpture with lapis eyes and ears. 'Claudette's going to love it. There's no way she has something this gaudy.'

Uncle Oswald's eyes lit up at the sight. 'Wonderful taste. Just wonderful. He's been calling out for an owner, um . . .'

'Tessa,' supplied Effie, setting down the agate coaster she'd just been inspecting. 'We've only been friends our entire lives.'

'Of course, of course. You must forgive me.' Oswald tapped his temple with a ringed finger. 'My fluorite memory crystals need to be recharged.'

'Well, there's a full moon coming up,' offered Effie drily, sparking some excited muttering from the students. 'You can leave them out with your potions and moon water. I find the bug corpses give it an extra kick.'

Oswald's brow furrowed. He knew he was being mocked, but didn't want to call it out in front of his customers, who were still whispering together about the tourmaline. Which was probably just polished glass, knowing Uncle Oswald.

'I'm definitely taking the cat. What's your best price?' asked Tess, her hand on the sculpture.

Uncle Oswald tapped the price tag, which had a number written in gold and was attached to the statue by a thin gold string. He might be a charlatan, but Uncle Oswald *did* know a little something about branding. 'The price is final.'

Tessa shook her head. 'The price is never final.'

'Let's start at half and go from there.' Effie regarded an ornate crystal grid, a decorative laser-cut board arranged with a rainbow profusion of crystals. It promised total calm for a mere thousand bucks (board included).

'Half!' If Uncle Oswald had magic, his wrists would've been crackling in indignation.

Effie raised an eyebrow. 'And throw in a pack of those tarot cards before I tell your shoppers about the source of your tourmaline.'

Uncle Oswald spluttered. 'I'm only discounting this because I have a familial responsibility to you. Because Lyra would have wanted me to help her girls.'

He plucked the cat from its velvet display and carried it off to the register, hopefully eyeing the students as he rang up the cat.

'And have we made our decision?' he called across the room, clearly hoping to get ahead of Effie's threatened comments about his tourmaline pricing.

'We're thinking about it,' said one of the students, who'd been regarding a price tag with raised eyebrows.

'Take your time.' Uncle Oswald said it cheerfully, but a scowl tensed his mouth as he finished ringing up Tessa's order.

Tessa returned with her carefully packaged cat sculpture, which swung in a gold-stamped paper bag with twine handles.

'Half price? You're definitely coming on my next yard sale adventure,' she whispered. 'That was some impressive haggling. Although don't you feel bad ripping off your own family?'

Effie waggled a chunk of heat-treated amethyst at Tessa. 'Honestly, yours is one of the better pieces in here. What he's done to this amethyst is criminal. And those crystal grids are just laser-etched cutting boards. If I were a betting person, I'd say the gems are ordered in bulk online, then dipped in nail polish for some extra shimmer.'

'Well, you have to give him points for creativity.'

Effie was unconvinced. 'Do I, though?'

Squaring her cardiganed shoulders, she went up to the students, passing out her head librarian business card. 'We're doing an evening class on crystals at the library later, if you're interested. It's mostly geology focused, but we can teach you how to pick out fakes.'

'Are fakes a problem?' asked the student in the pink beanie.

'Huge,' said Tessa, her naturally long-lashed eyes wide. 'Imagine thinking you're getting a crystal to help you sleep, and bam. You're grinding your teeth like you've been main-lining espresso all day.'

The student with the green-and-white striped hair grimaced. 'We'll think about it,' she called out to Uncle Oswald, whose eyes narrowed behind his ostentatious glasses, which were so on the nose (literally) that they made Effie feel bad about being a glasses wearer.

The door chimed as the students waltzed out, their reusable bags empty but their bank accounts full.

'You cost me a potential sale,' said Uncle Oswald, folding his arms.

'Are you sure?' asked Tessa, wandering off to inspect an alchemical singing bowl. 'They seemed like they were pretty au fait with all this DIY crystal stuff.'

'Besides, they said they'd think about it,' added Effie. 'And when they come back, they'll be informed buyers.'

'Informed *not* to buy,' noted Uncle Oswald churlishly.

Well, he'd said it, not her.

Effie jumped as Tessa ran a mallet over the edge of the singing bowl, sending a resonant tone vibrating across the room. Tessa grinned, then tested out another bowl.

'Go on. You and I both know that you're not on the up and up here. This isn't magic. It's snake oil. None of it works.'

Oswald snorted. 'Bah. Who cares as long as they *believe* it's working? That's what we're dealing in here, isn't it? Belief. Moon-charged water? Sure, it's nonsense. Crystals? They look nice. But if someone honestly thinks their necklace is helping with their mood or their memory potion is helping them pass that exam, what's the harm?'

'The harm is that it's fraud,' said Effie. 'And at these prices, it's also extortion.'

'I have expenses,' said Uncle Oswald icily. 'Besides, if certain individuals wouldn't gatekeep their magic, I could be more accommodating with my offerings.'

The hum of Tessa's singing bowl crescendoed.

Effie bristled. There was no gatekeeping about it! Magic was a form of power, and it had to be handled carefully. You couldn't go about casting spells and enacting charms

willy-nilly, thinking that you knew what was best for
everyone else. Every action caused a reaction, and every
spell had consequences. Which was why Effie kept hers
small and mundane.

'I'd like the picture of Mom you promised,' said Effie, 'and
then we're leaving.'

Uncle Oswald stuttered – this whole interaction clearly
hadn't gone the way he'd wanted. 'We got off on the wrong
foot,' he stammered, holding out a newspaper-wrapped parcel
like an olive branch. 'Let's start over.'

The singing bowl went silent.

'Sorry, dropped the mallet,' Tessa called, scrabbling around
on the carpet for it.

Grateful for the interruption, Effie took the parcel, holding
it to her heart as though Mom's warmth and goodness might
seep from the picture into her. But she didn't want to open
it right here, not in front of Oswald, whose presence only
ever darkened things.

She checked her watch. 'Make it quick. I have to get back
to work – I have a crystal display to put together.'

Tessa, who'd thankfully given up on becoming a professional singing-bowl performer, hefted her gift bag. 'And *I*
have a cat to mail to South Carolina.'

There. Effie put her hands on her skirted hips, admiring the
crystal display she'd set up in the reading room – a display
that couldn't be further from Uncle Oswald's expensive crystal
grids. They even had real samples, courtesy of the rock collection that the Grosvenors, one of the town's oldest families,
had donated a few decades back. The fancy art on the walls
was also from them. Effie wasn't sure that an art loan replaced
the taxes they'd avoided paying over the years, but a librarian
wielded only so much power.

The exhibit was aesthetically pleasing, and educational, for
she'd pulled as many geology books as she could find to

include as a backdrop for the display. She'd always prided herself on her strong science communication skills, an ability she'd honed from years of being asked to summarize books and articles for curious library patrons.

Uncle Oswald's student shoppers might not learn much about the metaphysical properties of tourmaline, but they'd come away experts on its pyroelectric properties, and the knowledge that it was used in hair-styling tools. If only Bonnie was here. She'd have a field day with that fact.

Now there's a magical property, she could imagine her sister saying as she fluffed her perfect blonde locks.

'Rocks!' exclaimed Bowow, who in today's adventures in sartorial clashing had paired a chevron-patterned shirt with floral pants. She'd topped the ensemble off with a polka-dot scarf. Dumping her stack of romance novels on a nearby table, she picked up a sparkly quartz cluster. 'Now we're talking. I could joust with this thing.'

'Please don't,' said Effie. 'Jousting is strictly against the library code of conduct.'

Bowow made a face. 'When did we vote on that?'

'At our March Friends of the Library meeting. It was after the whole Renaissance Fair debacle in the community room. The three smashed windows? *And* the gouges in the walls. You can check the minutes.'

Bruce the would-be rocker sidled up, pulling a basket of orange books behind him. All about portability and 70s cover design, he gravitated towards tiny vintage Penguin editions.

'Crystals,' he said appreciatively. 'I love a good crystal. All that glitters . . .' He picked up a piece of fool's gold and held it to an ear like an earring, making Bowow chuckle.

When he raised a bushy eyebrow at her, she cut her laugh short.

'I'm laughing *at* you, not *with* you,' she huffed, jabbing him with the quartz.

'There'll be no assault in the library, thank you,' said Effie drily. 'Although I won't report you if you help me put together a turtle display. It's to go with Tessa's craft session tonight. Apparently we're celebrating Shelby's centennial.'

Bruce frowned. 'I thought that was three years ago.'

Effie shrugged. 'Time moves differently when you're a turtle.'

'I can help with the turtle display,' came a low voice from behind Effie. It was Theo, dressed casually but immaculately, carrying a small chapbook volume of . . . was that poetry? Surely not. Bankers and poetry were inherently antithetical.

Perhaps he liked the short sentences. Or he'd picked it up from the Little Free Library down by the square.

'I didn't know you were a library member,' said Effie archly.

'I'm not yet. But could I be? I have all my ID.' Theo calmly waved his licence and a utility bill. How was his energy use so restrained, wondered Effie, glimpsing the monthly total at the bottom. And how was his payment so *prompt*, she thought approvingly, looking at the PAID stamp on the bill. It was the same date as the date of issue.

Poetry, timely bill payments, and now a library card? Effie wasn't even sure how to respond to this trifecta of desirability. She decided on her usual approach for when something seemed too good to be true: suspicion.

'Sure,' she said primly. 'The library always welcomes new members. And if you'd like to join our Friends of the Library group, here are the membership tiers.'

It was a standard part of the joining spiel – the Friends volunteer group was a major source of fundraising and support. All the author visits, the paint and sip nights, the silent auctions, the read with a service dog days, they were all thanks to the Friends. And assuming Theo decided to stick around in town, which was a big *if* given just how different life here was from the city, he could be a valuable asset. Not only was he good with money, but he *had* money, which was a handy thing to have in a Friends member. And yet, she desperately hoped he didn't want to join. The library was Effie's sanctuary, her quiet world away from the rest of the realm that Bonnie ruled over with such *vim* and *verve* and all the words that Effie quietly loved but could never in a million years inhabit. And Theo was clearly of Bonnie's world, not hers. The thought of those two worlds merging made Effie's stomach twist. Bonnie had the entire town. By virtue of her noise and messiness, she even had most of the house.

'Sign me up. And here, I'll make that donation, too.' Theo prodded at the largest dollar donation amount on the page as Effie typed in his details. His driver's licence photo was a good one, although old. From the looks of it, he was a bit scruffier now compared to the Theo of a few years ago. And there was definitely a sadness in those compellingly hooded eyes that hadn't been there before. And if sadness was going to show up anywhere, it was going to be in your driver's licence photo. Nothing sucked happiness from the depths of your soul like a visit to the DMV. Even Bonnie had had to demand a retake of hers. Retakes weren't standard procedure, but when you were Bonnie, there was nothing a little flirting couldn't get you.

'All right,' said Effie calmly, even as a voice inside her screamed, *No, don't do it! Let me have* something. She filled in his application, then offered him a pen to sign his name. Theo reached for it, but somehow fumbled, knocking over a tin of pens onto the library floor, and taking Uncle Oswald's photo down with it. Effie grabbed protectively for the photo, which showed Mom leaning back in her favourite armchair, a cup of tea in hand. Effie's wrists glimmered as she raced against gravity. She caught the photo just before it hit freefall, and crossed her fingers that Theo hadn't noticed the magical help she'd received.

'I was told that jousting wasn't allowed in the library!' shouted Bowow, cackling.

'Inside voice, Bowow,' warned Effie, scooting the photo back across the desk and out of reach of any additional mishaps. 'This isn't preschool story time.'

Muttering apologies, Theo stooped to pick up the wayward pens. Thankfully, he seemed oblivious to Effie's spontaneous display of magic.

'I'm a butterfingers lately,' he said, depositing the pens back in their holder. 'Did your sister tell you that I accidentally sprayed her with fire-extinguisher foam?'

'She did not!' said Effie, doing her best to fight back a grin. She leaned forwards, arms folded. 'This is the sort of general interest, high-action, high-stakes story the library needs to hear.'

'Well, I think you've got the gist. But that's why she was wearing my jacket.'

'Ah,' said Effie, trying not to be pleased that there was an explanation that didn't involve Bonnie throwing herself at Theo. 'It all becomes clear.'

'I hope so,' said Theo. He frowned. 'This is a weird thing to say, but is your sister . . .'

Here it came. The inevitable question. He'd tried buttering up the boring sister to get to the appealing one. And she'd fallen for it, as she always did. As used to this dynamic as Effie was, sometimes she wanted the guy asking to be interested in *her*.

Not that she'd know how to respond if ever the time came. What did one even do with a man?

'Worth the effort?' said Effie, handing over the library card.

Theo, who'd been about to offer his credit card in exchange, blinked in confusion. 'No, not that. Things keep catching fire when she's around. First the room at the bar, then my watch.' He tapped his scorched smartwatch. 'I was going to ask if she was a pyromaniac?'

Well, that was unexpected. But not unwelcome.

Could it be that Bonnie's charms didn't work on everyone, after all? Pondering this, Effie bit back a shy smile.

Next to her, Mom's image seemed to wink.

Chapter 6

THIS SPELLS TROUBLE

Bonnie

Bonnie wiped down the bar for approximately the thousandth time that morning. Was it dirty? No. Were they even open for business yet? Also no. Bonnie was procrastinating in the hope that her million unfinished tasks somehow took the hint and resolved themselves without her intervention. It wasn't out of the question. She'd been in enough group projects to know that eventually someone got the work done. And when it happened, Bonnie would be the first to volunteer to do the presentation part – she always got top marks for her presentations.

The morning wasn't going to plan. She'd finally shaken the hangover, but she wasn't able to shake the fact that Theo was apparently impervious to her charms. Was he a warlock or something? Had he bathed in some sort of attraction-repelling enchantment? Bonnie wasn't entirely sure that such a thing existed, but if you could repel coyotes with bear pee (as Bobby and his little brother Kevvie, both avid campers, vowed) presumably either science or magic could make it happen.

The thing was, she wasn't even *that* attracted to him. He was handsome, sure, and she appreciated a guy with smart footwear and a bank account robust enough that he wouldn't come begging for gas money or funds for an urgent tattoo cover-up, something that had been a frequent theme among the good-looking bad boys Bonnie tended to gravitate towards. But she didn't feel the spark she assumed she would have based on his on-paper stats. Could sparks be cultivated? They'd have to be, because when Bonnie had set her eyes on a prize, she was not one for going home empty-handed. Or empty-bedded, for that matter.

The bar's smart doorbell chimed, breaking through the sultry tones of her Lana Del Rey playlist. She squinted at the grainy video that showed up on her phone. A delivery guy, but hauling an enormous cart of something white.

What on earth?

Bobby, who had a truck, handled most of the deliveries, but every now and then an actual uniformed guy showed up to drop off something big. Meaning expensive, Bonnie thought with a sigh.

She stalked outside to help him in through the patio gate.

'Hi,' puffed the delivery guy, whose uniform was covered in sweat patches in spite of the mild weather. A blue evil eye pendant peeked out from behind his shirt. 'I'm Tristan. I'm taking over the account from Ned. He's retiring – said Madame Destinée's latest column gave him the final push he needed. He's a Virgo,' added Tristan, as though this explained everything.

'Like my sister,' said Bonnie, reminding herself to check Effie's horoscope when she got back inside.

'The librarian, right? I just dropped a bunch of books off there.'

'If she gave you a withering look over her glasses and told you to switch off the lights behind you, that was her.' Bonnie folded her arms, regarding the delivery van, which was parked in the square, hazards flashing. 'So, what have you got for me?'

Tristan slid open the van door, revealing more milk than the dairy aisle of the supermarket.

Bonnie recoiled. 'Do I look like I need all that? This is a

bar, not an elementary school. I make like two White Russians a day.'

Tristan shrugged. 'You could be on the GOMAD diet.'

'The what now?'

'A gallon of milk a day. It's a bodybuilding thing.'

'A lifestyle that bar patrons are famously into.' Bonnie smirked, then flexed a tanned bicep. 'Besides, who could possibly improve on this?'

'Love the confidence. I have an eight-year-old daughter and we're big on body positivity,' Tristan confided. He flashed his phone lock screen, showing off a cute little girl with freckles and a unicorn headband. 'That's her there. Here's the order, by the way. Placed by one Bonnie Chalmers.'

Bonnie checked the order, which he'd pulled up on his phone, then groaned. She must have typed an extra zero when making it – she'd been doing it while on hold with the people who serviced the bar equipment and simultaneously texting Flora from A Pocket Full of Posies about the care and keeping of the wisteria that overhung the patio frame. This was like that viral moment where instead of a bag of rice, a whole semi-trailer truck had pulled up in front of someone's house.

Where on earth was she going to fit all that milk? Worse, how on earth was she going to use it? Milk was hardly a bestseller. Maybe she could sponsor a Girl Scout gathering outside of regular opening hours.

'Is it too late to change the order?' she asked, batting her eyelashes for good measure.

'I wish, but I can't send back perishables. Do you want some help bringing it all in?'

Bonnie sighed in resignation. 'Sure, that'd be great.'

Bottle by bottle, Tristan started unloading the milk crates. But not onto a dolly or a cart. Onto the brick wall around the patio. Bonnie blinked. Wouldn't it make more sense to wheel the dolly into the bar and then unload it?

When she said as much, Tristan shook his head. 'But the cracks,' he said.

Bonnie didn't follow. 'In the milk bottles?'

'In the pavement.' He nodded at the flagstones that formed a tidy path between the patio and the bar, the gaps between them filled with soft green moss. 'It's just . . . a superstition of mine. Step on a crack, break your mother's back?'

Bonnie wondered whether she was being pranked.

'My mother's pretty frail, and I really don't want to risk it. I'll be quick, I promise.'

Maybe Tristan's mom should be drinking the milk. It was good for bones, after all.

'Are you sure you're suited to this line of work?'

'I've wanted to be a delivery guy my whole life,' said Tristan cheerfully. 'I was a UPS guy for Halloween three years in a row. And FedEx the three after that.'

'All right, then.' Bonnie sighed. 'Here. You load them onto the dolly, and I'll haul the dolly to the door. Deal?'

She was part-way through the hauling when Bobby showed up.

'Career change, Bon?' he asked curiously.

'It's complicated,' she panted. Then she paused. 'You don't happen to need an enormous amount of milk, do you?'

Bobby shrugged easily. 'Always. The bakery goes through it like you wouldn't believe. You'd think we were rearing a shop full of kittens over there.'

Oh, thank goddess. A solution. 'If you take this delivery off my hands, I'll be grateful to you for ever.'

'Sure. We'll do a special on tres leches cake this week – the college kids go wild for it. What do I owe you?'

Bonnie thought about charging him – she really could use the money, given that she'd just spent several hundred bucks she didn't have on dairy products, and the next payment on her Cadillac was due the following week. But just at that moment, Theo was strolling by, a pile of documents under his arm.

Here was her chance to work the whole jealousy plan that her entourage had recommended as the perfect method for sending Theo rushing into her arms. Yes, it was cheesy, but it had worked before. Most notably when she'd been dating one of the Chen twins, but had her eye on the other. Ah, the messy days of teenage Bonnie.

Donning her sunniest smile and doing the eye-crinkle thing she *knew* was irresistible, she lightly touched Bobby's arm. 'Put that away. You're doing me such a huge favour already.'

Bobby stared down at his arm, his dark eyes dancing. Bonnie was slightly worried he might get a tattoo on the spot she'd touched to make the occasion linger for ever. 'Sure, Bon. Wow. I'll definitely bring over some treats for you. Not that we could ever match your mom's brownies, but we'll try.'

'Great!' she said warmly. Then, in the most casual voice she could muster: 'Oh, hi, Theo!'

Theo pulled up, leaning over the patio wall. He greeted them both cheerily. 'Thanks for the party last night, Bonnie. You know how to make a guy feel welcome.'

Bonnie preened. 'I live to please.'

'How's town life treating you, man?' asked Bobby, cradling a milk crate.

'I'm just out seeing the sights. I'm actually on my way back from the library. I guess I'm on the same schedule as the delivery guy.' He waved to Tristan, who was typing something into his phone. 'We just unloaded a bunch of books together. Coffee's next on my list.'

He ducked to one side, letting Bobby past with the first of many milk crates.

'Coffee, huh?' Here was her chance to lure him inside. 'I have an espresso machine in here, you know.'

Theo blinked. 'Oh. But you're not open 'til noon, right?'

'I can make an exception.'

'Coming through.' Bobby squeezed through the gate again to grab another crate.

'Need some help? It'll be my resistance training for the day.' Theo grabbed one of the crates and followed Bobby over to his truck. 'Besides, I've always wanted to try GOMAD.'

Bonnie couldn't believe it. First Theo had ditched her for Effie, and now for *Bobby*? Everything was topsy-turvy. Had someone cast a bizarre spell on the town? Or maybe Mercury was doing its retrograde thing.

'Look at you, all helpful,' she said flirtatiously. 'Well, when you work up a thirst, you know where to come.'

'Thanks, Bon!' said Bobby, with a grin that suggested he thought that *he* was the subject of the invitation. 'All right, Theo, put your back into it.'

Well, it was slightly unexpected, but Bonnie had the bar to herself. At least she could count on Bobby to talk her up to Theo.

Fortunately, her pre-opening tasks kept her busy right up until the time she switched over the sign on the door, and soon Theo had slipped from her mind altogether.

For you, Mom, she thought as she opened the doors, as she did every time. Because this bar thing wasn't just for Bonnie. From the paintings on the stairwell walls to the brownies in the dessert case, this whole place was a tribute to Mom's memory.

Back in high school, the careers adviser Mr Nolan had asked Bonnie what she wanted out of life, and she'd shrugged – how could anyone answer that? Meanwhile, Effie had been set on a librarian career since she'd admonished Bonnie, then aged three, for arranging her picture books by colour instead of alphabetical order. Effie had always been fascinated by imaginative worlds; how knowledge could be contained and organized; by how, she said, one building on a hill could be a haven to everyone.

When Mr Nolan pressed Bonnie about her own goals,

Bonnie had stammered out something about being memorable. Because she didn't know quite what she wanted, but she did know what she *didn't* want. To be invisible, to be forgotten. Now Bonnie had her own building on a hill (all right, *near* a hill), and she was determined to make it the place where the entire town wanted to spend their time. And also, given the wholly unexpected expense of running the place, their money.

A few groups of hotel workers and college kids came in, including Terrance from The Winged Monkey, still in his barista T-shirt, who shyly ran his fingers through his hair when he saw her.

'How's the talent show audition going?' she asked.

'I'm really good at memorizing the jokers. It's the queens that get me all messed up.'

'Queens will do that,' said Bonnie with a grin. She poured him a glass of milk from the crate that Bobby had left her with, then slid it over to the barista, along with one of Mom's brownies. 'There. Calcium's good for the brain.'

Probably.

'Got it.' Taking a sip of the milk, Terrance produced a pack of cards from his pocket and handed them to her. 'Do you want to do the honours? You can be my good luck memory charm.'

'Only because it's quiet.' Bonnie tipped out the cards and quickly laid them out.

'First one's a queen of hearts,' he said approvingly.

'Correct! Now you just have fifty-one to go. Let me know when you need a top-up.'

She left him to his milk, then poured a jug of beer for a trio of girls she recognized as psych majors from the college. This was something she always found amusing, as they'd sit around the patio firepit for hours, textbooks open, reading each other's palms or wondering whether the lunar tide cycles were behind a professor's tough grading rubric. Bonnie was pretty sure she'd had the same professor before she'd dropped out in sophomore year.

'Here you go, babes,' said Bonnie, dropping off the jug, together with a stack of chilled glasses. 'How are the lifelines today?'

'Ugh, *awful*,' said a tiny, peppy blonde who reminded Bonnie of herself. She'd go far in life. The girl jabbed at her palm. 'See this line here? There's a callus on it. Disaster. There goes my future earning potential.'

'You *have* been putting in a lot of time on the rower at the gym,' said one of her friends, a brunette with morose eyes wearing a lilac pantsuit that Bonnie coveted.

'Combined with the change in my Mount of Mars . . .' The girl prodded at the fleshy pad of her thumb. 'You see what I'm seeing, right?'

'Sure,' said Bonnie, because who was she to argue with her patrons? Just so long as they paid their bills and tipped generously, they could read whatever they wanted in their palms. Or their beer foam. Or their napkin folds.

'Desdemona Nocturne did a whole video about it, and now all I can see is how my palms are all wrong.' The girl wiped her hands on her denim skirt. 'And sweaty, *ugh*.'

'But did you see the one from Lyriana?' countered the third girl, who was swimming in a hoodie she'd apparently borrowed from a boyfriend. 'You're emotionally resilient.'

'Well, there are always gloves,' said Bonnie cheerfully. 'You can go fingerless if you're feeling the 80s vibe.'

Other customers were starting to file in. Winston and his friends, some of the young creative types from the coworking space that had recently opened up above the old bank, and Bowow Walker with a corgi wearing a collar that looked like a crown. Bonnie left the psych students to their palm comparisons, which she was pretty sure weren't covered in their textbooks. But who knew, maybe their professor was giving them extra credit for considering additional diagnostic criteria.

Customers continued to stream in, and Bonnie lost herself in the work of it all: the mixed drinks, the bussing of tables, the keeping up with tabs and tips and change. At some point, the sun began to drift down in the sky, and outside, the fairy lights strung over the patio switched on. Things would start to get busy after this, but her friends would clock on to help. Hannah, who was still getting her foothold as a realtor, never minded the tips, and Kirsty fancied herself a maestro when it came to high-end mixology. Even Alana, who didn't drink, could be counted on to plate up some baked goods in a pinch. And of course, there was always Bobby. Who, despite his volunteer status, was the hardest worker she had.

She was returning to the bar with a stack of empty glasses and brownie-crumb garnished plates, when her mouth suddenly felt sour. Ugh, had her hangover caught up with her again? She reached for her glass of soda water, hoping to wash the taste away.

But then her vision blotched slightly, as though a migraine aura were starting up. Blobs of brown discoloured her peripheral vision – blobs the exact colour of Mom's disquieting painting in the stairwell.

She glanced up, knowing exactly who she was about to see. Uncle Oswald.

He was dressed ostentatiously as usual: pointed shoes, green pants, a voluminous shirt, and an ascot tie that sparkled with an emerald motif. And then there was the hat. It was impossible to be truly pretentious without the requisite headwear, and Uncle Oswald was committed to the part. Like some sort of 1920s gangster, he sported a bowler hat high upon his head. She imagined that beneath it, a slimy version of the rat from *Ratatouille* was tugging his oily hair and making him behave amorally.

'I didn't expect you to grace us with your presence,' she said warily, setting out a glass on the rich wooden counter. She'd never spent much time with Oswald one-on-one: his rocky relationship with Mom had made sure of that. Besides, what did they have in common?

'I thought I'd stop by while things were quiet at the shop. Good to see they're less quiet here.' Oswald set a fifty on the table and slid it towards her. 'Mint julep.'

Of course. Oswald loved his green.

After some careful muddling of bourbon, simple syrup and bitters, all topped with a generous mint garnish, Bonnie pushed the drink towards her uncle, swallowing as she caught a hint of Mom's features in Oswald's cheekbones and the shape of his chin. This meant there was a hint of Bonnie in there too.

Reckoning with what that meant, she took the money and popped it in the vintage till, hesitating for a few beats too long when it came to picking out his change. A few beats more. She was confident by now that Oswald wasn't expecting change. He'd tipped her an extremely generous amount for a very simple drink, which meant that he wanted something.

She wasn't silly. She might have been the pretty face, but she was wily when she needed to be.

'You're doing nice work here,' said Oswald, his gaze travelling across the room.

Bonnie tried to see it through his eyes. The groups of community college kids and young hotel workers laughing uproariously, if self-consciously, for everyone that age thinks that every eye is on them and them alone. Winston and the darts players clapping beers together when they made a tough throw. The coworking 'solopreneurs' trying to beat the pinball machines into submission. The endlessly changing faces of the tourists who'd sidle in for a weekend of fun, then disappear again as quickly as they'd come. To an outside observer, the bar looked like a success, all packed tables and glowing reviews. No one knew just how close Bonnie walked the line to insolvency each and every week, especially with quarterly taxes coming up. She made a mental note to ask Tessa about those when she next saw her. She was way less intimidating than Effie, who'd no doubt roll her eyes and admonish Bonnie for not filling out ten obscure forms or opening a special bank account or whatever.

'Thanks,' said Bonnie, as she mixed a G&T for a sparkly-looking girl with dark ringlets and incredible hoop earrings. 'I'm really happy with how things are going. I wish Mom were here to see it.'

She passed the drink across the bar to the girl, who leaned forward conspiratorially, her earrings waggling.

'You're so pretty,' said the girl, like she was sharing a deep secret.

'Aw, thank you!' said Bonnie, who never tired of hearing this. It was a sign that all was right with the world, after all. She slid over one of the cookies that became a crowd essential towards the end of the night. 'That's for you.'

The girl waggled her fingers and wandered off, drink in one hand and cookie clenched between her teeth.

'She'd be proud.' Uncle Oswald drank in infuriatingly tiny sips, dabbing his moustache with his handkerchief each time. Momentarily, he added, 'So, my reason for visiting is this: I was going to ask if you'd noticed something odd about the townsfolk recently.'

He cocked his head. Unfortunately, the hat did not fall off, and Bonnie was left none the wiser about the existence of Bad Ratatouille.

Bonnie propped her chin on her hand and regarded her patrons. Nothing seemed out of the ordinary.

'I mean, Effie might say they're a bit odd,' she said lightly. 'But that's Effie for you.'

'Hmm, as someone with your inclinations,' Uncle Oswald nodded at Bonnie's tattooed wrists, 'I thought you might have noticed it. The new-found reliance on *magic*. Forces they couldn't begin to understand.'

Bonnie shrugged. All right, sure, she could see a few evil eye pendants and witchy tattoos, but what of it?

'It's a free world,' she said. 'If someone's going to put some crystals out under the moon, that's their prerogative. I probably wouldn't go drinking any moon-bathed water, though. I prefer my fluids without added mosquito larvae.'

'It's not that I don't want them to enjoy the spoils of what comes so naturally to our family,' said Oswald. 'But I worry about their safety.'

'How so? Have they been riding around on brooms or something?'

Uncle Oswald huffed. 'The way they ride those scooters, the very prospect of that should terrify you. Look, you know that Yellowbrick Grove is a place where superstition and rituals loom large. How many black cats do you see around here? How much salt gets tossed over shoulders while cooking? These are exactly the kind of people who get swept up by the promises of online charlatans. Suddenly, they're curing cancer with a pendulum or quitting their jobs because they got a peculiar reading from one of those aura Polaroid cameras.'

Bonnie muddled a tall spoon through a rum and ginger beer highball cocktail. 'No offence, but you're sounding kind of like a boomer.'

Uncle Oswald adjusted his bowler hat primly. 'I get it. We're from different generations. And I know things could have been better between Lyra and me. Part of where we differed was that she was all about keeping magic to herself. Just like your sister.'

Bonnie raised an eyebrow. Was he really going there? Mom had believed that magic had to be wielded carefully, and with good reason. It wasn't a gatekeeping thing. It was that magic had a tendency to cause problems. And sometimes resulted in literal witch hunts.

'I'm not saying we advertise it,' said Oswald. 'I'm just saying that magic from the right source, a responsible source, is a good thing. It could be good for the townspeople. And good for business. Yours *and* mine.'

He clasped his hands over the top of his drink, then added, 'I have a proposal that would be mutually beneficial to our bottom lines.'

Seeing Winston waving from over at the darts board, Bonnie poured a fresh round of beers for the Old Darts. Something was going on here, and she wasn't sure she wanted to be a part of it.

'I know where Mom stood,' she said finally. 'And it's where I stand too.'

Uncle Oswald nodded thoughtfully, then shrugged. 'Your sister said the same.'

Bonnie's hands tightened on the beer tap. Of course he'd gone to Effie first. Of *course* Bonnie was the afterthought when it came to discussions of magic. 'When did you see Effie?'

Uncle Oswald's rings flashed as he waved her off. 'Oh, it doesn't matter. But I do hope the two of you enjoy the photograph of Lyra. I thought you should have it.'

What photograph? Effie had a photo of Mom that she'd been hiding? Bonnie was so flabbergasted that she managed to squirt beer all over herself. Dammit. Between last night and this, she'd managed to ruin two consecutive outfits.

'Well, you definitely know what you're doing,' mused Oswald, sliding down from his stool. 'The bar business is a hard one. The old owner, Harvey? He didn't have the touch that you do. I remember when he first opened. It was the place to be! But when the novelty faded, things dropped off. Such a shame. And so avoidable.'

Bonnie frowned. What was he saying? That her success was destined to be temporary? That her profits were about to circle the drain the same way her credit rating had before Effie demanded she freeze her accounts and pay down the balances she owed?

But she didn't have time to think any deeper on this, for a girl who'd been sitting quietly at one of the corner tables came up in tears, her eyes red and her mascara painting her

cheeks with inky stripes. 'Do you . . . have some tissues? I'm
having the worst night. I drew cards and checked my tea
leaves and *everything*, just like the video said, and he didn't
even show up.'

Bonnie's heart went out to the poor girl. Coming out from
behind the counter, she wrapped her up in a hug.

'It's okay, babe. You're a catch! This is a him thing, not a
you thing.'

'I mean, that's easy for you to say. Look at you.'

'That's right. That's how I know that if he doesn't show
up, it's a him thing.'

'It's a him thing,' repeated the girl.

'You'll forget all about him in a few days, I promise.' Bonnie
rubbed the girl's shoulders. Then she grabbed Uncle Oswald's
pocket square and handed it to her. 'That's what my mom
always used to say, and you know what? She was right.'

'Moms are the best,' sobbed the girl.

'Moms *are* the best,' agreed Bonnie, as she poured a glass
of wine for the girl. A small one, because getting just slightly
tipsy over your woes made for a better tomorrow than
drowning your sorrows. Damn, she missed Mom. She'd run
to her hundreds of times over the years, sometimes over small,
silly things, sometimes over ones that felt so existential that
she feared the very world might cave in. She remembered the
very last time she'd done it, too: how she'd cried in Mom's
arms about the thought of losing her.

A part of Bonnie hated herself for putting that on Mom,
but Mom knew it had come from a place of love.

As though she could read Bonnie's own heartache, the girl
began ugly-crying into Uncle Oswald's pocket square. The
look on Oswald's face was priceless.

'You can keep that,' Oswald said in disgust, as the girl took
her wine and retreated to the pinball machines. From all the
banging and clanging that followed, she was exacting some
serious revenge.

'Ugh, that handkerchief was born for better things,' muttered Oswald, shuddering. 'But now you see my point, don't you? The pain that people are experiencing from subjecting themselves to things they don't understand. It's not that they don't work. It's that you need sophisticated, nuanced knowledge to use them effectively.'

Bonnie thought about how her magic habitually backfired on her, often creating more drama than it was worth. What was she missing that Effie wasn't? Was it simply knowledge and skill, or something deeper?

'I have a proposal,' said Oswald. 'Between two of the town's most entrepreneurial business owners.'

'Oh yeah?' Bonnie made a show of looking around. 'Where are they?'

'Very funny. Look, I know that you're not as inclined to use your magic as your sister is. And I know it's because your magic is so much more powerful that you don't want to outshine her. After all, you already overshadow her in every other way.'

Bonnie mopped down the counter thoughtfully. She'd never considered that maybe the reason her magic backfired was because it was *more* powerful than Effie's. But it would explain so much.

'Look, what we need is simplicity. Simplicity makes life easier in every way. And it definitely helps business. I'm just talking about a tiny charm here.'

'To be used on people?' said Bonnie warily.

'Oh no! Not on people. On *drinks*. Some simple recipes to help guide townsfolk away from their reliance on internet influencers and pseudo-magical hearsay. I have a whole book of them. There'd be no more girls sobbing into handkerchiefs over some date who didn't show up. No more delivery boys picking their way around cracks in the ground.'

'Tristan visited you as well, I see.'

'They could come to me instead, and I'll guide them carefully, in a bespoke manner, towards the products and solutions that work best for them. Look, I know my products aren't magical in any real sense. But crystals and stones can be an invaluable source of comfort and protection. Especially if people aren't bogged down by a million contradicting hashtags and reaction videos.'

Bonnie gave a disdainful chuckle. 'Wow, you really have been researching this.'

'I'm just saying they can seek comfort in something that might be a placebo, sure, but it's not going to do *harm*.'

Bonnie considered. All right, so this didn't sound terrible, but it did sound one-sided.

'So, your business gets more sales. What about mine?'

'A cut,' said Oswald, jabbing the air with his cane. 'For every person you send my way, I'll cut you in on the proceeds. Think of the upside. You can launch a whole new line of unique drinks not found *anywhere* else. And you can finally use your' – he glanced around – 'magic for something good instead of hiding it for fear of making your sister look bad. It's not your fault she doesn't come across so well, is it? She's had every opportunity to become a shining light like you, and yet . . .'

And yet indeed, thought Bonnie, thinking of the way Effie's mouth had tightened the previous night at the bar. Bonnie's very presence had been enough for her sister to turn on her heels in exasperation and stomp off. Bonnie always tried to include Effie, but her older sister made it practically impossible. It wasn't just introversion. It was rudeness.

And then there was the magic. She'd never really been given a chance to prove her magic, to train it. Now with Mom gone, she knew that all Effie would want was for Bonnie's magic to be hidden away and forgotten about. But Bonnie deserved more than that.

'I'll think about it,' said Bonnie carefully. What Oswald had offered *seemed* sound, but she wasn't sure she could fully trust him. Mom never had, after all. And Effie loathed him – although, to be fair, Effie loathed most everyone.

Uncle Oswald finished his drink and reached across the counter to shake her hand with his clammy one. He left, leaving Bonnie to review with a sinking heart the overdue invoice that had pinged on her phone. She didn't even have time to think about that before another disaster struck.

'Bonnie,' groaned one of the psych majors, 'Megan's locked herself in the upstairs bathroom, and we all know what that means.'

Chapter 7

THE MOON MADE ME DO IT

Effie

Effie had read the same paragraph half a dozen times and still had no idea what it said. Something about mountains. There was definitely a goat, or perhaps a big sheep, or at least some kind of ruminant.

She resettled herself on the couch, snuggling into the nest of decorative throw pillows and blankets she'd made. Cosiness and bookishness went hand in hand, and the living room had a draught that she hadn't quite been able to conquer. The chill swept in around the ancient window panes and down the chimney, curling its fingers around the decorative tiles on the fireplace and onto the rug that Mom had inherited from some distant, apparently well-off, relative. Effie always loved its patterns: the floral swirls, the bright stars, the stylized protective motifs that kept their family safe. Even the threadbare bits had their charms.

You're distracted by a rug, Effie, she scolded herself. Ever since she'd come home from her shift at the library, she'd found her thoughts wandering. All right, not since then. Ever since Theo had shown up at the library, which was infuriating, because usually Effie's thoughts were logical, steadfast, focused. Tonight, they were as scattered as Bonnie's, and kept wandering off down alleys filled with coffee dates and garden paths abloom with studious conversations. Effie had been attracted to people in the past, of course, but attraction usually came on slowly for her. So slowly that by the time she was ready to properly entertain the idea, the other person had long since moved on. If they'd ever been interested at all, which, let's face it, was questionable at best. Bonnie had tried to nudge Effie into action a few times throughout her life, but Effie didn't do things Bonnie's way. Besides, the way Bonnie went about the whole business of dating was the antithesis of how Effie intended to. There would be no surprise poltergeists in Effie's bedroom.

If only Mom were here. She would've listened, leaning back on the couch, gently braiding Effie's untameable hair as Effie stuttered out her thoughts and insecurities, nodding in that quiet way to show that she understood, but without judging or trying to push her towards something she wasn't ready for. But no matter how hard Effie tried to hold on to the memories through the bookmark she carried around with her, those moments were lost in time.

There came a thud, then a bang, then a muttered *dammit* as Bonnie bashed into the grandfather clock in the hallway. Effie bit back a grin. All right, so maybe Effie had charmed the light in the room to make it slightly more likely that someone might bash into said clock, especially if one were texting at the same time, which Bonnie inevitably was.

'We're selling that stupid clock,' snarled Bonnie. She stomped into the living room, rubbing her shin as she went. After more ostentatious stomping that added a scuff to the rug, Bonnie dropped down on the long yellow couch that ran almost the whole length of the room. For years, the three Chalmers women had watched movies on it, sprawled over each other, with feet in laps and fingers twined, passing chocolate-smothered popcorn and tiny hot dogs and trying to guess the name of every actor on screen.

'You wouldn't believe who came into the bar tonight.' Bonnie stretched out, kicking off her shoes and prodding Effie with her pink-painted toes. Effie smacked her with the paperback she'd been trying to read. If only she'd been able to follow through with the Proust. That was a massive hardback that could do some damage.

'Henry Cavill,' suggested Effie, a little bit wistfully.

'I'd still be at the bar if that were the case,' noted Bonnie.

Effie felt her wrists glow. And perhaps her eyes as well, although that had never been documented. 'You saw Theo.'

Blinking, Bonnie shook her head. 'No, I actually meant—'

'He came into the library today. Insisted on applying for a library card.'

Bonnie raised an eyebrow. 'Criminal. How *dare* he.' She inspected the imminent bruise on her shin. 'How much do grandfather clocks go for online? We'll split the profits.'

'It's not for sale! It was Pop's!'

'Oh, who cares.' Bonnie pulled the leg of her jeans back down, hiding the bruise. 'He's been dead for how long? You think he's up floating around in the great wherever worrying about whether we're keeping his clock polished and buffed?' She cackled. 'That sounded crass. Sorry, Pop!' she shouted to the ceiling.

'Well sure, if family memories are meaningless, we'll just chuck out everything in the house belonging to a dead person.' Effie glowered. Bonnie was being her usual thoughtless, indifferent self. Couldn't she see what she was suggesting? That, post death, there was a time limit on your value on Earth? Once a predetermined socially acceptable amount of time had passed, you could bin anything belonging to a deceased person?

'Mom's been gone almost a year,' she added, running the edge of her bookmark under her fingernails. She always did this when she was anxious. 'Should we start forgetting her as well?'

'That's not the same. Sheesh, Effie. What's with the beehive in your stupid bonnet.'

'No beehive. No bonnet.' Effie sniffed. 'I can't believe you think I'd wear a bonnet.'

'I've seen you in worse.' Bonnie folded her arms, flashing her tattooed wrists at Effie. 'So, what happened after Theo got his library card? Did he check out anything good?'

'He joined the Friends of the Library Club.' Effie made a face.

'Oh no, anything but that.'

'He also made a sizeable donation,' admitted Effie, who felt conflicted about it. Donations were always welcome, but they also came with strings attached. And Effie was wary of strings.

'A monster. Did you report him to the police?'

Effie was tempted to charm a bigger bruise onto her sister's shin. 'You're not taking me seriously.'

'It's hard to take you seriously when you're mad that Theo joined your library, showed interest in the organization that supports your library, and then used his money to support your library.'

Well, when she put it like that . . .

Bonnie leaned forward to take a bite from the cookie Effie had been saving until she finished her chapter. 'Anyway. You should be nice to him. There's clearly something wrong with him, after all. Self-esteem issues, maybe.'

Effie bristled. 'What's that supposed to mean?'

'I mean that you should be grateful for the attention! For some reason, he seems to *like you*. The town . . .'

'The town what?' asked Effie quietly.

'Nothing.' Bonnie polished off the rest of the cookie. 'Nothing.'

Effie didn't comment on the cookie. She had better battles to fight. Besides, the cookie had chia seeds in it, and hopefully Bonnie would be picking those out of her teeth for the rest of the night. 'Better than the town narcissist. I've seen how you treat Bobby.'

Bonnie's eyes flashed, and Effie vaguely worried that Bonnie's wayward magic might set the entire house on fire.

'You don't know *anything*,' snapped Bonnie. 'You only see what you want to see.'

'I think I know what I see,' retorted Effie. 'And that's you swanning around expecting everyone to do your bidding. What will you do when you're not young or pretty any more?'

Bonnie jerked back as though Effie had slapped her.

'I'm more than just my looks,' she said, her voice quavering. 'Other people see it. Just not you. Why only tonight, Uncle Oswald offered—'

'Uncle Oswald!' scoffed Effie. 'You're using *him* to make your point? The man's a charlatan. No wonder he picked you to talk to.'

'Well, he certainly wouldn't have picked you, Little Miss Rules and Regulations!' snapped Bonnie, her wrists glimmering purple from anger. 'The only reason anyone shows up to your stupid library is because everything there is *free*.'

'At least you don't have to be drunk to enjoy the library,' retorted Effie, her own wrists crackling a furious green. 'Besides, unlike your bar, the library isn't all about *me*.'

'Well, that's fortunate, because it would be even more depressing if it were!' shouted Bonnie, a stream of purple exploding from her wrist and knocking a needlepoint off the wall.

'Oh good,' snarled Effie, waving a glowing hand at the broken frame. 'Yet another one of your messes for me to clean up. Just another day in the life of being Bonnie Chalmers' big sister!'

Bonnie glowered, but said nothing. Effie could tell her words had cut deep.

Well, good, Effie thought, trembling with indignation. It was about time Bonnie heard the truth. And she'd spoken only the truth, after all.

There was a beat as the two sisters tried to decide whether they'd gone too far and needed to resolve their argument, the way Mom would have insisted upon. She never let an argument extend beyond bedtime.

But pride won out. Instead of reconciling, both sisters raced to their respective rooms.

Effie's only regret was that her sister beat her to the door-slamming by a fraction of a second. *Damn Bonnie's athleticism.*

Chapter 8

BE CAREFUL
WHAT YOU WITCH FOR

Bonnie

Bonnie had never anticipated that Uncle Oswald would become a regular at The Silver Slipper, and yet here he was again. Perched on one of the bar stools in the pre-opening quiet, cane across his lap, he sipped his mint julep. Bonnie had never been a mint fan. Effie was, but Bonnie suspected that her sister had cultivated a taste for mint chocolate purely to keep Bonnie away from her kitchen stashes.

'I'm glad you came around,' said Oswald. 'It's a smart business decision. And most importantly, the right decision for the town as well.'

And an excellent way to spite know-it-all Effie, thought Bonnie darkly. At least now she knew how Effie truly felt. Last night she'd wanted to get Effie's thoughts on the collaboration, but being so summarily dismissed had made it an easy decision. Bonnie was all in.

'Mm-hm,' she said absently, turning her attentions back to the recipe she was working on.

Bonnie was making her third charmed tonic in a row, her wrists glowing purple as she tried to bespell the drink according to the simplest recipe in the ratty book that Uncle Oswald had slid across the bar after she'd agreed to his proposal. She still wasn't sure where he'd sourced the recipes from, because Oswald didn't have magic of his own, as far as she knew. But he might have learned a few things from Mom, even if he couldn't actually put them into practice.

This particular spell was meant to negate attentiveness to numerology, which as someone who was strictly anti-math, Bonnie had a vested interest in. She knew exactly who she'd test it on. Bowow Walker, who was always banging on about the connection between numbers and names and life paths. She'd come to numerology after going down a YouTube rabbit hole, and since then she'd made herself quite the pest when it came to her bar tab, which always had to be a perfectly round number lest a volcano erupt or something.

The drink fizzed as it was meant to. But the glass shattered.

'Dammit.' Bonnie grabbed the dustpan by the counter and went to sweep up the shards.

Oswald leaned over with his handkerchief, mopping up the puddle that hadn't been caught by the drip tray. Grimacing, Bonnie wrung out the green silk kerchief over the sink at the back of the bar.

'Do you want me to throw this in the laundry for you?'

Oswald's thick eyebrows rose over his spectacles as he sipped his drink. 'You could just use your magic to dry it, surely?'

Bonnie wasn't willing to risk another wayward spell. 'Stickiness is hard to remove magically. I wouldn't want to ruin the fabric.'

Oswald nodded, but Bonnie could tell that she'd slipped in his estimation. 'All right. I'll pick it up tomorrow.'

Bonnie set the handkerchief aside, trying not to imagine Effie's expression when she spotted Uncle Oswald's laundry mixed in with theirs. Effie could easily charm the kerchief back to normalcy, of course, but Bonnie was hardly about to ask. Not after their fight the other night. They'd each been carefully avoiding the other since, Effie heading out early to the library, and Bonnie hanging around as late as feasibly possible at The Silver Slipper. She'd even brought her sleeping bag up to the partly finished upstairs apartment, just in case sleeping over sounded appealing after a few post-closing beers. She'd given it a try, but after a princess and the pea-like experience where she'd rolled around agonizingly on a knot in the hardwoods, she'd decided that home was where the heart was. Just so long as Effie was asleep.

As Oswald observed judgementally, Bonnie mixed another drink, this time in a shatter-proof brass mug usually used for Moscow mules, before trying the charm once more. The drink fizzed, and although the mug grew warm to the touch, it held.

Bonnie set her head on her arms in relief. It had worked. As far as she knew, anyway. She needed someone to test it on.

With impeccable timing, Bobby came through the door pushing a dolly stacked high with crates.

'Hiya, boss!' he said cheerfully, waving at Bonnie and giving Oswald a nod. 'Got your deliveries. Wow, we're going big on the limes this week, huh? And the Himalayan salt. If it's the whole milk situation all over again, let me know, and we'll put key lime pie on the menu at the bakery.'

Bonnie nodded, but didn't comment. Both the limes and the salt were part of Oswald's enchantment recipe, along with gilded flakes and water charged with the essence of an eclipse-studded sun. Oswald had brought the sun water himself, thankfully, which meant slightly fewer questions. Although Bonnie was curious about why it had arrived in the form of a hundred bottles of Perrier.

'Bobby, can you give this a taste for me? Oswald and I are working on a collab and we need a test subject.'

Grinning flirtatiously, mostly to cover the fact that she was worried the recipe might cause Bobby's hair to fall out or his skin to turn green, Bonnie slid the fizzing drink across the bar and gestured for Bobby to take a sip.

Bobby nodded appreciatively as he regarded the drink, which was high drama in a glass. 'Are we doing flaming drinks now?'

'You know me. I'm all about theatre.' Bonnie waggled her fingers. Were her nails starting to chip already from all of this spellcasting? She'd just painted them!

Bobby took a sip, then smacked his lips thoughtfully. 'Citrusy. I think you have a winner there. I could see Gerald picking that over a shandy.'

'Good, good,' said Oswald, his rings flashing as he rubbed his hands together.

Bonnie, who was surreptitiously charming a quartered lime, nodded. 'That's what we love to hear. I'm still finessing the other drinks we're looking at introducing, but I'll get your expertise on those when they're ready. Oh, look at the time!'

The three of them turned to look at the clock on the wall. It was 11:11 precisely, something Bobby always pointed out with a reminder to 'make a wish'. Since they'd been kids, he'd set his clocks to twenty-four-hour time so he could see repeated numbers all the way through to 23:23. He wasn't a numerology person in the same way that Bowow was, but a fascination with number patterns had to count, right?

Bobby squinted, then shrugged. 'Sorry, didn't realize I was running late.'

Then he rubbed his forehead. 'What was I doing again? I'm having a complete brain-fart over here.'

'You were putting away the deliveries,' said Bonnie, frowning as the lime hissed like a deflating balloon. Unfortunately, magic was a bit like chemistry. Get your method a touch wrong and you ended up inventing the atomic bomb.

'Right, right!' Bobby grabbed his dolly and trundled off to the storeroom. Well, sort of.

'It's the second door,' Bonnie reminded him, as he almost dropped off the goods in the bathroom. Weird. The bar was strategically dim, but not *that* dim, and Bobby knew where he was going. Had Bobby missed his morning coffee?

'He didn't comment on the clock,' Bonnie pointed out to

Oswald, when Bobby was safely in the storeroom, unloading napkins and straws from his dolly. 'He *always* comments on a clock at 11:11.'

'And that was our numerology spell, yes?' said Oswald, leaning across the bar to peer at the heavily thumbed recipe book, which was opened to a drink-splattered page headed *By the Numbers*.

Nodding, Bonnie spun the book around and tapped the title.

Oswald fiddled with his ring. 'So, how long until we can officially move ahead with our partnership?'

Bonnie swallowed. There were dozens of recipes in the book, and she'd barely even mastered one. She'd tried a few of the others, and had come *this close* to burning off her eyebrows with one that targeted herbalism, while another that focused on lucid dreaming had scorched the counter. Not to mention the one aimed at tarot readers. When she'd tried that, an entire murder of crows had descended upon the wisteria overhanging the patio.

'A week, maybe?' she said. 'I want to make sure the magic is consistent.'

'Yes, don't want to be turning people into frogs or what have you. Still, better to move a tad fast than too slow, no? Especially with those start-up costs to recoup. And the loan you took out on the Cadillac.'

The sharp scent of lime filled the air as Bonnie's knife pierced the fruit's thick skin. How did Oswald know about the loan?

'I keep an ear to the ground,' Oswald said diffidently.

'I tried the Small Business Association,' groused Bonnie, 'but they rejected me. They said my business plan wasn't thorough enough. Apparently, the numbers were aspirational. But I did everything I was supposed to! I did a short course through the college and everything.'

All right, so her passing grade was mostly due to the fact

that she'd shamelessly flirted with the teacher. But she *had* attended. She'd even taken notes!

'It's this changing world of ours,' said Uncle Oswald, gesturing out at the square. 'People can't see past their screens. That's how you know we're doing the right thing. We'll succeed together, just as long as we don't lose momentum.'

Uncle Oswald tapped one of the branded coasters he'd brought over that morning. For every coaster one of Bonnie's customers brought over to his shop, he'd offer a discount on their purchase, and a kickback for Bonnie. Given the ambitious markup on Oswald's products, the kickbacks could be pretty solid.

And let's face it, Bonnie desperately needed the extra source of income right now. Her credit cards were so full that she crossed her fingers every time she tapped her phone to make a payment. Thankfully, she could easily survive on the baked goods Bobby brought over each day. As long as she remembered to take her iron tablet.

'I'll work fast,' Bonnie promised. 'I'll have them perfected before you know it.'

Uncle Oswald nodded. 'Let's aim for this week. Oh, and drop off the handkerchief when it's ready. Although given that I've now ruined two of them sitting in this exact spot, I might need to rethink my attire around you.'

Or he could stop haunting that bar stool and trust that Bonnie could make this thing work.

'Well then. Crystals await. I look forward to seeing drinks sparking on the patio and a surfeit of coasters making their way across the square.' Raising his hand goodbye, Uncle Oswald grabbed his cane and strode out with the trip-trap, trip-trap sound of a billy goat crossing a troll bridge. Only Bonnie was pretty sure that Oswald was the troll.

She sighed. Well, she definitely had some homework.

Bonnie set about preparing for today's opening when she

realized that she hadn't seen Bobby leave. Was he still in the storeroom?

Her heart squeezed. Had he had a bad reaction to her spell?

Heeled boots clattering on the floor, Bonnie hurried to the storeroom, shoving open the door.

'Bobby? How're you doing in there?' she called, trying not to let panic tinge her voice.

There he was, perched on a beer keg towards the back of the storeroom, looking dazed. Dazed, but alive. And not even transformed into a frog. Bonnie had never felt more relieved. She hurried over and wrapped her arms around him, whispering a thanks to the universe for not turning him into a slimy amphibian. Or worse.

Surprised, Bobby blinked at her, then smiled his easy smile.

'I'm fine, I promise. Just had a bit of a head-spin. Too much bending, maybe. Weird.'

'I'm just glad you're okay.'

Bobby chuckled. 'Why wouldn't I be? Although if I get a hug every time I need to sit for a moment, I'm going to start fainting all over the place like some sort of Victorian lady.'

'Please do,' said Bonnie. 'That sort of thing is great for my Yelp reviews. Suggests the drinks are strong.'

'Hey babe! Your girl's here to save the day!' came Kirsty's voice from the main bar, together with some overstated air kisses that Bonnie could hear from the storeroom.

'Where are you?' Kirsty's designer sneakers squeaked as she wandered around the bar, looking for Bonnie. Momentarily, she poked her head into the storeroom, jumping in surprise as she saw Bonnie and Bobby squeezed together on the keg.

'Oh, it's not . . .' Bonnie leapt up, grabbing an armful of lemons for reasons she couldn't articulate, but which sort of made sense in her head. 'I was just . . . he's not feeling well.'

Kirsty raised a slightly too thin eyebrow. Bonnie, being an excellent friend, would never inform her that her brows were anything less than perfect. 'Please don't tell me it's going to be like eighth-grade camp all over again. Because I still have PTSD from the bus trip.'

'He's fine,' said Bonnie. 'Just light-headed.'

Kirsty shrugged, which she probably would also have done had Bonnie told her that Bobby had suffered a severe head injury. Compassion wasn't her strong suit.

'Here, Bobby,' said Bonnie. 'Let's get some ginger beer into you.'

Kirsty strolled ahead of them as Bonnie helped Bobby out to the bar area, holding out an arm to stabilize him, just in case. He was steady enough on his feet, but seemed dazed.

'What have you been cooking up here?' asked Kirsty, waggling the drink that Bonnie had prepared for Bobby. She leaned over the bar, poring over the ingredients that Bonnie had left out: the blood-red citrus, the gold-dusted herbs, the rows of Perrier.

'I'll take that.' Bonnie took the brass mug from Kirsty and set it aside. Were those lipstick marks? Either the dishwasher wasn't working properly – ugh, another bill – or Kirsty had taken a sip. 'You didn't have any, did you?'

'As if,' said Kirsty, looking offended. Although she *did* dab absently at the corners of her mouth.

'The drink's strictly a work in progress,' explained Bonnie. 'It's part of a series of family recipes that Uncle Oswald dug up. We're calling the line "Perfectly Charming".'

Kirsty was now regarding the costings Bonnie had been working up. She jabbed a perfect nail at the total at the bottom. 'For that price, it'd better come with a prince.'

If only, thought Bonnie. There was an unfortunate shortage of princes in Yellowbrick Grove, where the closest anyone got to a ball were the silent auction nights up at the Toto Hotel. Or a drunken party by the grotto at the quarry. Besides, there was only one guy in town who could in any way be considered princely, and he'd been hanging out at the library, of all places.

'It's a fair price,' said Bonnie, an edge to her voice. 'Quality ingredients aren't cheap. And then there are the overheads.'

'Like all the free labour your friends provide?' asked Kirsty sweetly.

Bonnie set her hands on her hips. 'I pay you.'

'Bon, do you mind if I head out?' asked Bobby, interrupting their bickering. He massaged his temples, blinking blearily.

Bonnie frowned. He looked terrible. 'Are you okay to drive?'

'I'm fine. Just a bit off.' He mustered his usual smile. 'Whatever you put in that cocktail must have been seriously strong.'

Bonnie pretended to think about it. 'Ah, the Drano! I knew I shouldn't have put that in there!' She said it lightly, but felt a pang thinking that she could have hurt Bobby with a misspell. What if he didn't get better and she'd done some actual damage?

No, Bonnie. You know you can barely use your magic to fix your own hair. It's probably just a touch of food poisoning. Or a mild cold.

But she was worried about him. He wasn't far from home, but it only took an instant for things to go wrong behind the wheel.

Bonnie could drive him back, but she still had a million tasks to complete before opening.

'Kirsty, could you drive him?' she asked, sliding the mug into the dishwasher. 'Just in case?'

Kirsty made a face. 'Me?'

'Please. I'll owe you one.'

'Well, in that case, sure. But we're taking my car. I can't be seen in that truck.' Kirsty looked Bobby up and down. 'At least my windows are tinted.'

Bonnie was about to leap to poor Bobby's defence when a group of tourists burst into the bar, bragging among themselves about who would drink whom under the table.

'Are you open?' they called, weaving around Kirsty and the dazed Bobby, who made an extremely uncomfortable-looking pair.

Joy, thought Bonnie, as she regarded the excited tourists, who were snapping selfies and pointing at the neat rows of craft beer bottles behind the bar. Just what she needed.

But it *was* just what she needed. Because until she got her spells figured out, what she needed was tips.

Bonnie plastered on her brightest smile and smoothed back her hair. It was time to turn on her natural charm. Which was the only type of charm she couldn't mess up.

'Hey, babes!' she exclaimed. 'What'll it be?'

Chapter 9

CRAFTY WITCHES

Effie

It was craft night at the library, and Effie was rushing about printing last-minute signage and hunting for the boxes of safety scissors, which always seemed to go walkabout. Perhaps there was some connection between this and the missing pages in the *National Geographic* collection, thought Effie, as she rifled through the storeroom.

'It'll be fine, Eff,' called Tessa easily, leaning back in her chair as Effie hurried into the community room again, this time with a box of crayons, which she was fairly certain weren't needed for a crochet turtle night. But you could never be too prepared. Especially at this particular moment in time, where anyone could come striding through the doors with an armload of poetry and a giant donation cheque.

'Found the scissors,' she panted, setting down a red plastic tub shaped like a giant Lego brick.

'Brilliant,' said Tess. 'And I brought stress balls for when everyone gets stuck trying to figure out the slipknot and casting on. Well, not actual stress balls. Hacky sacks. But close enough.'

Effie and Tessa spent a few minutes arranging and rearranging yarn and crochet hooks until everything looked perfect, then slumped down in their chairs, ready for the chaos to begin.

'I do love these classes,' said Tess. 'Gives me something to do.'

Effie straightened the chairs around the table. 'The dog walking isn't fulfilling you, huh?'

'I'm starting to think I might need something that involves occasional conversations with someone of the human persuasion.' Tessa's phone buzzed, and she smiled down at the message. 'Oh hey, Claudette just received her cat statue. His name is KitKat, and he's going to have pride of place on her bookshelf.'

She flashed a photo of Claudette's room, which was packed like Tetris on hard mode with cat statues of all shapes, colours and sizes. Effie wondered how Claudette could sleep without worrying about being crushed to death.

'I'm glad Uncle Oswald was able to do some good,' Effie said, zooming in on the cat picture.

'Ah, he can't be all bad. He's Lyra's brother, after all.'

'I'll remember that when Claudette starts frantically texting you about the cursed cat in her bedroom.'

Tessa laughed. 'At least Claudette will get some good viral video content out of it. Which means dear old Ozzy will, too.'

Effie blanched. 'Uncle Oswald does social media?'

'Wow, Effie, we need to get you into the twenty-first century.'

'I've posted photos!' Effie did some simple posting for the library's social media accounts, which had been stuck at under twenty followers for three years. However, she'd never ventured into the world of short-form video. That was more Bonnie's realm.

'Anyway,' Tessa went on, 'he did this rant about how Gen Z's obsession with the New Age movement was bad for society. It was a full boomer moment. I wish I'd screenshotted it. He took it down almost immediately.'

'Sounds like a repeat of the infamous Chalmers family

dinner party five years ago when he got into the after-dinner port,' said Effie wryly. 'Mom had to drive him home.'

But Tessa had turned her attention to the door. 'Ooh, we've got some crafters!'

A small cluster of baggy-clothed teens loafed into the room, shouldering novelty tote bags adorned with fluffy animal keyrings and sparkly beaded adornments. From their woollen beanies and bracelets, they all looked as though they were old hands at crocheting.

'Welcome to craft night!' exclaimed Tessa, clapping her hands. Tessa loved a crowd almost as much as Bonnie, just a different type.

Then she faltered, for Alana was peeking around the open doorframe. She looked slightly nervous, as though she'd been swept up by a tornado and deposited into a strange land. A giant takeaway coffee cup from The Winged Monkey wavered slightly in her hand.

'*I* want coffee,' said one of the teens enviously. 'Being awake is so hard.'

'It's the worst,' agreed another, who was twirling the crochet yarn between their fingers.

'Come on in, Alana.' Effie pulled up a chair for Bonnie's friend, surprised to see one of Bonnie's entourage, who were well known for their preference for photos over words. But the library was for everyone, and it was Effie's goal to make sure every single person who entered was greeted with the kindness and inclusion that only a library could offer.

Alana perched at the edge of the seat, her floaty kaftan wafting like a peacock's feathers. She fiddled with the large wooden crochet hook that Tessa had set out before her.

'Hi,' said Tessa shyly. 'I really enjoyed yoga the other day. I think I discover new muscles every time.'

Alana idly spun the crochet hook on the table. When it stopped, pointing at Tessa, she clapped her hands over it, her cheeks growing red.

Effie felt a light twist of jealousy, but pushed it deep back down inside her where it belonged. Tessa was her best friend, and always would be.

'So, we're making turtles, huh?' Alana said finally, tapping the pattern with her rainbow nails.

Tessa nodded. 'In honour of Shelby's centenary, plus or minus ten years.'

Alana grinned. 'Hey, when you hit that age, you deserve every celebration. Anyway, my uncle has a tortoise habitat in his backyard. He has a whole arrangement with the zoo in Emerald. His birthday is coming up, and I thought he'd like one. And when I saw that you—'

She broke off as a knock at the doorframe interrupted them.

'Room for one more?' Theo shot the crafters a crooked smile filled with decidedly uncrooked teeth.

The pair of scissors Effie had been holding snapped shut. What was he doing here? When she'd said the library was for everyone, she hadn't meant interlopers from the city in fancy loafers and extremely well-fitting shirts that were most definitely professionally tailored. Even if they did read poetry and have lovely eyes.

'Always,' said Tessa, patting the empty chair next to Effie, who drummed her scissors on the table. 'Have you guys crocheted before?'

'Nuh-uh.' Alana rolled a length of wool between her fingers.

'A bit.' In demonstration, Theo made a slipknot and quickly knocked out a chain stitch. 'My mom is really into it. When I visited on weekends during college we'd watch 80s movies and make creatures to donate to local non-profits.'

Tessa, standing behind Theo, raised an eyebrow at Effie. 'A keeper,' she mouthed, jabbing a finger.

Standing, Effie set her hands on her hips. Everything felt unsettled and odd, like she'd been drawn into a game of musical chairs without knowing it. 'I have to do some reshelving. Let me know if things get unruly, and I'll bring the spray bottle.'

The teens looked alarmed at this.

'Not the spray bottle!' exclaimed Tessa in faux alarm. 'Won't someone think of the children?'

Effie shook her head and left Tessa to her crafting session. Tessa was a natural. From the murmuring and giggles that emanated from the room, the session was proving a hit. Alana looked surprisingly engaged, and even Theo was happily crafting away, Effie noticed, as she stood on her tiptoes to see over the Fantasy book display that took up most of the window space. Not that she particularly cared whether Theo was having a good time, unless it was reflected in any future reviews he might leave Tessa or the library. Theo seemed like a reviewing type, and you never knew what kind of rating system he might employ.

All right, Effie. Less hypothesizing, more shelving.

She pushed the books cart along the plush carpets, glancing about as she surreptitiously used her magic to scoot books back into place or return them to the top shelves. Yes, the library had ladders, and Effie had made good use of them early on in her career, but a quick flick of magic moved things along faster than her arms and legs could. Just so long as she stuck to her base rules: only use magic on non-human things, and even then, only use it when no one was around. Things got weird and complicated otherwise. Spells on people tended to backfire, as there were so many factors to consider. The ripple effect of shifting someone's behaviour could never be properly predicted, and even worse than that was the risk of becoming known as the person who could cast spells.

No, much better to simply use magic to clean up litter by the side of the road, or reach something on the top shelf.

Effie rolled the cart around, diligently returning books and gathering up the occasional baby sock or stuffed animal that a parent would no doubt shortly call about. Every book she put back, she gave a quick once-over, running her thumb over the jacket and scanning the back cover copy. She was always intrigued by the books that people picked out. Just what inspired an obsessive foray into the fauna of Papua New Guinea? How many tomes about artisanal cheese-making could one possibly flip through? Why were there so many folded pages in the ogre erotica? She suspected she knew the answer to this one, but didn't want to think too deeply about it.

She was returning the cart to the circulation desk when she happened across two of the library's most avid graphic novel readers browsing the crystal display she'd put together after her visit to Behind the Curtain the other evening.

'Wow, it's so shiny,' said one of the girls, who was studying for an audio engineering certificate and could often be found, headphones on, fiddling around on Pro Tools in the reading room. Amy something. 'And the descriptions. Can you seriously just find this stuff out on the trails? I don't know, I thought that you had to mine it or something.'

'From the moon,' agreed her friend, who was a tattoo artist apprentice, always sketching out designs in her notebook. Abigail.

Effie pulled out a map of the local trails from the set of wall pockets that housed the town's tourism materials and passed it to Amy. 'Here, you can use this if you want to go exploring. You can polish up anything you find in a rock tumbler, or even in a dryer, if you have one. Although I probably wouldn't take them to the laundromat.'

'A tumbler . . .' mused Abigail.

Maybe Effie should get one for the library. It could be her way of taking a stand against Oswald's Griftertorium and its overpriced sham magic.

Having waved goodbye to Tessa's group of crafters – most of whom had emerged from their session with something resembling a turtle, and in a few cases, something closer to a green worm – Effie sat down at her computer, ready to place an order for a rock tumbler.

But right as she went to hit the checkout button, a thud from the stacks startled her, making her wrists flash green.

What was that?

Heart thudding, Effie grabbed a hardcover book and made her way through the dark stacks. The library was closed, and Tessa's event had been an after-hours thing, so there should be no one here. Not Bowow searching for a few extra cowboy romances to add to her list. Not Tammi munching away on her latest library snacks. Not poor Thomas, who was outside in his truck.

'Effie?'

Spinning on the heel of her Doc Martens, Effie lunged with her book. The strike connected viciously enough that she could feel it reverberating up her wrists all the way through to her shoulders.

The intruder grunted in surprise.

'Ow! What the hell?'

Oh shit, it was Theo. Of *course* it was Theo, traipsing around here like his very generous donation meant that he owned the place.

Theo rubbed his arm. 'Wow, I guess the pen really is mightier than the sword. That hurt.'

'We're closed!' Effie snapped.

'I know. I just thought it would be rude to head out without saying goodnight. Are you okay locking up by yourself?'

Aha, thought Effie triumphantly. He was a white knight type who couldn't fathom a woman being able to fend for herself. She'd *known* he was too good to be true. Besides, she was a witch! She was perfectly capable of looking after herself. Not to mention that Yellowbrick Grove was safe to a fault. The worst that might happen here was that your pizza delivery came with the wrong toppings. Or maybe someone might cut a few roses from one of the bushes in the park.

'Why wouldn't I be all right locking up?' she retorted. 'I do it every night. And this is the first time a would-be serial killer has been sneaking around like a creeper.'

'A would-be serial killer? Do I *look* like a serial killer?'

Spoken just like Patrick Bateman. 'I can't think of anyone who looks *more* like a serial killer. You're well dressed. Quiet. You keep to yourself. I bet your neighbours say that you're polite.'

Theo raised an eyebrow. 'Well, yes. Except for a stint in my early twenties when my neighbours would have said quite the opposite. But anyway, I'm not big on blood. It's such a pain to get the stains out.'

'Maybe you're a poisoner, then. Like that mushroom murderer in Australia.'

'Fair. Remind me never to cook for you. Especially risotto.'

Effie, in spite of herself, was intrigued. She lowered the book, which she realized she'd been brandishing this whole time. 'You cook?'

'Sure. Who doesn't cook?' Theo checked his smartwatch, which looked a bit the worse for wear. 'Anyway, how about I leave you to whatever you were doing that got you all jumpy.'

There was something in his phrasing that put Effie back on the defensive. *He* was what had got her all jumpy!

'I was ordering a rock tumbler,' she snapped. What was wrong with ordering a rock tumbler? It was perfectly normal to order a rock tumbler.

'So you can lob polished stones at my head next time I darken the threshold?'

'Perhaps.' Effie was tempted to smile, but she held firm. 'Actually, you go ahead. I just remembered there's a report I need to file before I go.'

This was a lie, but it was better than prolonging this excruciating conversation. Besides, she'd walked to the library, and the thought of walking home with Theo beside her was too much to deal with. She could already see all the ways she surely fell short in his eyes. She didn't need to add to them.

Theo nodded slowly, then twined his scarf around his neck. 'All right. Well, I'll see you another time, I suppose.'

Effie nodded, directing him to the double doors at the front of the library, watching as he rubbed the nose of one of the stone gargoyles flanking the entrance. He waved, then made his way down the stairs and into the clear autumn night.

Effie sighed. A small part of her wished she'd taken Bonnie up on the discounted flirting lessons her sister had offered during high school. But what was the point? Theo wasn't her type, and she certainly wasn't his. Besides, it would probably be mere weeks before the bright lights and busy social calendar of the city lured him back.

Effie turned to shut off the lights, but as she did, another *thud* came from somewhere in the reading room.

She swallowed, her wrists glimmering green. All right, so *that* hadn't been Theo. But if not Theo, then who – or what?

Chapter 10

DOUBLE, DOUBLE, TOIL AND BIG TROUBLE

Bonnie

'Dammit!' Bonnie reached for a cloth to wipe away the pulp from the lemon that had just exploded all over the room.

Lemons were not only good conductors of electricity, but apparently, they were pretty good at channelling magic.

At least she'd had the good sense to bring over a pair of swim goggles from the house, or she'd be booking an emergency optometrist visit right now.

'Sorry, little apartment,' she whispered as she glanced around at the room above the bar. Sure, it was still mostly drop sheets and paint-swatch tests, and the floors were grooved from years of wear, but eventually it was going to be a cosy place filled with cushy seating and plush bedding.

Bonnie had fallen in love with it when she'd first toured the building with Hannah. It had been closed off, with a lock on the door, but Hannah had worked her realtor's magic using her skeleton key, and they'd snuck in.

'I had no idea this was even here,' Hannah had said, pushing up her blazer sleeves as her inner interior designer took over. 'Just imagine this with some cute boho furniture and soft rugs. And maybe a full rewiring so that you don't electrocute yourself. There's even a bathroom and a kitchenette!'

Bonnie had instantly seen its potential, and the opportunity to put some distance between her and Effie's smothering motherly ways. Bonnie was tired of being chided about her showers and her preference for putting the cereal boxes on the second shelf of the pantry instead of the third. Not to mention the whole outside porch-light situation. Or the endless battle over the order the cars should be parked in the driveway.

Anyway. The upstairs apartment still wasn't liveable. The wiring needed to be addressed, something Bonnie was working around with the strategic use of battery-powered string lights and tea candles in hurricane lanterns. And the plumbing was almost certainly possessed by the spirit of a sewerage demon who had a horrifying habit of making the toilet water bubble from afar. But a fresh coat of paint and an extensive array of throw pillows had gone a long way towards turning the apartment into a place for Bonnie to spend some time. On her own. Without judgement.

Nevertheless, until then, it was the perfect out-of-the-way space to work on finessing Uncle Oswald's bespelled drinks.

Bonnie flipped through the hand-printed pages of the mixology grimoire, her heart sinking. There were so many recipes, and they were all so complex, even discounting the whole magic part. The book wouldn't be out of place on display in a hipster speakeasy in the city, with snooty quotes from tattooed bartenders from competing establishments (all of whom would be vying for their own mixology book deal).

It was the enchantment side of things that truly worried Bonnie. These were spells designed for use on *people*, and people were already complicated enough. Bonnie, of course, had tried the occasional love spell as a teen, but it was always difficult to tell whether the spell had worked or whether her non-magical charms had drawn in the object of her affections. Not that she was complaining. She'd also tried a few boob-enhancement and leg-lengthening spells, but once again, it was hard to know where nature ended and magic began. Effie hated her for it, but Bonnie couldn't help being blessed in that area. Besides, it wasn't that Effie was bad-looking. She just hid her looks under baggy cardigans and those stern glasses.

Bonnie, you're getting distracted.

She closed her eyes, trying to focus on the task at hand. Uncle Oswald's spells each targeted a specific type of interest in magic, such as horoscopes, palmistry, or ghostly premonitions, and then diverted interest away from that specific magic. The agate coasters, which were hexed to entice people towards Oswald's shop, did the rest.

It was as easy as that, and as difficult as that. Especially when Oswald kept pestering her about how things were going. When she'd dropped off his freshly laundered handkerchief this morning he'd demanded to see photographic evidence of the hexed cocktails. He hadn't been impressed with the scorch marks and exploded lemons in Bonnie's videos.

'I was so sure you had it in you,' he'd said, with the kind of disappointed air that took Bonnie straight back to her high-school days. 'But if you don't, I understand. I'm certain you gave it your best.'

Bonnie had immediately raced back here to prove him wrong. Well, after stopping at The Winged Monkey for a takeaway coffee.

Now, she huffed out a dejected breath. There was no way she could master all of the spells in the recipe book. It would take weeks of dedication just to get the non-magical ingredients handled. And Bonnie wasn't exactly known for her keen study skills. Well, unless it came to the names of the nail polish colours in her drawer. She had a photographic memory there.

But she had to get this figured out before the repo guy came for her Cadillac, and Willamina from the bank started knocking very politely on the front door.

Maybe there was a handy catch-all recipe she could try.

One she could get a handle on before the bar opened for business tomorrow.

She flipped through the pages, looking for recipes that seemed both manageable for her and appealing to the townsfolk. She couldn't choose anything *too* out there. If people couldn't pronounce an ingredient listed in a cocktail, they'd probably avoid ordering it.

There. A concentrate called Memory Lane, comprising just four ingredients and a splash of enchantment. She could manage that. And best of all, it was purple, like Bonnie's magic.

Bonnie grimaced as she saw the magical annotations – there was a whole language to magic that, unlike Effie, she'd never properly mastered. A bit like musical notation, it guided you with gesture and language, helping you create the set of circumstances needed to bring the spell into being. But not all magic was like that. You could also cast magic just by directing your emotion at a particular target. Now *that* Bonnie was good at, even if it did tend to result in a touch of magical recoil.

Memory magic, though, that was tough. You had to be specific about what it was you were targeting, or you risked lobotomizing your audience. And people with no frontal lobes weren't great at ordering drinks, which didn't bode well for the bar's longevity.

Well, she'd manage. Because if she didn't, Willamina and the bankruptcy court awaited. Or worse, a despairing look from Effie as she bailed Bonnie out yet again.

Bonnie was done being bailed out.

She arranged the coupe glasses she'd carried upstairs in a triangle, then in a pitcher mixed together the sparkling rosé, candied plums, crème de violette and chopped mint the recipe called for. So far, so good.

Then, hands at the ready, pinkie fingers poised, Bonnie channelled her inner magic, feeling her wrists grow warm.

Purple swirled atop her floral tattoos as she directed her focus towards the pitcher, letting her mind's eye bloom with the image of smoother, less stressful times. But then the thing that she was determined not to forget, not ever, sparkled into the vision. Mom's smiling face.

Bonnie's magic flashed, shooting in a zigzag from her wrist to the pitcher, turning it a swirling purple and almost knocking it over.

'Dammit!' she shouted.

At least she managed to grab the pitcher before the entire thing spilled all over the hardwoods, creating an entirely new restoration issue.

Just then, there was a knock at the door. Bonnie swore as the cocktail sloshed over her hand, and her favourite magenta skirt.

'Bon?' Bobby's voice was muffled through the thick wood. 'Is everything okay?'

'Fine,' said Bonnie, trying to keep exasperation out of her voice.

'Do you want me to come in?'

She stood up to let him in, hoping he wouldn't find it odd that she was hanging out with a pitcher of purple liquid and two cocktail coupes too many. Not to mention the residual smoky smell that lingered from her wayward magic.

Bobby tiptoed in, looking awkward in the apartment. He thrust his hands in his pockets as he took in the messy scene.

'Drinking alone, huh?' he said lightly.

'Just working on a new cocktail recipe. How's your head?'

'Much better. I think I was probably dehydrated. All that running around on nothing other than a few bites of a pastry will do it.' Bobby made his way carefully around the ladder in the middle of the room – he'd always been vocal about the karmic risks of walking under a ladder – before perching on one of the taller stacks of cushions. 'I dropped off some ice for you, by the way. It's in the storeroom.'

'Thanks,' said Bonnie. 'You're sweet.'

Bobby rubbed his cheek, the way he always did when she said something to make him blush. Bonnie quite enjoyed having this superpower.

'Did you want to come to the basketball game at the college?' he said quickly, his dark eyes meeting hers before darting away. 'The coach gave me some free tickets as thanks for helping out over the weekends. I can get some extras for the girls if you want?'

Bonnie bit back a smile. Bobby was annoying, but kind. And she definitely appreciated the free labour and the endless dessert offerings. It was almost a shame that he'd only ever be the boy next door.

'I'll pass on the basketball. But can you do me a favour?' She raised one of the coupes, filling it with the bespelled mixture. 'Can you give this recipe a try for me, let me know what you think?'

She passed him a glass, then took one for herself.

'To fancy cocktails,' said Bobby, sipping from the cocktail. 'And fancy neighbours.'

'Indeed,' said Bonnie, pretending to sip from hers.

Bobby coughed, then rubbed at his throat. 'Wow, that's strong. Notes of burning. And crab apples. Does it contain crab apples?'

Bonnie chuckled. 'It does not. You remain undefeated at getting every cocktail ingredient wrong.'

'Well, there are worse flaws to have,' said Bobby with a grin. He sipped away, turning to take in the work she'd put into the apartment, and stifling cocktail-induced coughs as he did so. 'This is coming along. I see you've moved the furniture incrementally since you made me haul it up the stairs.'

Bonnie batted her eyelashes in faux apology. It wasn't her fault that quality furniture was heavy.

'Wow, this is even stronger than the last one you made me

try. Hits right behind the eyes.' Bobby rubbed the bridge of his nose, frowning.

Bonnie hoped this meant that the spell was working and not that she'd blinded the poor guy, because *that* was something her magic definitely couldn't undo.

'Are you having another dizzy spell?' Bonnie was a bit worried she was doing permanent damage to Bobby's brain. Was he allergic to her magic? Was that even a thing?

Bobby shook his head. 'I just need to work on my tolerance. Anyway, I'd better be off. Early start at the bakery tomorrow, and then the basketball game.'

The basketball game. Bonnie felt a mild pang for missing it. She probably should have said yes, considering all the help that Bobby had given her, with not a single complaint. Not just at the bar, but also in the wake of Mom's death. But if she did go to the game, there might be expectations. And while Bonnie was open to some fun, like with Theo perhaps, she couldn't possibly entertain anything that might be *real*. Not with the bar to wrangle and her looming debts. Ugh, *and* she was meant to meet Effie and Mom's friend Sabine at the Toto Hotel the following morning.

'Go, Munchkins,' she said half-heartedly, waggling her fingers in support of the college team.

With his usual shy wave, Bobby hurried out of the room.

Bonnie watched him leave with interest, and not only because she'd noticed how well his jeans fit. But rather, Bobby had done something he never ordinarily did. On the way out of the room he'd walked right beneath the ladder.

Oof, thought Bonnie. *Bad luck, here we come.*

Well, at least the spell seemed to be working.

Bonnie's phone pinged. It was Effie, who she'd renamed 'The Wicked Witch' in her phone.

Don't forget that we're meeting Sabine tomorrow. 10 a.m.

Of course Effie didn't trust her to show up. No matter what Bonnie did, Effie was always hovering about, looking for an opportunity to step in and prove that she was the responsible, functional one of the two. She was *insufferable*.

Bonnie sent a passive-aggressive thumbs-up emoji in response and got back to work.

Chapter 11

THESE MAGIC MOMENTS

Effie

If a hotel could be a gargoyle, the Toto Hotel was it. For a hundred years, it had sat upon the hills surrounding Yellowbrick Grove, all gables and turrets and ornamental fretwork that made it a favourite of photographers and art students – along with the hot springs that dotted its grounds, sending up steam and inviting the townsfolk and tourists to dip in year-round. Effie and Bonnie had spent an inordinate amount of time up here as kids, wandering the gardens while Mom worked, plied with tiny finger sandwiches from the kitchen and enormous cups of lemonade. Effie would read by the springs or in the soaring light-filled atrium, while Bonnie lolled about the lawns in her bathing suit, keeping an eye out for cute boys or gangs of teenage girls she could appoint herself leader of.

Mom had worked at the hotel for the girls' entire lives, but the hotel had looked after her as well. It had kept her on staff even when she was long beyond being able to work her job at reception, and she'd had access to the mineral pools whenever she wanted to soothe her aches and pains.

Effie felt a pang as she rolled up its meandering, shrub-lined driveway in the Jeep – Mom's Jeep. Now all the memories she had of the place were just that. Memories. And like the cushions on all the lawn chairs she was cruising past, they would fade over time, becoming threadbare, then unrecognizable.

There would be no new memories of Mom. No new stories they could share together.

I love you, Mom, she whispered sadly to the air as she pulled into a space. How much of the air she was breathing now was the same Mom had breathed for years? She'd spent decades here, after all, infusing every inch of the hotel with her sunny personality and the smiles she always had for everyone. Plying the gardeners and maintenance staff with the home-made brownies she seemed to have an endless supply of.

There was a reason Effie hadn't been back here since Mom's death, even though Sabine, who also worked at the hotel, had been so good about staying in touch and lending whatever support she could. It was all too hard. But a few weeks ago, Sabine had called, asking her to come by the Toto. And no one turned down Sabine, who had a welcoming, gregarious energy that dwarfed even Bonnie's charm. She veritably sparkled with joy and warmth.

So here Effie was, on one of her rare days away from the library.

'Effie!' came a familiar fluting voice. The voice wavered as its owner hurried down the wide, Spanish-tiled steps that led up to the hotel's wraparound porch.

Sabine embraced Effie, who found herself pressed against a dangly earring made of tiered bells and long greying waves of hair. As kids, Effie and Bonnie had always joked about drowning in the Sabine hair tsunami. Effie wasn't much of a hugger, but exceptions could be made for Sabine.

Sabine pulled back, looking at Effie with her gold-flecked eyes. As always, she wore a flowing outfit: a floral kaftan with a patterned shawl draped around her shoulders. Shimmery and rippling, her attire always reminded Effie of a gentle breeze. She dressed like a less self-conscious version of Bonnie's friend Alana.

'No Bonnie today?' Sabine adjusted her shawl, something she did when she was trying to ward off bad energy.

Ah. Of course, she'd figured that something was wrong. Sabine had spent a lifetime working with the public, and could instantly read someone's body language. It was a skill you quickly perfected if you wanted to stay ahead of angry calls to the manager.

Effie hesitated, not sure how to respond. How could she tell Mom's lifelong best friend that the two daughters who represented all that was left of the Chalmers family line (if you took a matrilineal approach, Uncle Oswald didn't count) were scarcely talking to each other?

'We'll see,' said Effie cagily. 'You know what Bonnie's like.'

Arrogant. Know-it-all. And willing to entertain the business ideas of Oswald of all people!

Sabine nodded. 'I'm sure she's busy with the bar. It's good to see that she's found a passion for something. Community building.'

Effie's immediate inclination was to retort that running a bar wasn't about community building at all. Now a library, *that* was doing something for the community. A free space where all were welcome, where you could expand your understanding of the world and hone new skills. As opposed to a bar, where people were plied with alcohol, unleashing their worst selves upon the town square at closing time.

But Sabine's gentle presence always brought out the best in everyone around her. Instead of giving in to her natural defensiveness – a protective mechanism honed over years of living in Bonnie's shadow – Effie simply nodded.

Running a hand over the porch railing, Sabine stared down the hill at the town, with its red rooftops and autumnal trees. She smiled gently, drinking in the crisp air of the season, which beckoned with promises of pumpkin patches and chrysanthemum planters.

'I suppose we can wait for her a little longer. Let's get some lemonade and sandwiches, for old times' sake. Ham and yellow pickles?'

Now it was Effie's time to smile. Sabine knew her too well. Effie might have switched to peanut butter and jelly in her day-to-day life, but at the hotel, ham and pickles reigned.

Sabine put in the order with the kitchen, then pulled out a black-and-white patterned chair for Effie to take a seat. She followed, taking the opposite seat. Lost in memory, the two of them sat quietly for a moment, watching a finch flick its tail atop the railing.

Maureen, one of the kitchen staff, hurried up with a silvery platter, dropping off their sandwiches and drinks, together with a bud vase of flowers.

'You're looking good,' said Maureen, shrewdly regarding Effie as she adjusted the barrette in her salt-and-pepper hair. 'I know that colour in the cheeks. What's their name, this new person in your life?'

Maureen had an incredible knack for spotting the lovesick in a crowd. But this was the first time she'd levelled it at Effie – usually Bonnie was the one she was quizzing about crushes and dates and matrimonial intent.

Effie blinked. 'No name. It's—'

Thankfully, Bonnie's Cadillac roared up the driveway just then, creating a rumbling distraction from Effie's non-existent love life. Crookedly parking the car in the widest spot, Bonnie strutted up to Effie and Sabine – Maureen had apologetically raced back inside to deal with a guest. She wore a skirt so short that Effie was sure her legs must have got stuck to the leather seats of her car, and boots that, no matter what Nancy Sinatra might have said, definitely weren't made for walking.

Bonnie waggled her fingers at Sabine, ignoring Effie.

'Love the spread,' she said, flicking her perfect blonde tresses and propping her sunglasses up on her head. 'Sabine, you look stunning, as usual. The shawl is giving me life. I brought you these.'

She set down a small box of brownies and a bouquet of

chrysanthemums on the table, deliberately blocking Effie's view.

Oblivious to the tension between the two sisters, Sabine embraced Bonnie, who hugged right back, rocking Mom's friend back and forth on the spot. Effie nibbled a sandwich, feeling instantly cast aside. Bonnie had arrived full of compliments and gifts, her sunniness overshadowing Effie's own reserved presence. And punctuality.

'Oh, it's so good to see you girls,' said Sabine gently. She pulled back to regard them both. 'You both remind me so much of Lyra. It's like you were both spun off her, in your own ways.'

'So, what's the surprise?' asked Bonnie, dropping into a chair and propping her booted feet up on the last remaining seat. Sabine had mentioned something in her messages about a surprise, but she'd been coy.

'It's something we at the hotel have been talking about for a long while. Come on.'

Sabine stood, leading the sisters off the porch and down into the manicured hotel gardens, which in their perfection rivalled the yard of the sisters' lawn-proud neighbour Freddie Noonan. Asters and geraniums brightened the walkways, their flowers vivid pinks and lilacs. Ducks waddled about, plumage shimmering green and purple.

Effie drank it all in. She'd made this same walk a thousand times, and before Mom's death, had assumed she'd make it a thousand times more.

'Here we go,' said Sabine.

There, at the end of the path, was a beautifully fashioned teak bench, its curved arms patterned with a design that combined flowers, stars and a sun and moon motif. Pink and gold cushions were strewn across it, and a plaque gleamed at its base.

Sabine took each of the Chalmers sisters' hands in her own and pulled them around to face the bench.

'Lyra's favourite spot,' said Sabine gently. Although she didn't have to, because the sisters knew it well.

Sabine sat, pulling the girls down with her.

Effie's eyes welled as she settled into one side of Sabine, her vision filling with wildflowers and trees, and at its edges, ghostly reminders of Mom. Mom spotting the fingers of the daffodils rising up from the damp spring ground. Mom hiding foil-wrapped eggs for them to find and then carefully unpeel, flattening the colourful wrappers into silvery rectangles. Mom twirling sparklers with them as they danced across the dusty fields as fireworks exploded overhead. Mom's endless smile, the one that Effie could still conjure in her mind's eye in a flash.

Sabine reached for the sisters' hands and clasped them together in her lap, giving them a gentle squeeze. As she glanced over to meet Bonnie's teary gaze, Effie smiled gently.

Bonnie smiled back.

'It's perfect,' Effie whispered.

Chapter 12

MAGIC IN THE AIR

Bonnie

Head turned to hide the spikes that her tears had made of her eyelashes, Bonnie dabbed at an eye with the back of her hand. Her heart swelled as she took in the colourful brickwork at her feet. It was so beautiful. So perfect. So *Mom*.

Everything about it, from the gently carved wood of the bench seat, which reminded Bonnie so much of the swirling landscape scenes Mom loved to paint, to the brightly patterned Spanish-style tiles that interspersed the path of yellowish local bricks stretching out from the bench to make a wildflower-smothered loop around the frog pond.

But the tiles weren't just patterned, she realized. Each was hand-painted with a tiny scene.

'They're memories,' she said, her throat thick.

Sabine's voice was as warm as a hug. 'Every one of them.'

And so they were: each brick at the base of the bench was etched with a few words or a little picture, illustrating a memory that the hotel staff had of Mom. *Smile like a swan*, said one, poking fun at Mom's insistence that swans were always smiling. You just couldn't tell because they had no lips, she'd say. *Rain is nature's soundtrack*, said another, referencing her love of sitting out at night reading as the rain pattered on the veranda roof. *To catch a butterfly*, said a third, reminding Bonnie of the time half of housekeeping had chased after her five-year-old self, demanding to know where she'd been going wearing a pool net over her head. *Brownies heal all*. And poignantly, so much so that Bonnie had to kneel to touch her fingers to it: *It's all for my girls.*

'It's a memory chair,' said Sabine. 'So that we always remember the wonderful times your mom gave us, and will continue to. There are many more tiles. We want everyone to contribute over time.'

'I love it.' Bonnie stood, nudging the toe of her boot over tile after tile, letting the memory housed within each spill up through her like sunshine peeping through the clouds.

'And you chose Mom's favourite place,' said Effie quietly. She turned a slow circle atop the spot where a fairy ring sprouted during mushroom season, and then again when the daisies popped out in spring. The three of them had enjoyed countless picnics here, sprawling on the thick blankets they'd carry down from the main building, picking out shapes in the clouds as they lay on their backs, bellies aching from thick sandwiches and too-big portions of cake.

'She was so proud of you girls,' said Sabine, wiping away a tear of her own. 'We all are. This last year has been hard beyond belief, for all of us. But Lyra's memory will live on. In this. In your home. In your work. And in your bond.'

In your bond.

Bonnie tried to catch Effie's gaze again, to see if she might put their fight behind them, but Effie had that blank look on her face she always did when someone spoke earnestly of them as a duo. That hard expression that said she hated being lumped in with Bonnie. Almost as if she was too good for the flighty sister whose wild ambitions didn't gel with Effie's structured aspirations.

Maureen, who wore her usual apron tied around crisp slacks and paisley shirt, came over with a bottle of wine. 'Isn't it a beautiful spot? It's so fitting. That one's mine.'

She pointed to a brick decorated with text that read *You are all my sunshine.*

'We were teasing her about a bright yellow dress she had on. She looked like she'd stepped right out of the sky.'

Even Effie smiled. Because Mom had always looked like that.

Maureen displayed the wine bottle label, which depicted a series of tall Douglas firs against a grey sky. 'Would any of you like a glass? We're trying out a new Oregonian supplier.'

'I don't day-drink,' said Effie stiffly. She took off her glasses to polish them. Although from the amount she was blinking, Bonnie suspected that smudgy lenses weren't really the issue here. Would it kill her to show a touch of emotion?

Actually, it might.

Bonnie retracted that thought, just in case.

'That's more Bonnie's thing,' added Effie.

Bonnie un-retracted the thought.

'I'll take one,' Bonnie told Maureen, although the thought of drinking after her week of late nights didn't particularly appeal. But it was worth it to position herself as Effie's opposite. 'It's one of the perks of being the most in-demand bar in town.'

Maureen poured her a generous glass of pinot grigio, stopping just before the glass overflowed. Effie eyed the glass. Bonnie could tell she was curious, but being Effie, simply could not abide the prospect of anything that didn't fit the Effie Chalmers Book of Appropriate Public Comportment. It was a long book.

'Wow. You should come work for me,' said Bonnie, taking a sip of the wine to avoid it spilling. It was lovely and light-bodied, with soft citrus notes. 'The punters would love you.'

She clinked her glass against Maureen's and then Sabine's. 'But both of you *should* stop by, really. We have a new cocktail range launching tonight. It's going to be magical, I promise.'

'Ooh,' said Sabine. 'Sold. If not tonight, then later this week.'

Bonnie sipped her wine, feeling a sense of pride as Sabine and Maureen quizzed her about the bar operations and the new menu. Effie, meanwhile, wandered off down the looping golden pathway, pausing to read each of the embellished tiles she passed.

She walked lightly, but the judgement that emanated from her was impossible to ignore.

Maureen brought Bonnie back to the present.

'Did you read Madame Destinée's latest horoscopes?' Maureen grinned, showing off the snaggle tooth that somehow suited her. '*Watch out, Tauruses, because the world knows that you're full of bull.*'

Sabine chuckled. 'Here, show me what it says for Aquarius.'

Maureen's eyes twinkled as she read out the horoscope for Mom's sign. 'She recommends water aerobics.'

It was such a Lyra joke, and the three of them laughed, just as they would have if Mom had been there.

And if you squinted, thought Bonnie, she almost was.

Chapter 13

THAT'S JUST MY RESTING WITCH FACE

Effie

A new day meant an opportunity for Effie to restart the timer on her daily caffeine consumption. And she dearly needed a coffee. She'd snuck out of the Chalmers family home without her usual morning cuppa, as Bonnie had been holed up in the kitchen, scrolling through videos on her phone with the volume all the way up. Obnoxious phone-scrolling aside, Effie still wasn't ready for a sit-down with her sister. She'd done her best to be the better person yesterday, but Bonnie had been so over the top in how she'd wooed Maureen and Sabine, and how she'd made the entire moment about *her*. How much attention did one person need?

Between her responsibilities at the library and the endless chores that somehow fell under her remit, Effie was finding it easier just to avoid Bonnie as much as possible. It wasn't a pride thing, not really. It was inertia.

Mindful that the skies above the house looked about to open, Effie shouldered her heavy book bag, then grabbed her favourite novelty umbrella, an old duck-handled one of Mom's made from vintage waxed canvas. Then she picked her way down the slippery front steps with the utmost care. Even with the tacky tape she'd added over the summer, the moss-covered stone became a trip hazard when damp.

Because Effie was prone to ruminating on all the embarrassing times of her life to date, she flashed back to the time that, around age fifteen, she'd slithered all the way down the front steps of the Toto Hotel, much to the amusement of Bonnie and her friends. It was one of those moments that stick with you for all eternity, and she was fairly certain that one of the decorative tiles she'd pored over yesterday had referred to the incident. She'd been too afraid to ask, lest the others, who were tipsy from the wine, affirmed her suspicions.

The rain rattled off Effie's umbrella as she thought back over the awkward meeting with Sabine at the hotel. She'd wanted to extend an olive branch to Bonnie over their fight, but Bonnie was being so insufferable. No matter the occasion, everything turned into the Bonnie Show. Even a thoughtful gesture for Mom had ended up being a boozy affair culminating in a sharing of star signs.

Okay, so Effie occasionally checked to see what Madame Destinée had in store for Virgos, but mostly because whoever the writer was had a snappy, charming style. Effie had never been able to pass up a witty barb. Especially one on paper.

Don't let your green eyes lose your green eyes, Effie's most recent horoscope had said, rather cryptically. Effie hadn't been able to figure it out. Was it a reference to jealousy? Or cats, perhaps?

Sidestepping to avoid puddles, she passed by Bobby's house, noting with surprise a grey sporty SUV with vanity plates and a *Honk If You Love Bloggers* bumper sticker parked in the driveway. It was Kirsty's car, of course. The 1 KB 1 plates were a dead giveaway. But Effie couldn't for the life of her figure out why Kirsty would have parked at Bobby's. Perhaps she was doing an interview piece about the family bakery and its new lavender-dipped croissant wheels. Maybe she'd been visiting Bonnie but had quickly pulled into the driveway to avoid the imminent arrival of the street sweeper and the resulting fine. Effie checked her phone. No, it was the wrong day for that.

Curiouser and curiouser.

In desperate need of caffeine before she started her shift at the library, Effie hurried down the street, marvelling at Freddie Noonan's perfect lawn and stooping to give Bowow's dogs a quick scratch on the head through the wrought-iron fence that ringed the ivy-smothered property. Bowow's home was famously haunted, and not just by the larger-than-life personality of its owner and her many yappy dogs.

As Effie strolled past the house Theo was renting – which, let's face it, was the entire point of the trip to the coffee shop – she made a point to keep her gaze pointed straight ahead, even as she drank in the property through what little peripheral vision she had. Bonnie was always on about her needing to try contact lenses for this reason, and perhaps, for once, her sister had a point.

But as she did, a gust of wind kicked up. A letter smacked her in the face. Rude!

She grabbed at the envelope, thankful that her rain-speckled glasses had saved her from some sort of papercut-related eye injury, then squinted at it.

It was addressed to Theo.

Effie glanced at the brick path that separated the sidewalk from the front door. Her heart skipped as she thought about walking its moss-filled length, climbing up the front steps and standing there, on Theo's porch, with only the vintage yellow door separating his public life from his private.

She could just give him the letter the next time at the library. But what if it was urgent? A letter from the IRS, perhaps. Or a bill. She didn't know an awful lot about Theo, but she did know that he was prompt when it came to paying his bills.

She'd better drop it off in person. Just in case. Out of the goodness of her heart.

There was nothing untoward, nothing sneaky, nothing voyeuristic about it. She didn't care to see how Theo lived, not really. The white Art Deco home with the curved corners and the dramatic stripes and the simply incredible geometric chandelier above the front door did nothing for her. Even if it did remind her of something straight out of *The Great Gatsby*, which, according to the book log she'd been keeping since elementary school, she'd read sixteen times.

Effie's umbrella bobbed as she picked her way along the garden path, then crept up the steps. There would absolutely be no slipping this time.

All right. Here she went.

She slid the letter through the flap in the door, but as she did, a curtain twitched. *Please let that be a ghost*, she thought.

Of course it wasn't. It was never a ghost when you needed it to be.

The front door opened, and Theo stood there, dressed in activewear and sheened with sweat from a workout. Effie had never really seen the appeal of working out, what with all the grunting. It felt too much in the realm of Bonnie's poltergeist hauntings. But, curiously, she was suddenly starting to come around to it. Theo held a protein shaker bottle in one hand, and clutched the doorframe with the other. Effie couldn't help but notice the curve of his bicep and how his shirt clung to his well-muscled chest. She swallowed, hoping that the flush creeping over her cheeks wasn't as vibrant as it felt.

'Are you delivering books direct to my door now?' Theo asked, nodding at her book bag.

Effie pointed to the mail slot. 'There was a letter kicking about in the rain. I thought I'd deliver it safely. In case it was important. What with all the move admin.'

Theo retrieved the letter from the mailbox and opened it.

'Thank you. I don't know what I would've done without this ten per cent off coupon for home surveillance.' He grinned. 'There's a smart doorbell on the place already. That's how I saw you coming up the driveway. Although I did assume you were a duck. They set it off every time they go by. There are so many ducks around here. Where *do* they come from?'

'Oh, there's a portal,' said Effie airily. 'We're just supporting characters in a duck's fantasy novel.'

Theo chuckled. 'You are extremely unexpected, Effie. And please don't take that as an insult the way you did at the bar.'

Effie exhaled slowly. 'All right. I'm just' – she hesitated – 'not used to compliments. They tend to flow Bonnie's way.'

'It must be hard living in her extremely loud shadow. I get it, a bit. My dad's the larger-than-life one in my family. Smart, successful, handsome. It's impossible to live up to him sometimes.'

Given that Theo was all of those things, Effie suspected that he was just being nice. And hated him a little bit for it.

'Are you getting coffee before work?' Theo added.

Effie froze. She'd been on her way to The Winged Monkey, but perhaps she could skip it and rely on the crusty machine at the library. Nudged with a strong enough charm, it put out something at least *resembling* coffee. If you added enough cream and sugar and about ten pumps of hazelnut syrup, you could choke it down without making a face.

'I'm going to take your delayed reaction as a "yes, I really need coffee",' said Theo, reaching for his wallet.

Yes, she thought, I really need a coffee. *Alone.*

But if that was so true, why had she come to his house? With a letter that had *clearly* been junk mail and which she could easily have thrown in the recycling at the library. But that was too much self-reflection for a librarian who hadn't had a coffee yet.

'After you,' he said, waiting for Effie to pick her way gingerly down the front steps. At the bottom, she turned, waiting for him to catch up. But as had happened that fateful day at the Toto Hotel, gravity and dampness intervened. Theo slipped on the step second from the bottom, his feet kicking up and his arms splaying.

Before she could even register what she was doing, Effie clicked her fingers and with a thin stream of emerald magic quickly righted him. Theo paused, frowning.

Effie could tell he'd figured that *something* weird had just happened, but exactly what was beyond his comprehension. She hoped.

At least her wrists were covered by her voluminous wet-weather wear.

'My mom always says I have nine lives,' he said, regarding his hands as though they contained the truth of the moment. 'Although I've always been more of a dog person, to be honest. Which reminds me, I've been meaning to talk to Bowow about fostering. Or adopting. Do you want me to carry that for you?'

Shaking her head, Effie grabbed protectively at the straps of her book bag.

'The umbrella, at least?'

All right. He was taller, so it only made sense. She grudgingly passed over the umbrella.

'An animal is a lifelong commitment,' she said stiffly, as they navigated the garden path. She'd heard the stories from Bowow of people giving up their dogs on a whim: the pet was inconvenient to their travel plans, or it needed too many walks during the day. Or it shed too much. 'Especially if you're just here temporarily.'

'Temporarily?' Theo regarded her curiously as he opened the front gate.

Had she misspoken? For someone so into poetry, he seemed to struggle with subtext.

'Yellowbrick Grove is a big change from the city,' she explained. 'In case you hadn't noticed, there's no stock exchange here.'

Theo chuckled. 'I had noticed that, actually.'

Effie's lips tightened. It was an unwritten rule that only locals were allowed to make fun of the town.

'There's not much for me back in the city, at least for now. It wasn't my doing,' he added, as though he'd read her thoughts. 'I was perfectly happy with how my life was going. But my ex apparently wasn't. And sometimes you need to step away to heal.'

Effie nodded slowly. All right, so he wasn't wrong about that. After Mom's death, she'd seriously considered fleeing to the city, a place where she could be anonymous and unknown, and where anyone who looked at her wouldn't instantly know her entire life story. One of the hardest parts of working through grief in a small town was the constant pitying looks and the *endless* questions about how you were doing and whether someone could do something to help. It forced you to face your feelings over and over, and constantly go on the record about how you were coping.

'I lost you for a minute there, huh?' Theo swiped the rain from his hair, his green eyes trying to find Effie's hazel ones beneath the safety of her oversized glasses.

It wasn't just grief Effie had been thinking about. It was whether she wanted to risk getting to know someone who might pack up and leave the next week. Effie had always been cautious with her attentions, even her friendship ones. And with good reason. Because usually when she opened up, mockery awaited.

'I was thinking about my coffee,' said Effie, as she turned the corner to the main square, which The Winged Monkey had laid claim to for as long as she could remember. The huge planters out the front overflowed with colourful wildflowers, and the hanging baskets swung gently in the misting rain. The paned windows were steamed up from the inside. Someone had drawn a heart on one of them, and Effie idly wondered if she'd ever be the subject of a heart drawing.

Shaking out the umbrella, Theo dropped it by the entrance with the others, then opened the door for Effie, gesturing for her to go ahead. The shop was busy, as it always was at this time of the morning. A line of customers hung out by the espresso machine, and a backdrop of murmured conversations was punctuated by the clinking of spoons and the rattle of coffee cups. Curious eyes followed the two of them as they approached the counter, and Effie immediately felt defensive. She could feel the questions on their lips, the way that people were trying to make sense of it. Effie, not Bonnie, walking into the coffee shop with Theo.

Terrance, the barista with the crush on the *other* Chalmers sister, took her order: a coffee for herself and a pastry for library parking lot Thomas. Then, finger poised over an iPad, he glanced at Theo, who'd sidled up next to Effie and was brushing down his damp jacket.

'Are you two together?' asked Terrance. She could hear the undercurrent of confusion in his voice.

Spluttering, Effie took a step to the side. 'Absolutely not. What a thing to assume.'

She would *not* be the subject of town gossip and judgement.

Terrance raised his hands to protect himself from her stark tone. 'I meant your order.'

'Sure,' said Theo easily, handing over his card. 'I've got it. Make mine a flat white.'

Effie rummaged in her purse for a five-dollar bill, handing it out to him. Amused, Theo waved it off.

'It's on me. As payment for lending me your umbrella.'

Effie put the bill in the tip jar, then hung back as Terrance set to work banging out the orders that were ahead of theirs. About half were coffee-based drinks, and the rest tea – after a recent video from someone called an 'influencer', the whole town had decided that it was very important to start reading their futures in their tea leaves. Or, in the case of the people ordering Turkish coffee, in their coffee grounds.

She was about to pick up a newspaper to try her hand at the word puzzles when she noticed Hannah and Alana lounging on the L-shaped sectional in the corner, sharing a croissant and a pot of tea, and no doubt some local secrets. It was strange to see just the two of them without Bonnie around. Until Alana had shown up at the crochet night, Effie hadn't even been sure that Bonnie's friends existed independently of her. Tessa always joked that they lived in a stairwell cupboard, coming to life like weird puppets only when Bonnie needed her entourage.

To Effie's surprise, Alana waved, the bangles on her slim wrist jangling.

'Hey, Effie,' she said.

'Alana,' responded Effie, baffled. Was this a trick of some sort?

Hannah waggled her fingers in an indifferent hello. She was clearly busy on a text thread filled with emojis of houses. Her nails clacked irritatingly against the screen as she typed.

'So, the crochet night was actually super fun,' said Alana, sipping her tea. 'I didn't have high expectations, given it was a library thing and all, but I had a good time. Everyone did.'

Effie smiled stiffly. *A library thing and all.* Well, a backhanded compliment was still better than an insult.

'Tessa is great,' offered Effie.

Alana nodded as she sipped again. 'How'd you enjoy it, Theo?'

'That's right,' said Hannah curiously. Setting down her phone, she looked askance at Theo. 'Library craft sessions over a visit to the bar. Interesting.'

'It was fun. I went home and made a koala,' said Theo, who was holding one of the for-sale plants from the plant wall – this one in a sausage-dog-shaped holder spangled with glittery gold stars.

'Someone must've put something in his drink,' muttered Hannah to Alana. 'It's the only way it makes sense.'

Alana regarded the tea leaves in the bottom of her cup. 'The library's not so bad,' she murmured.

'What's the verdict on this?' Theo waggled the ceramic dog

at Effie, drawing her attention away from the judgemental conversation going on right in front of her face.

Well, if this was the sort of dog Theo had meant when talking about getting a pet, Effie could abide it.

'Cute,' she said. 'Could do with some grooming.'

Theo chuckled, then whipped out his phone to pay using the QR code stickered to the dog.

'Coffee for Ebby and Neo?' called Terrance from the counter.

Close enough, thought Effie. At least it wasn't just her name getting butchered.

'Here, Longdog can live there while I grab our coffees.'

Theo loped off to get their drinks, clearing the mugs off an empty table on the way. Hannah and Alana watched him go with raised eyebrows.

Hannah turned a hawkish gaze to Effie. 'What's the story there? Did you buy a love potion from your uncle's shop or something?'

'We just bumped into each other. In the rain,' said Effie cagily. She tried not to flush as an image of the two of them huddled under her umbrella flashed through her mind.

'In the rain, huh?' Alana was not buying this at all. But beneath her bemusement she sounded almost pleased for Effie. At least one of Bonnie's friends had some semblance of empathy.

Hannah tapped her pouty bottom lip with a perfectly manicured fingernail. 'Does Bonnie know about your extracurriculars?'

Ah, that was more like it. It was almost comforting to be back to her usual defensive position.

'I think Bonnie would be more interested in *Kirsty*'s extracurriculars,' Effie retorted.

Before Hannah could ask for clarification, Theo returned, cups of takeout coffee in hand.

'Here ya go, Eff.'

'Effie,' she corrected. Effie did not abide nicknames. Especially from someone she barely knew. Even Tessa knew better than to try it. Still, Effie took the coffee, stuffing the pastry bag into her tote.

With Theo back, Hannah spun her phone on the table to face him. On the screen was a picture of the quaint cottage that everyone in town called the Dorothy House. Effie had always loved it. It felt like it had a thousand stories inhabiting its walls, and possibly a few ghosts as well.

A few years earlier, the owners had opened it up as part of a historic homes tour, with proceeds benefiting the Downtown Small Business Association. Effie and Tessa had spent hours poking around, investigating the decorative glassware on the mantels and conjuring backstories for the people in the watercolour portraits on the walls.

'Theo, do you know anyone interested in this place? It's a bargain compared with what you'd pay in the city,' she added.

'It's cute,' he said. 'I'll have a think.'

Effie checked her watch. The library awaited. And she needed an hour of peace and quiet before the patrons started filing in to ask about a book with a green cover by an author whose name possibly started with a T, or to insist that the library needed a donation of their outdated encyclopaedias.

'I'd better get to work,' Effie said, apologetically. Hopefully apologetically enough that Theo would get the hint and find something else to do with his morning. There was plenty to do in town: the parks, the hikes, the hot springs at the Toto Hotel. Even if it was pouring out.

As she hefted her book bag (the one that said *The Contents of This Bag Are Dangerous to Small Minds*), Bonnie's friends looked faintly relieved.

This shifted to amusement when Theo grabbed his sausage-dog planter and made to follow her.

'Let me know about the house!' called Hannah.

Effie shouldered open the door, awkwardly juggling the coffee cup and book bag as she tried to reach for her umbrella. If she were somewhere quieter, she'd use magic to protect herself from the rain, but she didn't want to run that risk in the busy town square, especially not with Theo in tow. She'd almost revealed herself a couple of times already, and Theo seemed perceptive. There'd be a point where he quizzed her about the green glow that seemed to show up whenever she was around.

Theo stooped to grab the umbrella.

'Not this time.' Effie snatched it off him, giving him a light jab with the not insubstantial spike on the top.

'Oof,' said Theo, feigning the weight of a mortal wound. 'Did you just stab me? On purpose?'

'Would you prefer I whack you with the handle?' Effie brandished the beady-eyed carved duck that comprised the other end of the umbrella. It was quite sturdy, and very good for whacking. In fact, she'd used it as an improvised croquet mallet during Tessa's *Alice in Wonderland*-themed twenty-first birthday party.

'You're going to *whack me* for my gallantry?'

'Clearly,' said Effie. 'Besides, you have your hands full.'

He did, somewhat, between the dog planter and the coffee cup.

He sighed. 'Who am I to argue with a champion fencer? Let's get this library of yours opened up.' Pulling up the collar on his jacket, he followed her out into the rain.

As they crossed the square and headed down the street towards the library, a gust of wind turned Effie's umbrella inside out. Her wrists glowed green beneath the cuffs of her cardigan, but she quelled her magic. Any other time, she would've quickly turned the umbrella back, but she didn't want to invite more questions from Theo. All right, so she did. Just not about her magic.

'Here.' Theo took the umbrella and turned it the right way. He passed it back to her as though it were a bouquet of flowers.

Effie flushed at the gesture. Figuring she was in his debt, even in a small way, she squashed her inner prickliness and asked him about his experiences in the town so far. His green eyes sparkled as he described the routes of his morning runs and the long chats he'd had with Bruce Dickens about hair metal music.

'That little bakery is good, too. The one Bonnie's boyfriend works at?'

'Bonnie's boyfriend?' Effie frowned. 'Oh, Bobby! He's not . . .' She paused, not wanting to say that Bonnie was single, actually, and that even though she and Bobby would actually make a lovely couple, she'd never consider it. That, in fact, *Theo* was more Bonnie's type. 'Bobby's our neighbour,' she finished, lamely.

'Ah,' said Theo thoughtfully. 'A good neighbour to have. You must be swimming in day-old pastries.'

'We're very popular with the ducks.'

They arrived at the library, which sat stately and quiet beneath the morning drizzle. Effie loved this time of day, even when the clouds sat dark and heavy. The morning sun still found a way to break through and sparkle on the leadlight windows, gleaming against the freshly painted railings and the planter that Effie had installed in honour of Mom. Lyra had spent every free Saturday morning here with Effie, picking through the vintage picture books at the shop where the library sold off its old volumes.

'Here, let me take Thomas his pastry first,' she said. She went round to the back of the library, where Thomas was huddled in his old truck in the parking lot. She popped the treat on the hood and gave him a thumbs up.

'I need to fill up the food pantry, too,' she told Theo, as she made her way up the steps that led to the front entrance, before shaking out her umbrella. 'The Friends are always after canned and boxed food for that. And snacks for the kids on weekends or when school's out.'

Theo nodded, waiting for her to unlock the door and disable the alarm. Then he frowned, pointing at a tear in the screen on one of the windows near the door. 'There's one to report to maintenance. A gust of wind must have got to it.'

Great. Mentally adding the torn screen to her list of things to deal with, Effie opened the door, gesturing for Theo to go ahead of her. As he went past, she was painfully and awkwardly aware of his proximity to her, and how they were both equally drenched from the morning mizzle. Theo removed his jacket, revealing a shirt that was see-through where it clung to his abs. What's more, the hair at his collar was damp. Jane Austen would have wept.

Maybe Theo wasn't so bad after all.

But then . . .

'What on earth?' she whispered.

'Oh shit,' said Theo.

Books and magazines were strewn all over the floor, in the children's reading area, between the stacks, around the circulation desk. And not just books. Effie's rock display was scattered all over, and the crocheted turtles were on their backs on the tables. Derek and George's chess pieces rolled sadly about on the carpet, with the board upended on a beanbag.

The library ghost had struck again.

Chapter 14

ABRACADABRARGH

Bonnie

Dammit! Bonnie grabbed a drinks menu, holding it over her head.

For the fourth time that week, one of her wayward spells had set off the bar's emergency sprinklers. The fire department had been highly entertained the first time, but seemed slightly miffed the second. The third time it happened, Bonnie had provided pizza and mocktails for the entire crew lest they send her a bill for the inconvenience. And now, well, she was hoping that they'd just leave her to it, because she was starting to feel like she ran a water park, not a bar.

At least she'd become a pro at wrangling the valves of the backflow device, she thought, swiping damp hair out of her face as she dried herself off in front of the hand dryer in the upstairs bathroom. The bar hadn't even opened yet for the day, so she hadn't drenched her customers. This time, anyway.

Emerging from the bathroom, she tromped down the stairs, giving a middle finger to the Uncle Oswald aura painting on the wall. If Oswald hadn't got her embroiled in this whole dastardly collab, she wouldn't be casting wonky spells and setting off every sprinkler within a mile radius. All right, so sales had been up in the two days since she'd introduced the Memory Lane menu, and Oswald had promptly paid her the agreed-upon percentage of sales the following morning, but this was all a huge pain. Bonnie missed the days when pouring a gin and tonic was enough to call herself a mixologist. This full-time spellcasting thing was far beyond the effort she was used to putting in.

'Everything all right, Bon?' asked Bobby, who'd come in early to help with the deliveries.

'Fine,' she said, with a fluff of her damp hair. 'The sprinklers are being temperamental again.'

'Do you need me to take a look?' There was an odd hitch in his voice that made Bonnie pause.

Bonnie shook her head. 'No, it's just a workflow thing. But thanks. You can help with prep, if you want?'

Bobby hesitated. 'About that. Since I'm not getting paid for the time, I'm going to need to set some boundaries. Work–life ones, you know?'

Bonnie did not know, actually. For a solid decade, Bobby had been a cheerful presence in her life, always happy to do her bidding. All right, so maybe she'd taken his generosity and reliability a touch for granted. But Bobby seemed happy to serve her, and Bonnie was certainly happier when Bobby helped take a chunk of her infinite daily errands off her plate. She was only one woman, after all, and everyone needed something from her at all times.

Something had changed, but what? Had Effie put him up to this? Her sister was all about unions and fair labour laws and blah blah blah. She'd been very proud of the display she'd put up in the library for Labour History Month a few years back.

She definitely wouldn't put it past her sister to get into Bobby's ear about unpaid labour.

'Sure,' said Bonnie easily, braiding her hair with as much indifference as she could manage. 'You know I'd never ask you to do anything you don't want to do. I thought you liked helping out.'

Bobby clasped his hands awkwardly. 'I do, I do. I did. I was just talking to Kirsty about it, and she isn't super into it. She thinks it's exploitative. And that you're using your social position to take power over me.'

Bonnie snapped her hair tie in shock.

Well, this was a plot twist she hadn't seen coming. Since when was Kirsty a psychoanalyst? No, blogging didn't count.

Not only that, but when had Kirsty decided to lend her new-found psychoanalytical talents to the relationship dynamic between Bonnie and Bobbie? Which she'd completely misread, of course, because there was no dynamic between them. There was just Bobby the puppy dog, and Bonnie the, well, queen bee. Who really could do with the free labour and kind words right now.

'I didn't realize Kirsty was a labour organizer,' said Bonnie archly.

'She's not. But we're kind of dating, I guess, so . . .'

Bonnie was too damp and frizzy and frazzled to properly compute this. When had this happened? And how? Kirsty had spent their entire childhood mocking Bobby for being too dull and too *nice*.

And what about the whole Make Theo Jealous campaign that Bobby was an integral part of? Not that *that* was going well, given that Effie had apparently recruited Theo full time at the library. Maybe the man had some community service hours he had to complete as part of a deferred sentence or something.

'But Kirsty hates you,' she said, voicing her thoughts in case it helped Bobbie come to his senses. 'She thinks you're destined for a small life in a small town.'

Bobby propped his arms on his dolly, which was marked *Property of The Golden Hour Bakery* – the bakery that he and his dad had built over the last decade and a half, and which Bobby would eventually inherit. 'Well, I probably am, aren't I? And anyway, is that so bad?'

Bonnie wasn't sure, honestly. Part of her had always wanted to try her luck in the city, just to see how far she could go.

But another part had told her to stay here, where she ruled the roost and was surrounded by people who happily did her bidding. It wasn't worth it to risk her big fish status here for who knew what elsewhere.

'But you hate Kirsty,' she said. Because it was true. Bobby had always warned Bonnie about Kirsty, whose friendship had a cutting edge to it. *She's rooting for your downfall*, he'd warned her earnestly one night after a few too many ciders, the drink he described as his own personal truth serum. And Bonnie knew it, always had. But she'd also known that she could handle having a frenemy, just so long as everything else stayed as it was.

Now she wasn't so sure.

'That's not true,' Bobby countered. 'When have I ever said that? I don't hate anyone.'

All right, so technically Bobby had never used the word hate. He was nice to a fault. And that niceness had led him into Kirsty's arms. Somehow. Some*why*.

Bonnie had to get to the bottom of this before she lost two friends, and the hierarchy of the town became irrevocably topsy-turvy. But not now. First, she had to make sure she had enough of her bespelled cocktail mix ready prior to opening, and that she wasn't going to set off the sprinklers for a fifth time. The hardwoods and pinball machines could only take so much water intrusion.

'Fine. You're easily replaceable anyway,' she snapped, her tone harsher than she'd meant. But once she'd gone off down that track, there was no reeling in the nastiness. 'I'll find someone else to do the deliveries. Someone with actual liability insurance. And a backbone.'

Bobby flinched, confused by how this conversation was turning out. Of course, none of this was Bonnie's fault. He was the one skewering their friendship.

'I'll drop the day's leftovers at your house, though,' he said. 'It's not like it's out of my way.'

Bonnie gritted her teeth.

'Don't bother,' she said. 'I'm trying to cut down on my sugar intake.'

Bobby didn't respond, but she could see the hurt in his eyes. He'd been bringing them leftover pastries for as long as Bonnie could remember. They'd started as his dad's recipes, and bit by bit, Bobby's own recipes and additions had crept in. It was a tradition Bonnie had secretly loved, even though she'd always pretended the whole ritual was beneath her.

Treat 'em mean, keep 'em keen.

It was the opposite of what Mom had always preached. Mom, whose personal mantra was more like *kill 'em with kindness*. But somewhere along the way, watching Mom work those long shifts and give and give and *give*, right up until the end, when she had nothing left to give but her spirit, Bonnie had found that kindness became equated with weakness. Especially when you were a woman. Bonnie didn't want to be steamrollered. And if that took *being* the steamroller, then so be it.

Still, watching Bobby climb into his old truck and pull away, Bonnie felt a pang. She'd never known life without Bobby. It was as though the world were conspiring to take the people she cared about away from her. First Mom, then Effie, and now Bobby.

But she didn't have time to wallow. She had debts to pay and a bar to keep afloat and a hole in her heart that she needed to heal before she could consider the mere possibility of letting someone into it. Besides, Bobby had decided that he wasn't the one to fill it.

As Bonnie prepared a batch of the Memory Lane cocktail that was proving so popular, a tear trickled down her cheek and landed in the pitcher. It hissed and steamed, sending a purple cloud of sparkling smoke into the air.

At least it didn't set off the sprinklers.

'Are we open for business?' asked Winston, poking his

balding head around the front door. Weird – where was his cap? 'Because I'm ready for a game of, ah, what's it called? Ooh, I'm having a senior moment. Fancy that.'

'Reckon it must be the stress of knowing he owes me a chicken and chips dinner if he loses,' teased Gerald, who was hot on Winston's heels and ready for his newly spell-infused shandy. It was the Memory Lane concentrate, but mixed with lemonade. Gerald didn't like to be left out. This was apparently a deep-seated fear that had its roots in New Zealand regularly being left off world map illustrations. 'Old what's-his-name here can't handle the pressure. Anyway, pop one on our tab, and give us a shout when you're ready.'

With a cheerful arm around Winston, Gerald ushed his friend towards the pinball room.

Bonnie frowned. This was an unusual development. Winston had long been a vocal opponent to the very concept of pinball. The only thing he loathed more was foosball (with oversized Jenga coming in a close second). Darts was a game of both skill and strategy, whereas pinball was, to quote him verbatim, the 'earliest form of button-mashing'.

'We might have added some new drinks to the menu, but we haven't started on the renovations yet. The darts board is that way.' Bonnie pointed with a sprig of sage.

'Oops, off we go, mate,' said Gerald, steering Winston back on track.

Bonnie went to work mixing their drinks, grimacing as she added a too-heavy pinch of pink sea salt, which she tried to offset with a smoked stem of rosemary. But now the entire concoction was unbalanced. She couldn't quite tell how, but she could feel it. She swore. She'd have to start over.

Thankfully, nothing caught fire this time.

After what felt like an hour, Bonnie carried the drinks, and an extra pitcher for the team members who would be arriving any moment, over to their usual table by the darts board, cursing Bobby for not being around to help.

But what she saw disquieted her. Instead of the usual jovial chatter about Winston's daffodils, which were fit to rival Freddie Noonan's, and the rude ribbing they gave each other over their wayward throws, Winston and Gerald were sitting in silence, each quietly regarding the dart they held in their hand.

'Everything all right, gents?' she asked, setting down their drinks. She'd never seen them manage more than a moment of quiet. The two were famously chatterboxes. Between their propensity for gossip and their shared habit of narrating their darts games, there was barely a moment of peace over by the darts board. 'Do you need me to take the first throw?'

Winston blinked, confused. Then realization showed behind his eyes. 'Oh, right! Just warming up the old throwing arm.'

He stretched his arm back and forth like an Olympian preparing to take on a world record. With a wink, he turned that move into one culminating in a grab at his drink. He knocked back the bespelled cocktail, then wiped his mouth with the back of his wrinkly hand.

Then, without reciting his usual prayer to the darts gods, he turned to the board, aimed carefully, and missed.

Chapter 15

ENCHANTMENT!
AT THE LIBRARY

Effie

The morning of her next shift, Effie opened the library door with trepidation. She'd begun bracing herself every time she unlocked the library doors, preparing for disaster and disarray. But apparently the ghost had taken the night off. The books remained neatly shelved and the toys in the children's section, well, remained somewhat neatly put away. And hopefully still sanitized, although if Theo came in, maybe she'd put him to work on that delightful job.

Overall, things were quiet. Students wearing massive headphones crammed for upcoming exams, enthusiastically highlighting their reading materials until whole textbooks turned yellow. Bowow and Bruce were glaring at each other over their paperbacks. Derek and George, the chess players, silently moved pieces in the game they'd restarted after the ghost had upended their last one. An exhausted mom whispered *Goodnight Moon* on repeat to a half-asleep infant. Agnes Audri, a retired elementary-school teacher, was making paper flowers at one of the group tables. Willamina from the bank, one of the library's major donors, was poring sadly over a set of tarot cards. Shaking her head, she'd gather them up, then pull a new set of cards, hoping for better news.

Effie knew how that went. She made a mental note to offer some upbeat book recommendations to Willamina before she left. After all, knowledge was empowerment.

Although with today's absence of ghostly destruction, and the dearth of callers demanding to know about the sleep habits of blue whales or the number for the local pizza shop, she'd been productive. She'd finished adding clear protective contact paper to what felt like a hundred picture books for the kids' section, and had moved on to one of her favourite jobs: repairing some of the well-loved books in that collection. The town patrons had differing ideas about the care and upkeep of the library's books, and it wasn't uncommon to find candy bar wrappers used as bookmarks, or rude marginalia that had to be dealt with, or even entire board books gummed together with sticky food that Effie couldn't begin to identify. Once, after finding mushrooms growing out of a volume on mycology, she'd set up a display on how not to treat a library book. The mushrooms, after an expert at the college had confirmed that they weren't poisonous, had made quite a nice stroganoff.

Humming along to some golden oldies on the record player, Effie taped up a few spines and set aside some older editions for more involved repairs at the desk downstairs. There she could repair freely and without the risk of prying eyes noticing the thin streams of sparkling green that accompanied her.

As Effie picked up a tatty Poe collection that should prob-ably go on the ever-growing weeding pile – a stack of books that had outlived their usefulness at the library – a slip of paper fell out.

She unfolded it, curious. She'd found all sorts of things in books, and even had a corkboard on the wall displaying the best of them: a butter knife, a friendship bracelet, a postcard from Latvia, a flattened four-leaf clover, some foreign paper currency and several photos of Very Good Dogs.

Hmm. A poem. She perused it, trying to read the chicken-scratch handwriting.

'What do you have there?'

Effie almost dropped the note in surprise.

It was Theo, again. He had a preternatural ability to appear over her shoulder, like an extremely good-looking Nosferatu. Today, he was dressed as usual in a simple, well-fitting outfit. Effie could smell the fragrance of the morning on him: crushed leaves, the richness of petrichor, and the spicy hint of the vibrant asters that burst from the planters lining the library.

He set a coffee from The Winged Monkey on the counter. It was marked *Ebby*.

Doing her best to pretend that she wasn't completely unmoored by his proximity – or the fact that they might just have an in-joke – Effie handed him the note.

'You *have* to stop sneaking up on me. If I didn't like coffee so much, I'd throw this cup at you,' said Effie. 'So, Mr Poetry Scholar, tell me your thoughts on this poem.'

Theo grinned. 'I actually minored in poetry during college.'

'You did not.' She knew he was interested in poetry, of course, but not that he took it so seriously. To be honest, she'd assumed that the poetry-toting thing was mostly for aesthetics.

'I'm even most of the way through a master's. Just an online thing I'm doing around work, though. *Was* doing around work.' He turned the poem around and around in his hand, as though it held all the answers to the world. 'I'm on a sabbatical. While I figure this whole situation out.'

Effie nodded slowly. She'd been right to assume that he was only here temporarily. Theo had probably only thrown himself into his Friends of the Library membership to keep himself occupied until it was time to head back home.

'It's a shame you didn't arrive a few months earlier,' she mused absently.

She could've kicked herself for saying it aloud. So much for her famous self-control.

Theo raised an eyebrow. 'Oh? You wish I'd arrived a few months earlier?'

Coughing from surprise, Effie had to take a sip of her

coffee. How were attractive people so *confident*? Theo had the same type of glamour and charm that Bonnie had been doused with. It was something that helped you walk through the world with ease, knowing that things would always go your way, that people would be nice to you. It was like every time they rolled a die, a six was guaranteed. Meanwhile, when you were an Effie, the die rolled off the table and got lost under a cupboard.

'I mean that the poetry lecturer at the college had to fly back to Germany for a family emergency,' she explained. 'Otherwise you could've sat in on the classes. I honestly don't know who else they're going to find to fill the spot. This town is hardly famed for its rich poetic heritage. We tried to fund a poet laureate position a few years back, but no one applied.'

Theo nodded thoughtfully. 'I see. Well, if I can't darken the doors of the college, I guess I'll just have to make this place my local for now. My horoscope said something about books being my future.'

Glancing up over her latest cowboy romance, Bowow grinned. Presumably she and Theo shared a star sign.

'So,' Theo said as he passed back the poem, 'since I'm here, do you need any help from your newest Friends of the Library member?'

Effie bit her lip. There were always tasks that needed doing, even if she preferred doing them alone and with the help of magic. But catching Theo's sparkling green-eyed gaze, she figured that perhaps it wouldn't hurt to do things the traditional way. Just this once.

'I could definitely use some help with alphabetization,' suggested Effie, supposing that he couldn't do too much harm there. 'No matter how many "Please do not reshelve the books" signs I put up, people just jam the books in every which way.'

Especially in the past few days. The shelves were an absolute shambles – it was as though the library patrons had forgotten their ABCs.

'Keeps life interesting,' said Theo, to Effie's absolute chagrin. *Interesting* was right up there with *disorderly*, which was something she strived to avoid.

'How about I sort them by colour instead?' he added.

Effie almost knocked her coffee over. How could he suggest such a thing? Had he been speaking to Bonnie?

'There are shelving standards we must adhere to,' she snapped.

Theo raised his hands in surrender. 'I should've read up on the cardinal sins of shelving.'

Effie folded her arms, narrowing her eyes behind her glasses. She couldn't figure out whether he was joking, or *teasing*. And if the latter, what was the intent behind it?

Before Effie could press Theo about it, a man in full pirate regalia stomped through the doors, waving a feather sword in one hand. Effie blinked. That *had* to be the ghost.

'Quite the outfit,' said Theo, regarding the pirate as he went off to sit in the corner, muttering at the wall.

'You can see him?' she mused. Not the ghost, then. Unless Theo had the rare ability to spot the dearly departed. But he hadn't commented on the oddly cold spot in The Winged Monkey, or the strange shadow that sometimes followed Effie when she passed between the park and the cemetery on her way to visit Mom.

Theo cocked his head. 'Why wouldn't I be able to?'

'I just thought . . .' Realizing how ridiculous she was about to sound, Effie pretended to be busy with a stack of books. 'That he might be a ghost.'

'A *ghost*?' Theo let out a guffaw so loud that it drew the attention of every patron. 'A pirate ghost? In a library? Wouldn't it be more sensible to think that he was just a snappy dresser? Or that he's a method actor researching books about shipwrecks?'

'I have my reasons,' said Effie, feeling extremely self-conscious at the fact that everyone was looking at her. Being perceived was something she did her best to avoid in her daily life. And yet, every time Theo showed up, she was suddenly the centre of attention.

She did indeed have her reasons for suspecting a ghost. Like the fact that this morning, she'd seen a pair of creepy golden eyes flash at her from impossibly high up on one of the reading-room windowsills.

Theo raised an eyebrow. 'You don't strike me as the super-stitious type. You seem so rational.'

'I *am* rational,' retorted Effie. After all, she hadn't said for sure that the library was being haunted. She had a hypothesis, but she was reserving judgement until she had evidence.

She felt her brow furrowing. Theo had already accused Bonnie of being a pyromaniac, and now he assumed that Effie was inclined towards woo-woo. But she couldn't defend herself without *revealing* herself. And she was certainly not about to do that in the presence of someone who might only be around for a few weeks.

'What's so funny?' she snapped, seeing Theo trying to stifle a grin.

'Nothing,' he said, shaking his head. 'How about I get to that reshelving. These books aren't going to colour-coordinate themselves.'

Actually, thought Effie, thinking about the disarray she'd come across the past several mornings, they just might.

Chapter 16

EYE OF NEWT,
SCORN OF FRIENDS

Bonnie

Bonnie glanced at her painstakingly waved hair and sighed as it immediately frizzed. Effie had *definitely* applied a hex here somewhere. Out of scientific curiosity (and feigned generosity) Bonnie had lent the curler to Hannah, who'd shown up with perfectly styled hair after using it, so it wasn't the curler itself that was hexed. Perhaps it was the location. She carried the curler into the bathroom, plugging it in and grimacing at the sparks that resulted.

Had that been a magic thing or an electrical wiring thing?

Not wanting to get the blame for anything electricity related, since Effie's grumbling about the bill was annoying enough, Bonnie unplugged the curler and hurried out to the hallway. Where else?

Effie's room.

Effie was out at some Friends of the Library meeting, so there was no way she'd catch Bonnie. Besides, it had been a while since Bonnie had snooped through her sister's things, and it was time for a refresher.

The trick was not to touch anything. Because Effie could always tell. Especially if you touched her books. She always knew if a book was in the wrong place.

Bonnie gently cracked the door open. Even though she knew full well that her sister wasn't home, she glanced around to make sure Effie wasn't about to pounce up from her reading chair or out from under the bed. Of course, Bonnie wasn't trespassing, not really. She was just availing herself of better humidity conditions. Like how she sometimes came in here waving her phone about her head under the guise of getting a better phone signal.

Effie's room was the spiritual opposite of Bonnie's. The bed was tidily made, her clothes were put away, and there were far too few cushions. Although the pothos that grew above the reading chair was in magnificent shape, Bonnie thought, slightly jealously. But it was easier for Effie to tend to something than it was for Bonnie – her job let her keep regular hours, and she barely went out otherwise. Honestly, there was no excuse for her *not* to have thriving houseplants.

Bonnie plugged the curler in, propping it up on a dinner plate to avoid scorching a hole in the ornate desk. No sparks, no crackling, which seemed like a good sign. She frowned in indignation at the round mirror propped up against the window alcove. What on earth were you meant to do with a mirror so lacking in dimensionality? Although that explained *so much*, truly. Effie had never seen her full reflection. Little wonder she got about in the outfits she did.

While the curler heated up, Bonnie poked about, looking for any evidence of Effie's dalliance with Theo – because there was *definitely* something going on between the two of them. Bonnie couldn't figure it out. Effie was like a holly bush – endlessly prickly in her defensiveness. It was nearly impossible to get close to her. Their mom had been the only one she'd truly opened up to, and without Lyra's mediating force, Effie was just getting sharper and more irritable.

Bonnie tapped her bottom lip, trying to make sense of it. Effie's room gave away no secrets – there were a few books of poetry on the desk, but that was no surprise. Effie loved pretentious things. And everything else in the room seemed so boringly Effie. The tidy bookshelves. The vintage brass quail sculptures, a gift from Tessa. The three-wick Paris-scented candle that had never been lit, a gift from Bonnie. The single tub of lip balm that Mom had given her after her lower lip split during a particularly bitter winter.

It was time to go straight to the source.

Glancing around again, just in case, Bonnie pulled out the diary her sister had kept under her mattress since the two of them had been small. Not the very same one, of course. The volumes had come and gone over the years, although Bonnie wasn't sure what her sister did with the completed ones. This volume, decorated with golden curlicues and imprinted with floral designs, seemed so small. It was barely bigger than Bonnie's hand.

Biting her lip, she glanced at it, willing a breeze to come through the room so that the book might open of its own accord. No luck.

Whoops, oh no. She'd dropped it.

Gravity, you cheeky thing.

The little volume landed spine-up, open just a few pages from the front.

Well, she had to pick it up now.

As she did, the last entry in the book caught her eye. It was from the day before Mom's death. Effie, a dedicated, lifelong diarist, hadn't written anything since then.

Bonnie swallowed. Maybe her sister wasn't infallible after all. Maybe there *was* some emotion in there under all the snide looks and curt comments.

Without reading that last entry, she returned the diary to its rightful spot, smoothing the comforter so that it was wrinkle-free. Then she set to work touching up her hair, drifting into that familiar meditative state as she twirled curl after curl around the hot wand. She thought about her sister and all the time she'd been spending with Theo. As frustrating as Effie was, she was still Bonnie's sister, and Bonnie didn't want to see her hurt. Embarrassed, sure. Put in her place a little, absolutely. But not hurt.

Setting down the curler, Bonnie jutted her face in front of Effie's tiny mirror, trying to get a proper glimpse of her hair. It *seemed* to be sleek and glossy, with the waves curling loosely as she'd intended.

Take that, evil frizz charm.

She unplugged the curler, letting it cool down. All right. It was time to head back to the Flamingo Room and raid her closet for her pinkest, most fabulous outfit.

'Welcome to Pink Wednesday!' called Bonnie as the front door swung open for the umpteenth time that afternoon. Her throat was hoarse. In between calling out names for the hexed drinks she'd been pouring, she'd been having an extremely high-energy discussion with Bowow Walker, who was clad in mismatching pinks that clashed so hard they *almost* worked. They were discussing Madame Destinée's latest horoscopes, which had specifically warned Leos about blood being thicker than rivalry.

'Mine said that the frenemy of one's frenemy was one to watch,' said Bruce Dickens, who was seated at the bar in a too-tight fuchsia T-shirt. 'I'm watching you, Bowow.'

'Oh, shut it, Bruce.' Bowow whacked him with one of Uncle Oswald's agate coasters. She put on her reading glasses to examine it. 'These are charming, actually. Does your uncle have anything for dogs? I have a Pomeranian with a dicky hip. And a German shepherd with terrible anxiety.'

'He does indeed,' said Uncle Oswald, who'd just now oozed in the door. Wearing green, of course. 'For your Pomeranian, I recommend a combination of onyx and rhodonite, with a touch of aventurine for the connective tissue. Just bring that coaster over and I'll honour the discount.'

'Discount? Don't threaten me with a good time, hon.'

Uncle Oswald smiled smarmily. 'Any time spent at Behind

the Curtain is a good time. I just wanted to stop by a moment in support of my wonderful niece, but I'll be heading back across the square shortly, should you care to join me.'

'Done, and done,' said Bowow. She finished her drink and gave the counter a cheerful slap. 'Let me powder my nose, and then I'm all yours.'

With Bowow gone and Bruce having turned to chat with another barfly about the karaoke numbers they had planned for later, Oswald pulled up a seat in front of Bonnie, popping his hat down on the table and grinning his usual oily grin. The tips of his fingers had a purple tinge to them, as though he'd been painting.

Bonnie fought the urge to recoil. There was just something about Oswald that left a bad taste in her mouth. Even though he hadn't ever done anything especially *wrong*. In fact, he'd been true to his word. For every customer Bonnie sent his way, he set aside a portion of his profits, and he was prompt about paying as well. Bonnie was actually beginning to make a dent in her bills.

'I see the new recipes are quite the hit,' he noted, counting the purple drinks around the room while Bonnie poured his usual mint julep. 'And overall, people seem more even-keeled. Wouldn't you think?'

Bonnie slid his drink across the bar. 'Sure. And the drinks are popular, which is the big thing.'

'I notice your sister isn't here,' said Oswald. He sipped his drink, then dabbed his moustache with his handkerchief.

Bonnie snorted. 'It takes a lot of arm-twisting to get her in here. And it's Pink Wednesday, so there's absolutely no way she's making an appearance tonight. Tessa does have a good record of dragging her along for Trivia Night, though.'

'Tessa. Ah, the girl with the cat statue. Not a friend of the store, I must say.'

'Oh?' Bonnie was curious. She couldn't imagine Tessa doing

anything that might put her on Uncle Oswald's bad side. She was a nerdy type, like Effie, but without the spikiness.

'Are we doing this, Oswald?' Bowow had barrelled back up, and was swinging her purse over her shoulder. 'Let's give my dogs some of the crystal magic.'

'Shouldn't you call Dr what's-his-name?' asked Bruce, turning back from his karaoke conversation. 'The vet.'

'Dr Freng,' offered Bonnie. It was hard to forget the name when it was emblazoned on the vet clinic wall in a typeface made to look like cats and dogs.

Bruce jabbed the air with a finger. 'That's the one.'

'Of course, of course,' said Bowow. 'But I want to try this crystal stuff. Don't you?'

Bruce didn't need much convincing. For as much as he pretended not to like Bowow, he was never far from her. 'I could stretch my legs.'

'Well, then, off we go,' said Uncle Oswald, donning his hat and reaching for his cane. 'I hope it's a monumental night for you. Drink up. Drink up!' he called across the room.

A subdued cheer went up as people toasted with their purple drinks.

'Just as long as Bruce makes it back for karaoke,' called Bonnie, as the trio loped off out the door.

Bonnie barely had a moment to feel relief at Uncle Oswald's departure, for just then Hannah, Alana and Kirsty sauntered in, all dressed in multicoloured outfits that did not include a hint of pink. Bonnie gestured at her own pink outfit, confused. Had their tradition withered like the succulent she'd purchased a few months back from The Winged Monkey, determined to keep something other than herself alive? She could barely look Tilda Harvey, the plant lady who stocked the plant wall, in the eye. Especially now that she knew how robust Effie's pothos was.

'On Wednesdays we wear pink?' she reminded her friends, her tone a touch quizzical. This had been a tradition of theirs for years, ever since they'd watched *Mean Girls* during a sleepover at Hannah's and had decided that the group dynamics of Regina and her entourage were thoroughly aspirational.

Alana's eyes widened. 'But Kirsty said—'

Kirsty jabbed her with an elbow, giving her a warning look.

Hannah glanced down at her fiery red ensemble and blinked thoughtfully. 'Well, red is *close*. In the right light it's practically pink.'

Bonnie folded her arms as she regarded the other outfits. 'But denim and daffodil yellow are not, by any stretch of the imagination.'

'Sorry,' whispered Alana.

Smirking, Kirsty toyed with the buttercup sleeve of her shirt. 'Look, traditions don't have to last for ever. Just because we've done something a certain way for however long doesn't mean we're obligated to keep doing it. Like when my dad decided he was just going to do brisket for Thanksgiving instead of turkey. Grandma came around in the end.'

Ah, thought Bonnie. Kirsty had done the cicada thing where she'd emerged from underground after seventeen years and then eaten every other cicada in sight. Bonnie wasn't sure that cicadas did this, but it seemed right. And Effie wasn't around to ask.

Kirsty regarded one of Uncle Oswald's coasters, then turned her attention back to Bonnie. 'Anyway, no one's going to stop you from wearing pink. Even if that particular tone washes you out just a little. Maybe you can keep repping the pink for us.'

'Sure,' said Bonnie uncertainly. She suddenly felt very off-kilter in her pink baby-doll dress, the one with the frilled skirt that ordinarily made her feel like a sexy birthday cake.

'Besides, I'm seeing Bobby later,' added Kirsty triumphantly. 'And pink's not really the vibe I'm going for.'

Bonnie swallowed. Kirsty's words had hit her right in the stomach, with an impact that surprised her. Hannah and Alana had made some evasive remarks about Kirsty and Bobby, and Bonnie had obviously noticed Kirsty's car in her neighbour's driveway, even though she'd pretended she hadn't.

But thinking about her friend and her neighbour together, actually together, made her realize just how much she missed having Bobby around, and how much a part of her life he truly was.

'Babe, could we get a pitcher of the Memory Lane?' asked Hannah, pointing at the purplish cocktail that Bonnie had snapped a Polaroid of and stuck to the menu wall as the Drink of the Evening. 'It looks so good.'

'It really is, though,' agreed Kirsty. She leaned in, confessing: 'I snuck some the other day when you weren't looking. The day you asked me to take Bobby home.' She said this last part with a smirk that seemed to carry a challenge with it.

So that *had* been Kirsty's lipstick on the brass mug. But she'd seemed fine that day, unlike Bobby. Maybe Bonnie's spell hadn't backfired after all. Maybe Bobby had just been coming down with something.

'Just sparkling water for me,' said Alana.

Bonnie nodded, although her hands shook with confusion as she poured the drinks. Everything was changing around her. Her friendship group was all askew, and now she couldn't even rely on Bobby. Not that she particularly wanted to ask anything of him, knowing that for some reason he'd started something with Kirsty. *Kirsty!*

But who else was she meant to talk to? In the past, there'd been Mom. Although honestly, she still often spoke to Mom.

Sometimes when the wind was right, she could convince herself that Mom was talking back.

Back before the Chalmers sisters had drifted off into their separate realms, there'd been Effie as well. But Effie had grown so cold over the years, and especially since Mom's death. Everything Bonnie did seemed to irritate Effie, and digging into why that might be terrified Bonnie.

The Effie of today certainly wasn't going to offer the kind of advice that Bonnie wanted to hear. She could just imagine her sister's dismissal of her friends: she would point out how they were focused on status and appearance over everything. How they were only interested in Bonnie because she helped elevate them. And, said a little voice, how Bonnie had lorded that fact over them ever since she'd suddenly risen to the top of the popularity ladder at the age of fourteen.

Bonnie sighed. Maybe Effie was right. She'd never needed to consider her sister's opinion on the matter of her friends before, which she'd always put down to jealousy. But maybe Effie had just been looking out for her.

Sliding the pitcher over to her friends, who headed out to the patio area to no doubt gossip about her, Bonnie hurried over with a top-off for Willamina from the bank. Once a week, Willamina would come in, drawing out tarot cards from a beautifully gilded deck she'd picked up while travelling in France, and grumbling at the results.

But this evening Willamina was quietly sipping her drink while flipping through a library book. A romcom with a brightly illustrated cover. She fiddled with a yellow crystal that hung from her neck on a thin silvery chain. Bonnie immediately recognized Uncle Oswald's handiwork.

'No cards tonight?' asked Bonnie, setting down a Memory Lane cocktail on one of Oswald's branded agate coasters.

'Cards?' Willamina blinked. 'Oh, right. No, I was thinking it was time for something different. A good, uplifting book. I think I'd prefer to have a bit of a laugh, you know?'

'Oh, I get it,' said Bonnie, clearing Willamina's empty glass. 'Well, I'm glad to hear you're making positive changes for yourself. I love your necklace, too.'

'Thanks!' Willamina's eyes sparkled happily. 'I got it from Behind the Curtain. And a huge amethyst for my shrine by the front door. Oswald said it offers cleaning energy, and I think he's right. It's the deepest purple you've ever seen. I can't stop looking at it.'

'I love that for you,' said Bonnie, trying not to think about the purple staining she'd seen on Oswald's fingertips. He wouldn't *dye* his crystals, would he? Surely not, given he was charging such a premium for them.

'And I got a discount thanks to your coasters here.' Willamina tapped the agate coaster. 'I might have to bring this one over later. I have my eye on a gorgeous singing bowl.'

Bonnie expressed her delight at length. Every sale at Uncle Oswald's meant money in her pocket, after all. She headed back to the bar where a wide-eyed girl with beachy waves in her hair was waiting. The things you could do with your hair when you didn't have Effie cursing it.

'Hey there. Are you Bonnie?' The girl toyed with a crystal charm around her neck. 'I'm Iris. I'm wondering if I can book your room upstairs for a birthday party next week?'

Brightening, Bonnie slid over the branded sheet she'd prepared with the rates and details for private events. She lived for private parties. They let her put on her party-planner hat, which was her favourite of all the hats. And they were lucrative. Between the room rental fee and her drinks minimum, *plus* the kickbacks from Uncle Oswald, this might just be her most profitable month yet. So what if her friends had reneged on Pink Wednesday and Bobby had defected to Kirsty's side? Bonnie was kicking butt at this entrepreneurial thing.

Now all she had to do was keep charming her way to a front-page feature on the *Yellowbrick Grove Gazette*. Without setting off the sprinklers again.

Chapter 17

BIBBIDI-BOBBIDI . . .
ME AND YOU?

Effie

Effie stretched out her back, wishing her magic worked on stiff muscles. The Friends of the Library group were part-way through an hour-long meeting about the many pressing issues facing the library. For example, the fact that the cowboy romance section was apparently lacking, a Bowow-specific complaint. And how Emerald's library was doing a much better job with its social media, a Bruce complaint, levelled at Effie, whose disinclination to dance on the internet was apparently a major limiting factor. And who was in charge of the signage for the upcoming weeding day, which would involve removing old and unloved titles from the collection to free up space for the new ones. And which book they should choose to display as part of the 'StoryWalk' initiative they'd just received funding for.

'What's a StoryWalk?' asked Theo, intrigued. 'Please tell me it involves books with legs.'

'Basically, you display an illustrated book page by page along a designated walking track,' explained Effie, pulling up an example on her phone. 'That way walkers can read while strolling.'

Theo considered. 'Do we have a location yet? Because that would influence the book, right?'

'Not yet,' said Effie. 'But probably one of the parks.'

'Maybe we could do a turtle book,' suggested Bowow,

toying absently with the collar of her polka-dot blouse. 'In honour of . . . what's-his-name.'

'Sheldon,' offered Bruce, making a rock 'n' roll gesture.

'Shelby,' corrected Theo. 'We go way back,' he added, when Effie shot him a surprise look.

And not just because Theo knew who Shelby was. Her concern was more to do with Bowow getting the turtle's name wrong. Bowow might be a tad scattered by nature, but she never forgot an animal's name. She wasn't the only one behaving strangely tonight. Tammi, famous for her library cookie-eating habits and therefore in charge of the Friends cookie catering, had shown up empty-handed, apparently having forgotten that she was responsible for the meeting snacks. Effie had called Bobby to place an emergency order.

'Any other business?' asked Effie, seeing that they'd worked through every item on the agenda. Well, except for the ghost stuff, but she hadn't found a good time to bring that up. And probably wouldn't. In any case, the library's resident spirit had been reasonably well behaved today, and nothing had shattered or fallen. And the books remained on their shelves, which was a relief given that Theo had spent a solid day working through them and checking for accurate alphabetization. Even if he had teased Effie by putting together an entirely yellow book display.

'We'll have to start thinking about the kids' summer program soon,' pointed out Bowow. 'My cousin's happy to handle the bouncy castles again.'

Effie nodded, making a note to add that to the next meeting's agenda. Summer would be here before they knew it, and putting together a calendar with something that could appeal to kids of all ages was a full-time job. *Her* full-time job, given that she was the only official staffer here, and the rest were volunteers.

'Here come the baked goods!' came Bobby's voice from the hallway.

He and Kirsty appeared, Bobby in his usual flannel and jeans and Kirsty in her designer athleisure. Each carried a platter of buttery pastries from The Golden Hour. These they grandly set down on the table, letting the Friends pounce on the chocolate twists and sugar-dusted beignets.

'This place is cute,' murmured Kirsty, glancing around the main downstairs reading area, with its lofty ceiling and stained glass. 'Great lighting. Imagine the videos you could film here. My followers would just die.'

She pulled out her phone and started waving it around the room, zooming in on the children's art up on the walls, the cosy reading nooks and the rock display that Effie had put back together after the recent ghostly incursion.

'You haven't been in here before?' Effie couldn't keep the astonishment from her voice. How did one avoid the siren call of the library? 'Ever?'

Kirsty shook her head. 'It's so imposing with all those steps.'

'We have an accessible side entrance,' said Effie, pointing. 'We put it in a few years back. So you're not a member?'

She was still trying to wrap her head around this. Even Bonnie had a library card! Effie had signed her up as a birthday gift years earlier. As far as she knew, Bonnie had only used it to borrow back issues of *Vogue*, but it still counted.

Kirsty shrugged. 'I mostly read e-books.'

The astonishment was not abating. 'But you can access e-books free through the library. Not to mention movies and TV. We have admissions deals with the nearby national parks, museums and zoos, too. Oh, and you can even borrow telescopes.'

In her excitement, Effie could feel her magic starting to crackle around her wrists. She willed it away. *Not now, magic.*

Her phone trained on one of the vintage light fixtures, Kirsty brightened. 'I do love stargazing. How about you get me signed up? How much does it cost?'

The bewilderment kept coming. There were people in the community that didn't know the library was free? Maybe Bruce was right. She *really* needed to work on getting the word out. How many people weren't members not because they didn't like to read, but because they were worried about membership fees or didn't know what a membership offered?

'It's free. All of it. Well, unless you want to print a PhD thesis in full colour. But other than that, free.'

Effie led Kirsty over to the circulation desk, quickly typing her details into the system, then presenting her with a pristine set of library cards. 'You're all set. You can even borrow something tonight if you'd like.'

Kirsty hesitated, and Effie steeled herself. Was she going to ask to film a multi-part influencer dance routine in the reading room?

'Can I borrow the telescope?' she asked, finally.

Well, that was a relief. 'Sure.'

As Effie grabbed a telescope kit to check out, Bobby held up a tatty card on a keychain, clinking it against Kirsty's new one. 'Twins.'

Against all that Effie knew about her nature, Kirsty smiled. 'Wow, that card looks like it's seen some stuff.'

'I'm OG. I've had this since I turned ten.'

Effie passed Kirsty the telescope, walking her through how to use it and where the best night-sky sites were. 'Actually,' she added. Her voice faltered. 'Could I get your help with something? You've probably noticed that the library's social media accounts are a touch under-served.'

Kirsty searched on her phone, pulling up the library's accounts. 'Oh, wow. Understatement of the century.'

Here it came. Effie was about to do something she'd never thought she'd lower herself to.

'Do you think you could give me some tips?' she asked tentatively. 'We can pay you, of course. Through the Friends.'

'Absolutely! I'd love to. Just let me know when.' A blast

of music spilled from Kirsty's phone as she scrolled back through the library's account, hitting on the 'bookworm POV' video that Bonnie had put together for Effie the previous year. It had received the most views of anything on the account. 'That video wasn't bad,' she added.

'Thanks,' said Effie. Bonnie wasn't here to take credit, so why not?

'You know, I've even got your first piece of content – the sign-up we just did.'

Effie swallowed. 'You were filming that?'

'Of course. And you were *amazing*. Who knew that libraries were free? And that you could borrow telescopes? I'll cut it together and send it to you later tonight.'

Effie wasn't quite sure what to make of this interaction. Kirsty was being affable. Helpful. *Kind*, even. There must be something in the town's water, because this was thoroughly unusual. Kirsty was barely even nice to Bonnie, let alone Effie.

Maybe it was the moderating force of Bobby at play. Although the fact that the two were apparently dating was baffling to Effie. Effie might not be especially well versed in all things romantic, but she'd always thought that Bobby had a soft spot for Bonnie.

But she supposed that even someone as sweet and doting as Bobby would only wait in the wings so long before he gave up.

Bowow came up, a selection of pastries balanced artfully in her palm. 'I'm out, Effie. But you'd better hear me on those cowboys, because these babies,' she tapped her bag, 'are the last three in the library I haven't read. What are my dogs going to do if Mama can't read to them?'

'Duly noted,' said Effie. She waved as the other Friends took their leave.

Kirsty blew Effie a kiss before sidling out after them, telescope case slung over her shoulder. 'I'll text you that video when it's ready to upload.'

'I really appreciate it.' And she really did. 'Thanks for the pastries, too,' she added, as Bobby followed Kirsty.

'Any time,' said Bobby, with his usual cheerful grin. He gave her a hearty wave, then followed Kirsty down the front steps.

According to Effie's math, which was exceptional, and the hair prickling on the back of her neck, only Theo remained.

Well, and the ghost, but she didn't want to think about that right now.

Theo's green eyes regarded her thoughtfully as together they tidied up after the meeting.

'So,' he said. 'Any plans for tonight?'

Effie shook her head. 'Just the usual. A hot date with my book, a pot of tea and my own uninterrupted thoughts. I've been dreaming about it all day, honestly. There's a point where I get peopled out. I don't know how Bonnie does it.'

She paused, wondering how her sister was doing. Things had been slightly *off* recently. She'd barely seen Bonnie since their fight, and the times that she'd spied her in their kitchen, she'd seemed exhausted. Effie suspected her sister was sleeping at The Silver Slipper, even though the apartment above was barely habitable, even by Bonnie's standards.

'Have you been by the bar since the other night?' she blurted, not even sure why she was asking. Or *what* she was asking.

'I haven't,' he said, his tone sounding oddly like an invitation. 'But I could.'

Outside, a gust of wind picked up, rattling the stained-glass windows and causing the whole library to let out a creaking sigh. Upstairs, somewhere in the upper reading room, Effie heard a distinct thud, followed by the most horrific hacking sound she'd ever heard. She swallowed. The ghost was back.

'So, are we going, or not?' clarified Theo.

Effie blinked. What was he talking about? 'Going where?'

Theo cocked his head, looking at her the way her sports

teacher had during Effie's first game of dodgeball. Like she was an alien. He opened his mouth, about to say something, then shut it again. His tone, when he finally spoke, was bemused, but gentle. 'You, Effie Chalmers, are harder to read than James Joyce. I'll see you tomorrow.'

With a wave, he headed out the front door, giving each of the stone gargoyles a pat, then clattered down the front steps into the night. Effie, meanwhile, headed upstairs, wishing that perhaps she'd asked Theo to stay. For ghost-busting purposes, of course.

Chapter 18

ALWAYS PRACTISE SAFE HEX

Bonnie

Without Bobby around to help, Bonnie's opening prep had been taking longer and longer. She was spending hours concocting her batches of Memory Lane, but perfection remained elusive. And so-so magic wasn't something she particularly wanted to embrace. Not only that, but the bar was growing in popularity. The familiar faces were bringing new faces along with them, and she'd had a slew of great reviews.

Want to forget your troubles? This is the place! was her personal favourite. She'd chalked it on a sandwich-board sign and popped it out the front.

Bonnie was resting against the bar for a moment, flexing her aching feet after running about with pitchers of Memory Lane and stepping in multiple times to remind a group of energetic college kids that while she didn't mind them ordering in pizza from the shop from across the square, they weren't allowed to plug in their own toaster oven and do the honours here, when a warm, familiar voice broke into her thoughts.

'Hey there, thriving woman-owned small business proprietor,' came a voice over the hubbub of the bar-goers.

Bonnie looked up to see a pretty woman in loose, artsy attire and huge statement glasses that said *yes, dammit, I'm smart as hell, so don't try anything.*

'Tessa!' Bonnie was oddly relieved to see Effie's friend.

Mostly because Tessa was as close as Bonnie was going to get to her sister at the moment, and Bonnie really could do with Effie's advice. 'Your usual?'

Tessa beamed. She hoisted herself up on an empty bar stool, stowing her macramé purse on the hook beneath the bar. Ignoring the wishful gaze of the middle-aged guy next to her, she tapped the agate coaster in a *hit me* gesture. 'I'm impressed you remember. Nice coasters, by the way. Very upscale.'

With a warning look at the middle-aged guy, who was *definitely* going to try something, Bonnie peeled back the foil from the lid of an ornate bottle and popped the cork, letting out the unconscious whoop she always did when she opened a bottle of bubbly. Tessa had been on the bubbly train for as long as Bonnie could remember. Definitely since sometime during their teens, because she distinctively remembered Tessa calling it 'fun wine' when Bonnie's friends had snuck a bottle of it into the house.

'I wasn't expecting to see you here,' said Bonnie as she carefully filled a flute. 'I know you probably feel like you need to take sides.'

Tessa cocked her head, her hair swinging. She had miraculous curls that Bonnie had always envied. No amount of fighting with the hot tongs could emulate them. Certainly not with Effie's frizz spell at play. 'Take sides? Are you and Effie at it again?'

Her tone of faux surprise was belied by her raised eyebrow.

Bonnie popped a sliced strawberry on the side of the sparkling glass, and slid the prosecco over to Tessa. 'Again is right. But honestly it just sort of feels like she's given up. She's avoiding me like the plague.'

'Ah.' Tessa sipped. 'Well, Effie's got a lot on her plate.'

'*I've* got a lot on my plate,' countered Bonnie, trying not to think about how appealing the glass of bubbly looked, and whether it would *really* be an unforgiveable act to pour one for herself.

Yes, yes it would. Bonnie's magic was unpredictable at the best of times. Add some tipsiness to that, and she'd definitely burn the place down.

Tessa raised her drink in salute. 'I can see that. The bar's packed. Kudos to you – I know running a small business can be rough. I've been trying to sell my crafts online, but nothing is moving. Markets can do okay, but only when the weather's good and there are no competing events.'

'You should bring some of your stuff in here.' Bonnie cracked open a beer and passed it to Bruce Dickens, who hadn't yet come around to the delights of Memory Lane. 'We could do a Booze and Schmooze event, maybe? Where people browse local makers' tables while getting extremely drunk.'

'Drunk people do make poor and expensive decisions,' mused Tessa, thoughtfully. 'Like your sister and roller-skating.'

'My sister and *what*?' Bonnie, who'd been pouring a bourbon and Coke, squirted the soda gun all over her shirt. She passed the drink to the patron, blotting her now see-through top down with a napkin. Oh well. A see-through top meant better tips.

'Oh shit.' Tessa tried to hide behind one of the agate coasters. 'Bubbly went straight to my head, I guess. We've been roller-skating. Just on the walking trails, nothing fancy. We're not beating each other up at roller derby or anything. Yet.'

Bonnie couldn't get past the mental image of Effie sporting a pair of roller skates. A puff of smoke spired up from the rosemary she was cutting for the cocktail garnishes. Rats, she'd been so distracted that her magic had made a surprise appearance. She was definitely doing too much, she thought, catching a glimpse of herself in the small mirror behind the bar. Her bright blue eyes had a slight red tinge, and there were hollows under them. She'd never say it aloud, but she missed having Bobby around. Although at least Tristan of the Milk for Days fame hadn't come back, so there was that.

'Wow, the roller-skating thing has made my whole day,' said Bonnie, taking a moment to touch up her lipstick. She couldn't look *entirely* haggard. She had standards to uphold. 'We should definitely do an event together if it means getting dirt on my holier-than-thou sister. How about the Thursday after Trivia Night? Although I *do* expect to see you here for Trivia Night. And maybe Effie as well, if she's come around by then. Someone has to set the bar for the town, and just quietly, it's not going to be my friends.'

Tessa winced around her prosecco. 'Ouch, is that truth serum you're whipping up there?'

Bonnie could only dream. Surely truth serum wasn't anywhere near as difficult to mix as Oswald's potions. Although the consequences were probably quite alarming, she thought, as her mind flashed back through all the moments in her life where she'd gently massaged reality to fit her version of it a tad better. Or all the times she'd told Kirsty that her hair looked fabulous in a side part or that pale yellow absolutely didn't make her look like someone expecting a liver transplant.

'Things are a bit weird right now,' she admitted. 'It's like allegiances are shifting.'

Tessa blinked rapidly, and Bonnie wondered if she had something in her eye. There was nothing worse than when a falsie slipped, or when your apparently waterproof eyeliner made its way into your waterline, burning your eyeball with the viciousness of a thousand fire ants.

'Tissue?' Bonnie offered Tessa the box, just in case.

'Thanks. Just a little something, from the smoke perhaps. You're really into these smoky drinks at the moment, aren't you?'

Bonnie chuckled. 'It's just a family recipe. But it goes way beyond my usual shake and stir approach. Back in a sec.'

Bonnie hefted a jug filled with purplish liquid to take to Winston and his dart-playing buddies, who tonight were *not* in fact playing darts, but were gathered around Gerald's phone, watching videos of ducklings wearing flower hats.

'No darts, boys?' she asked them as she set down the pitcher.

'No what-what?' asked Winston, frowning.

Bonnie repeated herself, since Winston's hearing was iffy at best. Apparently he'd been quite the concert-goer in his youth, and earplugs had been a sign of weakness.

'Oh right. Nah, not tonight. I've got no brains for numbers right now,' said Winston, topping off his drink from the pitcher. But he sloshed the drink, spilling it down Gerald's shirt and onto his bare feet. Despite the chilly weather outside, Gerald was wearing jandals. Probably so that he had a reason to say *jandals* over and over.

'Dammit, not my flip-flops,' he muttered.

Bonnie jolted. Flip-flops? Gerald had said *flip-flops*? What was next? Parking lot? Sidewalk? Y'all? The man was finally embracing the language of his adopted country.

'That should do it,' she said, passing Gerald a handful of napkins so he could dry himself off. 'Let me know if you boys need anything else.'

'Rowdy lot,' said Tessa thoughtfully, as Bonnie returned. She'd finished her prosecco and was looking around the cosy corners of the bar as though expecting a particular face to materialize in front of her.

She raised her eyebrows as a group of women at the back of the bar let out an animalistic roar.

'It's my birthday, bitches!' shouted a short blonde wearing a sash that said precisely that.

'*They're* the ones you have to worry about. Not Winston and his boys,' said Bonnie, with a nod towards the women, who looked awfully like they might climb up on the table.

Please don't, she begged internally. *You're not as good in heels as you think*.

'So, are you meeting someone?' Bonnie asked, catching

Tessa's roving gaze and realizing that there was probably a reason for Tessa's being here beyond simply wanting to drink prosecco with her best friend's sister.

Tessa cocked her head. 'Maybe. I'm not sure. I just thought they might be here. And Madame Destinée said that good things aren't about setting the bar, they're about sitting at it. Although now I say that aloud, I think that the mysterious Madame has been taking her inspiration from cryptic crosswords.'

'No wonder I can never make sense of mine.' Bonnie waggled the bottle of prosecco. 'Top-up while you wait? Just so long as you promise not to drink and skate.'

Tessa chuckled. 'Sure. Wouldn't want to get pulled over for embarrassing myself. Although that birthday girl and her friends might have the embarrassment market captured. Is one of them chasing after Winston?'

Bonnie spotted the opportunity for a handy gossip segue. 'Speaking of chasing, I hear Effie's been running after Theo.'

She eyed Tessa, curious to see whether she'd offer up any intel regarding Theo and Effie, who seemed to have a, well, not a *Thing* going, but at the very least a thing (with a small 't').

'I think it might be the other way around, actually,' volunteered Tessa, after a beat. 'Although he seems nice enough. 'He's a voracious reader of poetry. He's gunning for Bowow's borrowing record, I think.'

Tessa considered her prosecco, then spun her glass slowly on the agate coaster, leaving a condensation ring over Uncle Oswald's logo. 'Since we're on the topic of the library, did Alana say anything about the craft night the other night?'

'Alana?' If Bonnie's ears were capable of such a thing, they would definitely have pricked up. Were Tessa and Alana suddenly friends? Craft buddies? Something else? The years-long tension between them had not gone unnoticed by Bonnie. 'I didn't know she was a crafter. Were you weaving yoga mats or something?'

'Just crochet,' said Tessa. 'Little turtles, mostly for the teens,

but the group is open to everyone. I'm thinking of opening
a studio,' she blurted suddenly.

Bonnie topped up Tessa's glass. 'That one's on me. Very
cool. What kind of studio are we talking here? Do you have
a space?'

Tessa's eyes widened with excitement, and she pushed her
glasses up her pert nose. 'Mostly for kids, but with some
sessions for adults. We'd make upcycled crafts from string,
cardboard, stuff that local businesses are always getting rid
of. I've been thinking about it for a while.'

Bonnie was impressed. Tessa wasn't actually so bad, after
all. She was *interesting*. And definitely not as judgemental
as Effie.

'That's actually a really cool idea,' said Bonnie. 'I could see
people getting behind that. And the recycling angle is cool.
You could probably get some grant money for it. Talk to
Willamina at the bank. She's been in a good mood recently.
She's switched from tarot to romcoms.'

'I can see how that would be life-changing.'

Bonnie pointed the prosecco bottle at the plant wall opposite them. 'I got some funding for that, actually.'

'Wow, really?' Tessa snapped a picture with her phone for
future reference. 'Yes, I can send it to you,' she assured the
birthday girl and her friends, who were delighted at being
caught on film comparing how well their cleavage could hold
a glass of wine.

'So, is that why you want to talk to Alana?' said Bonnie,
who was inspired to try the cleavage trick herself. She'd definitely win, after all. 'About recycling and stuff? I can see how
that would be her thing.'

Tessa nodded, her cheeks slightly red. She was one of those
people who flushed when drinking. 'Something like that.'

The bar phone rang. Bonnie picked it up, wedging it
between her ear and her shoulder as she mixed up another
pitcher of Memory Lane for Terrance the barista, who was

working on his card memorization trick out on the patio. From the mild swearing that kept spilling inside, he wasn't having much luck with the cards this time.

'Gina?' she called. 'It's your babysitter.'

A thoroughly sloshed redhead from the rowdy group of women stepped forward. 'My name's Gina,' she said, somewhat dazedly.

'And do you have a babysitter?' This was sort of an important part of the conversation, after all.

'Do I *look* like I have a babysitter?'

Bonnie garnished Terrance's drink. 'I couldn't tell you that. But she's saying that her employer, whose name is Gina, said she'd be back by eight. The babysitter has a family function she needs to get to.'

'Oh shit!' said Gina. A horrified look of realization dawned on her face, and she pulled the base of her glass out from her bra. Bonnie made a note to double-sanitize the glassware tonight. 'I have *kids*! I'm *old*!'

Throwing a few twenties at Bonnie's tip jar, she raced out of the bar and out to the square.

'She's on her way,' Bonnie assured the babysitter, holding up a finger as the birthday girl pressed forward, her eyes bleary. Birthday or not, Bonnie was going to have to cut her off soon, before she started ugly-crying in the corner. Or before poor Winston made a formal complaint. There was, of course, a third possible outcome, which would require Bonnie to break out the cleaning chemicals, and which she didn't particularly want to think about.

'Can we have another pitcher of the purple stuff?' begged the birthday blonde, batting eyes dark with smeared makeup. 'And one for this one here. She looks like she needs it. Wow, has anyone ever told you you're so pretty?' The woman leaned against the bar, holding up one of the coasters to the light. 'I'm going to take this. As a birthday gift. And a glass. And maybe one of those long spoons.'

'Let's compromise and say just the coaster,' said Bonnie sweetly. 'Did you want one?' she asked Tessa, hefting the forget-me-not-hued pitcher of Memory Lane.

Tessa shook her head. 'Not for me. I'm already two bubblies deep. And I'm skating home. *I'm* not a danger. It's the kids on scooters I don't trust!'

'Scooters are the *worst*,' agreed the birthday girl. 'We've gone backwards as a society. Except for this cocktail. This cocktail is amazing. Hang on, what was I doing here again?'

With a sigh, Bonnie closed out the woman's tab. She'd had quite enough.

'Drinking,' she said. 'For your birthday.'

'Drinking!' shrieked the woman, spilling half the pitcher on the hardwoods. 'For my *birthday*!'

Chapter 19

LET'S SIT AND WEED A SPELL

Effie

'Welcome to weeding day,' said a despondent Effie to the empty library.

Not a single soul had shown up.

Well, this was disappointing, and rather surprising. The townsfolk of Yellowbrick Grove might be scattered, but they tended to support the library's initiatives. And Effie had heavily promoted this one. She'd put signs up throughout the library, sent out a newsletter, and had Kirsty put together a social media post which had garnered a record number of likes, and, in a library first, a comment! She'd even gone to the effort of ordering pizza, as well as treats from The Golden Hour Bakery, which she'd now have to consume all by herself, without even the Friends of the Library group to help.

The only upside was that if no one else was around, Effie could use her magic to help speed up the process. Her wrists crackled green as she pored over the weeding lists. If she focused, she could have this wrapped up in a few hours.

The warmth of her magic was just starting to pour from her wrists when the door swung open. A familiarly athletic, well-dressed figure stepped through, clad in a coat that Effie was a bit envious of, and beautifully shaped boots that Effie *definitely* coveted. She wasn't a fashionista like Bonnie, but she was a thoughtful thrifter, and she liked to think she had an eye for things that were classic and well made. Especially when said things were being worn by someone so good-looking.

She swallowed, willing her magic back inside, and tugging her cardigan sleeves down over her wrists.

'I hope I didn't miss the party.' Theo raised an eyebrow at the ample spread of snacks, and the clearly empty library.

Ah. So at least *one* Friends of the Library member checked their email. Effie felt slightly effervescent at the thought that Theo had made the effort. And slightly anxious at the fact that they were about to spend an evening together. Her and Theo! Never in a million years could she have anticipated it.

'You know readers.' Effie did her best to keep the dismay out of her voice. She really *had* wanted tonight to be a success. 'They like to be fashionably late.'

'To weeding day, the social event of the year?' Theo put his hands on his hips in a show of indignation that made Effie smile. 'I'm surprised they're not banging on the doors like a horde of invading zombies.'

'I know,' said Effie. 'I'm sincerely surprised that Freddie Noonan hasn't shown up.'

Theo frowned, then grinned as he got the reference. 'Ah, the guy with the fabulous lawn.'

'It really is fabulous,' agreed Effie. 'I think he does the edges with a ruler.'

'I'm just glad that I didn't wear my tuxedo. In case it was a typo,' Theo clarified.

Effie couldn't help but feel a bit disappointed. Theo in a tux would have been a sight to behold. Anyone who looked that good in sweaty running gear would be a force to be reckoned with in a three-piece suit.

'Oh, you were hoping for some library nuptials?' she teased, grateful that her nerves weren't coming through in her voice.

'Sure. Colour me curious. I've seen bookshop proposals, so why not a library wedding with an open guest list? And hopefully an open bar.'

'Paid for by your generous donation.'

'Yes indeed.' Theo shook his head sadly. 'But alas, a typo.'

'I don't make typos,' said Effie, with faux indignation. She divided her weeding printout in two, clipping one half to a clipboard that she passed to him. 'Well, I do, but I don't let them stand. And while we don't have an open bar, we do have an excellent array of off-brand soft drinks purchased from the on-sale section of the grocery store. Can I tempt you with some Banta or some Mister Pepper?'

'Mister Pepper?' Theo chuckled. 'The underachieving brother of the Doc, huh.'

'Their parents are disappointed, although they'd never admit it.'

'Ah, I empathize fully,' said Theo, jauntily opening and closing the clasp on his clipboard. So, paperwork was a novelty to Theo. The man had clearly never held an admin role in his life.

'Wow, how are there so many books that deserve weeding?' he asked as he flipped through the list. 'Some of these are stunners. *The Care and Upkeep of Anglerfish*? *Toilet Paper Tube Parade Costumes for the Frugally Minded*? And this one! *Frogs Are My Faves*! I'm going to borrow that one right now to keep it in circulation.'

He wandered down the stacks, frowning as he narrowed down his search to a particular section, then triumphantly pulling out a handbound green volume that had clearly been created by a child.

'It's magnificent,' breathed Effie. She'd never seen the little volume before, even though she'd wandered the stacks tens of thousands of times over the years. 'How did it even end up on the shelves?'

'It must be part of a class project or something.' He flipped open the book, looking for a date. Written in pencil on the inside of the back cover was *June, 1984*.

As he read, Effie leaned over his shoulder, shyly at first,

then slightly less so as she found herself caught up in the typewritten text and the cut-paper images that had been carefully pasted in by a grade schooler decades earlier.

'I think frogs are my favourite, too,' said Theo, chuckling at the particularly fat, big-eyed frog that spanned the midpoint of the book. 'We absolutely can't weed this.'

'Maybe we can do a weeded books display,' said Effie, drawing back as she realized she'd been about to touch the soft hair at the base of his neck. 'We could put the most intriguing titles out to encourage people to borrow them.'

'Or buy them,' added Theo. 'With all proceeds supporting the Friends of the Library, of course.'

Effie, now at a safe distance, raised an eyebrow. 'Look at you, Mr Non-Profit.'

'It sucks to see something taken out of circulation, but there's only so much space on the shelves. And in the basement,' he added, before Effie could jump in. 'I've come in a few times using the elevator, so I've seen the chaos down there. It's a paper fire waiting to happen.'

'It's highly organized chaos,' protested Effie. 'Every stack of paper has its place.'

'I'm not sure an insurance company would accept that argument.'

Effie gave him a good-natured shove. Theo turned to her, surprised at the contact, and their eyes met. For a fleeting moment, Effie wondered what it might be like to kiss him.

But no, it was impossible. She was at work, and she'd never do anything to jeopardize her position. Not to mention that for all she knew, Theo was planning an imminent return to the city.

'Come on,' she said, breaking his gaze. 'We've got thousands of books to weed, and if you're wanting a decent selection for the display, we'd better get to it.'

'How about we get some music going?' he asked.

Out of sheer habit, Effie almost used her magic to switch

on the vintage stereo that sat in the far corner of the down-stairs reading room. She remembered herself just as her wrists started to glow, and hurried over to turn it on manually instead.

As golden oldies shimmered across the room, earning a thumbs up from Theo, Effie reminded herself that she was going to have to find the books on her list the old-fashioned way, using her legs and hands rather than the magic that ran through her blood. It would take so much longer than her usual book tidying and sorting efforts, which she managed in a few quick minutes at the end of each night, humming 'Be Our Guest' as she did, but she supposed it was a chance for her and Theo to spend a bit of time together. Although not *together* together. Together in a way that allowed for some personal space, and that was generally quiet (Effie's preferred way of spending time with someone).

'Ben E. King,' said Theo approvingly as 'Stand By Me' came on. He sang along quietly, and surprisingly tunefully.

'I didn't know you were a karaoke fan,' she said, as she pulled out a couple of ancient geography books predating the current world map by several decades.

'Only in the comfort of my own shower,' said Theo.

Effie was suddenly beset by visions of Theo in the buff in extremely steamy environs and, goodness, was the air conditioning not working in here?

Of course not, Effie, it's jacket weather outside.

'Right. The acoustics,' she added awkwardly.

'A clawfoot tub just doesn't cut it when you're trying to hit those high notes.' There was a thud as Theo plopped a heavy tome down on his stack of weeded books.

'So,' said Effie, trying to change the conversation away from Theo's naked body, 'how have you been finding Yellowbrick Grove? Is it feeling like home yet?'

'It's quaint,' said Theo. 'I've been doing the walking tour with the app.'

'Really?' Effie puffed with pride as she considered a book about Venn diagrams called *Stuck in the Middle with You*. Its pages were falling out. 'That was one of my initiatives. We put it together last year. The StoryWalk is this year's.'

Theo's head popped up over the stack next to Effie's. He waved *Frogs Are My Faves* at her. 'The StoryWalk! This is perfect for the StoryWalk!'

Effie couldn't help but laugh. It *was* adorable. And if it was by a local author, all the better.

'We'd have to get the rights, though.' She pulled out a sad volume about rabbit psychology. 'We'd need a way to get in touch with the author.'

'Careful, I hear little kids charge a fortune for StoryWalk rights.' Theo was browsing the culinary section, which held all sorts of weedable wonders. He held up a recipe book showcasing the wonders of savoury jelly desserts. 'This isn't on my list, but for the safety of your readers, I think we should weed it.'

'But that's a local favourite,' said Effie. 'I'm surprised it's not checked out.'

Theo blanched. 'Please tell me you're joking. Nope, I just saw the docket at the back. You're right. Endless due date stamps. If this is the type of food the town appreciates, no wonder I haven't been able to find decent sushi.'

'I absolutely would not risk the local sushi. We do have a great Phở place, though.'

Theo raised his eyebrows, impressed. 'I could go for some Phở. Or a banh mi.'

'They do a great one. The bread's so sharp it cuts your mouth.'

'Shall we?'

Effie turned, confused. 'Shall we what?'

'Grab something more substantial than congealing pizza and flat soda?'

She tapped her list, which she was only halfway through. 'But we're weeding.'

Theo regarded her for a moment, then gathered his stack of books.

'We are indeed,' he said quietly.

He returned to his list, and Effie did as well, poring over the stacks as she searched out the seemingly endless selection of books on her list.

As she worked, the music on the record player appeared to increase in volume, until every note seemed to blare with nerve-jangling amplification. She wondered whether it might be the fault of the ghost, but as she crept over to the record player to adjust the volume dial, she realized that the seeming crescendo was actually due to the fact that Theo's easy banter had subsided entirely.

The next book on Effie's list was called *Signs You're Doing It Wrong*. She sighed. Maybe she should give it a read before weeding it.

Chapter 20

IN THIS HOUSE
WE BELIEVE IN MAGIC

Bonnie

Bonnie had been standing outside the cottage on Tintagel Lane for fifteen minutes, the plate of fresh cookies in her hands slowly cooling off. There was no sign of Hannah, who'd asked her to assist with the home open, just in case a serial killer showed up and decided to off her. Between the demands of the bar and Kirsty's weird dalliance with Bobby, Bonnie was extremely aware that her grasp on her friendship group was slipping away. So here she was, doing her bit to get things back on track. And this was how she'd been repaid. She nibbled a cookie, feeling miffed that she'd gone out of her way to help Hannah, only to be stood up.

A young couple with a red wagon containing a small, napping child hurried up. 'Did we miss it?' asked the woman, who had the slightly unhinged, ready-to-snap look of someone subjected to sleep deprivation over a period of several years.

'Not at all,' said Bonnie, pasting a smile on her face. 'We're just getting started.'

Thankfully the lockbox on the door had the same code that Hannah's agency always used, and Bonnie had been to enough of these things with Hannah that she had it memorized. She'd also enjoyed a party here just a few weeks earlier, although she wasn't about to mention that to potential buyers.

'It's such a cute place,' said the mom, marvelling at the neat rose bushes that framed the garden, and the lush lawn with its quaint flagstone pavers. 'It has a turret! I could do my art there. I'm Beatrice, by the way. And this is Todd. And little Olivia.'

Of course, thought Bonnie. It was always Olivia. There were so many Olivias that if you were going to name your kid Olivia you almost needed to give them an extra first name to differentiate them.

Introducing herself with a handshake, Bonnie grabbed the key from the lockbox and pushed open the front door.

'A yellow door!' exclaimed Beatrice. 'I've always wanted a yellow door!'

Bonnie set down the cookies on the entry table by the front door. 'We call this one the Dorothy House – because of the gingham and red trim, not because it got swept up in a tornado and landed on a witch.'

'Well, that's good to hear,' drawled Todd, pushing the stroller into the living room. 'I don't want to be dealing with foundation issues.'

Beatrice groaned, but Bonnie humoured him with a laugh. Whatever it took to show Hannah she was an excellent friend. 'Take a look around and let me know what you think. Um, I'll have you sign in, though.'

Hannah did this bit ordinarily, but if she was a no-show, Bonnie might as well help her out. She drew out one of her bartending notepads from her purse.

'Could I grab your emails and phone numbers? It's a head office thing.'

'Um, sure.' The couple wrote down their details, then, each with a cookie in hand, went to explore the house. Bonnie could hear Beatrice exclaiming about the home's various charms: its quaint carpets, the vintage hanging light fixtures, the bay windows with their plush window seats.

Bonnie checked her phone. Still nothing from Hannah. Hopefully she hadn't been murdered on her way – not that

Bonnie could remember the last time any sort of violent crime had happened in town. A few years ago, some of the high-school seniors *had* got a bit overexcited about egging the gymnasium, and there'd been a feuding couple who'd drawn rude pictures on each other's cars, but that was about it. Hannah was probably just sleeping off a date or a late-night *Lost* marathon.

A trickle of other visitors came through, mostly neighbours wanting a peek inside the house or a free cookie. Freddie Noonan even stopped by, although by his own admission only to compare the quality of the home's turf with his own.

'They were runner-up in the Yellowbrick Grove Garden of Perfection this year,' he admitted, pulling off a pair of gardening gloves so that he could partake in a cookie. 'I need to see what I'm dealing with. And perhaps get proactive if I'm going to keep my crown.'

Bonnie grinned. 'No one could ever take your flower crown, Freddie.'

'You're a darl. And you're right. That section under the fence is patchy.' He pointed triumphantly. 'Just don't tell potential buyers, or they'll come down on their offer.'

'Wow, I didn't realize grass could affect a sale price like that.'

'A perfect lawn is a perfect lawn. And with that, I'm off to the garden centre for some fertilizer.' Freddie sauntered off down the pathway, doing a little skip as he passed the section of lawn that he'd apparently found wanting.

Next through the door was Tammi, that weird woman who hung out at the library all day eating crackers. Adding a squiggle to Bonnie's sign-in sheet, Tammi grabbed half a dozen cookies and dropped them in her bag before disappearing into one of the bedrooms, presumably to eat said cookies.

As she kept track of the visitors, Bonnie kept texting Hannah, but to no avail. Had she forgotten to charge her phone? Surely not. Despite how airy-fairy she was, Hannah was chronically organized. Her wedding-planner mom was intensely high pressure, and her dad's memory condition required careful, coordinated care.

When the trickle of visitors slowed, Bonnie went to find Beatrice and Todd, who were still wandering around the house somewhere. They were upstairs, in a room with cathedral ceilings and a bed with a chiffon canopy that felt like something out of a fairy tale.

'The perfect princess room,' she mouthed, seeing that their little one was asleep on Todd's shoulder.

'Sorry! We didn't want to wake her,' Beatrice whispered from the plush Sherpa armchair she was perched on, obviously feeling awkward about sitting on someone else's furniture.

'It's fine,' whispered Bonnie. 'How are you liking the house? It can come furnished, you know. The owner is moving to Florida.'

Beatrice stroked the armchair. 'The furniture is gorgeous. Babe, I love it,' she told Todd.

Todd, who was rocking from side to side with Olivia in his arms, nodded. 'We're definitely interested, but we'll need to figure out a price. Can we give you a call tonight?'

'Sure, sure!' said Bonnie. She dug in her wallet, looking around for Hannah's card. She'd had one, but she'd given it to some property investor guy at the bar a few weeks back who wouldn't stop flirting with her. Thankfully, the prospect of tax-deductible income in a market that Bonnie assured him was booming for short-term vacation rentals had been enough to make him turn his attention away from her.

'Oh rats. I don't have the managing realtor's card on me, but I do have some drinks cards for The Silver Slipper.' She held those up, somewhat surprised at how savagely Beatrice snatched them out of her hands.

Mama wants a drink, she thought wryly.

'That sounds lovely. We'll be there. Oh wait, it's *your* place?' Beatrice's lips moved as she read the copy on the back of the voucher. 'That is so impressive. I've always wanted to be a small business owner. Maybe a plant shop. Or a bookshop. Or a plant bookshop.'

'The feminine dream,' said Bonnie, marvelling at the magnificent monstera in the corner. The plant was so big it was basically a botanical CPAP machine.

'Instead, I'm an engineer.' Beatrice made a face. 'Yay numbers and keeping bridges from falling down.'

'Oh, is that all?' Bonnie chuckled, but a wistful feeling overcame her as she glanced around the room once more. She'd never been one to think about settling down, but there was something about this cute little family in this cosy little house that called to her. Perhaps, one day, she'd be one half of a couple browsing quaint cottages and excitedly talking about where the furniture might go. Perhaps there was a future that involved nights sprawled in front of the television, and home-made pizza with his and hers toppings, and building a collection of seasonal decorations that would be added to each year.

But there was only one person who came to mind when she considered the possibility, and the last time she'd seen him, she'd thrown all of his kindness and generosity right back into his face.

'C'mon, I'll see you out,' she said, trying to keep her voice from breaking.

Bonnie was clearing empty pitchers and glasses from the bar's patio area when she felt a slightly queasy feeling in her stomach. She turned, knowing her uncle was somewhere in the vicinity. Ah, there he was, dressed not unlike the tree he was standing beneath. Only with more velvet and definitely more gemstones.

'Bonnie, my dear!' he called. 'Busy, busy, I see. I just thought I'd stop by to drop off some extra coasters. Don't want to ruin the wood of these tables, do we? Twenty per cent discount if you bring that to Behind the Curtain!' he told one of the teachers from the high school as he slid a coaster beneath her purple drink. She looked up from the tests she was marking, surprised.

'For you, I recommend blue calcite,' he said. 'It helps with communication when trying to impart those difficult concepts. Grades will soar.'

Once he was done explaining the wonders of blue calcite to the teacher, he made his way over to Bonnie, his cane tapping against the flagstones.

'Fabulous job, Bonnie. Just fabulous,' he said, sliding an envelope onto Bonnie's tray. 'I've sold five Bastet cats today alone. That said, if you want to dial up the intensity, I am all for it.'

Then he grimaced. He'd spied Beatrice and Todd and their wagon approaching.

'The arrival of a child signals that it's my time to exit,' he said with a shudder. 'If you need more coasters, just knock.'

He disappeared out the side gate, not bothering to hold it for the little family. Instead, Beatrice propped open the gate as Todd tried to angle the wagon with its sleeping passenger through the gate, punching the air when at last he succeeded.

'You made it!' said Bonnie, adjusting her grip on her heavy tray. 'Come on in and I'll get you hooked up.'

Todd eyed the bar door, and then the wagon. 'I'll pull up out here. I trust Beatrice to order for me. Just no Jägerbombs.'

Ditching Todd with alacrity, Beatrice hurried after Bonnie.

'Wow,' she said as she crossed the threshold into the bar area. 'It's so weird existing as an individual human again. You don't realize the freedom of just walking through a doorway until you've been trying to do it with a wagon for two straight years. Ooh, and you have darts! And pinball! And is that a magician?'

Bonnie glanced over at Terrance swearing at his deck of cards. Around him, a group of his friends heckled him for his inability to remember where the joker in the pack was.

'After the queen of spades, you ding-dong!' crowed a girl wearing three layers of fishnet tights, all in different colours.

'You're going to have to pick a different audition talent,' added a guy in a 90s band T-shirt. He definitely did not realize he was wearing a T-shirt from a band from the 90s.

'That's just Terrance,' said Bonnie. 'He's made it his life's work to memorize a pack of playing cards.'

'Pfft,' said Beatrice. 'How hard could that be? I've memorized every infant milestone all the way up to age five. Now that's dedication. What's that purple drink everyone's got? I'll take one of those. Assuming they're strong. *Really* strong. Because I'm not driving, or even pushing the wagon. That's Todd's job right now. I carried the baby, I nursed the baby, and now I'm drinking for one.'

Outside, little Olivia whined. Bonnie could hear Todd settling her, bribing her with smuggled-in goldfish crackers.

'Sure. One Memory Lane coming up,' she said brightly. 'I'll mix you a fresh one, extra strong. And if you want to get a little something for your future home, bring this coaster over to Behind the Curtain for a discount.'

Bonnie topped the drink with a garnish of wildflowers, then popped it on one of Uncle Oswald's coasters. She slid the order over to Beatrice, who wasted no time in taking a sip.

'Oh, that's good,' Beatrice said, eyes widening. 'And yes to the discount. I'll take a brownie as well. No, make it two.'

Bonnie plated up the brownies, popping them on a tray for easy carrying. Although this was apparently unnecessary, because Beatrice was halfway through one of them before she made it outside. Apparently juggling was a skill that new moms became proficient at very fast.

Bonnie was popping a stack of glasses into the dishwasher – the one thing about all these purple drinks was that it took an extra cycle to get the glassware clean – when Hannah hurried up.

'Well, look who the cat dragged in.' Bonnie slammed the dishwasher drawer closed for emphasis.

'Oh my god, Bonnie. Thank you so much for today.' Hannah made prayer hands and pointed them in Bonnie's direction. Her ponytail swung over her shoulder. Bonnie blinked. Hannah was vehemently against ponytails, which she believed were slovenly and lazy.

'I don't know what happened, I swear. I got my calendars mixed up, or the reminders on my phone wrong, or *something*. Did the clocks go back? Because that has *never* happened to me before.'

Hannah was right. Hannah's mom had trained her from an early age to create a colour-coded schedule together with a series of alerts, alarms and backups to ensure that nothing slipped by her. Hannah had somehow graduated with perfect grades while also being on three different sports teams, the head of yearbook club and vice school captain. (Bonnie, of course, had been school captain.)

'You blew me off like . . . like I was *Effie*!' snapped Bonnie, with an extra dishwasher slam for good measure.

'I'm so sorry. I'm the worst. I'll make it up to you, I promise.' Hannah made a pleading gesture, her huge eyes begging for forgiveness.

Bonnie glowered, then sighed. She knew Hannah had a lot going on with her dad. And besides, she was starting to run low on friends.

'It's fine, babe,' she said finally. And extremely charitably, given that Bonnie was not one to be stood up. 'You had five groups show up, with one maybe interested in putting in an offer. They're out there.'

Bonnie indicated the young family outside.

Hannah just about squealed with joy. 'God, thank you *so* much. I'm going to go talk to them. Can I get some of those brownies to ply them with?'

'They're already hooked up,' said Bonnie. 'But I have some

chocolate twists. And a bottle of prosecco if you think that'll help your case.'

'Done.'

Bonnie popped the spoils into a gift basket, and Hannah trotted off to her prospective clients.

Momentarily, she was back, still clutching the gift basket.

'*Rude!*' she said, popping open the prosecco bottle and pouring herself a drink. 'Can you believe this! I went up to them, introduced myself and explained about the situation today, how I had a scheduling conflict or whatever, and they just looked at me like I was an alien.'

Weird. They'd seemed so into the house, and just now Beatrice had seemed excited about buying one of Oswald's decorative knickknacks for it.

'Maybe because you were out of context,' offered Bonnie. 'Like, when third-grade me saw Mrs Ferguson at the grocery store and realized that teachers exist outside the classroom?'

Hannah flicked her hair in the manner of someone preparing to make a pronouncement. 'Oh no, it gets worse. I mentioned the house, and they made out like they had no idea what I was talking about.'

All right, now that *was* rude. Maybe she'd been wrong about Beatrice and Todd's interest in the house. Perhaps they'd just been play-acting at home ownership. Or they preferred ultra-modern builds but were being polite. Still, faking amnesia wasn't really the way to go about the whole situation.

'Sorry, babe,' she said. 'Although honestly, I think they're just exhausted. Maybe buying a house is too much for them to deal with right now.'

Hannah polished off her drink, then intercepted the glass of Memory Lane that Bonnie had just poured.

'Sorry, I need it more than you,' Hannah told the bald-headed guy who'd been about to grab the drink.

The guy shook his head good-naturedly. 'Pour me another? I'll cover both.'

'Thanks,' Hannah said flirtatiously. Hannah was a graduate of the Bonnie Chalmers School of Seduction, and knew how to turn on the charm when it meant she'd get something from it.

'Maybe I could get your—' began the guy hopefully, but Hannah had her phone up to her ear, listening to her voicemails over the thud of Bonnie's playlist.

'Well, some investor guy left a message about the Dorothy House, so I guess that's how it's going to go. Welcome to the neighbourhood, short-term renters. Don't forget to take a few selfies, scare the ducks and grab a commemorative moon-charged water-fountain ornament at Uncle Oswald's.'

Bonnie slid forward one of Uncle Oswald's agate coasters. If Beatrice wasn't going to use it, Hannah might as well. 'Twenty per cent discount with one of these.'

Hannah looked impressed. 'Really? Well, in that case, I'm off to do some shopping. My crystals aren't going to charge themselves.'

Chapter 21

PAYBACK'S A WITCH

Effie

Effie looked at the electrical panel in dismay. She knew nothing about them, other than that they were quite important, and that you could flip the various switches to toggle the circuits around the house. As far as she knew, the panel at the Chalmers family home was perfectly fine. The lights went on and off upon request, and there hadn't been any fires, other than the ones caused by Bonnie's hair curler, and those were due to a user error issue.

And yet here she was, holding a stern letter from the insurance company that said if she didn't upgrade the panel within the fortnight, her policy would be cancelled. Fabulous. Insurance was non-negotiable when you lived with someone who came close to burning down the house on a daily basis.

'Hey, Eff.' Bobby waved from over the fence that divided their houses. 'Did you blow a fuse?'

Only at my sister, thought Effie darkly.

'I'm just trying to figure out what's involved in an electrical panel upgrade. Is that something you can handle?'

Bobby whistled. 'Expensive job. Definitely not just a handyman thing, no matter how much Bonnie bats her eyelashes at me. You'll need a proper electrician, permits, sign-off from the city and the power company. It's a whole thing.'

Effie sighed. Of course it was. And it was something that

had to be approved by the insurer, so it had to be legit. She couldn't just snap her fingers and stream a bit of magic at it, the way she did with the temperamental toilet in the downstairs bathroom and the finicky kitchen fan that had a wobble to it. No, this needed proper mechanical intervention, which was definitely not where Effie's skills lay.

She pondered the numbers in her bank account. She was frugal, but a librarian's salary in a small town didn't exactly put her in the realm of the big spenders. Sure, she had her investments, but those were tied up, unless she wanted to pay a penalty for an early withdrawal. It wasn't like she was going to get any help from Bonnie, who'd probably spent whatever draw she'd taken from the bar on nail art and new shoes.

Oh, if only houses could run entirely on magic! The world would be a better, and cheaper, place.

'Do you know anyone who'll do it cheaply?' Effie asked forlornly.

'Let me run in and grab you some business cards. Hang on. I'll get you some pastries while I'm at it. We have some pistachio-dusted cornetti I think you'll love. Assuming Kevvie hasn't eaten them all.'

Bobby rushed back inside, leaving Effie wondering for the thousandth time in her life why Bonnie had been so determined to keep him in the wings. Bobby was kind, and thoughtful, and cute, too, with his shock of wavy hair and those dark eyes with their long lashes. And he baked!

All right, so it wasn't Bonnie's obligation or responsibility to reciprocate just because someone had shown interest, but Effie had always quietly thought they'd make a lovely couple. They balanced each other. Which was probably the whole problem. Bonnie didn't want someone who balanced her. She wanted *more*. She wanted *everything*.

There was no one in the entire town who could live up to

her standards. Which was why she solely dated tourists and the contract staff at the college.

Speaking of.

'What's going on out here?' asked Bonnie, sidling out in a pair of satin pyjama shorts and a tank top. And Effie's robe. Judging from the way her hair floofed at one side and the slightly puffy look to her eyes, she'd just rolled out of bed, but in a movie star sort of way, not an Effie way. 'Did your e-reader short circuit the kitchen or something?'

Effie didn't even know where to start with that.

Instead, she passed Bonnie the letter from the insurance company. Bonnie gave it less of a perusal and more of a glance, but Effie saw her eyes widen at the bit that said 'cancellation' in bold.

'That seems bad,' she offered.

Ah, there it was. The propensity for understatement you could enjoy when you'd never faced a consequence in your life.

'Excellent reading of the situation. Bobby's going to see what our options are.'

Bonnie adjusted the robe, tightening it around her waist and settling it on her shoulders, transforming her from sleepy-eyed ingenue to slumber goddess. 'Bobby is?'

As the side door of Bobby's house swung shut with a click, she quickly scraped her fingers through her hair, then stuck a seductive pose straight out of a magazine. By the time Bobby was back at the fence, basket of pastries in hand, she had a handle on whatever feelings had swept over her when Effie mentioned their neighbour's name.

'So, I called my friend Nick, and he said that you're looking at four, five thousand dollars at least. More if you're going to get it done in that timeframe. Oh. Hey, Bon.'

He said it oddly politely, the usual excitement at seeing Bonnie absent from his voice. His tone made Effie's heart twist. It was a tone *she* usually heard when someone had to talk to her instead of her sister.

'Hey, Bobby,' said Bonnie, who was faux absently styling her hair into a loose braid, a skill that Effie did not possess.

The energy between the two of them was odd, but Effie couldn't put her finger on it.

'Do you think they'd do instalments?' asked Effie, mentally adding up the bills she anticipated over the next month. With Bonnie in the house, it was always better to estimate generously, especially since their water usage had ticked up into extreme levels this month. Apparently, Bonnie had been filling an invisible Olympic swimming pool.

'I can help.' Bonnie tied off her braid with the pink elastic that lived around her wrist. 'The bar's been doing well recently.'

Effie balked. *Bonnie*, helping? Everything Effie knew about the universe was upended at the very thought. Bonnie wasn't a helper. She wasn't the financially secure one. She was the unpredictable one whose antics required endless mitigation and apology notes and 'please forgive us' baked-goods hampers.

If Bonnie was able to step up and do her part financially, then what exactly was Effie's role these days?

'Are you sure? Shouldn't you build an emergency fund?'

Bonnie looked amused. 'I think this would count as an emergency. Just encourage your library people to come by the bar and we'll call it even. Besides, I have a . . .'

She trailed off, probably because she'd been about to say something rude about the library patrons.

Effie regarded her sister, struggling with something somewhere in between pride and envy. She *wanted* Bonnie to do well, after all. Didn't she?

'Thanks, Bon,' she managed eventually.

'Don't mention it,' said Bonnie with a casual shrug that sent her dressing gown sliding off her shoulder. Bobby averted his eyes – but there was a twinkle in Bonnie's that said she was *quite* pleased with herself indeed.

Bonnie Chalmers, entrepreneur extraordinaire. She could add it to all the other ribbons that dangled from the display case in her room.

Chapter 22

EVERY LITTLE THING SHE DOES IS MAGIC

Bonnie

Bonnie arrived at The Silver Slipper feeling like an 80s business mogul. In honour of the occasion, she was even wearing a pair of colour-block heels that Mom had nabbed from their gran's wardrobe years back. 'You look, um, professional,' Effie had told her.

She'd never before been able to volunteer to help out with a bill, especially one bigger than a split meal or a coffee order. All right, she couldn't *completely* cover it, but she knew she was on track to get there just so long as the numbers for this week stayed where they were. And it had been more of a pride thing, really. She'd seen that look in Effie's eyes, the tired, motherly one that she always affected when it came to day-to-day life stuff, as if she hadn't taken it upon herself to claim the mantle of Queen of the Domestic Realm. That judgemental look that assumed Bonnie would beg Effie to cover the expense. Those days were over, thanks to her arrangement with Uncle Oswald.

All right, so Uncle Oswald wasn't her favourite human, and the items he stocked in his shop were all flimflam (a word Effie overused when she'd gone through her hardboiled crime paperback phase, and which Bonnie found hilarious to parrot). And he still made her feel queasy whenever he was around. But there was no denying that their arrangement had single-handedly changed Bonnie's fortunes. So much so that not only was she ahead on payments for the Cadillac, but she could finally afford to hire some extra help behind the bar. Someone who wasn't Bobby or one of her entourage, who were becoming increasingly flaky (Hannah), increasingly bitchy (Kirsty) and increasingly absent (Alana).

Obviously, Bonnie would have to be the one who remained in charge of the specialty drinks, but an extra set of hands would free her up to focus on planning the events the bar needed to become sustainable in the long term. And give her more time to finish renovating the upstairs apartment so she had an option to move out of the Chalmers residence, away from the stifling memories of Mom and the endless pressure and judgement from Effie. Besides, she was spending so much time at the bar these days that the idea of being just a few steps from her bed appealed enormously.

Bonnie pulled up a shortlist of résumés on her phone. They'd come in from all over the place via email, text, Instagram messages, scrawled notes on napkins. Bonnie didn't mind so much, as it wasn't like bartender was a gig that needed a standard CV. She didn't even have one of her own. Her social media pages and the online reviews of her bar were résumé enough. And she had her reputation, which was all the calling card you needed in this town. Well, assuming you had a reputation like Bonnie's.

She scrolled through the selfies and copy and pasted bulleted text, looking for someone who might be a good fit. Hmm. Sara Settimana, current poli-science major and pole-vaulting champ. She'd probably be good for reaching things off the top shelves, but Bonnie could imagine some heated discussions between Sara and the darts-playing gents, who had *opinions* about things. Then there was Lily Nakamura, who was currently one of the baristas at The Winged Monkey, and who famously got everyone's orders wrong. People tolerated it because Lily was adorable, but Bonnie probably didn't need to add extra chaos to her business right now. What about

Clark Grenier? He was a PhD at the college, and with those dark eyes and stubble, he wouldn't be a bad asset to have behind the bar. He'd attract a whole new cohort of patrons, *and* he'd give Bonnie something to look at. Besides, with the whole Bobby and Kirsty situation, Bonnie felt she needed to up her game to stay competitive.

She considered texting, but decided to do right by her new entrepreneurial identity and make an actual phone call.

To her surprise, Clark picked up.

'Hey, Clark? This is Bonnie from The Silver Slipper. How'd you like to come in for an interview?'

Clark's voice was slightly gruff, but with a mirthful undertone that she liked, and he agreed to come down after his next class. Maybe this could work.

While she waited for Clark to arrive, Bonnie busied herself preparing the bar for midday opening. Much of this prep work now involved making room for the pre-made Memory Lane concentrate used in the new cocktail series. She hadn't seen people get so excited over a drink since kombucha had first hit the market. Bonnie banged around in the cabinets, trying to find more space for the concentrate. She liked to minimize storeroom runs during opening hours, but soon they'd be unavoidable. Unless she expanded the bar area. It was times like this she missed Bobby's easy presence – he had such a good eye for design, and he *got* what Bonnie was trying to express, even if she wasn't so sure. They'd always been on a very similar wavelength, even though they were so different.

There was a knock at the door, and Bonnie jumped up, almost smacking her head on the bar counter. Her heart sank slightly as she saw it wasn't Bobby, but immediately perked up when she realized it was someone just as welcome: Sabine.

'Bonnie,' Sabine breathed, in that zen, hippie tone that even Alana hadn't mastered. If you were looking for an individual with their chakras aligned and their energies balanced, it was Sabine.

'Sabine!' Bonnie drew her in for a hug. 'I'm so glad you came by.'

'I'm afraid I'm here as the Toto Hotel's sole ambassador. Maureen had good intentions, but we've had a wedding party making our lives miserable for the past few days. She sends her love.'

Sabine spun a slow circle, making appreciative noises as she took in the bar that Bonnie had worked so hard to bring to life.

'There's an upstairs as well,' said Bonnie, feeling suddenly shy. She was so proud of the bar, and part of her worried that Sabine's practised eye would find it lacking in some way.

'May I?' asked Sabine. 'If it's anywhere near as gorgeous as downstairs, I know I'm in for a treat.'

'Of course,' said Bonnie, feeling a flicker of pride at Sabine's kind words.

Sabine made her way up the stairs, running a hand over the ornate banister as she went. Like everyone, she stopped when she saw Mom's paintings, her hand reaching for the locket she kept around her neck.

'And these are the event rooms,' said Bonnie, opening the doors so that Sabine could explore. 'Birthday parties, engagements, things like that. Obviously on a smaller scale than the hotel.'

'I hope so,' said Sabine with a chuckle. 'Because the other way lies madness. And the next floor?' she asked curiously, as she stepped back out to the landing.

'My apartment. It's strictly a work in progress.'

Bonnie unlocked the door for Sabine to take a look. The renovations were still underway, but now that she had some extra spending money set aside, she'd be able to hire someone to help out with the bathroom and kitchenette areas. She'd painted, and had found a gorgeous vintage light fixture to go with the retro lamp that currently lit the space. Maybe whoever they hired to do the electrical panel could throw in a free installation.

'Your mother would have loved this,' said Sabine, as she picked her way back downstairs, pausing for a few moments to drink in the warmth of Mom's paintings once more. 'It's absolutely perfect, Bon. You've outdone yourself.'

Bonnie felt a lump grow in her throat as she imagined Mom sitting at the bar, sharing a brownie with Sabine as they chatted about Freddie Noonan's lawn or the latest adventures of Pickles the wayward French bulldog. Bonnie knew she had to hold on to what she actually had, her memories of Mom, but it was so hard not to focus on what might have been. What would never be.

It had been almost a year, she thought, although how that was possible she'd never know. How had she survived a year without Mom in her life? A year of silent evenings in the living room and outfits that didn't get commented on and solo breakfasts in the kitchen.

Which reminded her: during one of their awkward kitchen interactions, Effie had suggested they visit Mom's grave to honour the day. Bonnie had half-heartedly agreed, not wanting to make Mom's absence any realer than it was. Effie had made a point to visit Mom regularly, but the length between Bonnie's visits had been growing. It was too hard.

'Are you free on Thursday?' Bonnie asked. 'We're going to visit Mom. For her . . .' She trailed off, then started over. 'It'll just be us.'

Sabine squeezed Bonnie's shoulder. 'I'd love nothing more. Besides, there's strength in numbers.' Then, picking up one of Uncle Oswald's coasters, she added, 'Now, what does an old hippie have to do to get one of these famous purple cocktails I keep hearing about?'

'Coming right up.' Bonnie couldn't wait to show off her most popular drink.

Sabine was sipping the cocktail when Clark waved from the door, which Bonnie had locked after Sabine's arrival to avoid the inevitable drop-ins who didn't think that opening hours applied to them. He was dressed simply in dark jeans and a T-shirt, with his hands shoved in his pockets as he peered through the stained glass. He was gorgeously handsome, and definitely gay. Which was actually somewhat of a relief, as Bonnie probably didn't need the extra drama.

Sabine gave Clark an approving up-and-down look through the glass. 'He's hired.'

Bonnie chuckled. 'I think you might be right.'

She opened the door to let him in.

'Thanks for coming down so promptly,' she said, batting her eyes in that way that, unlike her magic, never backfired. 'Have you tended bar before?'

Clark gave an easy smile. 'Of course, hon. In Boston, during undergrad. And I make a mean mixed drink at a house party.'

'And you know how to work a till and fend off the advances of drunken tourists?'

'Yes, ma'am.'

'You can lift heavy objects?'

'Say, ones of up to about 140 pounds?' broke in Sabine.

He laughed at this. 'Would you like me to demonstrate?'

'Please,' purred Sabine.

'I think we'll take your word for it,' said Bonnie, amused. 'Are you free tonight?'

Clark's blue eyes twinkled. 'I'm free right now, if you need help opening.'

'Well, then. Welcome to The Silver Slipper.'

She said it coolly, but inside she was screaming with delight.

Between the soaring profits, her new status as the fiscally responsible sister, and the presence of a hot bartender who posed no risk of distraction, things in Bonnieland were on the up.

Chapter 23

MAGIC DELAYED IS MAGIC DENIED

Effie

Effie sipped her terrible library-brewed coffee, grimacing. Today, no amount of magical tweaking could transform the black concoction that came out of the machine into something drinkable. Sometimes she wondered if she was actually dealing with some sort of dark magic cauldron that had just been hexed into looking like a coffee machine. But she'd already finished the coffee she'd brought from home, *and* the one she'd ordered from The Winged Monkey, and she couldn't in all good conscience splurge on a second takeaway coffee for the day. Not even if she'd brought her lunch for a full sixty days straight, which was a personal record.

She'd spent the morning setting up the Weeded Book Sale, which had involved dragging out shelves and tables for display, and sorting out pricing and payments. The initial goal had been an honour system where people grabbed a book and popped whatever amount they thought appropriate in the change tin, but said tin had quickly got clogged up with chewing gum and CVS receipts. After she'd cleaned it out for the third time, she printed off a sign telling people to bring their books and payments to the circulation desk.

There'd also been the small matter of putting together a short video about the sale to go on the library's social media accounts. This had been by far the most challenging part of the whole ordeal, and had made Effie realize that perhaps she wasn't the patient, even-tempered person she considered herself to be. Who knew that it took a full hour to film a ten-second video and close to that again to actually get the video cross-posted to everywhere it needed to go? And that no matter how articulate you considered yourself, it was a physical impossibility to speak into the camera without flubbing a key detail.

And then there was the choreography, but the less said about that, the better.

Oddly enough, Madame Destinée had warned that her day would involve *dances with wolves (and shelves)*. The woman's crystal ball certainly had a wit to it, thought Effie drily, as she handed a patron change for their used books and popped the money in the lockbox she kept behind her desk. The sale was going surprisingly well – they'd sold over a hundred books, which meant extra funds to help support the summer programs and the food pantry.

'It's because of your video,' Kirsty had said, when she'd come in with Bobby to return the telescope. Effie still wasn't used to seeing them together. It went against the narrative she'd concocted for Bobby, where he and Bonnie finally admitted their feelings for one another. Not that Effie had romance on the mind.

'What do you mean?' Effie had responded.

Kirsty had pulled up a screenshot showing the stats for Effie's video. A mind-boggling number of people had watched it. Were there even that many people in town?

'You're trending on LibraryTok,' Kirsty had added, sounding almost impressed. But then she'd added, 'You know, if you're going to trend online, it might be a good idea to update your wardrobe.'

If Effie had been Bonnie, she might have whacked Kirsty with the telescope. But instead, she'd smiled tightly and pretended to check in a stack of books on the desk. To be honest, she *had* been thinking about going clothes shopping. Every time Theo came through the door in his neat, well-fitting outfits, Effie felt frumpy and underdressed. She was getting tired of hiding herself out of fear of being judged or teased. If Theo wanted to spend time around her, that surely meant she wasn't some hideous abomination. Perhaps it was time to add just a touch of sartorial magic to her comfortable outfits. Just a touch. In the name of her new-found LibraryTok fame, of course.

Effie wasn't sure what LibraryTok was, but she planned to do what she did with any new concept she was unfamiliar with: look it up. It was the librarian way, after all.

She was deep down a rabbit hole of long-form articles when a woman she recognized from a Friends of the Library paint and sip event a few months back strode up to the counter with that *I need a book* look on her face. Serena Murphy, that was it.

'Oh hi, Bonnie's sister.'

'Effie,' said Effie, trying to keep the ice from her tone. Now Bonnie was encroaching upon the library?

'I'm looking for *Battle for Hearts on Horseback*.' Serena leaned closer, adding conspiratorially: 'I'm on a gallant romance kick. The slow burn is real when everyone's wearing armour.'

Effie knew this well – in solidarity with Bowow, she'd read just about the entire romance catalogue, and had come to the same conclusions about the challenges of medieval clothing. The poor authors of said volumes had some serious logistical challenges to consider.

'That one's currently out,' she said, frowning as she browsed the record on the system. 'And overdue.'

Serena pouted. 'How about *Hot Knights with Gawain*?'

Effie checked. 'Also overdue.'

'*Your Sword, My Liege*?'

Effie pulled up the listing for that one. Same story. This was unusual, she thought, as she absently browsed through the overdues on her system. There'd been a sharp uptick starting a few weeks earlier, but there hadn't been any library closures or system outages to explain it. The library didn't charge fines – this had been one of the first things that she'd campaigned against upon taking the job – but they still discouraged people from hanging on to their books for ever. Books were like money. They were made to be circulated, not hoarded. It sounded like Effie had a book return drive to add to her endless administrative to-do list.

Perhaps Theo could help with that, she thought idly. He seemed eager to do his part, and apparently, he didn't need a job, so he might as well do something useful with his time. Besides, Effie was starting to quite enjoy his company.

'Would you like some other recommendations?' asked Effie.

'Sure,' said Serena. 'The more spice, the better.'

Well, then.

Effie walked Serena through some of the spicier selections on offer, digging behind the shelves and under a display table for the ones that she'd seen an apparently scandalized Mrs Brewster hide away after browsing them quite thoroughly. Mrs Brewster had made the sign of the cross before going back for seconds.

'Banned in Australia,' mused Serena, as she perused a well-thumbed volume with a grey and white cover and a suggestive title about sharks. 'Must be good.'

'Oh, it has nothing on this series.' Effie deposited a trio of cowboy werewolf books atop Serena's ever-growing stack. Bowow had discussed them at length at romance book club, growing hotter and more bothered by the second.

'I mean, some like them hairy.'

As she helped Serena with a comprehensive selection of glasses-fogging reading that should not be attempted on public transportation, Effie kept a close watch on the library doors, waiting for them to swing open under the shoulder of her favourite banker. Who knew it was possible to have a favourite banker? Especially when you were fundamentally anti-capitalist. Well, he was a former banker, which had to count for something.

The doors did swing with alarming regularity. A school group coming in for a guided story time and borrowing session handled by Bowow, who volunteered on Thursdays; the Scrabblers, a gang of oldies who'd come in every morning to best each other's triple word scores; Winston Ho, who had a thing for nautical maps; and Lily and Terrance from The Winged Monkey, who were whispering together about a job they'd both missed out on.

Once Serena was content with her huge stack of blush-worthy books, Effie hurried back to the circulation desk, where Babs, who worked at the Toto Hotel, was frantically dinging the bell that sat atop a copy of *The Bell Jar*.

'There you are,' said Babs, with her usual attitude. Effie never quite understood how someone so acerbic had managed a fifty-year career in hospitality, or how she was universally so beloved in spite of her habit of snapping at people should they get in her way. Especially if she was grocery shopping. Or waiting for a good parking spot. 'I'm trying to borrow a book over here, if you hadn't noticed.'

Effie took the book, a weighty non-fiction tome about cannibalism. Very revealing, Babs.

'Sorry about that,' she said. 'I was with another patron. Let's get you sorted out.'

She scanned Babs' card, then pulled up her account. Oh dear. The account was flashing bright red, like the background lighting in Effie's frequent anxiety dreams. Effie

scrolled through Babs' borrowing record, which was extensive, and rather gory.

'Babs, I can't let you borrow this. You have twenty-seven
books overdue.'

Babs folded her thin arms. 'Lies!'

'Let me print them out for you.' Effie printed off a receipt
listing Babs' overdues, then circled the amount at the bottom
showing how much money she'd saved by using the library,
and how much money she'd saved thanks to the new fee-free
overdues program.

Babs took the receipt, puzzling over it as though it were a
cryptic crossword.

'Something's afoot,' she said, waggling a finger. 'Maybe I've
been hacked. I attended your online safety awareness sessions.
I know all about phishers and the like.'

'Well, you keep an eye on your credit, and I'll keep an eye
out for those books in the drop box,' said Effie.

But it was odd, though, wasn't it? That so many books
were overdue at once?

She was so busy searching through her files to count
the overdue books that she didn't notice a certain broad-
shouldered guy come through the door until his elbows
were on the desk and he was rearranging the bookmarks
Effie kept by the monitor.

'There you are!' she said, before she could catch herself.

'Here I am,' said Theo, amused. 'Were you waiting for
me?'

'No, absolutely not. I just meant . . .' Effie cleared her
throat. Better to course-correct and hope he forgot about it,
rather like when you ended a work call with 'love you!',
which Bonnie was notorious for, and which Effie prided
herself on never having done.

Never having done yet, a little voice in her head noted.

Shut it, little voice.

'There's something up with the overdues,' she said.

'They're out of control. I'm going to have to do a drive-around or a book amnesty if we're going to ensure everything is returned.'

'You're right, the shelves are practically bare,' drawled Theo, amused. 'So bare it's indecent.'

Effie coughed as his words conjured thoroughly inappropriate images in her mind. It was like walking into a particularly spicy edition of Bowow's romance book club.

'Indecent is a matter of perspective,' she managed finally.

'Would you like me to join you on this drive-around thing? I can be quite persuasive when I need to be.'

I bet you can, thought Effie, her mind briefly turning to a particularly memorable scene from one of the novels she'd just loaned out to Serena. A scene that if spoken aloud would absolutely result in her being stripped of her head librarian status.

'You know what? Sure,' said Effie, pretending that she hadn't already decided that he was going to be a part of all of this. 'That'd be great. There's one more thing, too, actually.'

'Wow, none of this was on the intake paperwork when I signed up for the Friends of the Library.'

'Well, no one's ever made a donation like you have before. I have to assume that anyone who lends that degree of financial support wants to be involved. Come on.'

Effie led Theo over to the small downstairs conference room used for craft sessions and Bowow's Read to Dogs story-time sessions. She switched on the striped schoolhouse light that overhung the space, illuminating the row of signs propped up against the back wall.

Well, not signs, really: spreads from a book, each enlarged and displayed individually on its own thick plastic backing – and with a clear protective plastic front for when they were eventually installed outside.

'*Frogs Are My Faves!*' Theo exclaimed, making his way from sign to sign and marvelling at the vibrant crayon art and handwritten text. 'Wow, you got this done fast.'

Effie nodded, beaming. 'Tessa and Alana stayed back after craft night, and we went through all the yearbook records until they found someone called Elana C, then combed through the phone book. Well not the phone book. Google. And Tessa did the calling. That's more her thing than mine.'

Theo chuckled. 'But I've heard you read during story time. I wouldn't mind picking up a call from you at all.'

Effie pretended to regard a particularly excellent frog illustration. 'I'd have to get your phone number first.'

'I'm honestly astonished you haven't asked.'

'I'm astonished I should have to ask,' said Effie, with a boldness that surprised her.

'Touché,' said Theo. He gestured for her phone, then typed in his number. 'Now you have no excuse.'

Effie felt her cheeks flush as she took back the phone, even if her heart flip-flopped slightly as she saw the area code that preceded his number. The area code for the city, not the town, and a reminder that he could step back out of her life at any moment.

A text from Tessa popped up, but she muted it. *Not now, Tessa.* Effie needed to focus.

'Anyway, it turns out that our author lives a few towns over these days,' she said finally. 'She gave us permission to use the story, and offered to donate her licensing fee to a local tortoise society.'

'She moved on from frogs, huh?' Theo tutted.

'Well, not *that* far on. And surely it's better to kiss a tortoise than a frog prince.'

'I'll have to take your word for that.' Theo gave her an assessing look. 'Well, I guess I'd better add a detour to the hardware store to my to-do list, because I'm going to install these along the StoryWalk trail myself.'

'I think there's an ordinance against that,' said Effie. 'We'll get someone licensed and bonded to do it. And also less clumsy.'

'I have to have *some* flaws.' Theo cocked his head. 'But there's no law against me doing the overdues drive-around, right?'

There probably was some sort of potential liability issue, actually. Although she'd been going to invite Tessa, so she was flouting that law anyway. But Tessa surely wouldn't mind sitting this one out, not just this once.

'We should do a launch or something,' said Theo decisively. 'A ribbon-cutting for the StoryWalk. We could invite everyone. Maybe your sister could help with refreshments, or an after-party.'

'Perhaps,' said Effie diffidently. Ribbon-cuttings weren't exactly her thing, although it never hurt to get eyes on the library. Eyeballs meant funding, and funding meant more programs to help serve the community. But she didn't particularly like the idea of bringing Bonnie into her library activities. The library was her one refuge from her sister's larger-than-life presence.

She'd figure it out. But first, she was going to write up an email blast letting everyone know about the new door-to-door overdues retrieval campaign. She'd have to do it tonight, because she was off tomorrow for Mom's memorial.

'Effie,' said Theo, momentarily. His green eyes met hers, making her feel shy. Shy, but also . . . powerful. 'Before you change the topic back to library business, I'm going to ask you something right out, if I may. Would you like to go on a date with me?'

Effie almost said no out of sheer force of habit. After all, she'd been the invisible sister for so long, and the times when she hadn't been weren't particularly ones she wanted to relive. But Theo was kind, and interesting, and he made her laugh. And even if he might not stay in town for ever, he was here *now*, and she wanted to spend some of that time with him.

'I would like that,' she said at last, trying, but absolutely failing, to hide an accompanying grin.

Chapter 24

A GATHERING OF MAGIC

Bonnie

Late. She was late. And while Bonnie enjoyed the attention and awe that came with being fashionably late, there were certain things even she didn't want to be late to. Like the one-year memorial of Mom's death that Effie had circled on the calendar in the kitchen. Which she should be at right now. But she'd spent the morning trying to help a patron who'd fallen asleep in the patio hammock the previous night find their way home – they must have been a tourist, because apparently, they had no idea where they lived – while dealing with calls about no fewer than five lost wallets.

Bonnie floored the Cadillac, pulling out from her dedicated parking spot behind The Silver Slipper with a roar that made Paige at Girl with a Curl poke her head out the door, checking whether the Moody boys in their lifted truck were at it again.

'Just me, Paige,' Bonnie muttered, waving as she hurtled through the quiet square, rolling through the stop sign that led to the town's main thoroughfare. To her right, something flashed silver, and she was vaguely aware of movement in front of her car. The car jolted as she slammed on the brakes. Hands pressed against the hood of the car as a scooter rider braced against the car, pushing himself backwards and out of the way.

Bonnie put the car in park and jumped out. Under the car was one of those annoying rental scooters that jammed up the square and the college, and which no one ever put back in the racks. Well, except for Effie, who did so quietly with magic under the cover of night. And Bobby, but Bobby hadn't been by much these days. The last time she'd seen him, he'd been walking hand in hand with Kirsty with what looked like a telescope slung over his shoulder. Bonnie had crossed the street to avoid them.

Oh shit. It was Bobby's little brother, Kevvie.

'Are you okay, Kevvie?' Bonnie went to grab his shoulder, but decided against it, checking him over for injuries from afar. She couldn't see any scrapes or bruises, although he was breathing hard.

Kevvie nodded – he seemed fine, just shaken.

'I'm so sorry. I didn't see you there. Forgive me?' She offered him the fist bump that she knew was the standard of communication between Kevvie and his friends.

Kevvie bumped her fist and stooped down to pull the scooter out from under the car. 'All good, Bonnie. Although the scooter's having a bad time.'

Bonnie grimaced. She wasn't sure what the proper course of action was to repair one of the communal scooters. She supposed she'd have to call the phone number emblazoned on the side, but later. She had to get to the cemetery.

'It'll survive,' she promised. Then she hesitated. 'Hey, how's Bobby doing lately?'

Kevvie made a face. 'He's been so weird. And Kirsty is always over. She keeps asking me to be in her videos, too. I always thought you were way better. Why did you stop hanging out?'

Bonnie wished Kevvie was still small enough that she could brush that cowlick of hair away from his cute little face. But those days were long gone.

'It's complicated,' said Bonnie. 'I still care about your brother, though, I promise. But I really have to go. You sure you're okay? Do you need me to take you to the doctor?'

Kevvie snorted. 'I've done way worse on my skateboard. You should know, with Effie on her skates and all.'

How come everyone in town other than Bonnie had seen the mysterious skating Effie? When had the sisters become so separate?

'I'm just glad you're okay,' she said, pushing all thoughts of Effie out of her head. 'And that I finally clobbered one of those annoying scooters.'

'They're the worst,' agreed Kevvie. 'But I snapped my skateboard the other day, so.' He shrugged.

Bonnie dumped the scooter on the sidewalk and went to hop back in the car. But a swirl of red and blue lit up the street. Officer Brigsley, the town's police officer. They'd become quite well acquainted through Bonnie's shenanigans over the years.

'Hi, Terry,' she said, flashing her biggest smile and crinkling her eyes. 'All good, just a mistiming. I was on my way to the cemetery for my mom. Grief plays funny tricks on your peripheral vision.'

'You rolled through the stop sign,' Terry pointed out. His mouth turned down at the corners, signalling a very specific dad kind of disappointment.

'Barely,' she said. 'I was going, like, fifteen. Kevvie was cruising faster than I was.'

Terry shook his head. 'Maybe, but I can't let this one slide, Bon. I'm sorry. It's a blind intersection. Anything could've happened.'

'But Kevvie's fine,' she protested. 'No one got hurt.'

'Because you got lucky,' said Officer Brigsley. 'Next time, you might not be so charmed.'

Charmed, thought Bonnie darkly as he wrote out a ticket. Apparently the Chalmers family luck only applied to one sister at a time, and this time for once it wasn't her. No, Bonnie was breaking her back trying to keep the rowdy bar patrons in line, whip up commercial quantities of Oswald's magical cocktails, and pay for the new electrical box, while Effie sat around at the library reading books, eating cupcakes and complaining about Bonnie using up all of the hot water. Bonnie deserved those showers! She needed them to get the tension out of her shoulders, because unlike Effie, she couldn't cast a spell to get the knots out.

Needless to say, by the time Bonnie arrived at the cemetery, she was in a sour mood.

'Nice of you to stop by,' said Effie drily.

It was all Bonnie could do not to shove her into the duck pond.

Instead, she turned towards the vast weeping willow that marked Mom's resting place, its leafy boughs lush and laden with memories and dreams. The tree calmed Bonnie. It made her feel like Mom was still there, watching over them, her spirit twining through the branches and streaming foliage, reaching down to hug them in the only way she still could.

This had been a special spot for the trio long before Mom's death. The three of them would come here for picnics under the tranquil shade of the giant tree, basking in the dappled light it cast. They'd share all the stories they could remember of the people buried around them, doing their bit to keep their memories alive. So it had seemed fitting to make this Mom's own place, to have endless reasons to return and continue the tradition.

Fitting, but not easy. They'd managed a few quiet picnics together in the year since Mom's death, occasionally with Tessa or Sabine joining them. But the gaps between each gathering were growing. Effie was better about coming than Bonnie, although not because Bonnie didn't care. Quite the opposite. Bonnie hurt so much at the loss of Mom that being this close to her was unbearable. Worse than that was how these visits brought out something dark in her. A resentment at Mom for leaving them, at all the moments and milestones they'd never share, at how *alone* she was when she was barely an adult. Effie at least had been guided into adulthood by Mom, had had someone beside her to help her become who she was. But Bonnie? She'd barely made it into her twenties before Mom's diagnosis and the vanishingly small distance between that and what came after.

Where had the magic been then? Why hadn't the special talent the Chalmers women shared been able to save her? Why had Mom accepted so easily the words of doctors and the hand of fate? Oswald had hinted that there might have been another path, and maybe he'd been right. They should have at least tried.

Bonnie clenched her fists, the purple sparkle of her magic crackling around her wrists.

Seeing Bonnie's anguished, empty hands, Effie passed her one of the small wildflower bouquets arranged in the effusive style of Flora from A Pocket Full of Posies.

'Here, I brought two.'

Of course she'd brought two. Of *course* she'd assumed that Bonnie would arrive empty-handed.

Bonnie wanted to snap at her sister that she hadn't forgotten. She'd meant to stop off for a bouquet of her own but fate and circumstance were conspiring against her today. But she didn't want to fight with her sister in front of Mom's resting place. She didn't need dark energy polluting the beautiful willow tree and the serene space it offered.

'Thanks,' Bonnie said, trying to keep her voice level. Maybe Effie was just looking out for her.

'They had a buy one, get one free,' said Effie. 'I figured Mom wouldn't mind.'

Bonnie frowned. 'I'm surprised Sabine isn't here yet. She said she was coming.'

Effie checked her watch. She still pointedly wore one, even in a world where cell phones existed. An analogue watch as well, as though she was making a statement about other people's ability to read analogue time. 'Sabine's never late. She's early, even by my standards.'

As much as it pained Bonnie to admit, Effie had a point. Like Hannah, Sabine was chronically, frustratingly early. She was the kind of person who'd show up fifteen minutes early to a coffee date, or who'd get Taylor Swift tickets within seconds, or who'd be at the front of the line at The Golden Hour Bakery when they announced a new pastry.

'Maybe she got into an accident with one of those scooters in the square,' said Bonnie. 'Traffic's chaotic today.'

Effie cocked her head. 'That's oddly specific. Maybe it just slipped her mind.'

'I doubt it. I saw her the other day at the bar. We talked about it then.'

'Ah, of course, at the bar,' said Effie stiffly. She adjusted her glasses, then added, 'I would've stopped by to see her if I'd known.'

Effie, wanting to come to the bar? Had she been bopped on the head?

Bonnie fiddled with the bouquet Effie had given her, thinking it could do with a touch more colour and character. 'I thought you hated the bar.'

'Obviously it's not my preferred scene. But I'm not entirely a hermit. I'm perfectly willing to stop by if it means seeing someone I care about. Like Sabine.'

'Well, I'll let you know next time. Promise.'

'All right,' said Effie, even though saying so seemed like it hurt.

'You should come to the next Trivia Night, perhaps,' offered Bonnie, trying to assuage her guilt. 'It's not far off. And someone needs to keep Winston and Gerald in their place. I mentioned it to Tessa the other day, actually. I'm surprised she didn't pass it along.'

Effie frowned. 'Tessa came by as well?'

Hmm. Interesting that Tessa hadn't mentioned it to Effie. Bonnie had thought they shared everything.

'She was looking cute,' offered Bonnie. 'I think she was meeting someone, but she was a bit coy about it.'

She waited to see whether Effie would dish any gossip, but of course not.

'Speaking of meeting someone,' muttered Effie, a look of disdain flitting over her face. Not that this look was *so* different from her usual expression. 'Look who it is.'

Uncle Oswald's cane clacked as he came up, in full fusty magician-wannabe regalia, clutching a fistful of lilies in his free hand. Mom had always warned about lilies, which were deadly to cats and had an energy that scared her.

'Well, if it isn't my magical nieces,' Uncle Oswald said, adjusting his waistcoat and straightening his paisley bow tie. 'You're both looking beautiful as usual. Even on such a sad day as this.' He didn't seem especially sorrowful, for he immediately added, 'I went by your bar, Bonnie, but that new bartender of yours told me you were down here. How about we head back up together when we're done showing our respects to my loving sister?'

'Um, sure,' said Bonnie, feeling suddenly off-kilter. Was he checking up on her? And if so, why?

'Which reminds me,' went on Oswald, 'her loopy friend from the hotel – Sabine, that's it – stopped into the shop the other day. She shopped up quite the storm as well. Excellent job on that, Bonnie.'

Effie raised an eyebrow that could do with some threading.

'I, um, recommended some of Oswald's crystals,' Bonnie told Effie, hoping that her sister wouldn't press her any further on this. She was absolutely not about to explain the specifics of the business arrangement. Certainly not with Oswald leaning over her in his trademark slimy, leery fashion.

'Oh, here's Sabine,' said Bonnie, relieved. She waved as Sabine made her way over, all flowing skirts and dangly earrings – and a new bracelet that gleamed with crystals.

'I'm so sorry,' said Sabine as she joined the group, sounding slightly out of breath. She embraced the sisters in turn, then gave Oswald a quick hug. 'My head's just full of fog today. Just a touch of hay fever, I'm sure, but I'm all out of sorts. Shall we get started?'

Chapter 25

THE WITCHING HOUR

Effie

Mom's memorial had unsettled Effie in a way she hadn't expected. Both Bonnie and Sabine being late had carried a particular weight, and Effie could feel it hanging from her shoulders for the rest of the day. She'd even pulled out her diary for the first time in a year, preparing to get her feelings out in the only way that made sense to her. *Weird*, she thought. *Had that crease in the spine always been there?*

As she wrote, she understood why Theo had such a soft spot for poetry. Words could hold deep, precious meanings in ways the human body wasn't built to. After jotting away for a half-hour or so, she realized what she'd been trying to convey. That Bonnie's and Sabine's late arrivals had made her feel as though she alone was responsible for keeping the memory of Mom alive.

She considered dropping into The Silver Slipper for a glass of wine. Bonnie had invited her, after all. And as much as her sister vexed her, Mom's memorial had reminded her that the two of them shared a bond that no one else could ever come close to. But the thought of braving the busy bar while Bonnie was working was too daunting. What if she had to make small talk with drunk college kids? Or got drawn into a darts game?

She considered texting Tessa, but her friend was on a craft deadline for an upcoming market. Although she'd still made time to visit Bonnie, apparently. There was Theo, but was it too early in their . . . whatever this was to show up at his door in her present fretful state? He'd seen enough of Effie's neuroses on display already, and she didn't want to send him racing back to the city with tales of the strange librarians who inhabited the countryside. At least not before their upcoming library date.

No, she'd just do what she had as a kid. Climb into her reading chair and read until her eyelids were heavy and the book ended up draped over her slumbering face.

This was precisely what she did. But a book only offered so much protection against the world and it wasn't long until her dreams turned sour from the anxiety of the day. Nightmarish images of Mom sinking into the ground, of Uncle Oswald and Bonnie laughing together, of the purple and brown portraits that hung in Bonnie's bar swirled together into a foul, muddy colour, then coming at her in a stream of magic with a howling face.

Effie jerked awake, her heart pounding so fast that it barely had a rhythm. She tried to grab on to the beat, but it galloped away. Sitting up, she focused on her breathing, calming herself, seeking out those moments of peace that for now lay out of reach. The part where the nearby trail turned off slightly, leading to a trickling waterfall in a basin of ferns and soaring trees. Sitting on the front porch licking the beaters from the bright red KitchenAid after baking with Mom.

A younger Effie might have asked Mom to perform the special nightmare spell that had always worked on Bonnie, the one that had involved them speaking certain memories aloud as a way of erasing the memory of the nightmare. Bonnie's night terrors were the rare time that Mom allowed magic to be used on another person, and that she'd involved a non-magical person in the spell – Bobby. But this was no longer then, and Effie couldn't ask that of anyone. She'd have to find her own way through.

Finally, Effie's body started to relax, her heart slowing as her breathing deepened. She felt human again, rather than a set of screaming electrical impulses. Or, perhaps, a ball of uncontrolled magic. For that was her fear: that her magic would escape and run riot, become unpredictable, just like Bonnie's.

Effie snuggled up against her pillow, the thick one she turned sideways and spooned when she needed the comfort. Bonnie had always teased her about it – *why not make it a real someone?* But the pillow didn't demand anything of Effie and it certainly didn't judge her for her preferred choice of pyjamas. These consisted of one of the oversized button-down shirts Mom had used as a smock while painting and a pair of ratty sweats that had seen better days. And years.

Trying to will herself back to sleep, Effie played her usual game of picking a letter of the alphabet and trying to run through as many words starting with it as she could. At intervals, when she got stuck, she'd squint at the wall clock, which was at that frustrating in-between time where it was too late to go back to sleep, but too early to get up. Not the witching hour, of course. In Effie's mind, the witching hour was one of power and strength. This, *this* was a deeply human hour.

Ugh. Effie turned on her night light to read for a few minutes before sleep beckoned again, but the words simply weren't going in. Every sentence was punctuated with visions of Theo's charming smile, or of the discomfort she'd felt learning that Bonnie had sent Sabine over to Oswald's. Or, worst of all, of the ever-fading image of Mom. Effie's greatest fear was forgetting Mom, and it was happening, day by day. She still had countless photos and videos on her phone, but they never captured the whole person. There was less tethering Mom's memory to the world. The letters and junk mail had stopped coming, and the family friends came by less often, talking for shorter durations and with less passion and care. If Effie called Mom's phone, the familiar voicemail greeting no longer warmed the line. Instead, a robotic voice told her the number was no longer available. One day, it would be recycled, and a whole new person would take it on, and Effie's calls would be sent to spam.

Effie was hot now, and panicky.

First the nightmare, then the heart palpitations, and now that prickly feeling of anxiety. This is how nights like this always went. She'd be frantic and out of sorts until she gave up and climbed into Mom's bed. But Mom's bed was cold, and the only other option was Bonnie. Who was probably sleeping at the bar, anyway. And if she wasn't, she'd hardly appreciate being woken up. She was famously like a bear that way.

But Effie had to get up and moving before anxiety devoured her. Cool air. That always helped.

It was dark out, although the moon sailed high amid the pointed stars, guiding the way. Effie hesitated, then laced up her roller skates and buckled her helmet. There'd be few souls around to see her slithering around off balance. And anyone who did was probably in a particular state that meant they'd barely register it anyway.

Mindful of the areas of the path that angled up from the aged, sprawling tree roots of the enormous oaks that knitted the street together, Effie skated off the narrow pavement and onto the wide, empty road. The breeze cut at her skin, sloughing away her nightmare and scrubbing her of the anxiety that had been prickling under her skin since she'd woken. She cruised down the street, ducking through the yellow hugs of the street lamps, counting the porch lights that remained on and the interior lights here and there that signalled either someone was up, or they wanted the world to think as much. Theo's house was dark, she noticed, with a pang of regret. Although even if his light *were* on, she'd hardly go banging on his door to see what he was up to. At least, probably not.

So distracted was she by what Theo was up to that she almost tripped on a divot in the road. She righted herself with a quick burst of magic that fought the good fight against gravity. Effie had never broken a bone, and she didn't plan to start now. Not with the health insurance plan the library offered, anyway. She'd be better off buying some trinkets from Uncle Oswald's and crossing her fingers.

As Effie found her footing, she could've sworn she saw a curtain in Theo's house twitch. Surely not. That was just her anxiety talking. Or perhaps a ghost. A ghost was better than the alternative, which was that Theo had climbed out of bed for a glass of water just in time to see the green sparks of her magic lighting up the night. She'd have to put in a call to the local paper complaining about kids lighting off fireworks, the way Bonnie did on the occasions where her wayward magic had caused fires, electrical blackouts, and worse, bad hair.

Effie skated on, drinking in the picturesque town and the way it slumbered under the spell of night. She loved Yellowbrick Grove, mostly. It was home, and all her memories of Mom were here. All right, so the townsfolk could be a tad closed-minded, and the way everyone followed Bonnie as though she were the Pied Piper of Popularity certainly landed a particular way. But there was the library, the coffee shop, the tiny college, the beautiful parks with their rose gardens and hedges and verdigris-tinted sculptures. And the people: sweet Tessa, bossy Bowow, tough-guy Bruce, generous Sabine, and the always cheerful Bobby. And Theo. If the tiny town was good enough for someone from the city, then it was enough for Effie. She just had to find her way through, even if Mom wasn't there to guide her.

Effie made a slow loop around the town, trying to take in the quietude and draw the stillness of the night into herself to quell the anxiety that wouldn't settle after her nightmare.

She skated past the local landmarks: the belltower was all that stood of the church that had burned down a decade before after votive candles and pigeon nests had come together to cause a terrible (but memorable) conflagration. The Wall of Moss by the old theatre. The huge oak that soared over the garden park not far from the library, which all three of the Chalmers women had chalked their initials on over and over with every visit – Mom had made them promise never to etch their initials into a tree, for doing so caused a rift between you and its spirit.

They'd stuck with chalk, although Bonnie had famously made her mark on various bits of wet cement over the years, and there was a patch of graffiti on one of the underpasses that Effie had her suspicions about as well.

The night remained quiet. It was just Effie and the nocturnal animal denizens out and about now. A possum's eyes glowed, regarding her from the safety of an azalea bush as she skated past; a thatch of raccoons paused their looting of a dumpster; an owl gave a staccato serenade to the moon. It was hard not to be mesmerized by it all, by the spell that the dark cast over the town, like they were all Sleeping Beauty under the magic of the stars.

Everything in its own way was magic.

Her anxiety slowly gave way to the different kind of heart-pounding that came with physical exertion. She started to retrace her steps – glides, perhaps – continuing her loop back towards the stately family home that Effie was determined to hang on to, no matter how much of the wiring needed to be replaced or the plumbing redone, and no matter how much Effie's librarian salary did not stretch that far. Hopefully her patchwork of hexes and charms (and Bonnie's help with the electrical box) would stave off the worst of it for now.

Ah, the familiar Yellowbrick Grove of Garden Perfection sign that meant she was a few scoots from home. But as Effie got closer, she frowned. Something was amiss with the house,

which was known for its dramatic floral displays (Freddie
had spent countless hours in the library researching how to
achieve pH neutral soil conditions). And, of course, its lush,
rolling lawn, which had somehow been kept safe from moles
and gophers, something she considered Freddie's own
particular brand of magic.

Effie pulled up on her roller skates, albeit not very well.
She had to grab the fence to stop from falling over. Although
even if she'd been wearing regular shoes, she might still have
toppled over in shock. For Freddie's magnificent, putting-
green-worthy lawn was . . . ragged. There were yellowy bits
like a dog had been peeing all over it with a vengeance. (Effie
had learned from Freddie's library expeditions about the high
nitrogen levels in dog urine, which could alter lawn pH levels
and kill grass. This was the primary reason that Freddie was
an indoor-pet kind of guy.)

And it wasn't just the lawn that was in sorry shape. The
shrubs were unkempt, the pretty pansies were dehydrated,
and the usually voluminous hydrangea bushes looked like
they were hanging on for dear life. Moreover, was that a
weed?

Effie tried to think when she'd last seen Freddie. She had
bumped into him at the supermarket a few days earlier, and
he'd seemed well enough. They'd laughed over how he
couldn't remember where he'd parked his car, and that every
car these days was a silver SUV. Effie had told him he needed
a golf cart, or a membership to the rental scooter company.
Besides, Freddie was only sixty or so, and extremely spry
from all that gardening.

A light was on inside, so presumably he was up. Would it
be wrong to go and check on him?

Effie steeled herself. Introverted as she was, she couldn't
abide the thought of bypassing someone who needed her help.
She swung open the perfectly balanced gate – much smoother
than the one at the Chalmers house, which had seen better

days and sagged like the ultra-comfy bra Effie couldn't bring herself to throw out.

Pulling her sleeve down over her wrist, she knocked lightly, hoping that would be less startling than ringing the doorbell in the middle of the night.

'Hello?' she called. 'Freddie?'

Relief as she heard some shuffling and scuffling about inside. Freddie was alive at least. Although now she felt a bit silly, banging on someone's door to do a welfare check when they were probably just up watching *Golden Girls* reruns. She waved awkwardly as she saw a shadow pass over the peephole on the door.

'Hi,' she called, trying to look unassuming and not like a weird stalker as Freddie opened the door. 'It's just me.'

'Who are you?' he asked, looking judgementally down at her roller skates.

Effie stammered. This wasn't the greeting she'd been expecting. 'Effie. Effie Chalmers. I live a few houses down.' And then, because it tended to help people place her, 'Bonnie's sister.'

'Oh, right,' said Freddie, in a tone that didn't sound any less confused. 'Well, that's good to know.'

'So, you're okay?' she pressed, giving him a once-over to make sure he wasn't sporting a head wound or something that might indicate why he'd suddenly let his beloved lawn quite literally go to seed. She sniffed. No gas leak that she could smell. Although it could be carbon monoxide, which was unfortunately odourless.

Freddie squinted at her. 'Why wouldn't I be? Are *you* okay? You're the one coming to my door in the middle of the night. Is someone chasing you? Do you need me to help you get home?'

Effie shook her head. 'Everything's fine. Nothing to worry about. Sorry to bother you.'

As Effie carefully made her way back down the front steps,

she couldn't shake the feeling that something odd was going on in the town. Sabine's tardiness, Freddie's lawn, Bobby's shift in allegiance from Bonnie to Kirsty – it all felt so strange. Was Effie just being hypercritical and overly set in her ways, the way Bonnie always said, or was something else at play?

Chapter 26

IT'S FEELING A LITTLE CAULDRON IN HERE

Bonnie

With a yawn, Bonnie stepped back to admire the display she'd put together for Iris's birthday party. She'd woken up multiple times throughout the night, convinced she'd heard the front door bang, although the only explanation for that was that Effie had snuck out, which was impossible. Whatever the cause of the wake-ups, there was not enough coffee in the world. This was evidenced by the three empty takeaway cups from The Winged Monkey that sat on the trestle table, amid the dips and snacks she'd carefully arranged, and pre-mixed pitchers of Memory Lane-infused cocktails, which Iris had personally insisted upon. Fuelled by three double-shot caramel lattes, Bonnie had draped, arranged and constructed with an intensity that rivalled Hannah's wedding-planner mom.

Fairy lights twinkled all along the back wall, and balloons wafted gently in the breeze from the pedestal fan that kept the air moving around. She'd even brought in a photo booth for good measure. Next to it sat a huge box of props, and in a rare win, the Bluetooth speaker was working. Love it as she did, the device was usually only good for picking up Bruce Dickens' Saturday evening radio show, whose 80s hits Bonnie would never admit had helped her through a ton of cram sessions during high school and the few semesters of college she'd managed. Currently it blasted a solidly boppy

Bonnie-crafted playlist of 90s and early 00s pop, and Bonnie was mouthing along to Britney Spears.

The only thing that wasn't quite right was how empty the room was. Surely *someone* would've peeked their head in by now? If not the guest of honour, then one of her friends, or a date, or a mom.

Bonnie checked the time on her phone. Weird. All right, so being fashionably late was something she personally approved of. In fact, it was a vital part of the Bonnie make-'em-squirm philosophy. Maybe Iris lived her life by the same personal mantra. But she hadn't seemed like the type. She'd mentioned needing to leave early just in case there was traffic on the way to her part-time job, and traffic, frankly, did not exist in Yellowbrick Grove.

To be fair, Iris *had* booked a daytime party, which was easier on the finances than a prime-time one. It wasn't out of the realm of possibility that her college friends were still asleep.

She might as well go help Clark downstairs until the guest of honour showed up. She enjoyed working alongside the new bartender. He was affable and focused, and being in a self-described long-distance relationship with a gent in Barcelona, not desperate for her phone number either. A few weeks ago, Bonnie might have been miffed by that, but she'd been somewhat off men since the Bobby and Kirsty situation, which unsettled her in a way that she couldn't quite put her finger on. Well, she might be able to if she thought about it at length, but she didn't have the time to do that, *or* to deal with the consequences of any realizations that might come out of it.

'How's life at the college?' she asked Clark as she restocked the caddies under the bar.

'More of the same,' he said, as he sliced up citrus for garnishes. 'But apparently they're on the hunt for new poetry adjunct. The girls are swooning at the thought. And half the guys, too. Including yours truly.'

'Poetry, huh?' Bonnie chuckled. 'Unfortunately, I've been on the receiving end of too much of it to be a fan.'

'Poets are a unique breed indeed.'

The two fell into an easy rhythm as they finished their prep work and started serving the trickle of customers who came in once the doors opened. Thankfully Clark had a smoother temperament than Bonnie, because the patrons were even more scattered than usual. If Bonnie hadn't known better, she might have assumed they were already drunk. She had to give directions to the downstairs bathrooms (the signs for which were visible from the bar) no fewer than five times, reassure a woman freaking out about her lost spectacles that she was actually already wearing them, and help an older regular through the security questions on her bank account. This involved a good deal of guessing.

On the plus side, at least no one was sobbing over their palm's heart line or having a panic attack about whether they were astrologically compatible with their love interest, so at least Uncle Oswald's hexed recipe was doing what it needed to. Although Bonnie was starting to wonder whether it was doing a tad more than it needed to. Was everyone always this airy-fairy? Perhaps she was just noticing it more now that she was so busy and every little miscommunication or delay messed up her schedule.

Oh goddess, was this how Effie felt about her? No, surely not. Effie was just unreasonably grumpy.

Bonnie's phone buzzed, startling her.

The Dorothy House sold, texted Hannah. *Cash offer, over asking. Investor. Let me know when you're free to celebrate!*

Bonnie texted her back a series of celebratory emojis, although she felt conflicted about it. Happy for Hannah to receive her commission, of course, but disappointed to hear that the young family she'd liked so much had missed out on the house.

It wasn't until a full hour later that Iris, in a profusion of tulle and perfume, finally burst through the doors. Erroneously assuming she was part of the night's entertainment, the patrons burst into applause at the dramatic entrance.

'I'm here!' she called breathlessly. 'I'm so sorry I'm late, Bonnie. I forgot all about it until my mom texted me.'

Bonnie passed a beer over to a student and gave Iris a hug. 'Oh, it's fine. It happens all the time when you book a party after the actual birthday.'

Iris looked relieved. 'I suppose you're right. Everyone's not mad I left them hanging, are they?'

Bonnie cocked her head. 'Everyone?'

'Everyone up there waiting for me.'

Oh, this was going to be awkward. Because when Bonnie had come back down the stairs about half an hour ago, not a single person had been up there. And since then, she'd seen a sum total of three people head upstairs: Winston, who preferred the height of the upstairs toilet, and a former classmate of Bonnie's called Greenly, who wanted to show his boyfriend the weird paintings on the wall. All had returned and were presently sitting downstairs. Winston was musing over a stack of Jenga blocks, while Greenly was considering the various Camemberts on their cheese plate as he sipped his charmed cocktails. Greenly's boyfriend, meanwhile, was regarding the agate coaster with Uncle Oswald's details on it.

'This place looks cute,' the boyfriend was saying. 'We should get some charms and crystals and things. Don't you think a huge crystal would look amazing in that nook by the entryway? Especially if it wards off evil spirits.'

Bonnie exhaled. Given the extent of the no-shows, she'd assumed that Iris would be bringing the party with her.

'Everything okay?' pressed Iris.

Bonnie poured a glass of Memory Lane, garnishing it with a gold-dusted sprig of lavender and a handful of edible flowers. Iris was going to need it.

'Do you happen to remember if you sent out the invitations?' she asked gently.

Iris's eyes widened. She reached into her purse, drawing out a stack of cards. 'Oh no. It completely slipped my mind. No, wait.' She frowned. 'I was going to deliver them, but I had this weird brain fog. I couldn't remember anyone's addresses. I thought maybe it was a post-Covid thing or something, so I went back home and napped. And I guess I just forgot.' She grimaced. 'I don't still owe you for the room rental, do I?'

Bonnie's heart clenched. She'd spent a small fortune on the decorations and the food, and if Britney Spears sued her for failure to pay her music licensing fees, she'd be out on the street selling wildflowers to pay for a lawyer.

But Iris looked so forlorn. She'd ruined her own birthday. Or rather, thought Bonnie, *Bonnie* had ruined Iris's birthday. Because the niggling feeling she'd been having before about the townsfolk's capriciousness was growing strong. There was definitely something more to Uncle Oswald's cocktail spells than the recipe book suggested. But was it her wayward magic at fault – or something more?

'Of course I wouldn't expect you to pay,' said Bonnie, grimacing as the numbers in her bank account dwindled before her eyes. 'Unless . . .' she began. An opportunity to make things right, and profitable, was coming to her. 'Can you give me half an hour? We'll have this place rocking in no time.'

Iris's eyes widened. 'Really?'

Bonnie pulled out her phone. 'I have the phone number of every single individual who's ever stepped foot in this town. Particularly the hot guys. Just let me work my magic.'

The magic she could actually control, that is. Because when it came to social charms, no one had a patch on Bonnie Chalmers.

Bonnie was on top of the world as she cruised home after her shift. Iris's party had become quite the rager (a term Bonnie loved because it always elicited such a pained response from Effie), and although the guest list hadn't been quite what the birthday girl had originally intended, she'd rounded out the afternoon, and then the night, full of cake and smiles. Bonnie had almost decided to crash upstairs in the half-finished apartment, but after her poor night's sleep the night before, she needed a date with her own bed.

She took the long way back, the way that took her past the Dorothy House that she'd been so certain Beatrice and Todd were going to buy, and which had been snapped up instead by someone who'd never even live there.

The FOR SALE sign had been taken down, and a work truck belonging to Bronson, the town handyman, was camped out the front. Giant tubs of white paint sat on the porch, next to a stack of mass-produced canvas prints featuring geometric designs of famous cities and boxes of flat-packed furniture. Bonnie didn't have to see the pictures on the front to know exactly what they contained: cheap mid-century knockoffs with splayed pin legs and chevron wood patterning. And definitely an oversized backyard Connect Four set.

Her heart twisted as she thought about the young family who'd loved the house so much, and who'd been so keen on making an offer. They could be in here right now, putting up toys on the built-in shelves and hanging their family photos (and adding child locks and safety gates to every cupboard and doorframe). Olivia could've grown up here, and Beatrice and Todd could've grown old here. And instead, the house would most likely sit empty for most of the year, except on weekends or holidays. But at least an investor from the city was making money on it, she thought angrily.

Bonnie wondered if it was too late. If she could figure out a way to get the family into the house. Maybe she'd look into the zoning laws. Or attend a town planning meeting to protest all the short-term rentals.

But tourism traffic is essential to your business, she reminded herself.

Her business that might have had a hand in this whole thing. Because there was something going on with her drinks recipes that was doing more than just helping people forget their psychic troubles. And as much as Bonnie had been trying to convince herself otherwise since the realization had struck her this afternoon, telling herself that the townsfolk were just naturally flighty, that modernity had people scattered and torn between a million different responsibilities, whatever Uncle Oswald had set into motion was going way beyond what it said on the label.

Bonnie squared her shoulders. That was it. She'd visit him. Right now. On behalf of the family who'd missed out on their dream home. On behalf of Iris, who'd almost missed her own birthday party. On behalf of her own conscience.

She climbed into her car, getting ready to head to Behind the Curtain.

Her phone dinged. Ugh, the autopayment for her car insurance was about to go out. And the electrical at the bar. And her health insurance.

But the sinking pit in her stomach she usually felt at this time of the month didn't gnaw at her the way it usually did.

Because for the first time in the past year, she was confident that she could cover all the bills without having to check her bank balance, and more importantly, without asking Effie to spot her. There was such a relief at the thought. That low-level fear of living on the precipice at all times had ebbed.

Maybe she just needed to be more selective about who she served the drinks to, and how often. Because the townsfolk were better off overall, weren't they? Even if they were slightly more ditzy and forgetful than usual, at least they weren't sobbing over star charts or anguishing over tea leaves.

Off she cruised, trying to focus on her new-found success instead of the creeping sense that it came at a cost.

Pulling up at a stop sign – she was not about to roll through one after the incident with Kevvie the other day – she adjusted her rear-view mirror. The charm hanging from it, a gift from Uncle Oswald, gleamed and flashed as it caught the soft light of a street lamp.

Everything was fine. Sparkly and fine.

It was a mantra she repeated all the way home.

Chapter 27

HEX AND HEXABILITY

Effie

Effie couldn't believe it: she was shopping for a date.

All right, not this very second. But she would be when Tessa arrived. Meanwhile, Effie was standing in the crisp autumn sunshine outside Second-Hand Magic, the vintage shop where she and Tessa had sourced almost the entirety of their wardrobes from the age of twelve. Although Tessa was much better at upcycling her clothes with quirky embroidery and decorative patches than Effie was. Effie's clothing tended to wear her instead of the other way around.

You and I are the difference between 'worn' and 'styled', Bonnie had pointed out more than once. Effie knew it, but she wasn't about to give Bonnie the satisfaction of asking for her help.

And especially not when the situation involved a date with Theo.

A kid on a rental scooter clattered past, balancing his coffee cup on the handlebars. The shop was tucked back in one of the alleyways that meandered off from the square, close to The Winged Monkey and on the opposite side to Uncle Oswald's shop. This was a relief, as she'd been distinctly uncomfortable when Oswald had shown up at Mom's grave the other day. There was something about his energy that made her stomach churn.

'Always listen to that instinct,' Mom used to say. 'It comes from millennia of experience, all passed down from woman to woman.'

But Bonnie seemed to be spending quite a bit of time with Oswald these days. From what Effie had gleaned, they had some sort of business arrangement going on, although Bonnie had been coy about the details. Maybe it was some sort of Chamber of Commerce initiative where businesses encouraged cross-traffic with punch cards and treasure maps. Bonnie *did* love a punch card.

Here came Tessa, hurrying down the alleyway in a swish of loose fabrics and flying curls. Her boots splashed through some of the residual puddles that lingered after the overnight rain, speckling the decorative pumpkins and foliage arrangements out the front of the little shops.

'Sorry.' She was clearly bursting with news she was dying to share. 'I was looking at a space for a possible shop.'

Effie raised an eyebrow. 'Sounds promising. Do tell.'

'Soon. I don't want to curse it.' Tessa zipped her lips. 'Still, it's not as important as helping you find something to wear for your date.'

'It's not a date,' lied Effie.

'Your not-a-date,' agreed Tessa, eyes twinkling behind her glasses.

Effie had downplayed the night to her friend, worried that it was going to end as disastrously as the handful of dates she'd attempted in the past. It wasn't Tessa's judgement that she worried about so much. It was more Bonnie's. But Tessa had been hanging out at Bonnie's bar, and Bonnie had a supernatural ability to coax gossip from people. Effie didn't want to risk it.

The motion-sensor crow by the door cawed as they entered. Dierdre, the owner, waved at them from behind her magazine, which today wasn't her usual horoscope super-edition, but rather a celebrity gossip rag. Odd. Effie had only ever known Dierdre to read New Age magazines. The shop music that piped through the hidden speakers was different, too. Usually it was Yanni on repeat, but today she was listening to a pop radio station. Effie pretended not to recognize the Ariana Grande song playing as Tessa mouthed along.

Perhaps Dierdre was going through something. A breakup. A TV show binge cut short by the streaming platform abruptly removing said show. Or maybe one of her horoscopes had told her a change was coming.

'Let me know if you need any help,' Dierdre called, although it was purely a nicety. She wasn't one of those shop owners who followed you around until you bought something. When it came to the hard sell, she was the opposite of Uncle Oswald.

'So, we're looking for a sexy number for a hot night in at the library, no?' Tessa raised an eyebrow as Effie flicked through the colour-coded shirts on the rack, pretending to consider a striped number.

'We are absolutely not,' Effie protested. She held up a slouchy burnt orange cardigan with an interesting knitted pattern. 'How about this?'

'I hate to sound like Bonnie, but you should be ashamed.'

Effie waved a shirt that said *I Brake for Huts on Fowl's Legs*. 'This one?'

'Too niche,' said Tessa, regarding a silvery belt studded with Medusa heads. 'And definitely too Baba Yaga.'

Effie groaned. 'I have no idea what I'm doing. I'm not used to someone being interested in me. It's disconcerting.'

'It's about time, if you ask me,' said Tessa, with a grin.

Effie balked at a hat that had Uncle Oswald vibes. She hid it under a Stetson. 'You know as well as I do that the only action I ever saw was when everyone was worried about failing their SATs and used me to help them cram.'

'At least you got a lot of chocolates and roses out of it.'

'I know my worth. How about these?' Effie held up a pair of high-waisted dark green slacks. 'With a T-shirt.'

'Actually, the slacks aren't bad. But you're not doing a T-shirt. Promise me. Swear to me. Aha!' Tessa pulled out a sparkly high-necked shirt that looked extremely sheer and extremely fitted.

Effie shook her head. 'That's a Bonnie shirt.'

'Bonnie doesn't have an exclusive claim over sparkles. Trust me. Off you go.'

She pointed Effie in the direction of the changing room.

Effie obediently pulled aside the curtain, shimmying into the outfit as Tessa wandered around outside, sifting through the dresses and coats. Tessa never tried anything on: she had a knack for knowing at a glance what would work on her. And it was never things you'd expect. No matter the garbage bag-ness of a jacket or uneven hem of a skirt, it all worked on Tessa.

But Effie, well, it wasn't like there was anything *wrong* with her, she thought, as she regarded herself in the mirror. She and Bonnie were a similar height and similar build. But that was where the similarity ended. Bonnie was simply imbued with the magic of charisma, which had somehow bypassed Effie entirely.

Averting her gaze, Effie dragged on the outfit, wondering how it could look so good on the rack and so *awful* on her.

Oh shit, she'd knocked over a crystal in the corner. She picked it up, frowning. It was one of Uncle Oswald's. Strange. She couldn't imagine Dierdre darkening the door of Behind the Curtain. She had so much of her own spiritual knowledge. Why double down on Oswald's cheap trinkets?

'How's it going in there?' asked Tessa.

Ah, the moment of truth.

Effie pulled back the curtain, standing awkwardly on her tiptoes so that the slacks wouldn't drag on the floor.

'Here.' Tessa pounced, twisting and tweaking, pulling the sleeves this way and the waistband that. Then she came at Effie with a thin belt and some shimmery gold earrings.

Effie blinked. Tessa had worked her magic on the outfit. Before, it had hung inelegantly and sat awkwardly. Now, it skimmed her frame perfectly, the fabric flowing as she walked. And the cut of the shirt was perfect.

'Glamorous,' said Dierdre, with a wink. 'Can I ring it up?'

'You definitely can.' A delighted Effie smiled.

'So, what does the zodiac have for us this week?' she asked as she waited to pay at the register.

Dierdre looked up from folding Effie's new clothes. 'Huh? Oh, I gave all that up a few weeks ago. Never looked back.'

'Wow, really?' Tessa set a huge patchwork coat down on the counter. 'But you've been the town's horoscope guru ever since I can remember.'

'Too much hassle. Besides, they never had anything nice to say about Capricorns.'

'Fair,' said Tessa, although Effie thought she heard a touch of suspicion in her friend's voice. But why? It was good that the townsfolk were moving on from their bizarre superstitions and fascinations. It never hurt to be grounded in the real world.

'Nice to meet you both,' said Dierdre, with a wave. 'I hope you come in again.'

'I'm sure we will,' said Effie, slipping her new outfit into her ever-present tote bag.

As they emerged from the shop, Tessa folded her arms. She frowned as she peered in the window of Second-Hand Magic, like she was weighing something up.

'Don't you think that was weird?' she asked. 'The whole one-eighty on the horoscopes, and then acting like she didn't know us? We come in at least once a month.'

Effie shrugged. In her experience, the townsfolk were always weird and scattered. 'Maybe she misspoke. Like when you say "you too" when the ticket registrar says they hope you enjoy the concert. She'll probably be kicking herself about it for weeks. I would be.'

'Hmm,' said Tessa.

Uh-oh. A *hmm* from Tessa meant that this was not the last Effie would be hearing of this. But Effie had a not-date at the library to prepare for. Which was going to involve a lot of educational videos and some careful raiding of Bonnie's makeup drawer. And maybe even the hair curler.

Effie adored the peace and calm of the library at night. Not to mention the sweeping views it had of the town's glimmering lights. And best of all, there was absolutely no risk of Bonnie sauntering in to judge Effie for her hair, or her outfit, or her Saturday night schedule. Besides, this Saturday, she actually *had* something in her schedule. All right, so it was work-adjacent, but it did involve another human being, and in a rare event, one who wasn't Tessa. It also, thought Effie as she dimmed the schoolhouse light fixtures, involved mood lighting.

The doorbell by the circulation desk chimed, and Effie looked up to see Theo waving from the front door, a bouquet of paper flowers in his hand. A reusable shopping bag sat at his feet.

Straightening her outfit the way Tessa had shown her, Effie went over to let him in.

'Security's tight on this place after hours,' said Theo. Then he paused. 'Wow, you look gorgeous.'

Effie swallowed as she tried to come up with a confident Bonnie-style response. She knew she didn't look terrible, because she'd styled her hair and put on a coat of mascara and a dash of rouge. And even a soft-blur lipstick, which was about as close as she could get to a red lip without racing to the bathroom sink to wipe it off. But *gorgeous* was an intimidatingly effusive compliment.

'Thanks,' she said finally. 'You too.'

And he did, in his neat pants and the merino cardigan he wore over a simple T-shirt. (Maybe Tessa had been right to guide Effie away from the cardigans earlier, or they might have looked like twins.)

'I brought you these,' he said, passing her the paper bouquet, which she saw was crafted from book pages. 'Don't worry, the pages are from weeded books. That retired teacher showed me how to make them.'

Deeply aware of his presence, Effie led Theo over to one of the empty reading tables, where she'd set up a simple platter of snacks and baked goods.

'From The Golden Hour?' he asked, perusing the spread.

'Home-made,' she said shyly.

'You *are* a woman of many talents,' said Theo. 'Mine's store-bought. I hope you don't mind.'

He plonked the shopping bag on the table, pulling out a bottle of Argentinian malbec, and a wide-ranging array of dips and pita.

'Tonight, we feast,' he said with a chuckle. He uncorked the wine, then frowned. 'Damn, I forgot the cups. Do you have anything?'

Effie held up a finger and went off to the kitchen area, using her magic to quickly send two mugs flying across the room and into her waiting hands. Alas, this type of catching finesse only extended to her own spells and not sports, or else she'd have enjoyed a full-ride scholarship to an Ivy playing Division-I sports.

'"People Displeaser", huh?' Theo turned the purple mug in his hands as he filled it with wine.

'I aim to displease.' Effie took the mug and made a cheers with it.

She'd just realized what was on the mug she'd handed to Theo: *Yes, I'm a librarian, and I'm checking you out.*

The mug had been a joint gift from Mom and Bonnie for Effie's birthday two years earlier. The two had thought it hilarious, and Effie had too, honestly. It was impossible to feel churlish when Mom was around. Even her teasing was good-natured.

Effie felt a pang. She couldn't imagine Bonnie giving her such a gift now.

'I didn't realize you librarians were so saucy,' said Theo, filling his own cup. 'Cheers to that.'

Effie had never before in her life been called saucy. In fact, she'd never heard the word not followed by 'wench'. But coming from Theo, it didn't sound rude or debasing. It sounded charming. Sweet. Sexy.

'Nice wine,' said Effie, sipping from her mug.

'Wait 'til you try the dips. They're not my handiwork, so I won't be offended if you don't like them. Although I do make a mean hummus.'

Effie dipped a triangle of pita into a purple dip – baba ganoush. 'Is that so?'

'If it requires a blender or a food processor, I'm an unparalleled talent. My protein shakes are works of art.'

Effie chuckled. 'I see. I'm a whiz with a skillet or a baking tin.'

Theo was making inroads with the hummus. 'Yep, mine's better. Cakes or cookies?'

'I do both. I actually thought about going professional for a while there.'

'With Bobby and his family?'

She shook her head, marvelling as her new curls bobbed about. 'No, baking was a passion of my mom's.'

Theo regarded her quietly as her voice hitched. Ah, so he knew about Mom. One good thing about small-town life was that you never had to share your own bad news; other people did it for you.

'I think I wanted to share in it with her. In the end I figured there was enough competition. And transitioning something from a hobby to a job can be fraught.'

'I understand,' said Theo, sipping his wine. 'I'm trying to figure that out for myself at the moment.'

His green-eyed gaze broke away from hers as he reached for a pastry. 'Actually, I had a job offer,' he continued. 'Back in the city.'

Effie bumped her mug, almost knocking it over.

'Are you thinking of taking it?' she asked, as she mopped up the wine she'd sloshed with a napkin, dreading the response.

'I'm not sure yet. The pay's good, but it's not something I'm particularly excited about. I've done the money-making thing. Now I think I'd like to do something more meaningful.'

Effie nodded, but as she went to respond, a thud behind her made her jump.

Right into Theo, who gently held her shoulders. 'Are you okay?'

'Did you hear that?' she whispered.

The hair on the back of her neck was at attention, and not just from the tension between the two of them. Because on the heels of the thud had come a high-pitched wail.

'The ghost,' she whispered.

'The ghost?' Theo repeated. He frowned as he tried to make sense of this. 'Do you mean that pirate guy you were talking about the other day?'

Effie's new curls flicked as she shook her head. 'No. You're going to think I'm mad, but something weird has been going on. Strange noises. Flashing eyes. Books being scattered all over the place.'

Theo considered this. 'But it can't be a ghost, surely. It could be any number of things. But not a ghost.'

'You sound so sure,' said Effie, 'but I've been Bonnie's sister long enough to know that not everything is easily explained.'

'Fair enough,' said Theo, chuckling. 'All right, ghost it is. I wish I'd brought my vacuum cleaner. I hear they do the trick. How about a heavy hardback or something? Just in case we need to whack it?'

'Ghosts are incorporeal,' Effie reminded him. Even though she had pulled the hardback-book-as-weapon move herself a few weeks back. 'And I don't appreciate your tone.'

'I mean just in case it's not a ghost. In case it's *real*.'

'Well, it's obviously real,' said Effie. 'We're both hearing it.'

'You know what I mean!' Theo blew air through his lips. 'Do you do that on purpose? Twist my words?'

Effie's eyes narrowed so much that her glasses prescription felt off. People were always accusing her of this, when all she wanted was clarity. *Well then, don't say stupid things*, she wanted to say.

So this date was going well.

'Come on,' she whispered, trying to redeem herself. She crept stealthily through the book stacks, trying to pinpoint exactly where the sound had come from.

From above came a huge thud, as though a dozen books had slipped from the shelves and fallen to the floor.

'It's in the upstairs reading room,' she decided. With a fortifying breath, she headed for the curving stairwell that led up to the soaring space, one of her favourites in the library. Theo at her heels, she picked her way up the stairs, squinting in the dim moonlight that filtered in through the stained-glass windows.

'Now that I think of it, are we *sure* we want to be chasing a ghost?' whispered Theo, catching at her arm. 'What if it's malevolent?'

Effie's wrist sparked at the contact. Oh shit, not now. Not when she had a ghost to deal with. She focused her magic, pressing it deep down inside, hoping Theo hadn't noticed her wrists glowing green.

But of course he had. How could you not notice being zapped by someone every time you touched them?

Theo drew back, surprised. 'Wow, talk about sparks. That's the second time that's happened, you know.'

'It's these shoes,' whispered Effie. 'Static electricity. Don't worry, ghosts are afraid of it.'

So she hoped. She'd only ever properly met one ghost: Jean Floyd, who hung out in the ballroom at the Toto Hotel. Jean was quiet, and never bothered anyone. She perched on the plush silver chair that no one at the hotel had the heart to move, waiting to be asked to dance. Effie wasn't the only one who'd seen her. Maureen from the kitchen had mentioned seeing a young woman dressed as a flapper dancing the Charleston alone as she'd cleaned up after an event one night, and Sabine always commented on the strange energy in the room.

Effie didn't know if Jean was the norm for ghosts, but she couldn't imagine a library ghost being cruel. A library ghost would surely want to sit around reading and sipping cups of ghostly tea.

Effie swallowed. She was at the top of the steps now. Ahead of her was the moonstruck upper reading room, with its shelves and tables picked out by the gentle light of the night sky. The globe on the stand in the eastern corner spun slowly. Hopefully because of a draught.

'Okay, I'm going in,' she whispered.

'I'm right behind you,' murmured Theo, so close that she could feel her wrists glowing again. *Dammit, magic, not now.*

Tugging her sleeves further down her wrists, Effie tiptoed into the reading room, casting her gaze around for any sign of the poltergeist that had been rampaging through the jigsaw puzzles in the kids' section and knocking the books off the returns trolley.

Hiss!

With a shriek, a dark blob scuttled past them, disappearing down the stairs.

'Come on.' Unthinking, Effie grabbed Theo's hand as she hurried back down the stairs.

Downstairs was dim: the lights had blown. Effie wondered whether the glimmer of her magic earlier had done it. It wouldn't be the first time, after all. And it was a more pleasant thought than the idea that the ghost might have done it.

But she didn't have long to ponder the thought, for there was movement in the non-fiction stacks.

'You take the 300s, and I'll take the 400s,' whispered Effie, creeping through the stacks. She knew the room so well that even in the dim light she could navigate around without tripping over a stepladder or a reading chair. Theo did not have this advantage, and she heard a few groans and moans as he bashed his shins into low shelves or sculpture plinths.

There!

From deep within one of the shelves, yellow eyes glowed.

Mrow!

The ghost was on the run once more. A vase tumbled to the floor, landing with a dull thud that Effie knew all too well. It was the unmistakable sound of something landing on the thick rug that covered the parquetry flooring found only in one section of the library.

'It's in large-print fiction,' murmured Effie, grabbing Theo's arm as he rounded the aisle ahead of her. Her wrists sparked once more, but she ignored it, hoping Theo was too preoccupied to notice that she was glowing like uranium glass.

The two of them raced towards the looming shelves, Effie grabbing a tablecloth from one of the reading tables on the way.

Mrow!

The shadowy apparition disappeared over the gap above the storeroom door at the back of the library's main floor.

'Okay, it's trapped now,' said Effie. 'There's no way out of there.'

'I thought ghosts weren't bound by things like walls and ceilings,' whispered Theo.

Good point. Effie pulled out her huge ring of library keys, flipping through them as quietly as she could. Oh goddess, it was pointless.

'Can you turn around for a second?' she whispered. 'I can't open locks under pressure. It's a whole thing.'

'Um, sure.' Theo sounded baffled, but he did as he was asked.

Shielding her wrist with one hand, she used her magic to pop the lock while feigning opening the door with her keys.

'Just like magic,' he said, turning back at her signal.

The storeroom was silent. Banker boxes and propped-up tables made a dark, angular skyline at the back of the room, and props from story time and seasonal displays bristled on chairs and stands at the front.

Effie stepped into the room, breathing as quietly as she could. Nothing.

Then at their feet, sudden movement.

'It attacked me!' howled Theo, grabbing at his leg. 'The ghost has furry little paws! And sharp little claws!'

'Furry little paws and sharp little claws?' repeated Effie, mirth welling up inside her. All this for . . .

'A cat,' said Theo, wincing.

'A cat,' said Effie, piecing together all the clues from the past few weeks. The holes in the window screen, the flowers pushed from shelves, the scratching noises, the weird hacking sounds, the glowing golden eyes.

'Well, it's better than a ghost,' Theo pointed out, rolling up his trouser leg to reveal several long slashes, as if a tiny Freddie Krueger had attacked him.

'And fluffier,' agreed Effie, laughing. Her laugh was interrupted by a tiny, high-pitched squeak, and then another. Kneeling, Effie ducked under the table, where atop a scarf from the lost property box, four tiny fluffy heads bobbed awkwardly.

'Not just a cat,' marvelled Effie, her heart swelling. 'Kittens!'

Chapter 28

A WITCH'S FAMILIARS

Bonnie

Bonnie lived for Saturday nights, but this one had been particularly epic. It was 2 a.m. when Bonnie pulled her Cadillac into the driveway, ears still ringing from DJ Scarecrows, and the thudding memory of the bass still pounding in her chest. The moon was at its peak, and stars threaded the sky, bobbing and bowing between the reaching arms of the trees that lined the street. It was the peace she needed. The bar had become wild and unruly as the so-called witching hour approached, although quietly she thought that had had less to do with witches and more to do with the cocktails being enjoyed. Bonnie had cut off a record seven people, including Bowow and Winston, Dierdre from Second-Hand Magic, and Freddie Noonan of the perfect lawn fame.

It wasn't just that the crowd had become raucous. The Silver Slipper was a bar, after all, and some degree of wild and uninhibited behaviour was to be expected. It was more that Bonnie was having to be everyone's mom, making sure they weren't overdoing it on the cocktails, and helping them remember their own addresses (and not to text their exes until they'd sobered up). That, and the fact she hadn't had a day off for over a month now.

Having Clark around made things a tad easier, at least when it came to breaking up imminent brawls, but it wasn't like she could just hand everything over to him. Especially not the spells. As demand for the cocktails grew, so too had the demand on Bonnie's powers, and she was feeling like she had when she'd tried to cram a whole year's worth of study in the day before her final exams. She'd almost been able to see through space and time. There was only one other person who could pick up the slack with Uncle Oswald's recipes, and she'd be beyond furious at the suggestion.

Speaking of that one other person, Bonnie certainly hadn't expected her to still be up when she pushed open the front door.

Effie's usual bedtime was approximately when the sun went down, or so it seemed to Bonnie. Her sister was very proud of the fact that she'd figured out the scientifically ideal time of day to switch from coffee to herbal tea, something she probably had a spreadsheet for. So, seeing her not just awake, but fully dressed, was quite the shock.

Although Effie did seem to be tending to a cat, so at least that particular part of the equation was on brand.

'Wow,' said Bonnie. 'Your transition to witchy cat lady is complete.'

'Thanks,' said Effie drily. 'I've been working on it my whole life.'

'Is that Bonnie?' Theo came out from the kitchen, a couple of small dishes in hand. 'Wow, you really are nocturnal.'

'Theo's here?' Bonnie couldn't compute this. She'd been happily working alongside Clark, enjoying being proximate to a good-looking guy who had absolutely no intentions towards her. Meanwhile, Effie had been upping the ante by spending extracurricular time with Theo. In their home, no less!

It wasn't that Bonnie had anything against Effie finally starting to date, or whatever this was. It just didn't seem fair that she was doing it with the most eligible bachelor in town, all while Bonnie was spending inordinate hours slinging drinks and juggling complicated open tabs and being ignored by Bobby, of all people.

This whole thing was a mathematical impossibility. The universe was out of balance.

'It's not what it looks like,' said Effie, finally, as though Bonnie was an overbearing parent, and not someone who'd been dubbed 'Most Likely to Party All the Time' in their high-school yearbook.

'We thought there was a ghost at the library,' explained Theo.

'Only, the ghost turned out to be of the feline variety,' said Effie. 'And the new mom kind.'

The situation might be thoroughly strange, but Bonnie couldn't resist an *aww*. The four tiny kittens were snuggled into their mom's plump body, so close it would be hard to tell them apart, save from the fact that each was a different colour. The mom was a beautiful black cat with yellow eyes, and her babies were in turn white, grey, tabby and tuxedo, like a greyscale rainbow.

'They're tiny,' observed Bonnie. 'Do we need to call Dr Freng?'

'He said to just make sure the mom is fed, and that they're all warm and feeding.'

'Ah,' said Bonnie. 'Hence why you have a fire going. And the heater as well. Have you stepped down as the Karen of the Electrical Bill?'

It was odd to be in the draughty old Queen Anne and not feel the chill of the New England air seeping into her bones. Despite her utter exhaustion, Bonnie felt almost cosy.

Effie pushed her glasses up her nose the way she did when she was spoiling for a fight. 'Pardon me for sticking to a budget.'

'At least our new energy panel helps with that,' said

Bonnie snippily. She regarded Theo curiously. 'Very chival-rous of you to see my sister home. Are you planning on staying?'

Effie cocked her head, as though wondering about the answer to this question as well.

Theo raised an eyebrow. 'How about I leave the two of you to it. I have meetings back in the city tomorrow, but I'll pop by when I can. And definitely for our overdues ridealong.'

'I'll let you know if anything changes with them,' Effie promised calmly, although Bonnie thought she heard a slight crack in her sister's voice. She'd definitely frowned when Theo had mentioned the city.

'Enjoy the rest of the dips,' said Theo, gesturing towards the kitchen as he made for the front door. 'All yours. Night, Bonnie. Night, Effie.'

The door creaked, then clicked.

'Don't be dim,' hissed Bonnie. 'Walk him out.'

Effie blinked behind her glasses. 'Why? He's a healthy adult. He can manage the stairs.'

Shaking her head, Bonnie grabbed Effie by her sparkly shoulders – she was actually wearing an outfit that Bonnie *might* be caught dead in for once – then spun her around towards the door. All right, so she and Effie weren't seeing eye to eye right now. If they ever had. But she couldn't let Effie fumble what might turn out to be one of the most momentous moments of her life.

'Night!' called Effie, waving awkwardly at Theo as he made his way down the driveway. He turned and waved back, shooting a sunny smile at Effie, then jogged backwards down the driveway, almost tripping over a wayward garden hose.

'Happy now?' muttered Effie, closing the front door on Theo's clumsiness.

'Well, I tried,' said Bonnie, pulling a slice of cold pizza (the best kind) from the fridge. Effie was a hopeless case. Absolutely hopeless.

As she sat down, she opened the copy of the *Yellowbrick Grove Gazette* that sat folded up on the table, flipping idly to page 23, where the horoscopes lived. But not tonight. The page usually dedicated to Madame Destinée's spirited forecasts was blank.

Chapter 29

HOCUS, POCUS, LIBRARY FOCUS

Effie

When Theo showed up at the Chalmers family Queen Anne two days later, ready for their overdue book collection ride-along, Effie was deeply ensconced in her cat mom duties. Which, as it turned out, was somewhere she quite liked being. She'd always had a soft spot for cats, but she now properly understood Bowow's fascination with her furry friends.

Tessa had come by with tiny handmade collars for the kittens, and an etched nametag for the mother cat, whom Effie had called Agatha, due to the mystery she'd generated. She was stroking Agatha, whose neck shone with a gleaming bell and a glittery charm.

'You have such a talent for crafts,' said Effie admiringly, watching the soft living-room light play off the charm. 'How's the shop-hunting going?'

'Actually, not badly. Hannah's been showing me a few places.'

Effie nodded stiffly. She was still coming to terms with the odd way that her and Bonnie's friendship groups were starting to overlap. In the past few weeks, Effie had spent quite a bit of time with Kirsty, discussing social media strategy. And Alana had been attending the library's craft nights. But she still wasn't quite sure how she felt about Tessa hanging out at The Silver Slipper, or Hannah being the one to browse shop locales with her friend.

Between this and Theo talking about a job back in the city, Effie's whole world was topsy-turvy.

'Hannah, huh,' she said, trying to keep her tone neutral. She failed.

'Yes, Hannah.' Tessa frowned, like she wanted to add something, but wasn't sure how to put it. 'Actually, I think something's up with her. She's been really away with the fairies. Missing appointments, forgetting to text, showing up without the keys. Do you think it's related to the situation with her dad?'

Effie pondered this. Hannah's dad had been diagnosed with early onset dementia a few years back. It had been a difficult time leading up to the diagnosis, with Hannah's mom making up every excuse under the sun to explain it away.

Peter's just overworked. He's low on B vitamins. He hasn't been sleeping well. We all have our little moments.

'Hannah probably just has too much on her plate,' said Effie. 'It's not easy keeping up with the latest in eyeliner trends.'

Ordinarily, Tessa might have laughed, but today she frowned. 'They're not all bad, Effie. Don't you think we're past this whole teenage clique thing?'

'Easy for you to say when you're the one in the clique,' she snapped, hating herself even as she said it.

Tessa's mouth tightened, but she didn't respond. She was too kind, too good, to let herself go there.

Thankfully the doorbell rang before Effie could double down on her cruelty.

'Knock knock!' It was Theo, who'd arrived with a basket filled with cat toys and catnip. 'For Mom and the littles,' he explained. 'The kid at the pet shop gave me a ton of recommendations. I just about maxed out my credit cards.'

This was hyperbole if ever Effie had heard it, but she appreciated the sentiment. And the gifts, for she was quickly realizing that hosting a family of kittens was an involved endeavour. The kittens were still tiny, but it wouldn't be long until they were wandering all over and testing the limits of the upholstery fabric or Effie's makeshift litter box.

'Hey, Tess,' said Theo easily. 'How's the crafting going? I'm on turtle number four. Shelby's never been so spoiled.'

'Look at you go. You'll have to join me for a class when I open my new studio.' Tessa's tone was warm. She wasn't going to betray Effie for her sharp words. 'I'm not sure of the when or where yet, but it's in the works.'

'Sign me up for a membership, or whatever you have going on.' Theo knelt down by the fluffy bed that housed Agatha and the tiny kittens. 'Ready to pry these overdue books out of the hands of the local book hoarders, Effie?'

'Want to join us, Tessa?' asked Effie, trying to throw her friend an olive branch. It wasn't always easy for Effie to pick out when she'd misstepped in a conversation, but it seemed to happen often. Sometimes she wished she had Bonnie's unique brand of social magic.

Besides, it was the first time she'd seen Theo since his trip to the city, and she was worried that he'd decided to take the job offer after all. Tessa would be a welcome buffer.

Tessa's face darkened slightly as she shook her head. 'If you'd texted me earlier, I would've said yes. But I've signed up for a yoga class at Alana's studio. Send me photos of the kittens, though. I'll try to think of some names for them.'

'Big car,' observed Theo, as Effie unlocked the Jeep. 'I thought you'd drive something more like a Vespa.'

To be honest, a Vespa was Effie's dream vehicle. She'd always had visions of herself cruising around the tiny villages of Sardinia, fresh market produce in a basket on the back, silk scarf fluttering in the breeze. But there was a huge disconnect between the Effie of her dreams and the Effie of reality, with the latter fiendishly aware of the dangers of riding a

motorbike. At least in books there was no way to get hurt.
Other than emotionally. Unless papercuts counted.

'It was my mom's,' she explained, reaching reflexively for
the broomstick that hung from the rear-view mirror as she
pulled out of the driveway. 'She was a larger-than-life character. Like bottled sunshine, which is a cliché, but clichés are
clichés for a reason. She could make anyone laugh. And she
was an amazing haggler. The best. Everyone at the farmers'
market quaked in their boots when she arrived. We used to
get our radishes and cucumbers practically free.'

'Does that explain the *Caution: this vehicle makes frequent
stops at yard sales* bumper sticker?' asked Theo.

'It explains so many things,' replied Effie. She rubbed the
bridge of her nose beneath her glasses. 'I miss her.'

Theo was quiet next to her. 'I can't even imagine what it
might be like.'

'I'm terrified I'm going to forget her,' admitted Effie. 'One
of our friends' dads is having memory issues . . .'

Theo nodded. 'I heard.'

Effie swallowed. 'Oh. Basically, every time I hear anything
about him, all I can think of is that our memories are all that's
left of Mom. And once they're gone . . .'

Theo nodded. 'I get it.'

She pulled up at Willamina's, a charming cottage bright
with hanging flower baskets (a brightness darkened by a
surfeit of hideous garden gnomes).

'How did your meeting go?' she asked after a moment.

'It went,' said Theo with a chuckle. 'But I have a few days
to make my final decision.'

Effie's fingers tightened around the steering wheel as she
thought about Theo leaving Yellowbrick Grove for good. But
should she be surprised, really? He had a whole life back
there, a whole world of opportunities. Whereas here he had
just the Friends of the Library group. And Effie.

'Are we going in?' he asked, shaking her from her thoughts.

Effie unbuckled her seatbelt. 'We are.'

They came back with a stack of books and a few slices of carrot cake. After Willamina's, they stopped at barista Terrance's apartment (how could so much laundry fill one small space?), a new mom's house (where Effie held the baby while the poor woman showered), and then the Dorothy House, which Bronson was busy painting grey, inside and out.

'It's hideous,' breathed Effie to Theo, as she grabbed the stack of overdues off the porch. 'Criminal.'

Theo grimaced in agreement. 'They probably only coughed up the overdues because they're not monochromatic enough.'

They spent the entire morning driving around chasing down books and being plied with baked goods and coffee, which honestly was not a bad way to pass the time. Especially when you had good company along for the ride. Even if that company was only temporary.

'Wow,' said Theo, when they'd reached the last of the houses on their list. 'You're going to need new suspension after this.'

The poor Jeep groaned under the weight of what was easily several hundred books, not all of them only recently overdue. They'd managed to collect a few that, according to the date stamp in the back cover, had been due back thirty years earlier. They were so old that they weren't even in the system – Effie hadn't even known they were outstanding.

Thankfully, she was an old pro at declining book 'donations', or it would've been worse. Effie had learned the risks of accepting mildewy basement boxes, because you never knew what you were going to infect the rest of the collection with. Mould. The plague. Impossible-to-remove mouse-pee smells.

'I've never been this flush with cookies and cake in my life,' said Theo, through a mouthful of carrot cake. 'I think I pursued the wrong line of work.'

You did! Effie wanted to shout. *Because it's taking you back to the city!*

But instead, she exhaled quietly.

'Speaking of,' said Effie, as diffidently as she could manage, 'the college is looking for an adjunct poetry professor to replace the one I told you about, who had to fly back to Germany. It's not tenure track, and I know it's not a particularly prestigious school, but if you wanted to, you could apply.'

Theo cocked his head. 'How did you find out about this?'

'I asked,' said Effie quietly. 'I mentioned that you're almost done with your master's, and that you've basically been acting as an employee of the library. And that I'd write a letter of referral if you needed it.'

Theo almost choked on his cake. 'You did? You would?'

'I think the town would love to have you,' she said quietly. 'Whether you'd love to have the town, that's up to you.'

Having recovered from his coughing bout, Theo regarded her thoughtfully. 'You, Effie Chalmers, are an enigma.'

Effie pulled the Jeep into the library parking lot. 'I've certainly heard worse. Now, are you up for helping lug this first batch of books inside?'

Theo opened the door, dusting carrot cake crumbs onto the pavement. 'Let's do this,' he said.

Chapter 30

SUPPORT YOUR LOCAL COVEN

Bonnie

If only Uncle Oswald's recipe book had a wakefulness potion, thought Bonnie, who was presently being buffeted by wave upon wave of exhaustion. She was starting to feel like the subject of a psychological experiment. The busy nights and long days of prep and admin were already a major undertaking.

Bonnie checked the Memory Lane recipe store in the massive fridge out back, which Clark had helped her lug inside a few days earlier. Demand for the charmed concentrate continued to grow. She'd gone from a few pitchers a night, to a bar fridge, to this huge industrial beast whose energy consumption would surely give Effie a fit. Although handily, Bonnie was now in a position to cover it.

It was hard to deny the profitability of this enterprise, she thought, going over the takings from the past week. The margins on the magical cocktails were excellent, and the high demand combined with the kickbacks from Uncle Oswald had taken Bonnie out of the red and into thriving local business status. So much so that Oswald had come in the other day talking about scaling up to other locations.

'We could even franchise!' he'd suggested, pulling out a set of numbers that the bank would love but that had just about made Bonnie break out into hives. The thought of unleashing her wayward magic on whole cities and states terrified her, especially now that she was almost certain that the recipes were having more than the intended effect.

But when she'd tried to broach the subject with him, he'd waved her off.

'Drinking makes people forget their heads,' he pointed out. 'Isn't that the whole point?'

Bonnie had pressed him about it, but to no avail.

'Magic has side effects,' he'd said, his eyes glinting with a darkness that had made Bonnie glance away. 'And you're the one with the magic, after all.'

Oswald was right. Anything that happened was *her* fault, really. She was the one preparing the spells. She was the one passing out the drinks.

'But I'll make sure this is our little secret,' he'd said soothingly, with a thin smile. 'Just so long as you do, too.'

She'd nodded, but her stomach had refused to settle.

'Cassandra's here, hon,' called Clark from the patio.

Great. On top of the issues of conscience and the endless demand for the hexed liquor, a journalist had just arrived to interview her about the business's success. All right, so it wasn't for the *Yellowbrick Grove Gazette*. But student journalism still counted. Even if said journalist had mostly gotten wind of the story because she'd bumped into Clark at the college library and had stopped by over the weekend for discount cocktails. At least the mates' rates paid off with some good PR.

Ah, there she was now.

Bonnie opened the door to Cassandra, who had a penchant for the structured but baggy look, and fiery hair that matched the chrysanthemum planters outside.

'Sorry I'm late. I decided one of those scooters was a good idea, and I took a wrong turn. No sense of direction, I suppose!'

Bonnie winced. It was absolutely impossible to take a wrong turn from the college to the bar: the two were a straight shot from each other. Not to mention that the college–downtown trip was the one journey that every freshman mastered (mostly drunkenly and on the first night of semester). Were her drinks at fault? Or was Cassandra just terribly disorganized?

'Happens to the best of us,' said Bonnie brightly, just in case.

She cleared a table, inviting Cassandra to sit down. 'Um, you're welcome to record. Especially if it involves video. I'm at my best on video.'

'Oh, I don't need to record. I have a photographic memory.'

'Right. Like Terrance,' said Bonnie.

Cassandra frowned. 'Terrance?'

'He's memorizing a deck of cards as part of a College Kids Got Talent audition.'

'You interviewed him, hon,' Clark reminded her as he pulled a stack of dishes from the dishwasher and started putting them away. 'You did a two-page piece, with sidebars including the probability of drawing a certain card, and ways that he could conceivably cheat.'

Bonnie swallowed. Poor Terrance. He'd never get past the first round unless he went cold turkey on the pitchers of Memory Lane. But he hadn't been great at his chosen talent prior to trying Bonnie's hexed drinks, so was she really to blame here? Maybe he could switch his talent to latte art or something.

'So, tell me about your bar. You just opened, right? This week.'

'It was a few months ago, actually,' said Bonnie, trying to keep the alarm from her voice. 'But we changed the menu recently, which might be what you're thinking of.'

'No, I don't think that's it.' Cassandra leaned forward, eyes sparkling. 'So, everyone's obsessed with this, um . . .'

'Memory Lane,' supplied Clark.

'That's it! This Memory Lane drink of yours. Tell me, what

makes it so unforgettable?' Cassandra held up a finger. 'You know what? I think I will record.'

For the first time in her life, Bonnie was sweating with anxiety. Her underarms prickled and her heart thrummed. Her words felt thick in her mouth, and instead of charming and chatty, she felt awkward and unbecoming. Was this what it felt like to be Effie?

But then, a reprieve. Tessa and Alana were pushing their way through the patio side door. Bonnie could've kissed them. Although, from how close together they were standing, it looked like she might be the third wheel in that situation.

'I'm so sorry, but I've double-booked,' she said, doing everything in her power not to crow with relief. 'It's a business thing. Could we reschedule?'

Cassandra hit pause on her recording app. 'Sure. Anything for the proprietor of The Golden Stiletto.'

Bonnie didn't even bother to correct her. Besides, the poor girl would probably have forgotten about this whole interaction by the time she got out to the square. Which was a relief, because Cassandra gave Alana and Tessa a look that suggested she might not entirely have believed Bonnie's excuse. But there was nothing Bonnie could do about that now.

'Hey, babes,' Bonnie said, giving Alana a hug and, in a first, extending the same to Tessa. 'Given up yoga for day-drinking, huh? Now this is a quality-of-life choice I love to see.'

'Glad you're looking out for us.' Alana shook out her auburn hair. 'We just came from a session in the studio. We're going to go check out Tessa's new space.'

Bonnie raised an eyebrow. 'You're really going for it, huh. Well, let me know if you still want to collab. A craft market, maybe. Or a pot and papercraft night.'

'Beers and beading,' suggested Tessa.

'Chardonnay and crochet,' added Alana.

Tessa and Bonnie both laughed.

'ABC. Anything but chardonnay,' Bonnie and Alana chimed in together, courtesy of a twenty-one-year-old Bonnie's favourite catchphrase.

'Noted for future reference,' said Tessa. 'Do you want to see the space? Hannah's meeting us in a few. Hopefully.'

'She completely flaked last time,' confided Alana.

Bonnie swallowed. This was at least the second time Hannah had flaked on a client appointment. And who knew what else she was flaking on in her life – hopefully not her responsibilities to her dad, who needed her now more than ever. She might have to switch her friend to wine only until she sorted herself out.

Perhaps it was time to go back to the recipe book and give some of the other spells a try. But where would she even get the time for that? She was already run ragged with just the Memory Lane concentrate.

'Babe,' said Alana, who was squirming on the spot, 'I gotta pee. Way too much reverse osmosis water. Is that okay?'

Bonnie stepped aside – she'd never stand between a famously small bladder and a bathroom. 'Be my guest. You know where to find the good paper.'

'Always.' Alana hurried inside, doing the thigh-squishing pee walk that Bonnie saw all too often among her patrons.

Watching her go with a lovesick gaze, Tessa plonked down on one of the plush outdoor couches that packed the patio area. At Bonnie's request, Clark brought out some lemonade and brownies, which Bonnie had taken to outsourcing since the introduction of the Memory Lane concentrate. A girl could only juggle so much.

'So, how're things going with the two of you?' Bonnie asked, curious. It was so odd to see one of her friends spending time with Effie's one and only friend, but stranger things had happened in the past few weeks. And besides, she was beginning to quite like Tessa. She was like Effie, but less likely to tell you off.

Tessa smiled shyly. 'Really . . . well. It's new, obviously, and we haven't put a label on it yet – I don't even know if *I'm* ready for a label – but it's great.'

'I love it for you,' said Bonnie, who meant it. Tessa's interest in Alana hadn't gone unnoticed over the years. Not with Bonnie, anyway, and she'd long thought that the feelings had been reciprocated. Alana had always lingered at the door of the Chalmers house whenever Tessa was over. She'd even signed up for a library card after Bonnie had mentioned that Tessa spent almost as much time as Effie at the library. And in recent months she'd taken a surprise interest in crocheting, despite having had a lifelong passion for one hundred per cent cotton clothing.

'I'm glad at least one sister does,' said Tessa.

Bonnie was surprised at this.

'Has Effie said something? Because she's not a bigot or anything. She's the biggest champion of Pride Month the library has ever seen.'

'Oh, it's not like that,' said Tessa. 'It's more . . .' She waved her arms in a circular motion, encapsulating their two very separate friendship groups.

'It's me,' realized Bonnie. 'In the iconic words of our goddess Taylor Swift, *I'm* the problem.'

'It's Effie,' corrected Tessa. 'She's been pretty preoccupied with Theo, to start. And on top of that, I think she's worried that I'm going to defect to your side.'

'My side,' said Bonnie, amused. Fair. She sipped her lemonade.

Tessa held up her hands. 'I am absolutely not getting in the middle of that. But come on. We all know that the two of you have a weird dynamic.' She let out a breath. 'Which is why I wanted to ask you something.'

'Go on,' said Bonnie warily. This was going to be an Effie thing, wasn't it? Tessa was going to ask her to be extra nice to Effie and say something to give her self-esteem a little boost.

'Is there something going on? With the bar?' asked Tessa. Bonnie almost choked on her lemonade. 'What do you mean by "going on"?'

'It just feels like there's maybe something in the water recently. Everyone's . . . forgetful, even for Yellowbrick Grove.'

Bonnie chuckled, but she could feel the hysteria bubbling up as Tessa trained that thoughtful, bespectacled gaze on her. Tessa was no fool. Bonnie had been around while Effie and Tessa had watched dozens of murder mystery shows together over the years, and Tessa *always* guessed whodunnit. But the murderers on TV didn't have Bonnie's charm. Or facility at lying, which she'd honed over years of truancy and reassuring her friends that cutting your own bangs was a great idea.

'I haven't noticed anything out of the ordinary,' she said, pretending to think on it. 'Although to be fair, I'm mostly dealing with drunkards. And I mean, the two of you seem fine, and you're in here all the time.'

'You're right,' said Tessa slowly.

Alana emerged from the bar, looking triumphant. 'I hope you don't mind, but I helped myself to some cookies. Oh, and barista Terrance left these.'

She held up the ratty pack of playing cards that Terrance had been working so hard to memorize.

'See?' pressed Tessa, as Bonnie took the playing cards, admiring their quaint folk-art style. Maybe she'd do him a favour and drop them off at the coffee shop. It was the least she could do. Well, that and bring up the latte art talent option instead.

'See what?' asked Alana, but only with passing interest. She checked her phone. 'It's Hannah. Hey, babe!' she said, putting it to her ear. 'No, not the Dorothy House. Tessa's art studio. And don't park near the hydrant. Officer Brigsley's on a rampage at the moment. Yes, I *know* you're terrible at parallel parking.'

She rang off.

'Want to join us?' she asked. 'Hannah's on her way. Or so she says.'

Bonnie yawned. 'Sure,' she said. 'So long as we have time for a coffee first.'

Fifteen minutes later, coffees in hand (and playing cards delivered to Terrance), the trio arrived outside what might become Tessa's new art studio. Hannah was parked wonkily down the tiny laneway to one side of it, the trunk of her car far enough out in the street that she was definitely risking a ticket. But at least she wasn't in front of the hydrant. This time.

'Got you a matcha,' said Alana, passing a giant smoothie to Hannah, who was in somewhat of a state. Her usually perfectly flat-ironed hair was damp and twisted up in a clip, as if she'd just stepped out of the shower, and she was wearing false lashes on her right eye only.

'Roll out of bed on the wrong side today?' asked Bonnie.

'Ugh, that's not even the half of it,' groaned Hannah. 'My alarm didn't go off, then I forgot to put the pitcher under the drip coffee – it went everywhere. Everywhere! Then my hair straightener didn't heat up. Then I put cold-sore cream on my toothbrush. And then I apparently forgot to fill up the car last night, so I had to stop for gas. But no one was there, so I drove here on fumes. Well, the Dorothy House first. And then here. It'll be a wonder if I make it back home. I think' – she lowered her voice – 'I'm cursed. Do you think curses could be real?'

'I mean, sure,' said Bonnie, sipping her coffee as she tried to hide her growing sense of panic. 'But think about it. Why would anyone go to the effort of cursing you?'

'Plenty of people hate me, Bonnie,' Hannah snapped. 'I'm *just* as influential as you. Realtors are highly controversial. People loathe us for our success.'

This was a better take than Hannah pinpointing the real

culprit here: Bonnie's delicious yet mind-numbing charmed drinks.

'How about we just go inside?' suggested Alana calmly.

Hannah glared at the digital door lock flashing at her as it demanded a code. 'Hang on, it's in my notes app . . .'

She pulled out her phone, which flashed, then promptly died. A bestial groan started up in her throat.

'Here, let me,' said Bonnie, stepping in before Hannah transformed into a werewolf or something (stranger things had happened in this town, after all). 'Can you turn away for a sec? I don't want you to be accessories to a crime. And not even matching accessories.'

The others did as requested.

She held her hands over the lock, letting magic sparkle through her wrists. It was coming more easily to her now, even if she was exhausted. The lock beeped, then smoked, and the door opened.

'How did you do that?' marvelled Alana.

'Hairpin,' said Bonnie, hoping that Alana wouldn't think about this too deeply. In fact, only Tessa seemed to suspect that more was at play – her left eyebrow seemed to have stayed raised pretty much ever since they'd left the bar. Tessa had never explicitly mentioned the sisters' magic, but Bonnie knew that between them, it was a bit of an open secret. Like Tessa's decade-long crush on Alana.

'You might want to let the landlord know that they need a new lock,' said Bonnie as she opened the door, heading inside in front of the others.

The studio space was small but homely. Like The Silver Slipper, it was all creaky polished hardwood floors and stained-glass windows, with a hammered-tin ceiling that had rusted in places.

Watching Tessa's expression was everything. Bonnie could remember how she'd felt when she'd first stepped into what would become her bar. How every step rang out with possibilities. The furniture that could go here. The lighting fixture she could add there. The signage that could go up on the back wall.

'Imagine all the cute little beasties you could crochet in here,' marvelled Alana, turning a circle in one particularly well-lit part of the room. 'And I'm thinking a Moroccan lamp in that corner.'

'Built-in shelves!' exclaimed Tessa. 'They'd be perfect stacked with materials. Pottery blanks. Fabric bolts. And my extraordinarily expansive glitter collection.'

'Don't forget Effie's book overflow,' added Bonnie.

Tessa laughed. 'There aren't enough shelves in the world.'

There was a rumbling outside as a car pulled up. Bonnie hurried to the window to check that Hannah wasn't going to get a ticket. Surely, after the side effects of Bonnie's charmed drinks, she'd hit her limit for bad luck for the day.

But no, it wasn't a police cruiser. It was Mom's Jeep. Well, Effie's Jeep now, since Bonnie had her own ride. One that didn't come with memories of Mom every time you climbed into it. Like the twiggy broomstick that hung from the rear-view mirror. Or the old CD player with the Cranberries CD Mom had always sung along to, belting out 'Dreams' in a passable Dolores O'Riordan imitation. Or the glovebox she'd kept filled with emergency sour gummies. Or even the way she white-knuckled the handlebar above the door when Bonnie had first been learning to drive.

Effie pulled over, parallel parking flawlessly (she'd spent hours as a teenager perfecting the art), and leaving plenty of room for the fire hydrant. Moving carefully in what looked like new shoes and wide-leg pants Bonnie actually quite liked, Effie climbed down from the Jeep, Theo following after her.

'Now here's a crew with overdues, if ever I saw one,' said Theo, with a wave at the girls who'd appeared at the building door. He hefted the library tote bag he was carrying

(obviously one of Effie's, for it read *Get Lit at the Library*).
'Got books, folks?'

'Mine are all on my Kindle,' said Alana, shaking her head.

'Here.' Wincing, Hannah passed Effie a crumpled twenty-dollar note. 'That's for the one that I spilled a glass of water on this morning. It was on the counter because I got your email and was planning on returning it. I had good intentions. Really.'

'Right,' said Effie, although she did pocket the money. She glanced around at the airy space, and then the unexpected group of people in it. 'I didn't realize we were missing a party,' she said, with a smile belied by her furrowed brow. Who knew that a person could smile and frown simultaneously? Scratch that. Who knew Effie could fake-smile?

'Oh, we were just checking out the new studio space,' said Tessa, awkwardly. 'Everyone was in the area, so, here we all are.'

'So not yoga class, then?' said Effie pointedly.

Tessa swallowed. 'No, we already—'

'It's great,' interrupted Effie. 'I could definitely see your craft classes in here,' she added slowly, although Bonnie could hear the hurt in her voice. Bonnie had heard her complain a million times about being cut out of things, or being the last to know about a social gathering she'd never attend anyway. But Effie made it so difficult. She was always lost in one of her books or hiding behind the library stacks, and you always felt so *guilty* for interrupting her, like whatever you had going on was horribly inferior to the themes and topics of whatever she was reading.

'Thanks, Eff,' said Tessa.

'I'm just glad I could see it,' said Effie archly. 'Even if it was just by luck.'

Bonnie's friends exchanged glances that spoke volumes. Here Effie was, ruining a perfectly pleasant moment with her jealousy. And Effie had the cheek to say that *Bonnie* made everything about herself!

'How much is the rent?' asked Effie, running short finger-nails over the wall panelling. There was an edge to her tone that grew sharper as she went on. 'Did you talk to the Chamber of Commerce about a business plan? Because it's different when it's free at the library as opposed to people paying out of their own pockets.'

Tessa's shoulders slumped a little, but she smiled gamely. 'I've run the numbers.'

'She's run the numbers,' echoed Alana in a sing-song voice, like a 50s chorus girl.

Effie didn't hear this – she was wandering around the room with a frown, adding her usual Effie doom and gloom to what *had* been a joyful outing. Effie's lifelong streak of raining on people's parades remained unbroken.

'She'll do great,' said Bonnie, stepping in to save Tessa from Effie's inevitable questions about diversification and lines of credit. 'Besides, we're going to do a cross-promotional thing.'

'I'm sure you are,' sniped Effie. 'Maybe you can get Uncle Oswald in on it as well.'

Bonnie felt as though she were about two inches tall. Effie could be so imperious when she wanted to be. And she knew exactly what to say to make you hurt.

'Maybe we should get going, Effie,' said Theo, gently touching her arm. He gave Tessa and Bonnie a softly apologetic look. 'We have all these books to unpack and get back.'

Effie took off her glasses and polished them with her cardigan sleeve. 'Fine. The Jeep's full anyway. I love the space, Tessa. Really.'

Tessa gave a small smile. 'Thanks, Effie. Sorry I didn't text you after yoga, but it was all just kind of impromptu.'

'And you seem to be busy anyway,' said Bonnie, her gaze tracking from Effie to Theo.

'I'll see you in a bit for craft night?' added Tessa, hopefully.

'Of course,' said Effie, although her voice wavered. Bonnie had the very strange sensation that her sister might be about to cry, something she hadn't seen her sister do since the day of Mom's death.

Bonnie might ordinarily have felt sympathy towards her sister, but frankly, she was getting tired of tiptoeing around Effie's moods. So what if Bonnie had a popular bar and Tessa preferred Bonnie's company? Why couldn't Effie be grateful with what she had instead of complaining about what she didn't? Moreover, wasn't it about time she learned to share? Who cared if Bonnie happened to be available to take a peek at Tessa's new shop! Especially since Effie had apparently had more important plans anyway.

Overdues ridealong *indeed*, she thought with an internal snort.

'I for one am very excited about carving soap,' Alana was saying with exaggerated cheerfulness, as Theo guided the huffy Effie back out to the Jeep. 'So long as it's vegan.'

Bonnie folded her arms and watched her sister climb dejectedly into the Jeep. Effie just couldn't help being Effie.

Although she did have to admit that she liked her sister's new shoes.

Chapter 31

SNAKES AND SNAILS
AND PUPPY DOGS' TAILS

Effie

Was it possible to live the rest of her life in a cave? Because a cave sounded quite pleasant right now. It had worked for the Oracle of Delphi, after all. And most importantly, Bonnie would never follow her into a cave.

Smarting from being made to feel like an outsider, Effie couldn't get away from Tessa's potential new shop fast enough. Unfortunately, the Jeep was so laden with books that she had to drive twenty miles under the speed limit. It wasn't out of the question that she'd have to pay for new suspension after all this – or worse, new tyres. But at least her brakes were in good shape, because when she suddenly slammed her foot down on the pedal, the car jerked to a halt.

'Did you see that?' she asked Theo, who was in the passenger seat, half buried under a stack of books and a box of cupcakes. 'Something moved.'

Theo adjusted the book stack in his lap, peering around to try to catch a glimpse of whatever Effie was talking about. 'We caught the ghost,' he reminded her. 'Well, ghosts.'

They had indeed, although Effie hadn't quite figured out what to do with them yet. Perhaps a cat adoption initiative through the library, with proceeds supporting the summer program. Or maybe when the kittens were big enough, Effie could just move the whole family into the library's basement area. Or, and this was the option she was most leaning towards, she could keep them all. Were five cats too many? Surely not. Besides, the thought of separating them from their mom, Agatha, or from each other, seemed cruel. Effie knew first-hand just how painful it could be to no longer have your most treasured person around – or even your sister.

A point that had been driven home just now at Tessa's shop. Effie's social circle had never been heavily populated, and now it seemed that Theo was the only one left in it. Although Tessa had been right that Effie had invited her to the ridealong last minute. But still, Tessa could have texted her when she was done with yoga!

This was all Bonnie's fault. She'd clearly been getting in Tessa's ear.

'There! There it is again!' Effie exclaimed, grateful for the distraction from her woes.

It wasn't a ghost, or a cat. A terrier with eye patches and a brown spot on his back was running in cheerful zigzags all down the street. His pink tongue lolled as he merrily cocked his leg on a fire hydrant, a mailbox, and a rubbish bin awaiting pickup. Sniffing at something near the bin, he flopped over on his back and proceeded to roll in it.

It wasn't even Pickles, the neighbourhood's usual escapee. Effie knew this because Pickles was on a lake vacation with his owners (she'd learned as much when her efforts to retrieve their overdue books had been met with a *gone fishing* sign).

'There's another one.' Theo pointed at a fat corgi who was happily lying in a triangle of sun, his head atop a freshly delivered newspaper.

'A third.' Effie nodded at a golden retriever balanced on its hind legs as it tried to coax a squirrel down from one of the massive oaks that lined the road.

There were at least ten, Effie saw, glancing around at the furry faces universally delighted at their new-found freedom – there was plenty of butt-sniffing and lawn-digging and shoe-chewing going on. The dogs all wore distinctive purple collars: collars that Effie had seen on the ever-changing lock screen of one of her most dedicated library patrons.

'They're Bowow's,' she said in realization. 'How did they get out?'

'Maybe there's a hole in her fence or something,' suggested Theo. 'But we should round them up before one of them gets hurt. Let's do the corgi first. He's definitely the slowest.'

He climbed out of the Jeep, gently approaching the fat-butted corgi, who had rolled over and was baring his fuzzy belly to the clear autumnal sky. The dog's nubby tail wagged as Theo knelt to give him some belly scratches. Looping his hands gently around the corgi's ample girth, he picked it up, grunting a little.

'Surprisingly solid,' he said, holding the baffled dog against his shoulder. 'Now what?'

Thankfully Tessa always kept a few spare leashes in Effie's Jeep just in case an emergency dog-walking opportunity popped up. Effie dug around in the side-door compartments – ugh, where were they? Checking that Theo was distracted by the corgi (he was still muttering to himself about its heft), she used her magic to pinpoint the leashes. Under the passenger seat. Of course.

Leashes in hand, she hurried over to Theo, clipping one of the leashes to the corgi's collar.

Meanwhile, the terrier had approached and was running circles around them, barking like this whole situation was a grand game.

'That one's trouble,' said Theo with a chuckle. 'I like him.'

'We'll bribe the others with the baked goods,' decided Effie. 'But no chocolate, I promise.'

She grabbed a paper plate of angel cake and waggled it, wafting her hand to spread the scent of the food. The golden retriever perked up, lumbering over with curiosity in its eyes.

'Gotcha,' said Theo, clipping a leash on the dog and stroking its soft head. 'There's a good boy.'

Using a combination of cake bribes, whispered invitations and (when Theo wasn't looking) the odd sparkle of magic, they slowly rounded up the others, using Theo's belt and Effie's purse strap as emergency leashes when Tessa's leash collection ran low.

In true terrier form, the patch-eyed dog remained elusive, darting back every time Effie or Theo tried to catch him. But he remained close by, happily barking up a storm.

'Now what?' said Theo, who was being pulled in all directions by the dogs, like a balloon seller on a windy day.

'They're not going to fit in the Jeep,' said Effie. 'Well, maybe that little guy.'

The terrier ruffed joyfully.

'Why don't you let him ride with you, and I'll follow on foot,' said Theo.

'Deal,' said Effie. She tempted the terrier inside the Jeep with the promise of even more baked goods. He climbed on her lap, poking his head out the window and barking the entire way as the car crawled down to Bowow's, Theo and his profusion of dogs following after them.

Watching him in her mirrors, Effie couldn't help but laugh. This was all so silly, and she was loving every minute of it. The awkward situation with Tessa and Bonnie earlier had all but slipped from her mind.

'Bowow's house is that one,' she called out the window, pointing at an enormous manor of a place with a wrought-iron fence decorated with gilded dog medallions. The house was a gorgeous red-brick estate with decorative masonry and wraparound verandas, on which Bowow's extensive canine family napped on sunny days. When they weren't running around the streets.

She pulled over, waiting for Theo to catch up.

'Wow, she's committed to the whole dog thing, isn't she,' marvelled Theo, taking in the dog statues dotted around the ample lawns. Effie's favourite was the fountain sculpted to show three dogs playing, with the top one leaping for a frisbee. In the summer, Bowow would have the water on, and the frisbee would spurt water from all directions back into the base of the fountain.

'Truly. I was the notary on her name change.'

'Really?' Theo blinked in surprise.

Effie laughed. 'No. My goodness. Come on – let's get these poor dogs home.'

She turned the Jeep into the driveway, preparing to type Bowow's gate code into the keypad (the birth year of her favourite romance cover-model). But there was no need, as the gate was wide open.

'I think I see the problem.' Theo grimaced. Then he turned his attention back to the dogs, patting them in turn as they clamoured for his affection.

Maybe there was something wrong with the gate mechanism. Effie couldn't imagine Bowow leaving the gate open, not with all of her pups running around. She was the kind of person who double-checked everything: whether she'd turned the stove off, the front door locks, the prognostications of her horoscope.

They hammered on the door for what felt like hours until Bowow answered, clad in Dalmatian robes that she was very hasty to explain were not from real Dalmatians.

'Do you know what time— Oh!' Her tune changed immediately when she realized that the duo had come bearing a veritable army of dogs on leashes. 'Are you volunteering to walk them?'

'They were running about all over the place,' said Effie. (The unleashed terrier still was, in fact.) 'I think your gate is broken.'

Bowow's brow furrowed as she stooped to hug her dogs. 'It can't be. I had it serviced just last month. And I definitely . . .' She squinted over at the gate. 'I definitely *think* I closed it.'

'I think they're all accounted for,' said Effie. 'We didn't see anyone else running around.'

Kneeling, Bowow patted the velvety heads of her dogs, murmuring gentle words to them in a tone that sounded to Effie almost like a spell. Because that was what so many spells were, something spoken with heartfelt intent, a cadence with intonation that meant something. There were whole phrases in the language that changed the state of the world – pronouncing two people married, for example – and others that reshaped or reinvigorated emotion, feeling.

'Maybe I've bitten off more than I can chew, taking in all these extras,' said Bowow with a sigh. 'I haven't been feeling myself these past few weeks.'

Effie understood how that went. Everything had felt topsy-turvy of late, although she couldn't pinpoint why.

'I think we all just need to do less,' she said gently.

'Maybe I can help with that,' said Theo, with one of his easy smiles. Still scratching the terrier's head, he turned to Bowow. 'Do you think I might be able to foster this one?'

Effie almost dropped the leash she was holding. All right, so he hadn't said adopt, just foster, but surely that meant Theo had plans to stick around, at least in the short term. Which meant that he might not be taking the job in the city?

The little terrier panted away, giving the cutest doggy smile imaginable. Then he nudged Theo's leg, as if to say *this is him. This is my human.*

Bowow beamed. 'Bernard? I think you might not have a choice.'

Chapter 32

IMPRACTICAL MAGIC

Bonnie

Trivia Night had rolled around far too quickly, thought Bonnie, waving as the mainstays of The Silver Slipper piled through the door. She'd barely had time to put the questions together, let alone check that they were simple enough for the townsfolk to answer after consuming a pitcher or two of Memory Lane. Just so long as they remembered to buy their drinks and tally up their responses, all would be well. She hoped.

Oh thank goodness, here was Tessa, who was not only one of Yellowbrick Grove's more intelligent residents, but whose preference for bubbly had kept her safe from the befuddling effects of the charmed drinks. At least someone would be earning some points tonight. And Bonnie would have plausible deniability. Especially since Cassandra of the student newspaper had apparently thoroughly forgotten about their interview.

There was no sign of Effie, though, she noted. Bonnie had barely seen her sister since Effie's embarrassing display at Tessa's possible shop space. Apparently she'd been throwing herself into her librarian responsibilities, but really, how many responsibilities could a librarian possibly have? Lots, she supposed, if they involved Theo.

But Bonnie *had* explicitly invited Effie to Trivia Night a few weeks back, before things between them had taken a turn for the worse. And Effie wasn't one to renege on anything written down on the kitchen calendar, no matter how much pride was involved. But it was odd that she hadn't shown up with Tessa. Even after their little tiff at Tessa's shop.

Bonnie wrapped Effie's friend in a proper, voluminous hug – she'd decided it was time to upgrade Tessa from acquaintance to friend. 'Good thing you came, because you're a shoo-in for the prize tonight.'

'What's the prize?' asked Tessa curiously.

'A gift voucher for Uncle Oswald's shop. And a meat tray. Ugh, I should've prepared a vegetarian option, shouldn't I? I'll check with the butcher.'

'Ah, the butcher. The perfect place to get your veggie treats,' joked Tessa. 'But I'm in. You know I love to wipe the floor with the townsfolk.'

'I do indeed, and I appreciate it,' said Bonnie. 'Saves me having to mop.'

'Alana's on her way, too. She's just finishing up a class at the studio.' Tessa toyed with one of her perfect curls. 'I texted Effie as well, just in case. But I can't promise anything, even though I mentioned . . .'

She trailed off, then course-corrected. 'She's been pretty busy recently, I guess.'

Wondering what Tessa had been about to say, Bonnie busied herself popping open a bottle of prosecco for Tessa. The pop of the cork – and Bonnie's accompanying yelp – coincided with the swinging of the front door, which gave way to reveal a familiar T-shirt and cardigan combo. But styled in a more put-together way than usual.

'Speak of the devil,' muttered Bonnie, as Effie strode into the bar with something approaching confidence. She couldn't wait to hear all the complaints Effie had about the bar and its patrons. Not to mention the dressing-down she was about to be subjected to for daring to speak with Tessa.

'You made it!' said Tessa, sounding surprised, but also a

little relieved. She angled away from Bonnie, as though trying to show that the two of them weren't *that* close, not really, and that Effie didn't need to be jealous.

'You invited me,' said Effie. Fiddling with one of Oswald's coasters, she turned to Bonnie. 'And you as well.'

'Well, aren't you a regular social butterfly,' said Bonnie. She paused, then added, 'You look nice.'

Effie did, actually. She was wearing a habitually terrible T-shirt, yes, but there was something different about her. She'd parted her hair differently, giving extra pop to her white streak, which Bonnie secretly liked, although she'd never admit it. There was a dusting of eyeshadow on her sister's eyes – not to mention a coat of mascara. And, most important of all, Effie was wearing a *skirt*! One that reached mid-calf, which in Effie hem-length parlance was positively scandalous.

This, all of this, was the equivalent of Sandy in *Grease* making herself over at the end of the film. Effie might as well be in skin-tight black leggings and red heels, with a serious bouffant hairdo and a new-found smoking habit. (As much as Bonnie would never admit it, Effie would actually look brilliant in such an outfit – if she ever had the guts.)

There was no denying it: Effie was in love.

'Thanks,' said Effie awkwardly, pulling her cardigan around herself. She swallowed. 'Besides, Tessa and I are on a team together. Right?'

She sounded a little nervous as she said it, as though she was worried that Tessa might disagree.

But Tessa nodded. 'Of course, Effie.'

There was a sense of palpable relief between them.

'You know I can't let any question go unanswered,' added Effie, an odd tone to her voice. She and Tessa exchanged a look that felt a little too pointed. Bonnie faltered. Was something going on here that she wasn't privy to?

As Effie slid over the sign-up payment, Tessa pulled a

hand-drawn sign from the purse she'd hung beneath the bar. She'd adorned it with a generous number of sparkles and bottle caps. 'We're going to be Tea for Two.'

'I've got you down,' said Bonnie, writing their name up on the chalkboard behind her. Her hand shook slightly as she noticed Effie glancing around the bar, settling her judgemental gaze over the patrons. Effie seemed to be looking for something. 'Nice sign – you could use that as advertising for the new shop.'

'Believe me, out of financial necessity, there'll be a ton of DIY branding,' said Tessa. 'Maybe you can help me, Effie. We can gather up the kids from craft night.'

'Sure,' said Effie, with surprising readiness.

Tessa sipped her prosecco. 'Is Theo coming? We could be Tea for Three. Or four,' she added quietly.

'He's on his way,' said Effie, with a quick glance at her watch. 'Apparently there's no limit to the amount of walking a terrier needs. Bernard is quite the distance runner.'

Effie didn't even sound slighted, even though she was obsessive about punctuality. She sounded *happy*. Bonnie hadn't thought such a thing possible. Who was Effie without something to gripe about?

'But let's keep our team name,' Effie added. 'There's magic in twos.'

Bonnie glanced up, wondering if perhaps Effie was speaking to her. There was something in that little phrase that resonated, reminding Bonnie that in spite of everything that had happened this past year, they were sisters. And that perhaps, whatever happened, maybe Effie really did have her back.

She hoped.

But no, Effie was looking at Tessa.

'Anything for you, Effie?' asked Bonnie at last, her hand on the soda water dispenser.

Effie considered. Bonnie could see she was intrigued by the vivid purple Memory Lane concentrate, which patrons were ordering practically in bulk. But with a slow furrow of her brow, she shook her head.

Bonnie's smile wavered. First the look between Effie and Tessa, and now this hesitation to order a drink. Was Effie on to her? She could sniff out magic like a bloodhound, after all. And the magic was thick in the air tonight.

'Just a wine,' said Effie eventually. 'A malbec.'

'Wow, look at you.' Bonnie raised an eyebrow. 'Let me guess, you found some dusty old books in the wine bit of the non-fiction section. Here, I've got one from Mendoza.' She hefted the bottle, feeling the damp prickle of anxious sweat, something that the beading of her fabulous minidress did not need.

'All right. I trust your recommendation.' Effie's tone said the opposite, but she took the glass of red and slid over a generous tip.

'It's on the house,' said Bonnie, though it pained her to say it.

'No, it's fine. I'm not going to take money out of the till of a small business. Besides . . .'

Besides. That one small word held a world of meaning. Bonnie's eyes narrowed as she read the reams of judgement in Effie's statement. She looked around, taking in the bar she'd worked so hard to get off the ground. Yes, so she'd fallen behind on some of the repairs with her busy schedule and without Bobby around to help, but she *was* going to get that window fixed, and she already had the paint to touch up the mysterious scrape that had appeared on the back wall the other day. And sure, the crowd had been a little odd recently, but that wasn't entirely her fault. Oswald deserved some of the blame as well. Especially given how sharply he'd responded to her suggestion that they pause the bespelled drinks until she'd figured out the side effects.

Remember, it's our little secret, he'd snarled. The threat had been clear.

Taking Effie's money, Bonnie affected her biggest, fakest smile.

'Well, grab a table and do some last-minute studying. We'll start in about half an hour.'

Chapter 33

QUIT YOUR WITCHING

Effie

'You don't believe me, do you?' said Tessa, the 11s between her brow deepening. 'That the purple drinks are hexed. And just the purple ones, which is why I'm fine, and you're fine, and Alana's fine.'

Effie hesitated. She glanced around the room, taking in the odd but deeply human sights. Winston and Gerald were sitting beneath the darts board, cheerfully whittling away at chunks of wood. Willamina was staring in deep fascination at the plant wall, marvelling aloud about how on earth plastic plants could grow so well. In one corner, Terrance the barista was tearing up a pack of playing cards one by one.

'I'm free!' he shouted, as he scattered the pieces over the table. 'Memorize *this*!'

And at the far end of the bar, Freddie Noonan had placed some squares of AstroTurf on the counter and was investigating them with a magnifying glass.

'I'm done with lawn,' he sobbed, pulling out his prized blue ribbon from his pocket and attempting to light it with a cigarette lighter.

'I'll take that,' said Bonnie, grabbing the lighter from him. 'And the AstroTurf as well.'

Meanwhile, Winston and Gerald had taken up in the games room and were playing ten pins with empty beer bottles. Bonnie's new bartender, Clark, had to run in and stop them before everyone ended up dancing about on broken glass.

'You truly think this is normal?' pressed Tessa.

All right, so the townsfolk were being a tad dramatic and performative. But assuming that Tessa was right, that meant that Bonnie had somehow got her hands on a huge amount of hexed cocktails, or she'd made them herself. Which, knowing Bonnie's wayward magic, was impossible. The whole bar would've burned down if she'd been spending her time bespelling drinks. Bonnie could barely hex the wrinkles out of a wool shirt.

Besides, bars weren't places where people went to be normal. Even Effie, whose malbec had gone straight to her head, was feeling less inhibited than usual. Another few glasses, and maybe she'd be the one tearing up playing cards.

'The townsfolk are always like this, and the tourists are even worse,' Effie said stubbornly. 'Tell me you've seen any of this lot in the library recently.'

Tessa took a fortifying sip of bubbly. 'Wow, Effie. You know that e-books exist, right? And that people can access the entire library through their phones now? And that as much as I revere the library as an institution – and that I out-read you during three of our high-school read-a-thons—'

'Because you read shorter books,' pointed out Effie.

Tessa gave one of her famous huffs, which Effie knew meant she was treading on thin ice. Tessa was a fair person, but she was also fiery, and every now and then she'd turn that fire on Effie.

'Yes, because of that, but who cares! They weren't *worse* because they were shorter. They were still books! And you're proving my point! Knowledge doesn't just disappear outside the hallowed reading room.' Tessa sipped her drink. 'Look, all I'm asking is that you look around, *without judgement*, without thinking that you know better than everyone, and tell me what you think.'

Effie folded her arms. 'I'm not judgemental. Bonnie's the judgemental one!'

Tessa cackled in disbelief. 'Effie. You're in a fight with Bonnie purely because of pride. Until it was proven otherwise, you assumed Theo's poetry books were hollow cases stuffed with cocaine and gold ingots. And then there was what you said about my studio the other day. You really don't think I have an intense set of financial projections? Sure, I walk dogs now, but I'm a CPA! I've been biting my tongue because I know it's been a difficult year for you, but you have to do something with this chip on your shoulder before you push everyone away. Including me. Because I have a right to spend time with other people, even if you don't think those people are good enough. After all, *you* get to spend all your free time with Theo, and I don't get a say in that. You know I would've helped with the overdues ridealong if you'd asked more than five minutes beforehand.'

Effie didn't know how to take this. Tessa had *always* been there, and Effie couldn't imagine a world where she wouldn't be. They'd written letters to the Tooth Fairy when they'd lost their first teeth and had each worn thick sanitary pads in solidarity when the other had got their first period. They'd got their driver's licences together, signed up to vote together, attended their first protests together.

Effie's heart twisted. 'I'm sorry, Tessa. I didn't—'

'Because you never listen!' interrupted Tessa. 'I love you, Effie, but my *god*! I've never met someone so self-involved. So *self-important*!'

Effie's malbec was virtually empty, but she took a final valiant sip. These weren't accusations that should be levelled at *her*. These were the things they always accused Bonnie of! Bonnie of the too-long showers and the always-open doors and the endless parade of men that she tossed aside, leaving Effie to make them an awkward post-sleepover omelette in the morning.

'I just wish you'd take me seriously when I say that some-thing is up,' Tessa said quietly. Then, to Effie's extreme surprise, she grabbed one of the purple cocktails from the Quizotics' trivia group table – to a rousing chorus of cheers – and chugged it.

She slammed the empty glass back on the table and dabbed her mouth with a napkin. 'There. Cursed drink, straight down the hatch. Come check on me in an hour or so.'

Bonnie's eyes widened. Tessa must be fully behind her conspiracy theory if she was going to put herself at risk by trying one of Bonnie's apparently tainted drinks. Clutching her empty glass, she returned to the bar, surreptitiously glancing around at the other patrons. A group of college kids were playing a game of Uno and arguing over the rules, which apparently were extremely complicated and difficult to remember. Out on the patio, a woman was screaming at a robotic voice on loudspeaker, bellowing that *no*, she didn't know her PIN, and could she speak to a . . . what do you call it, please! By the back wall, Winston Wakefield and Gerald Ho, who'd been kicked out of the games room after the unconscionable ten-pins behaviour, were sitting quietly, batting an agate coaster back and forth.

The coaster. It was just like the ones she'd seen at Uncle Oswald's shop. And they were all over the bar. Under every pitcher, every glass, every plate of brownies.

Effie's stomach churned, and not just from the extremely dry wine she'd chugged. (She should've stuck to the cheerful pinot grigios or effervescent rosés she actually liked, but she wanted to impress Bonnie, to suggest that the librarian life she lived wasn't so sheltered after all. That she was cultured, even if she'd stolen that culture from Theo.)

Alana, who'd just arrived and was still in her yoga clothes – and yet somehow looked more put together than Effie – picked her way over. Her brow was furrowed.

'Effie, do you know what's going on with Tessa?' She

turned, pointing at Tessa, who had found an empty spot and was swaying in place, completely out of time with the 90s bops playing over the sound system. Tessa was less of a dancer than Effie was, and Effie had never seen her voluntarily hit the dance floor. Never mind *start* the dance floor.

Now Sabine had joined her, swirling away in a profusion of garments, like a slow-moving pinwheel. Effie felt a pang. She hadn't seen Sabine arrive, but even so, why hadn't Sabine come up to say hello?

'Effie!' Alana grabbed Effie's arm and shook. 'I swear she has amnesia or something. Do you think someone spiked her drink? She didn't know me. *Me*. Her girlfriend.'

Effie's head swirled with realization. Of course. So much had been going on right under her nose, but she'd been so wrapped up in her own woes that she'd failed to see how the people she loved were changing. Growing, she realized with a pang.

Bonnie was clearly up to something that was more than a mere 'collaboration' with Uncle Oswald, and at some point Tessa and Alana had started actually, properly dating.

But the fact that Tessa hadn't told her all about it the way she might have in years past made Effie feel even smaller than her five-foot three-inch height. Effie *had* been selfish. She'd been wrapped up in Theo and her work and her grief. She'd made everything as much about herself as Bonnie was in the habit of doing – but she'd justified it by the fact that she'd felt shut out and ignored.

Struck with the pain of recognition, Effie turned towards Bonnie, determined to make things right. She met her sister's blue-eyed gaze, which welled with tears. Dabbing her eyes with a thumb, Bonnie shoved Clark behind the bar and hurried over, her heels clacking on the antique floorboards.

'Effie,' she began, her voice trembling. Effie had never heard Bonnie sound so scared and anxious.

'Bonnie, what's going on?' she hissed. 'What's wrong with Tessa?'

'It's not just Tessa . . .' Bonnie carefully wiped the makeup from the corners of her eyes, trying to compose herself. She pointed at Sabine, who was waving her fingers deliriously at the ceiling. 'It's Sabine. She doesn't . . . she doesn't remember Mom.'

Bonnie's voice broke as she added, 'I really need your help.'

Chapter 34

CHARM OFFENSIVE

Bonnie

Effie grabbed Bonnie's wrist and pulled her towards the stairwell. She didn't stop until they reached the landing, and the two of them stood there in the dim illumination of the stippled Moroccan lamps, surrounded by Mom's aura paintings. The ugliness of the Uncle Oswald painting, as always, set the hairs on Bonnie's neck to attention – but mostly because now she wondered if that's what her own aura looked like. Ugly and dank. Marred by the way she'd leapt at Uncle Oswald's business plan to make some quick cash, and at the chance to prove to Effie that her own magic skills were equal.

And look how that had turned out. She'd proven the opposite: that she was hasty and untalented and sloppy. She could've tried to perfect the individual recipes in the grimoire, but she'd been determined to launch the new range of cocktails as quickly as possible to take advantage of Uncle Oswald's promised kickback. She could've stopped serving them once she realized they were having effects beyond losing interest in dream interpretation or astral projection. And let's face it – she'd known for a while now. But admitting it would have meant that she'd messed up. Yet again.

But now she had no choice but to come clean.

'Effie, it's all my fault,' she blurted, getting out the words as fast as she could. 'Uncle Oswald came to me with these hexed drink recipes that were meant to steer people away from their influencer-created New Age woes and encourage them to shop at his place instead. He paid me every time they bought something.'

'I see,' said Effie. Bonnie could just tell she wanted to say something about the electrical box, but to her credit, Effie kept her mouth shut.

'But I messed up the recipe. Or the recipe was wrong to begin with. I don't know. Everyone's losing their minds. I called the newspaper, and apparently Madame Destinée keeps forgetting to write her horoscopes. Dierdre from Second-Hand Magic has turned into a sceptic. Freddie Noonan is excited about fake grass. And Sabine . . . how could she forget Mom?'

Her voice hitched as she said this, for it had been the final straw. The one thing that had set her conscience screaming.

Turning a nervous gaze on Effie, Bonnie took a deep breath. 'Can you . . . turn them back?'

Effie's eyes were narrowed behind her glasses, but to Bonnie's relief she didn't start yelling. Which, honestly, Bonnie deserved.

But how she *did* respond was arguably worse.

In a small, hurt voice, Effie whispered, 'Why didn't you just ask me for help?'

Bonnie burst into tears. How was she meant to explain to Effie that she'd been trying so hard to be a proper adult, one that Mom would be proud of, and Effie too? That she was more scared of Effie's judgement than anything else, because Effie was all that she had left?

Slowly and awkwardly, Effie wrapped Bonnie in a hug. 'I know I haven't been here for you the way you needed. I'm sorry, Bonnie. You messed up. Really and truly messed up. But it shouldn't have taken Tessa begging me to come down here to see that you needed help.'

Something damp fell upon Bonnie's shoulder, startling her. Was that a tear? Was Effie crying as well?

Bonnie drew back, gently touching her sister's face. That thoughtful face whose seriousness was partly Bonnie's fault.

'I'm sorry, too,' Bonnie said. 'I've been awful. I was just trying to prove to you that I could do this. That you could just be you and that you didn't have to try to replace Mom.'

Effie reached up to touch the painting that represented Mom's own aura. 'No one could replace Mom.'

Bonnie nodded tearily. Her sister was right, of course.

'You know I don't do magic on people,' said Effie slowly. 'It's too risky. There are too many variables, and you never know how things might backfire.'

'Things are definitely backfiring,' came Theo's voice from behind them. 'It's a zoo out there.'

Scrunching her eyes closed, Effie gathered herself, then turned to face Theo, who was regarding them with a mix of curiosity and alarm.

'But you're okay?' said Effie.

He did look somewhat mussed, as though he'd had to fight his way over to them. His hair was more tousled than usual, and his shirt was creased.

'I'm okay, but I would really love to know what's going on out there. Because even by city standards, it's wild.'

'It's magic,' said Bonnie.

'Bonnie!' snapped Effie.

'Magic gone wrong,' added Bonnie.

'*Bonnie!*' snapped Effie again.

'What? You think he's trustworthy, right? Or you wouldn't be dating him.'

Effie turned bright red. So did Theo.

'You're taking all of this quite well,' Bonnie told Theo.

Theo made a so-so gesture with his hand. 'I'm definitely a

bit freaked out. But I've had some time to come to terms with this whole Chalmers sisters thing.'

Effie groaned. 'But we work so hard to keep our magic under wraps.'

'Really?' Theo said. 'What with the whole weird uncle with a New Age shop, Bonnie's habit of setting stuff on fire, your uncanny ability to produce a requested book in seconds, and the weird green light that's always emanating from you whenever you're feeling emotional.'

'I don't get emotional,' snapped Effie.

'She absolutely does,' said Bonnie. 'I put her bookmark back in the wrong spot once and she put a glamour on my eyebrows that made them looked overplucked for *six months*. I had to take my yearbook photos with a hat on. It's one of my most painful memories.'

Effie, who'd been staring once more at Mom's aura self-portrait, clicked her fingers. 'That's it. Memories. Mom had a spell that might work. When you had nightmares and you needed to forget them. She'd bring Bobby over to help. I was thinking about it just the other night when I . . .'

She trailed off, letting Theo twine his fingers through hers.

Bonnie scrunched up her face, thinking. That was right. She'd forgotten all about that. By design, apparently.

'But Bobby's not here,' she said. 'He's off with Kirsty.' She could hear the pang in her own voice.

Effie shook her head. 'The spell doesn't require Bobby specifically. Just an unmagical person. I'd take Tessa, but—'

'But she sacrificed herself to the memory spell to make you finally believe her?' pointed out Bonnie. 'Friend of the year over here.'

'Like you can talk. You threw Bobby to the she-wolves.'

'One she-wolf,' corrected Bonnie. 'And not by choice. I didn't know that all this was going to happen. I was just trying to be entrepreneurial.'

'How about me?' interjected Theo – quite gallantly, Bonnie

had to admit. 'I'm unmagical. Bonnie can handle things here and make sure no one forgets their own head, and I'll come with you to the library.'

Bonnie shook her head. 'This is my mess. I'm coming too.'

There was a clatter downstairs, followed by an unnerving amount of laughing and jostling. Glass tinkled against the walls, and chairs rattled as they were upended. The sweet aroma of freshly spilled Memory Lane liquor wafted upstairs.

Either zombies had invaded, or . . .

'Bonnie, hon!' cried Clark from downstairs. 'I could really use some backup down here! Your Trivia Night people are really pushing their luck!'

'Oh shit, they've breached the bar,' said Bonnie. 'Come on. Especially you, Theo. You can be the brawn.'

'Glad to hear my GOMAD diet wasn't for nothing,' said Theo.

With Theo and Effie in tow, Bonnie clattered down the stairs to a group of would-be quizmasters, who'd taken it upon themselves to mix their own versions of Uncle Oswald's cocktails. Everywhere she looked, she could see purple-tinged mouths and lilac-stained fingers. Had the patrons' obsession with Memory Lane reached tipping point, or had she made a bad batch?

Whatever the case, this had to end now.

'Did you forget you weren't supposed to be back here, Gladys?' she said, shooing the elderly woman back to the floor of the bar.

'Just like you forgot to restock the hand towels,' snapped Gladys, retreating behind an overturned table, where she started fighting Willamina for a half-empty purple pitcher.

'I've never seen anything like this!' shouted Theo, protecting Effie with an angled arm.

'This is why I prefer the library!' Effie shouted back.

Bonnie caught sight of Alana crouched in the corner, hiding

from a group of students howling like werewolves, looking very confused and rather perturbed.

'Alana, babe,' she called over the ruckus, 'I need your help!'

Alana shook her head. 'You always need my help.'

All right, so this was true. She changed tack. 'Do it for Tessa. Believe me, she needs it.'

This got Alana's attention. 'What's going on? It's like a full-moon situation or something.'

Or something was right.

'Tessa's being really strange – pretending that she doesn't even know who I am. But I never pegged her as the cold-shoulder ghosting type. That's more . . .'

Bonnie sighed. 'Go on.'

'Your thing.'

Bonnie took a deep breath. 'I know. I'm trying to make it right. All of it. Effie has a plan to fix it, but she and I have to leave for a bit. Can you manage the bar for me until I'm back?'

Alana looked around in panic, combing her fingers through her hair as she tried to come to terms with what she was seeing. 'How am I meant to manage this? It's like a wrestling match. Is everyone on drugs?'

'Clark can help,' said Bonnie, pointing at poor Clark, who was extracting a small bottle of Memory Lane out of the hands of Dierdre from Second-Hand Magic.

'I'm second-guessing this job!' shouted Clark. 'No offence, hon.'

'None taken!' yelled Bonnie, who didn't blame him at all. Even she'd prefer to be studying for a PhD right now.

'Use the soda water guns,' called Effie, between cupped hands. 'They're pretty high pressure.'

'Set off the sprinklers if you have to,' added Bonnie. 'They're really sensitive.'

Taking a deep breath, Bonnie grabbed Effie's hand, then pulled her outside.

'Whatever you have planned, hurry!' came Alana's voice over the thronging crowd.

Heart pounding, Bonnie pulled open the door to her Cadillac.

'Hurry's my middle name,' she muttered as she revved the engine.

Chapter 35

BOOK, BELL
AND SISTERLY SPELLS

Effie

Mentally applauding herself for managing not to berate her sister the whole ride over, Effie unlocked the library's side door and ushered Bonnie and Theo into the elevator. The elevator whisked them down, and Effie felt a stomach-twisting sensation that might have been due to the elevator's movement or to the way that Theo's hand grazed her arm. Or maybe the fact that half the town was hopped up on Bonnie's wayward magic. How many times had Effie reiterated that it was dangerous to use magic on people!

The elevator came to a jarring halt, its doors sliding open to reveal the dim basement area, which was presently lit only by a few exit signs and the light of the moon pouring in from the glass bricks set into the ground around the library's foundations.

Effie flicked a row of switches by the elevator doors, and rows of antique light fixtures and lamps slowly hummed to life, casting the basement in a soft golden light, and revealing endless orderly stacks of storage boxes, overflow shelves for the big folio-style books, and the antiquated card-catalogue cabinets that Effie couldn't bear to part with.

'This way,' said Effie, leading Bonnie and Theo through the stacks and towards a small room off to one side of the basement – the one she secretly called her Speller Cellar, but whose unassuming metal sign read 'Storeroom'. Rather than bothering with her keys, she pressed a hand against the lock instead. The green crackle of her magic lit the air, and the door swung open.

'Um,' said Theo, impressed, but clearly a little unnerved. 'Cool.'

Effie ushered the others into the Speller Cellar.

'Don't bump anything – you could cause an explosion. And we have the books to think about.'

Theo hugged himself, keeping his hands safely around his sides. 'Noted, Oppenheimer.'

'Wow,' said Bonnie. She poked at a stack of dusty spell books that Effie had purchased from an estate sale and was slowly putting into the library system. 'I never took you for such a hoarder.'

Leave it to her sister to find a barb with which to poke her when Effie was cleaning up yet another mess of Bonnie's.

'It's not *hoarding*,' said Effie, slapping Bonnie's hand away from an ornate hourglass filled with ground amethyst. 'It's collecting.'

Bonnie perused a stack of hammered-metal spice jars decorated with lunar symbols. 'Spoken like a true hoarder.'

Theo jumped as he bumped into a pot filled with crow-feather quills. 'So, um, not to be that guy, but it would be really great if someone could explain what's going on.'

'Effie's amazing at womansplaining,' said Bonnie.

Effie shot daggers at her sister. 'Shouldn't you be more contrite, given the entire reason we're here is because you erased the memories of everyone in town for, what was it again? A kickback from Uncle Oswald?'

Bonnie cast her gaze downward. 'I didn't mean to wipe everyone's memories. They were miserable with all their New Age stuff. You saw them. It was information overload. All the lunar cycle apps and horoscopes and tarot cards and crystals – it was all too much to handle.'

'So what?' said Effie. 'We live in an overwhelming world.

We're bombarded with news and horrors and new technology and a constant need to be available. Is it ideal? Not at all. Believe me, I'd rather be reading.'

'According to your shirt, anyway,' said Theo.

Effie glanced down. He was right. But she wasn't done. 'Just because people are poor at dealing with something doesn't mean that you simply take away their ability to parse what's going on. You teach them critical thinking. Media analysis. You steer them towards resources and skills that might actually help them deal with the problems they're facing.'

'Like your crystal display,' mused Theo.

'Exactly.'

Bonnie threw her hands up. 'But you use magic all the time!'

'On little things! The laundry! The book return chute! The elevator close button! Never on someone's *memory*.'

'Yes, because you don't have *debt*. Do you know what it takes to run a small business?'

Effie gritted her teeth. Typical Bonnie. Even with the consequences of her actions blazing in front of her face, she tried to defer responsibility.

'I do, actually. In case you haven't noticed, I've been head librarian here for three years now. Managing the budget is one of my key responsibilities, and I do a damn good job of it.'

Theo stepped between them. 'Holy shit, you two! Look, clearly you have some stuff to work through, and I appreciate the open dialogue – and I have a great psychologist if you need one – but should we maybe deal with the situation at hand before we try to tear each other's throats out?'

Effie caught herself. Theo was right. This wasn't just a Bonnie problem. If Bonnie hadn't felt scared to come to Effie earlier, this whole situation could have been completely avoided. She could have helped out with a business plan. She could have helped Bonnie apply for the small business loan she knew Bonnie had been rejected for.

Or honestly, she could have just *given* Bonnie the money, because she had it, and what good was having savings if you didn't use them when they were needed? She could bang on about fiscal responsibility all she wanted, but maybe sometimes it was better to be empathetic than right. Besides, Bonnie was trying. Perhaps a bar wasn't the business that Effie herself would've staked her inheritance on. But Bonnie *was* striving to make something of it. And she was continuing Mom's legacy in her own weird way: the brownies on the dessert menu, the patio film nights, the paintings on the walls of the landing.

They were opposites in every way, but they were still sisters. They were all that was left of Mom. Well, other than Uncle Oswald, and Effie had a good mind to scrub him from their family tree entirely.

'I'm sorry, Bonnie. I should've helped you. I should've seen what was going on. But I was so caught up, you know.'

She trailed off, shooting a meaningful glance in Theo's direction. Fortunately, Theo was busy dangling a witch pendulum from his fingers, his brow furrowed as it swung gently from side to side.

Bonnie raised an eyebrow. 'Well, that all worked out.'

'What did?' asked Theo.

'I'll take that,' said Effie, pulling the pendulum from his fingers. A witch pendulum helped channel one's sixth sense to make the answer to questions clearer. Effie wasn't sure that was precisely what Theo needed right now – *Effie* was the one who was going to try her best to explain the situation.

'Right now, I need your help,' said Effie. Pulling one of the quills from the holder, she scooted it, together with an inkwell, over to Theo. Then she produced a sheet of handmade paper, one of the beautiful marbled pieces that Tessa had made for her as a birthday gift the previous year. She felt a pang as she considered all the hard work and love that Tessa had put into the gift just a few months earlier, and the hurt way that Tessa had spoken to her tonight.

She'd make it right, she vowed. She'd make it all right.

'Theo, I need you to write down a memory for me. A special one, though. One you hold very dear.'

'I'll try. I haven't handwritten anything longer than my signature in years. Especially not with a quill.'

'I believe in you,' said Effie drily. 'But there's a caveat.'

'Sounds bad,' said Theo, lifting his quill from the page.

Bonnie sighed. 'There's always a caveat with magic.'

'You'll lose the memory.'

Theo frowned. 'I thought we were trying to *restore* memories?'

'We are. But magic like this involves giving something of ourselves in return.'

Theo nodded slowly. 'I'm beginning to see why you stick to elevator doors.'

'Bonnie, can you do the same?' Effie slid a quill and sheet towards her sister.

Bonnie was frowning. 'Wait, so you're saying that every time I had a nightmare,' she said slowly, 'Bobby was giving up one of his memories?'

'He always offered,' said Effie quietly.

'And Mom was okay with that?'

'He only ever gave up memories of you,' said Effie. 'Because he knew that he could always make more.'

Bonnie went silent as she considered this, turning her quill over and over in her hand.

'We'll speak them aloud,' promised Effie. 'So that even if one of us is giving up a memory, the others will remember.'

'All right,' said Bonnie in a small voice. She scratched down a memory on her page.

'Mine is when Mom showed us how to French braid our hair, and we all sat in front of that antique mirror practising and practising. Even you, Effie, even though you're still terrible at it.'

Effie's eyes brimmed at the memory. 'I remember,' she said.

Grabbing a quill herself, Effie carefully wrote down her own memory.

'My memory,' she said, trying to keep her voice calm, 'is when I was trying to do that enormous jigsaw puzzle over the summer, but I'd bitten off more than I could chew, even though I refused to admit it. You and Mom spent a whole week working with me on it, pretending that you actually wanted to.'

'I remember,' said Bonnie, blinking away tears.

'Mine's from when I first met you, Effie,' said Theo, his green eyes gentle as they met Effie's. 'I remember the way the fairy lights on the patio hit you just so. Like magic. You were so proud and so strong and so curious to me, and I desperately wanted to get to know you.'

Effie smiled. 'I remember.'

'I remember, too,' murmured Bonnie, giving Effie's hand a squeeze.

With their memories spoken aloud, Effie collected them, together with a sprig of rosemary, in a special obsidian mortar, which she set down on a small decorative wooden table grooved around its edge so that it could easily hold a ring of black salt. Lighting a match, she set the notes aflame. The fire licked slowly at them, casting a gentle curl of smoke up in the air.

The smoke alarm beeped, but Effie shut it down with a click of her fingers.

Theo's eyes widened, but he said nothing. Apparently he knew enough about magic to keep his mouth shut during a spell.

Effie reached for Theo and Bonnie, and they stood, hand in hand, in a small ring around the table.

'*Pen, paper and rosemary,*' Effie intoned, '*may my truth return to me.*'

The smoke from the folded pages started to change colour, from black, to grey, to purple, and in it flickered images of smiling people, sun-kissed places, and, of course, of Mom.

'Pen, paper and gifted detritus,' Effie intoned, 'may our truths return to us.'

The smoke spun around them, growing thicker and more colourful. Effie's own magic sparked alongside, her wrists afire with the Chalmers gift that coursed in every vein, every cell, every heartbeat. Through the hand clasped around her sister's, she could feel her own magic twining with Bonnie's, the tentative purple that marked her sister's less practised efforts streaming gently from Bonnie's tattooed wrists and into the air around them. Theo's hand, in contrast, was cool and calm, a grounding element that kept the sisters' magic focused. His strong, unflappable presence soothed Effie, helping her stay attuned to the spell.

The magic reached its apogee, then suddenly exploded out through one of the glass bricks above them. It shattered, and would've showered down upon them if it hadn't been for Effie's quick magical reflexes. Dropping the others' hands, she clicked her fingers, directing the shards to land in a nearby trash can.

'Wow,' said Theo, clenching and unclenching his hands. 'I feel like I was just gently and lovingly electrocuted.'

'Did it work?' asked Bonnie, staring up at the hole in the wall above them, through which a possum looked curiously down at them.

The possum's face was promptly replaced by Bobby's. He looked down at them, extremely confused. 'Bonnie? Are you all right?' Rubbing at his forehead, he sniffed. 'Has someone been smoking down there? In the *library*?'

'Bobby! Oh my goddess, I've never been so happy to see your stupid face!' Bonnie exclaimed. She seemed as though she was on the verge of jumping up and down. 'I've missed it so much. You have no idea.'

Bobby blinked, then broke into a delighted smile. 'Wow, really? Are you sure?'

'Yes I'm sure!' cried Bonnie, clapping her hands to her throat. 'Are you okay? What are you doing up there?'

'I have no idea,' Bobby admitted after a moment. His voice was thick, and he sounded dazed, as though he'd just woken up from a deep slumber. 'For some reason I was in the car with Kirsty. Neither of us had any idea how that happened. I pulled over and let her out so she wouldn't have to let her friends know she'd been anywhere near me.'

A huge grin broke across Bonnie's face. Then, with a quick glance at Effie, she said, 'Bobby, I promise it's the last time I'll ask, but could you do me a favour?'

'For you, Bon? Always.'

Effie felt herself grinning as well. It was about damn time that Bonnie realized Bobby was as good as they came. Not to mention that in addition to the endless moral support, he also came with a lifetime's supply of pastries.

Bonnie cupped her hands around her mouth. 'Can you help Alana hold things down at the bar, just for a few minutes? Effie and I need to have some words with Uncle Oswald.'

Bobby gave her a thumbs up. 'On my way. By the way, I have a ton of supplies for you in the back of my truck. For some reason I never dropped them off. Must've slipped my mind. Oof, do I have a headache, though.'

'There's some Tylenol behind the bar,' said Bonnie. 'And some stronger stuff, if you need it. I call it the Sunday Morning Tonic. But stay away from the purple cocktails, whatever you do.'

'Got it. See you in a bit!' With a cheery wave, he disappeared from view. 'Don't burn the place down!'

There was a roar and a chug as he started up his truck, then rolled down the street towards the square.

'Ready to give Uncle Oswald what for?' Effie asked Bonnie.

Bonnie frowned at the ashes left in the mortar.

'I can't remember what I . . .'

Effie understood, because she too knew that she was missing a small, treasured part of herself.

'It's okay,' Effie promised her sister. 'We'll make new memories.'

Chapter 36

IF THE BROOM FITS, RIDE IT

Bonnie

The beaded strands that covered the door to Behind the Curtain clicked as Bonnie shoved through them, Theo and Effie right on her sparkly heels.

'Ouch,' muttered Theo, as a bead whacked him across the cheek. 'Solid security system.'

'Luckily I find welts becoming,' whispered Effie.

At any other time, Bonnie would applaud her sister's sudden facility for witty repartee. Only the stars and moon themselves understood how diligently Bonnie had been trying to school Effie in the art of flirtatious conversation. But right now, it was Bonnie's own gift of the gab that was needed to save the townsfolk of Yellowbrick Grove from the threat that Uncle Oswald represented.

'Where is he?' Bonnie's words bounced off the multifaceted stones and metallic incense lamps that cluttered the shop, hiding the leaky bits and the bowed sections of floor that Uncle Oswald tried to wave off as being examples of 'character'.

Seen in the sharp light of her new-found awareness, the shop had lost whatever charm it had held in Bonnie's eyes. The string lights screamed *scam*. The giant amethyst chunks bellowed *one thousand per cent markup*. The alluring scent of vanilla and sage reeked of the off-brand plug-in air freshener she could see peeking out from behind a $300 broom with apparent aura-cleansing properties. And that damned Enya playlist . . .

How had she been taken for such a fool? Bonnie had been known to play the guileless ingenue, sure, but only when she had something to gain. And not in a *bad* way. Just, say, when an extra piece of Toblerone was on offer, or a movie discount. Not when it came to fleecing people. Or wiping their memories. Bonnie had worked so hard to hold on to the fading mental snapshots of her mother, and the thought of someone siphoning them from her mind for the sake of a quick buck filled her with a boiling rage.

'There's a sale on those at the pharmacy,' Bonnie told a wide-eyed tourist frowning at the price tag on one of the wire-wrapped crystal mushroom charms that Bonnie knew in her heart had been ordered in bulk from an online vendor she absolutely wouldn't trust with her credit card details. She nodded at the door.

'Good to know!' The tourist dropped the mushroom with a plink and hurried off into the misty night in search of a more affordable trinket, leaving just Bonnie, Effie and Theo in the shop.

Impressed, Effie raised her eyebrows. 'You're good.'

Pride bubbled up amid Bonnie's rage. A compliment from Effie was a rare thing. 'I might not have your spell skills, but I have my own magic.'

Effie's eyes sparkled. 'That you do. Oof!'

She grabbed at Bonnie as Theo stumbled into her, having tripped on a tasselled rug that stuck out from a fake tree-stump display. The display had, until a second earlier, sported a bowl of yellowish crystals that looked an awful lot like glass beads that had been sitting for decades in a pack-a-day smoker's house. These were now all over the floor – along with a hand-scrawled sign that read 'rare yellow obsidian'.

'Sorry. I swear that rug jumped out at me,' said Theo,

rubbing his shin. Effie was giving him a slightly hungry look that suggested he was welcome to stumble into her any time.

Bonnie, meanwhile, was tapping one of the stained crystals with her sharp heel. Yellow obsidian. There was no such thing as yellow obsidian!

She clenched her fists in renewed fury. Every hanging trinket basket, every artfully arranged display on a mirror-studded wooden elephant, was a lie.

As Bonnie's manicured nails dug into the soft skin of her palm – it had been a while since she'd made a fist – the air crackled with the electricity of a coming storm.

'Wow, your hair,' marvelled Theo, pointing to the gold-rimmed Medusa mirror leaning against the wall opposite.

Wow, their hair indeed.

Bonnie and Effie were quite the sight. Their hair had risen up under the invitation of magic in the air, revealing all the ways they were alike beneath their vastly different hairstyles. Their cheekbones, their lips, their strong don't-mess-with-me-buster chins – she and Effie were just as similar as they were different.

She met Effie's gaze, and though unspoken, their words fizzed across the room: *Let's do this, sis.*

'Uncle Oswald!' Bonnie shouted. 'Get your—'

'—fatuous butt out here!' yelled Effie, looking very proud of herself for speaking up.

Theo gave her a thumbs up.

'I mean, let's not fat-shame,' said Bonnie.

'I wasn't . . .' Effie shrugged, then put away the pocket dictionary she'd produced the way Crocodile Dundee might a knife. 'Another time.'

There was a rattle and a clatter from the back of the shop, and then some choice swearing. Momentarily, the green velvet curtain along the rear wall swung aside, revealing Uncle Oswald, who was peering over an old book, halfway through concocting some sort of potion out of what seemed to be tea leaves. And was that a bag of guinea pig straw bedding?

The sham never ended with this man. Bonnie was offended to think that they shared a branch of the family tree.

Oswald's oversized emerald ring glinted in the dim light as he gestured sardonically at them. 'Oh good. It's the whole posse. Is it about that Bastet cat statue? Because I don't do refunds.'

'It's over, Uncle Oswald,' snapped Bonnie. '*You're* over. You've done enough damage. We want you out.'

Uncle Oswald snorted, amused. 'Damage indeed. I took your little business from abject failure to profitable enterprise in mere weeks! You certainly didn't seem to mind bespelling your friends and loved ones if it meant you could buy a new purse or get that silly car of yours detailed.'

'I didn't . . .' Bonnie had been about to say *know*, but that wasn't true. She'd been just as much a part of this as Oswald had. But just because you'd done a bad thing didn't mean you had to keep doing it. It was better to see the error of your ways than double down on a bad decision out of stubbornness.

'Of course you didn't.' Uncle Oswald regarded her over his tiny spectacles. 'So, what's the plan here? Are you going to bat your eyelashes at me and have me do your bidding? Or maybe your sister will present me with a petition?'

'Petitions can be very effective.' Effie tugged meaningfully at the sleeve of her cardigan. Beneath its woollen edge, the green marks on her wrist glowed. The book Uncle Oswald was poring over clapped shut on his hands, then flew off out the front door, which the crystal-shopping tourist had failed to close properly.

'Hey!' he howled. 'I was using that!'

'It was overdue.' Effie's voice was as clear as Bonnie had ever heard it. Turned out her sis had sass. 'You can borrow it again once you've returned any other outstanding books.'

'Which will never happen,' snapped Bonnie, so harshly that her throat burned. 'Because you're leaving. Now.'

Uncle Oswald's moustache twitched with scorn.

'You can't bully me out of my own town! After all, *you* were complicit.' He jabbed a finger at Bonnie, that awful emerald flashing as though it contained lightning.

Bonnie folded her arms, flinching at the fervent heat of her wrists against her ribcage. It was a feeling she hadn't had since childhood.

She didn't dare break Oswald's gaze, but she knew, just knew that beneath the tattoos on her wrists, the ones that she'd commissioned as a teen to cover up her magic, her skin glowed lavender.

The static in the air heightened. Now even the fake taxidermied animals on the walls were rocking mohawks.

Oswald snorted. 'Your housekeeping spells don't scare me. Please don't vacuum me to death!' he pleaded mockingly.

Bonnie unfolded her arms, staring down at her hands. They glimmered with violet light. Her pink-tipped fingernails flashed and gleamed, growing hot with the strength of the magic she'd kept deep within her for so long. She was more than a pretty face. More than a social butterfly. She was *more than she appeared*.

In a movement so deft she'd recount it a thousand times over breakfasts to come, she bent and whipped off one of her sparkling heels. Then she flung it with all of her might at Uncle Oswald. Its sharp heel, helped along by a crackle of magic, pinioned his chunky-knit scarf to the wall behind him. Uncle Oswald whimpered.

'Holy shit,' whispered Theo to Effie. 'Your sister is like if Carrie Bradshaw and Bruce Willis in *Die Hard* had a magical baby.'

'She's pretty great,' Effie whispered back.

Even sans heels, Bonnie felt ten feet tall.

'Taunt my magic again and the other shoe will aim for a more sensitive bit,' she snapped. 'Out.'

Uncle Oswald swallowed, then lunged forward. He grabbed one of the potion jars next to him, gave it a quick shake, then lobbed it in their direction. Its glass container shattered as it hit the hardwood floors, erupting in a sudsy foam that hissed and seethed. A solid splash hit the Bluetooth speaker hidden behind the record player, cutting Enya short mid-vocalization (thank goddess for that).

Effie grabbed her sister's hand, pulling Bonnie back to safety.

Bonnie sniffed. A familiar lemony scent filled the air. 'It smells like . . .'

'Lemon sherbet.' Theo gingerly prodded the foam with the handle of the $300 broom, then did the same with his finger. His skin, fortunately, did not dissolve. 'It's just cleaning solution and detergent.'

Of course it was. Like everything Uncle Oswald touched, the whole thing was a pretence.

'That *fraud*!' Effie's eyes were wide with disbelief. 'Wait, where'd he go?'

In the ruckus, Uncle Oswald had disappeared into the back of the shop – no doubt hightailing it out to his gleaming green Beetle, the way he'd done last year when a student journalist had asked one too many pressing questions about the provenance of the moon-charged water he'd been selling on a subscription basis online (no refunds).

Bonnie reached for Effie's hand. She marvelled as she felt their magic twine together, coursing up through their arms and creating a warmth that connected them, always, for ever. They were sisters, and nothing would come between that. Not jealousy. Not their different ways of seeing the world. And certainly not some *guy*.

Beneath her cat's-eye glasses, Effie's eyes glowed with the hues of an unearthly sunset. Bonnie's contact lenses felt dry, and she knew her own eyes were doing the same.

Damn, the Chalmers sisters could be impressive when they wanted to be.

Bonnie squeezed her sister's hand. Effie squeezed right back.

'Let's get him,' said Bonnie.

With Theo trailing nervously – and looking appropriately awestruck – behind them, they strode through the back of the shop and out into the misty night. Clouds gathered around them, deepening from white to pink to purple, then bursting open in an outpouring of magical rain that travelled upwards somehow. Up from the homes and businesses of the town and away into the night. Sparks of purple, gold and green flickered, creating brilliant new stars in the hidden sky. The puddles on the cobblestone alleyway steamed.

Uncle Oswald was in his vintage car, hunched over the steering wheel as he turned the ignition key over and over. The car clicked and ticked as the engine strained to start.

'Sorry,' called Bonnie. 'Magic and motors are a bad mix. It's a domestic charm thing. Do you want me to bring out the magic carpet you've got sitting in the shop?'

Uncle Oswald made a noise of strangled anguish that was up there on the list of the best sounds Bonnie had ever heard.

Finally, he clambered out of the car, dragging a suitcase with him. He always had one pre-packed, ostensibly because of potential disasters, but now Bonnie was seeing the real reason.

Effie clicked her fingers, tipping the suitcase sideways so that it burst open into a particularly oily puddle.

'You think you've won,' snapped Uncle Oswald, scrambling to shove his sodden clothes back into the misbehaving suitcase. 'But just wait until you hear from my attorney!'

'Oh no,' said Bonnie, with faux despair, 'a sternly worded letter! Whatever shall we do!'

'My dad can help with that side of things,' whispered Theo. 'If you need it. Which . . . I'm not sure you do.'

Abandoning the suitcase, Uncle Oswald tossed a few items of clothing over his shoulder, then grabbed an e-scooter that a tourist had dumped by the side of the road and zoomed off into the night, his torn scarf whipping behind him. Ah, what a damp, pitiful figure he cut.

'Well, this calls for a cocktail,' said Bonnie, blowing on her fingernails to cool them off. They smoked lightly from the ribbons of magic that had coursed through them. 'Hex-free, I promise.'

Effie hesitated, but only for a second. 'That sounds magical, sis.'

Bonnie's grin was as bright as the path the moon was cutting through the clouds. 'Well then. Let's go make some memories.'

Chapter 37

SOMETHING CHARMING THIS WAY COMES

Effie

Cleansed at last of the spell, The Silver Slipper was back to being the cheerful gathering spot where Effie had first met Theo. Knots of gaudily dressed tourists sipped away on beers and cocktails in every colour but purple, and couples curled up on the cosy outdoor seats. A group of older women from the romance book club nursed generous pours of rosé while they compared scandalous book covers around one of the firepits, and an academic from the college marked essays on a candle-topped table.

The skies had cleared, creating a vast velvety blanket overhead, and the rows and rows of string lights knotted around the huge wisteria and draped over the perimeter shrubs lent a magical air to the space, setting the colourful plants and bright couch cushions aglow.

It was the first time Effie had truly seen the bar – truly, properly seen it and all the work Bonnie had put in.

'You've done a really great job with this place, sis,' Effie said. And she meant every word.

'Thanks, Eff,' said Bonnie, tapping her wrist against her sister's so that their shared magic sparkled softly. 'That means a ton coming from you.'

Leading Effie and Theo up the pathway through the patio area, Bonnie shoved open the bar's main door with a confidence that for once didn't make Effie jealous.

Inside was just as busy as outside had been – and just as cosy. Effie was relieved to see that the townsfolk had returned to their usual selves, and that everyone had pitched in to clean up the mess from earlier. Although poor Alana was looking a tad the worse for wear and was taking a breather on a stool towards the back of the room. And Hannah was frantically scrolling through emails on her phone as she stress-ate a cookie.

'No idea what happened,' said Bobby, who was mopping up a particularly purple patch of fur. 'A rabid raccoon is my best guess.'

'Gross,' said Kirsty, making a face as she used a pair of bar tongs to pick up a used napkin. She took a few steps to the side. Ah, this was the Kirsty that Effie knew and, well, *loved* was definitely not the word for it. 'Of course you'd suggest something foul like that. I'm working alongside him, Bonnie. Not with him. Just to make that clear.'

Bonnie shot Effie a look of sheer joy. 'So you don't remember the whole Bobby situation?'

'I remember that he wrote your name in chocolate chips on the eighteenth birthday cookie he made you. Mortifying.'

'But nothing about purple cocktails?' Bonnie pressed.

Theo squeezed Effie's hand, making her wrist glimmer green. She squeezed back, stepping closer so that she could lean into him the way she'd been dying to for weeks now. Their bodies seemed to fit together perfectly, even allowing for Effie's book bag.

Kirsty frowned as she regarded her purple-stained athlei-sure in dismay. 'You know, I sipped something out of that Moscow mule mug that time. Not to be rude, but that recipe could have done with some refining.'

'Agreed,' whispered Effie, with a wink at Theo.

Bonnie bit her bottom lip, then, with uncharacteristic humility, said, 'As much as it pains me to say it, I think you might be right.'

'Hey, city boy!' Winston called over to Theo from over at the darts board. 'Up for a game of darts?'

'I'll shout you a shandy if you win,' added Gerald Ho.

'Just pretend you understand what he says,' whispered Bonnie. 'That's what I do.'

'Give me a few, and I'll be there,' promised Theo. 'But I want to buy this lovely individual a drink first. What would you like, Effie?'

'I hear she's on malbecs these days,' said Bonnie, with a raised eyebrow.

Theo shot Effie a grin. 'Is that so? A woman of culture, I see.'

Effie folded her arms. 'I'd actually love a G&T.'

'A gin and tonic it is,' said Theo.

'Coming right up,' said Bonnie, heading behind the bar and mixing up the classic drink in her favourite lowball glass.

'Cucumber and all,' said Theo approvingly as she slid it over. 'You know your stuff.'

Setting his mop aside, Bobby joined Bonnie behind the bar, where he proceeded to mix up a lemon, lime and bitters, which he passed to her with a tenderness that made even Effie smile.

'Since you can't drink on the job,' he said.

'Thank goddess it's not purple,' muttered Bonnie. Then, hesitantly, as though it hurt her to say it, 'Thanks, Bobby. For everything. Not just tonight. Over the years.'

Blushing, Bobby knotted a dishrag around his hands. 'Any time. You know that.'

Bonnie reached out to touch his arm. 'Actually, I do.'

Effie was no expert in love, but she *was* an expert in sparks, and purple ones were definitely flying.

'Hey, Bonnie,' called Freddie Noonan, who'd been chatting at length about grasses and hardiness zones with a poor tourist who looked quite anguished indeed. 'When's Trivia Night starting? I studied all week.'

The tourist took the opportunity to escape to the bathroom.

Effie raised her eyebrows at Bonnie, who broke her gaze away from Bobby long enough to shrug. Had all the bar-goers forgotten the absolute debacle of the past few hours entirely? Were they really going to blame the whole thing on a rabid racoon?

'Effie.' Tessa came up to them, with a relieved-looking Alana beside her.

Effie dropped Theo's hand and embraced her friend with as much emotion as she could muster. Which it turned out was actually quite a bit. 'You were right about it all, Tessa. And I'm so glad you're okay. Angry at you for doing that to yourself, but angry at myself for putting you in a position to have to do that. Especially the dancing in public bit.'

Tessa blinked. 'I did what? And *what*?'

'In that case, you definitely didn't dance,' lied Effie. 'Neither you, nor Sabine.'

Alana twined her fingers around Tessa's. 'Absolutely no dancing. I promise.'

In fact, according to some of the patrons, Sabine had danced up such a storm that she'd had to leave. Effie made a note to check on her in the morning.

'Well, in that case, how about we give the people their Trivia Night?' said Tessa. 'I'm going to sit this one out. Give everyone else a chance to win that not-so-vegetarian meat tray, for once. Besides, I'm going to be too busy opening my new business to find the time to cook it.'

Effie raised her glass. 'I'm so proud of you, Tessa, really. And I bet if I ask the Friends of the Library, they'd be happy to sponsor a craft night appearance or two. Paid, of course.'

'Seconded,' said Theo, toasting with his malbec. 'I'll even volunteer my services if you need crochet support.'

Tessa beamed. 'Really? Thank you! Here, let me give you my card.'

She passed him a card decorated with a potato-stamp print.

Theo chuckled. 'Love it.'

By the time Effie had finally extricated Theo from his new fans, the gin from her drink had started to go to her head. She was feeling slightly uninhibited, a sensation that was not particularly familiar to Effie, who liked to keep things buttoned up and manageable. After all, life was unpredictable enough, and Effie didn't need to add to it.

She led Theo outside, to the quiet spot with the Balinese love seat where she always found herself hiding when Bonnie twisted her arm into visiting the bar. Rose bushes and flower baskets shrouded them from the other patrons.

'Ah, the best seat in the house,' said Theo, as they settled in beside each other. He placed his malbec down on the table in front of them, scooting aside a tea candle in a hurricane vase. 'This is where I hid that first night as well. That feels like years ago now. I barely remember any of it.'

Effie swallowed, thinking of how he'd chosen the memory of their meeting to give up.

'Good years, though, right?' she murmured, looking down at the candle.

'Mostly good. With a few strange moments.' He nudged her thigh lightly with his knee.

Effie broke her gaze from the candle, turning instead to meet his green eyes. 'That's what happens when magic is involved. Things get weird.'

'You don't say.' Theo chuckled. 'But I think I might like weird, actually. I can't say I hate the idea of making my home in a place filled with haunted libraries and spotty-eyed dogs throwing themselves at me. And the occasional witch.'

'I never threw myself at you!' exclaimed Effie.

Theo's eyes sparkled with mirth. 'Those were two separate sentences.'

Effie exhaled slowly. 'So, you're definitely staying.'

Theo regarded her seriously. 'Would you like me to?'

'Is it up to me?'

'Not entirely. But I'd never presume to tread on a witch's territory.'

Effie grinned. 'There is nothing that no mere mortal man could do to tread on me.'

Theo chuckled. 'I love your confidence.'

'My confidence?' Effie had never been accused of having that. She'd founded the Low Self-Esteem club in middle school.

'Always do, always have.'

Effie regarded him, amused. 'I was always under the impression that Bonnie was the confident one. I've always been the opposite.'

'From where I've been sitting, it's the other way around. You seem to know exactly what you want. Exactly how things should be. Your moral compass is like one of those witch pendulum things in your secret cellar. It knows precisely where it's going.'

Effie considered this. 'Perhaps that's true.'

And then, Effie did something that she'd never allowed herself to do – and in fact, had never thought she would. She leaned forward and tentatively grazed her lips over Theo's. Then less tentatively.

Theo lifted a hand to her face, his thumb light against her cheek. The feeling of him was electric, like the magic that coursed through her veins, only at a different frequency. Effie's wrists warmed, glowing softly green in the dim patio light as she ran her fingers over his arms, his shoulders, then tangled them in his normally tidy hair, which presently was unruly from the events of the night.

Theo leaned into her, his lips warm, firm against hers, the smell of him intoxicating. They bumped teeth slightly, then redirected. A small part of Effie nervously considered all the things she was doing wrong, the awkwardness of connecting with someone new, but she shook that little voice away. The awkwardness was part of the joy of it all. She was done not letting herself enjoy things just because perhaps she wasn't good at them. In case people might laugh.

'How about,' she said, 'we go back to my place?'

Theo kissed her forehead. 'I'd like that. But just one thing.'

'What's that?' she said, suspiciously.

Theo burst into a high-wattage grin. 'Are we walking, or skating?'

Effie gasped. 'How did you know about that?'

'You have your skills; I have mine.'

She could hardly argue with that. 'I can see that. All right. Come on. But if you see Bonnie in the morning, make sure *she* cooks you breakfast. She owes me.'

Theo held up his hands. 'I'm not even going to ask.'

Chapter 38

WICKED SMART

Bonnie

'I don't see her, Bon,' said Bobby, having returned from a reconnaissance trip to find Effie and bring her back in time to join Trivia Night.

Bonnie pretended to be unimpressed, but secretly, she had a feeling she knew exactly where Effie had disappeared to. And with whom.

'Well, we're just going to have to start Trivia Night without her.'

'And without me,' said Tessa. 'Tea for Two are generously sitting this one out.'

'Finally, someone else gets a chance at the meat tray,' said Winston, rubbing his hands together in delight. 'Gerald, have you scrubbed up on your history?'

Gerald guffawed. 'Mate, you know my head is full of nonsense. Although I do speak six languages.'

'I thought you were going to say you played six sports. That's far more useful in a trivia setting. Languages, schmanguages.'

'You say that, but I'm useful as a travel buddy.'

Winston thought about this. 'We should do it, shouldn't we? The Old Darts World Trip.'

'I'll make the T-shirts,' offered Tessa, passing out another business card.

'I'm impressed with your business acumen already,' said

Bonnie. 'If you want to collab, you know where to find me.'
She paused. 'But I'm going to be very picky about what any
future collaborations entail.'

'I'm glad to hear it,' said Tessa, eyes bright.

Bonnie clapped her hands.

'All right, everyone. Trivia is starting. Who's ready?'

Tessa clenched her fists. 'Oh, but it's hard to sit out Trivia
Night. It's not even the meat tray. It's the sheer joy of wiping
the floor with everyone else.'

Alana reached for Tessa's hand. 'You could always be on
my team.'

Tessa considered, then flicked her curls dramatically. 'Only
if we can be the Crafty Bitches.'

'Oh, that we are.' Alana smirked. 'Bonnie, do you have a
lipstick?'

Bonnie scoffed good-naturedly. 'Do *I* have a lipstick?'

She pulled out one of the top drawers behind the bar,
revealing a display to rival Sephora. After all, what was the
point of having your own bar if you couldn't also have your
own dedicated lipstick drawer?

Tessa grabbed a napkin and scrawled her trivia duo's team
name on it with a purple lipstick.

Kirsty and Hannah came up, Kirsty looking nosy, and
Hannah sporting the same dazed expression that Bobby had
worn when he'd shown up at the library.

'Um, could we join in as well?' asked Kirsty, who despite
her outward cattiness feared being left out more than anything.

Alana gave Tessa a questioning look, giving her the out that
Bonnie wished she'd afforded Effie more often in life. But
Tessa seemed happy to add a few extras to the team, even if
they were probably going to be more hindrance than help.
She waved Bonnie's friends in with welcoming arms.

'The only caveat is that you have to come to my opening
night,' Tessa said.

'Deal,' said Kirsty and Hannah.

'But only if you let me cater,' added Bonnie.

'And let me help with the decorations,' added Hannah, glancing down at her phone, which kept buzzing. 'I have about a thousand notifications on this thing. Was there an outage or something?'

'Something like that,' said Bonnie gently. 'But we're all back on track now.'

She hoped, anyway. Because she was ready to put this whole ordeal behind her.

She drew Bobby in, sharing her question sheets with him.

'Bobby, do you want to do the honours?' she asked.

'I'd love to,' he said, beaming.

Bonnie passed him the microphone. Bobby tapped it, sending a screech of feedback through the room.

'Sorry, sorry,' he said, with a crooked grin. 'Well, not really. Thanks for coming out to The Silver Slipper tonight, everyone. I know it's been a bit of a weird night, what with the weather and the raccoons, but I think we're on top of it. Before we get started, I just wanted to give a shout-out to my favourite girl in the world. And no, it's not my budgerigar, although she comes close. Bonnie, you're a champ, and I can't think of anything better than running quiz night with you until neither of us can think of another question.'

'Ask Effie to help!' called Tessa.

'Good point. There's no excuse for us running out of questions with a librarian in the house . . . family . . . you know what I mean.' Bobby blushed. 'Anyway, Bon-Bon, Bons, Bonnie-Bee, thanks for letting me hang around and keep you flush with pastries.'

Bonnie dropped her gaze. 'And thank you for lifting heavy things so I don't have to.'

'As you can see, we're a team.' Bobby reached out an arm to pull her in against him. He gave her a kiss on the forehead, a tender gesture that would have made the Bonnie of old roll her eyes ironically. But the Bonnie of tonight broke into a deep, genuine grin.

'All right, question one: who thinks someone else should take over this quiz so I can buy my girl a drink?'

A whoop went up throughout the crowd. Bowow and Bruce Dickens pressed forward, holding hands. (It had been a big night for romance in Yellowbrick Grove.)

'The Number of the Pooch relinquishes its place at table number six,' called Bowow. 'Now gimme that mic and give that woman some sugar.'

Bonnie, for the first time in her life, was beetroot red. She didn't even have to see a reflection to know that her cheeks were veritably on fire.

'What'll it be?' asked Bobby, heading behind the bar. Now that she was off the clock, he could finally make her something stronger than a lemon, lime and bitters.

'Anything as long as it's not purple,' said Bonnie ruefully. 'Or chardonnay.'

As Bowow and Bruce bellowed out questions about local lore and customs to the crowd, Bobby mixed up twin apple martinis. He slid one across the counter to Bonnie, then grabbed the other for himself.

'Almost done,' he said, holding up a finger. He snuck into the chilled cabinet where Bonnie kept the bar snacks, and pulled out the remaining brownies.

'Now we're talking,' said Bonnie, as he plated them up.

'They might not be your mom's, but they'll do. She always made the best brownies. Like magic in your mouth.'

'That's how Mom did things,' said Bonnie with a smile. 'You're so much like her, you know. You both are.'

Bonnie grinned. 'You know, you're not the first person to say that.'

'I'm sure I won't be the last.' Bobby's gentle gaze met Bonnie's. 'Shall we take this upstairs?'

Bonnie grabbed her drink. 'Let's.'

They tiptoed around the perimeter of the room towards the stairwell, heading up past the private events room on the first floor and up to the apartment.

'Sorry about the seating situation,' she said, grimacing at the drop sheets and paint tins.

'There's plenty of room,' said Bobby. He pulled over a handful of rags, laying them out like a picnic blanket. Setting down the drinks and the brownies, he pulled a candle and a stick lighter from his pocket.

Bonnie laughed. 'Wow, okay, I'm impressed.'

Bobby cupped his hands around the wick, letting the lighter click until a soft flame spilled forth. 'I've been waiting about fifteen years to hear you say that.'

'And I've been pretending I didn't feel that way for about as long,' admitted Bonnie. She picked up her cocktail and raised it in a tentative toast. 'To magical new things?'

'To magical new things,' said Bobby, clinking his glass against hers.

'And now, please, for goddess's sake, would you kiss me already?'

Bobby didn't need to be asked twice. He leaned in, his fingers finding the nape of her neck, and his mouth at long last finding hers.

Bonnie wasn't sure what was sweeter: the cocktail, or his lips.

Chapter 39

BESPELLED BY FROGS

Effie

Effie stood nervously in front of the soon-to-be-launched StoryWalk. Launches and festivities outside the library weren't particularly her thing, but Theo had seemed so delighted by the idea of bringing the StoryWalk officially to life that she hadn't had the heart to turn him down. And besides, it was good for the library's KPIs. And its social media following, which had grown into the tens of thousands since Effie had enlisted Kirsty's expertise. Her library cats videos were, as Bonnie might put it, 'doing numbers', and she had a literal song and dance planned for *Frogs Are My Faves*. Although Theo would be the face of that. Like Tessa, Effie drew the line at public singing and dancing.

And then there was the fact that they'd found the most perfect spot for it: the looping yellow-brick path that spilled out from Mom's memorial chair at the Toto Hotel. The Friends of the Library had suggested a variety of locations, but in the end, they'd all agreed that there was no better place, especially since the lush pond at the end of the loop would by spring be vibrant with flashing tadpole tails and froggy croaks. Anyone was welcome to visit – no hotel reservation was needed.

A red ribbon waved from the StoryWalk entrance, courtesy of Dierdre of Second-Hand Magic, who'd had a bolt of appropriate fabric sitting out back of the thrift store. (The local movie theatre had donated it after they'd tired of vacuuming popcorn out of the velvet.)

Cassandra from the student newspaper was already there and waiting, although she *did* look almost as nervous as Effie felt. Perhaps because Bonnie had absolutely lambasted her over her article about The Silver Slipper. The article had come out the day after the magical reversal, and had managed to get not only the name of The Silver Slipper wrong, but every other detail as well (although this was not necessarily a bad thing given the events of the previous few weeks).

'Photographic memory, my ass!' Bonnie had griped, reading the article. 'More like a Snapchat memory. Tell the college to send someone else to do your page-stroll thing.'

'StoryWalk,' Effie had corrected.

'Eh, semantics.'

'Semantics matter! The meaning of the words you use matters! It's the whole point of communication. Besides, she probably had good reason for her memory not being all that, remember?'

Bonnie had responded with a particularly rude example of non-verbal communication.

But at least the newspapers were back to publishing on time – even Madame Destinée was back in fine, sardonic form. When Effie had mentioned this, Bowow had winked, but said nothing more.

A few dozen people had turned out for the StoryWalk opening, which was not *huge* by any means, but certainly wasn't an insignificant number in a town of only a few thousand permanent residents. And a StoryWalk launch wasn't exactly Touch-a-Firetruck or the read-a-thon, which were renowned as two of the library's biggest summer events. (The read-a-thon wrapped up with a splash-pad party, something that even Bonnie showed up for.)

Effie smiled as she saw Bonnie's trio of friends there, and Tessa as well, looking as though she'd come straight from yoga with Alana. Kirsty was livestreaming for her TikTok, and Hannah was snapping pictures to add to her 'Perks of Living in Yellowbrick Grove' page on her realtor's website.

'Every extra photo drives buyer interest,' she confided.

Even Bonnie had shown up, looking her usual glam self as she'd stepped, together with Bobby, out of her Cadillac, which after some accounting advice from Tessa she'd finally paid off. Effie hadn't realized how much she'd missed her sister's impeccably put-together outfits and perfectly waved hair. (Effie had finally relaxed the hex she'd placed on Bonnie's room.) It was only when something was gone that you truly realized how much you needed it there.

Like Mom, she thought. Mom, whose favourite place was right here, and who could now read *Frogs Are My Faves* every time she needed to stretch her ghostly legs.

'I called around during my morning run with Bernard,' Theo told her as he waved to the crowd. 'Went door to door across every house on the street.'

Effie smiled. Of course he had. Theo might not have magic like hers, but he had a particular knack for making people feel at ease. And apparently for getting them to attend community events on a whim. Although having a cute dog probably helped.

'And I grabbed anyone I encountered on the way here,' said Bonnie. 'Turns out I can fit seven people in my car. Eight, if someone rides in the trunk. Even though I promised to stop doing that after that whole quarry-diving incident in junior high.'

But Effie had stopped listening. Her attention was on the wild-haired, kaftan-clad woman holding the framed photograph of Lyra that usually lived on the library circulation desk. Sabine. Sabine, with the warmth and recognition in her eyes that had been absent just days before thanks to the machinations of Uncle Oswald. Tears welled in Effie's eyes as Mom's warm hazel ones, just like Effie's, smiled back at her.

'Let's get on with it,' said Effie, at last.

With Theo's help, she cut the ribbon using a huge set of shears she'd borrowed from Freddie Noonan, who had passionately recommitted to returning his lawn to its rightful state. Freddie, who'd come straight from working his garden, waved a weed puller in a garden-gloved hand.

'I hope you all enjoy *Frogs Are My Faves* every time you stroll through here,' she called.

'Or rollerblade,' added Theo, with a wink.

Effie folded her arms. 'You keep saying that, but really, how did you know about that?'

Theo tucked Effie's lock of white hair behind her ear. 'I happened to look out my window during the witching hour one fateful night a few weeks back.'

Effie covered her eyes in shame. He'd seen the near-butt plant and all, and still wanted to be associated with her. There was something seriously wrong with Theo, but just this once she wasn't going to question it.

'Sorry, sis,' said Bonnie, who'd wasted no time at all in winning back her famous smirk. 'I for one am done with the forgetting spells. You're going to have to own the whole roller-skating thing. Maybe it's something the two of you can do together. Like Barbie and Ken.'

Effie went to protest, but then gave up. Maybe Bonnie was right. Maybe Barbie and Ken weren't so bad after all. And besides, there was something flattering about having your ridiculously popular sister decide that *you* were Barbie.

Bobby put his hand around Bonnie's waist. 'I'm game to try roller-skating if you are.'

'Try?' scoffed Bonnie. 'Are you forgetting my roller derby obsession back in eighth grade? Wrists were snapped. Teeth were broken. None of them mine. You'll be eating my dust.'

'And yet,' said Bobby, 'I'm still game.'

'All right,' called Sabine. 'Are we walking this StoryWalk, or what?'

Water bottles at the ready and shoes laced, the group of townsfolk strolled the sixteen stations that showcased each spread of the cheerful picture book, chuckling at the crayon art and the effusive text. As they walked, the sun broke out from the clouds draping the sky, casting a rainbow that seemed to run from one end of the StoryWalk to the other.

'Magical,' whispered Sabine, looping her arm through Effie's.

'I think Mom's looking down on us,' Effie whispered back.

'I think she always has been,' said Bonnie, her smile sparkling as she drank in the spangled colours of the rainbow's arch.

'Is it rude to walk five abreast?' asked Theo, who'd commandeered Effie's other arm.

'Only if there are cyclists,' decided Bobby. 'Or someone making business deals on the phone while power-walking.'

'In that case, human chain, here we come,' said Effie.

Chapter 40

THERE'S NO PLACE LIKE SISTERHOOD

Bonnie

If you'd asked Bonnie a few weeks earlier if there was any probability of her sitting down for dinner with Bobby, Effie and Effie's *boyfriend*, she would have laughed in your face. It was all too preposterous and absurd. She and Effie had been navigating a rift more turbulent than the San Andreas Fault. And the prospect of either of them being partnered up certainly hadn't been in any of the tarot readings or horoscopes that had come her way – and living in Yellowbrick Grove, there had been many.

And yet, here they were, gathered around the kitchen dining table, where no more than one person at a time had sat since Mom had died. Bonnie had topped the table with a pink floral tablecloth that Sabine had borrowed from Mom years before, and had found while clearing out her attic. The table setting was perfectly mismatched, with glass and ceramic crockery in all sorts of whimsical combinations, and the aroma of home-made pizza and carrot cake and eucalyptus candles warmed the air.

Over by the butcherblock counter, Bobby tossed an immense salad loaded with sliced pears and feta cheese, and Theo was industriously slicing a pizza.

'So, when do you start, Theo?' asked Bonnie, nibbling a hummus-dipped carrot. 'Or should I say, Professor.'

'Not quite professor. I'll be an adjunct, starting next week,' he said, helping himself to a slice of pepperoni. 'I've been knee-deep in lesson plans since they sent me the offer letter. Not to mention cramming every night so that I can get these last few classes for my master's wrapped up.'

'It must be a bit of a change of pace after the city,' said Bobby, popping a square of feta into his mouth.

'Which is precisely what I like about it.' Theo leaned over to give Effie a kiss on the forehead. 'Besides, I have a formidable librarian on speed dial. If anyone asks me a too-hard question, she'll be straight off to the catalogue in search of an answer.'

'I can hardly say no to the man who single-handedly created an endowment for the Friends of the Library group,' said Effie with a tone imbued with . . . was that warmth?

Wow, Theo was a miracle worker.

'And how's the apartment going, Bobby?' asked Theo, wiping down the pizza cutter.

'Almost there. Hannah's going through the tenant applications right now. Once we have someone in there, the rent will be enough to cover the overheads at the bar.'

Bonnie flushed. Who could have known that the answer to her money woes had been so simple all along?

'And no one will mind that it's possibly haunted?' pressed Theo.

At that, Agatha meowed, sparking a grin from both Effie and Theo.

'Are you kidding?' Bobby chuckled. 'They'll pay a premium for it. Especially if we add some ghostly sound effects and—'

'We absolutely will not,' said Bonnie. 'We're doing it legit, or not at all. Besides, ghost hunters don't actually want to *see* a ghost. The whole appeal is the *will they, won't they*. It's like romance readers with a slow-burn book.'

'See,' said Effie. 'One session at the romance book club, and Bonnie is steeped in tropes.'

'Like friends to lovers?' teased Bobby, stooping to give Agatha a gentle pat on the head. 'I like that one.'

The fluffy black cat headbutted him gently, demanding more attention. As witches were wont to do, thought Bonnie with a wicked grin.

Never far from their mom, the tiny kittens tottered around beneath the table, mewling plaintively and batting at feet with their tiny paws. Bonnie and Effie had discussed what to do with the kittens once they were big enough to leave their mom – perhaps set them up as library cats or bar cats or yoga studio cats – but every proposal felt wrong. A mom and her kids deserved to be together for as long as possible. And if Bonnie and Effie could help make that happen, well, they would. There was plenty of room in the old Queen Anne, after all, even if the boys eventually decided to move in. Cat trees and cat beds and cat toys bristled all over, like a forest of fluffy feathered trees, and everywhere you went, huge eyes blinked up at you.

The house felt alive again, the way it had when Mom was here, sitting at the table making up nonsense answers to the crossword because her version was more poetic, or hunched over her desk, beading earrings to swap with Sabine, or humming golden oldies as she sat on the stairs folding the laundry and musing on the lonely existence of mismatched socks.

Theo uncorked a wine bottle, setting it down on the table as he reached for the glasses. One of the kittens chose just that moment to lunge up onto one of the dining chairs and then across the table with a caterwauling scream.

The wine bottle momentarily considered remaining upright, then decided that horizontal was the way to go. It teetered, wobbled, then angled itself towards the table, its contents sloshing from its open neck.

Bonnie didn't even think – she just reacted. Her wrists sparkled with magic.

So did Effie's.

Green and purple threads poured from the sisters' wrists as they simultaneously reacted to the toppling bottle, unthinkingly trying to right it in the way that seemed completely natural to them.

The bottle wobbled, then came to rest upright.

If Effie had been the high-fiving type, Bonnie would have raised her hand in invitation. Instead she just winked.

'Nice job, sis,' whispered Effie. 'You didn't even smash the bottle or set the wine on fire.'

'I've been practising,' said Bonnie. And she had been. Not because she wanted to impress her sister, but because she wanted to know how to properly manage this part of her that was going to be with her for life. This part that made her a Chalmers sister, and which she might one day pass down to a Chalmers girl of her own. And to do that, she had to work at it, not just do what came easily to her.

Although she might be getting ahead of herself there. Maybe she'd try out the aunt thing first. Better to mess up Effie's kids than one of her own, after all. Besides, Effie just inherently knew what she was doing.

'Wow,' said Bobby, shaking his head. 'This whole magic thing is going to take some getting used to.'

'I truly can't believe you had no idea,' said Bonnie. 'Especially with the bar thing. I mean, you practically lived there. And you've been our neighbour for two decades!'

'I mean, I always thought you were magic,' said Bobby. 'Just not literally.'

'How about you?' asked Bobbie, rounding on Theo. 'Were you Mister Oblivious as well?'

Theo raised an eyebrow. 'I might have had an inkling.'

'When did you first suspect?' pressed Effie.

'That very first day at the bar,' admitted Theo. He rubbed his forehead. 'Although I can't quite remember why.'

Bonnie felt a pang. Of all the memories for Theo to give up, he'd given up the one where he'd met Effie.

'I remember,' said Effie, squeezing his hand. 'It's because I used my magic to pick up the flower basket of yours I knocked to the ground.'

'That sounds about right,' said Theo, smiling gently. 'Apparently you made such a strong impression that my memory just can't handle it.'

'Well, I appreciate your not saying anything,' said Effie, smiling up at Theo. 'Yellowbrick Grove might be full of people who want to believe, but I don't think the town's *quite* ready for the truth about the Chalmers sisters just yet.'

Theo chuckled. 'Deal. Although my silence comes at a price. And that price is using just your magic to top up my glass of wine. The biggest slice of pizza goes to whoever does it first.'

Now there was a challenge.

Meeting each other's gazes, Bonnie and Effie grinned. They focused their energies, their magic shimmering in the air as they considered the laws of physics that needed to be overcome. Their twin streams of magic poured from their wrists, twining together then shooting out to lift the bottle, pouring a perfect measure into each of the glasses on the table in turn.

Not a drop spilled.

All right, so the two of them had their differences, and always would. But they also had something that bound them together for ever – in this life and whatever came after. And not just their magic. Their sisterhood. The bond that connected them in times good and bad and everywhere in between. The fact that their lives had been shared since day one, and always would be.

The doorbell rang, setting Agatha yowling, along with the kittens.

'That'll be Tessa and Alana,' said Bonnie. 'And probably

Kirsty and Hannah, if they all came together. Door's open!' she shouted.

'The more the merrier.' Theo got up to pull a second pizza from the oven.

Effie looked like she vehemently wanted to disagree. But she adjusted her glasses and took a measured sip of wine. 'Just so long as things don't get too rowdy. We do have neighbours, after all.'

'That's as close as Effie comes to saying "let's party",' said Tessa, setting down an enormous plate of chocolate-coated macaroons on the counter.

'Oh god, it's going to be eighth grade all over again,' teased Alana. 'Remember the Great Gummy-Worm Sleepover Incident?'

'Got any of that Memory Lane left over?' whispered Effie to Bonnie.

'Only for very special occasions,' said Bonnie. 'All right, who's up for Celebrity Heads?'

Everyone groaned. Bonnie was famed for her ability to stump crowds using D-grade celebrities from the 00s.

'We also have Twister. And the perennial favourite: darts.'

'Not darts,' said Effie. 'I don't trust any of you not to put holes in the wall.'

'Oh go on, Effie,' said Kirsty, who had famously busted through the panelling in the upstairs hallway wall years back in an effort to string up Halloween decorations. 'Would we do something like that?'

Everyone burst out laughing. Even Effie managed a small smile, although Bonnie could see that she was adding up the potential repair costs in her head.

'First we eat, then we Twister,' said Tessa.

'I think that might be the wrong order,' said Alana, grimacing. 'Isn't Twister better on an empty stomach?'

'I thought you were a yoga instructor,' pointed out Bobby.

Alana sighed. 'Well, those are fighting words. Pizza me up, Theo.'

Crammed into the cosy kitchen, surrounded by cats and friends and laugher, Bonnie had never felt happier.

Life felt whole again: all the greens and purples and everything in between.

'A shooting star!' cried Kirsty, who'd been by the window keeping an eye out for the meteor shower that the student newspaper had been heavily reporting on (Cassandra was back in fine journalistic form, and had been collaborating closely with the astronomy department).

Grabbing pizza slices and wine glasses, the group hurried out to the front porch, watching as the sky sparkled with the lights of clustering stars, and taking turns peeking through the telescope that Effie had borrowed from the library. Kirsty gave the telescope a curious look, as though trying to pull up a long-forgotten memory, then shook her head.

'Nerds,' she said, disparagingly.

'I wish Mom were here to see this,' whispered Effie, squeezing Bonnie's hand.

'You know,' said Bonnie, as a particularly bright meteor streaked across the sky, spinning a gold-hued trail behind it, 'I think she is.'

Their wrists glowing, the two sisters leaned against the doorframe of the home that had housed so much love over the years, watching the sky put on a display for the ages – and cheering along with their friends as the meteors stitched streams of light behind the clouds. Neither sister would ever replace Mom, and nor should they. But Mom lived on through them in every action they took and every bit of good they put into the world.

Not to mention the brownies that Bonnie had baked this afternoon using Mom's famous recipe. Well, a slightly illicit twist on Mom's recipe. But Officer Brigsley didn't need to know about that.

Bonnie ducked back inside to grab the platter, then passed them around, smiling at the chocolatey grins her friends threw her way. On went the memories, new and old, and those in between. She and Effie were stewards of them – and would do them proud. Because that was the magic of being one of the Chalmers girls.

ACKNOWLEDGEMENTS

There is a special kind of magic involved with turning an idea into a physical book you can hold in your hands, and it's a magic that extends far beyond my own laptop. There are so many wonderful people who have helped shepherd this book into being, and I'm enormously grateful for every one of you.

To my wonderful agent, Joanna Rasheed, I think you must secretly be a Chalmers sister, because every time you wave your wand, an idea becomes a book! Thank you for all of your cheerleading, and thank you to Elizabeth Aaron of Ultra and Imogen Bovill of Abner Stein for keeping the enchantment flowing back and forth across the pond.

To my husband, Wes, thank you for your unending support throughout the many early mornings, late nights and weekends that this career has demanded of me – I truly could not do this without you. And to my darling Leo and my good boy Samson, thank you for the endless inspiration. Leo, *Frogs Are My Faves* is my gift to you, although of course it has nothing on your hand-crafted seal book, which I will treasure forever.

To my lovely editors Emily Sumner and Raphaella Demetris, thank you from the bottom of my cauldron for giving me the opportunity to bring Effie and Bonnie to life, and for your boundlessly brilliant input in terms of time, place and character. This book is so much stronger (and less rainy) for it.

To Holly Sheldrake, Amber Burlinson, Rebecca Needes and Victoria Denne, thank you for all the behind-the-scenes bookmaking and finessing, especially given the Bonnie-esque timeframe we were working to! I'm so thankful for the Effie-level care and attention this book has received.

To Kieryn Tyler and Julia Murray, I am bespelled by how your beautiful cover perfectly depicts the Chalmers sisters and their differences, and I think we can all agree that it will have readers entranced! It truly is one of the most gorgeous covers I've ever seen.

To Charlotte Dixon and Lucy Doncaster, there is a special magic in connecting a book with its perfect reader, and oh, I am so thankful for your tireless efforts to help *Two's a Charm* find an audience who delights as much in autumnal settings, cute animals and sisterly shenanigans as I do.

To my coven of bookish friends – Breanna Wright, Chris Modaffieri, Svani Parekh, Aneta Cruz, Sofia Aves, Brenna Jeanneret, Kate Farrell and Linda Bennett – thank you for the support as I've fretted about deadlines and eaten my bodyweight in croissants while trying to figure out those pesky subplots.

To my sisters Darcie and Anna, there is nothing more magical than a sisterly bond. This book is a love letter to all the stories, memories, habits and quirks we share – and always will.

And to you, delightful reader, thank you most of all. This story would not be real without someone to read it, and I'm forever grateful that you decided to cast your readerly spell upon these pages. I truly believe that each of us has our own magic – whether it's baking, dog-whispering or styling the perfect outfit – and I hope this book has helped you see your own.